GONE OUTLAW

GONE OUTLAW

A SUNSET LEGEND

MADISON K. THAMES

Cataloging-in-Publication data:

Thames, Madison K., author.
Gone outlaw / Madison K. Thames.
Sunset Legends

Madison K. Thames, 2023.

LCCN: 2022920932 | ISBN: 979-8-9872811-1-6 (hardcover)
979-8-9872811-0-9 (paperback) | 979-8-9872811-2-3 (eBook)

LCSH Kansas—History—19th century—Fiction. | Women pioneers—Fiction. | Revenge—Fiction. | Historical fiction. | Western stories. | Christian fiction. | Love stories. | BISAC FICTION / Romance / Western | FICTION / Christian / Western | FICTION / Westerns

LCC PS3620 .H36 G66 2023 | DDC 813.6—dc23

Printed in the United States of America

www.madisonthames.com

ACKNOWLEDGEMENTS

Thank you to my cousin, Maegan, who probably didn't know what she was getting herself into when she agreed to be my first reader. The value of her listening ear and honest feedback throughout this process cannot be over-stated. I'm eternally grateful to my parents for encouraging me to chase after my dreams and for doing everything in their power to help me achieve them. Special thanks to my editor, Susanne, without whom this story wouldn't be what it is today, and to Mike, who helped me across the finish line.

PROLOGUE

"**R**obbery! Robbery at the bank!"

Gunfire erupted on Santa Fe Avenue. Dinah pushed off the brick wall she'd been leaning against and hurried to peek around the corner. Gunpowder clouded the air. Horses reared and screamed. A mother scooped up her child and ducked inside the general store next door.

Dinah's heart lurched. Her friend Ophelia was at the jewelry store right by the bank, buying a locket with the money she'd gotten from her parents for her eleventh birthday.

Dinah raced toward the store faster than she'd ever run before. A riderless horse charged out of the smoke, eyes rolling and nostrils flaring. She dove into the dust, and it thundered past her.

Coughing, she scrambled to her feet and kept going. A rifle fired from the sidewalk on her left. Dinah covered her ears as she stumbled around a man sprawled facedown in the dirt.

Was he dead? He wasn't moving.

She skidded to a stop just short of the jewelry store, gulping air into her burning lungs. A stranger in a rust-colored coat stood over a body—a girl in a white dress with pink flowers and lace ruffles. Dinah went cold.

Ophelia.

The man's black eyes met hers, his face hidden behind a bandana. Frozen with fear, Dinah glanced at the gun in his hand. Would he shoot her too?

He turned and walked away.

She released a shuddering breath and rushed to Ophelia. Her legs weren't working right. They moved, but she couldn't feel them.

"Ophelia!" she exclaimed as she fell to her knees beside her.

1

Blood soaked the front of Ophelia's birthday dress, spilling from a hole in her stomach. Dinah looked away, palm pressed to her mouth as she fought the impulse to vomit.

"Di…" Ophelia croaked.

Dinah swallowed and lowered her hand. She pushed both palms against the wound to stop the bleeding, and Ophelia yelped.

Dinah didn't care about the robbery anymore—what was stolen or how much.

"You're gonna be okay. You'll be okay," she repeated over and over.

Tears leaked down Ophelia's cheeks, the silver locket in her white-knuckled grip. As the color drained from her face, Dinah prayed for a miracle.

None came.

When the dust settled, her trembling hands were still pressed against Ophelia's stomach. Her unblinking eyes stared at the sky, but Dinah stayed with her.

Until a bloodcurdling scream shook her to her core.

She scrambled backwards as Ophelia's mother collapsed at her daughter's side. Mrs. Larson threw herself over Ophelia, wailing and rocking her like an infant. Her wild eyes helplessly searching.

But there was nothing she could do. Nothing anyone could do.

Only God could've saved Ophelia, and he'd taken her instead.

CHAPTER ONE

"I had another dream last night. About that day."

Dinah bowed her head and plucked a blade of grass, turning it over in her gloved fingers. A frigid breeze sighed through the cemetery, the hillside bleak and treeless even in spring. Red curls fell from the messy coil at the crown of her head and fluttered in front of her downcast eyes.

"'It's been ten years,' Mama said to me. 'Find a way to move on.' She's tired of my mopin'. Wants me to be more like Daniel. She's so proud of him, always goin' on about how great he is for gettin' outta Kansas and leavin' us in this mess."

Dinah huffed and threw the grass into the wind, her weary gaze wandering west toward Salina. Once so small and barely civilized. Now a burgeoning city sprawling along the snaking path of the Smoky Hill River.

"I wish I was somewhere far away," she confessed. "Somewhere no one knows me."

Dinah squinted at the clouds drifting across the deep blue sky. She used to believe she could reach up and touch them if she tried. That she could go anywhere. Do anything.

"Is it selfish?" she asked. "Wishin' I could forget?"

The grave gave no answer.

She shifted onto her knees, tears stinging her eyes and blurring the words inscribed on the weathered headstone:

Ophelia Larson
May 3, 1862 – May 3, 1873
Verily I say unto thee,
Today shalt thou be with me in paradise.

Someone had left lilies, probably Ophelia's parents, and Dinah scolded herself for her negligence. Today was the tenth anniversary of Ophelia's death, and she'd come bearing nothing but the burden of her grief.

An invisible fist squeezed her heart. Dinah's tears spilled over, sliding down her cheeks and dripping into her lap. Her blood boiling even in the cold.

Ten years is long enough to wait.

Didn't anyone care that her best friend had been murdered? That the monster who'd killed her still walked free?

He'd shot Ophelia amid the chaos of a bank robbery in Salina. Stolen every penny Dinah's father had ever saved. Left her family drowning in debt and chained her to this place she both loved and hated. Her home and her hell.

"He can't run forever." Dinah's fingers curled against her thighs. "He's gonna pay for what he's done."

"Dinah."

She started at the sound of her father's voice and wiped her tears on the back of her sleeve.

"It's time to head home."

She rose, dusted off her black split skirt, and trudged toward him. His brows furrowed under his wide-brimmed hat, a frown deepening the lines in his bearded face.

"I know you're still angry," he said as they wove between the headstones. "I know you want justice."

She squinted up at him, her searching gaze finding no judgment in his wise blue eyes.

"So do I," he admitted. "But sometimes—a lotta times—bad men don't get what they deserve in this life. That ain't easy to swallow, 'specially when it's personal. I take some comfort in knowin' their days are numbered."

Dinah clenched her jaw and glared down the path where he'd parked the wagon. Dusty waited patiently, his golden coat gleaming in the morning sun.

"How am I supposed to sleep at night," she asked, "knowin' he's still out there?"

Her father sighed as their footsteps crunched through the grass. "Some mornin's I wake up thinkin' I'm still in the uniform. Used to do all kinds of things to keep from fallin' asleep."

Dinah glanced at him in surprise. "You did?"

He had that look in his eyes, the one he always got whenever he mentioned the war. Distant and haunted. "I was tired of fightin' the same ol' battles night after night. I wanted to forget 'em. One day, I realized the only power they had over me was the power I gave 'em. And you know somethin'? It got easier."

She stopped beside the wagon, and he gave Dusty's neck a solid pat. Shame made her hesitate as she wrestled with her festering anger. "Every night, I ask God to take away the nightmares. Why won't he?"

The question emerged as less of a plea and more like an accusation. Her father faced her, and Dinah braced for a scolding.

"Don't ask him to take 'em away," he advised. "Ask him to get you through 'em."

That's it? That's the best I can hope for?

How could he be so calm? How could he just accept it?

Her father canted his head and raised a thick brow. "That Bible of yours is gettin' awful dusty."

Guilt panged in her chest. Dinah's face heated.

He sighed and adjusted his hat. "I went by the post office while I was in town."

"And?" she prompted, grateful for the change of subject.

"There's a letter from your brother. He wrote it to your mama. I shoulda waited, but…"

Her heart beat faster. "What'd he say?"

He thought a moment, then stuck his hand inside his weathered brown coat and produced an unsealed envelope. "You'd best read it for yourself."

Dinah took the letter and climbed onto the seat as he went to the other side of the wagon. She pulled the folded paper from the envelope with nervous fingers, holding it open in her lap as the wind tried to snatch it from her grasp. Her father scooted in next to her, picked up the reins, and gave them a good snap.

My dearest mother,

I hope this letter finds you well. Three weeks ago, I arrived in New York City, and it is a wonder to behold. A modern marvel.

I have found a job as a telegraph operator that pays better than farming ever did, and with far less labor. Life is easier here, Mama. Safer and superior in every way. There are theaters and restaurants on every corner and galleries filled with the finest art I have ever seen. This city is the paradise the West was promised to be.

I hope that Dinah's anger toward me has faded with time, but I know better. She will understand someday, and when that day comes, there will be a place for her here, a place of culture and opportunity. The kind of life a lady deserves.

Please write soon.
All my love, Daniel

"The *nerve* of him," Dinah growled. "Less than a month in a big city, and he already thinks he's better than us."

She shook her head in disgust as the wagon jostled along the familiar meandering road east toward home. She had a good mind to rip the letter to pieces and let the wind take it. One thought stopped her: *Mama will never forgive me.*

Her father shifted and wouldn't meet her gaze.

Dinah arched an eyebrow. "Well? Aren't you gonna say something?"

He gave a halfhearted shrug. "Truth is, Dinah, I don't know what to say."

I do, she thought, riled and ready to let loose.

"We *need* him. The cattle, the harvest—he won't be here to help us." She shoved the letter back into the envelope and stuffed it inside her jacket. "He'd rather strut around dinner parties and art galleries all day."

"I didn't want him to go, and I told him that," her father replied. "But he's his own man now. The life he leads is his to choose, and so is yours."

He cast her a sideways glance as she clung to the jolting seat.

"I can't leave you like this, and you know it," Dinah shot back.

"I can hire a couple hands."

"You can't pay 'em."

He sighed and closed his eyes.

The debt weighed heavy on him. On all of them. The little he made was like throwing a bucket of water on a wildfire.

She wanted to scream. How many months—how many *years*—would she waste because her father had borrowed money from the wrong man? How could they pay off a loan that never stopped growing?

"Let's talk about this later," her father said. "The sun's out—weather's nice. We should take time to enjoy it."

Dinah's gaze swept over the vastness of the prairie, green and teeming with new life. Blooming with wild indigo and dandelions and yellow sundrops. She breathed in the fresh air, sweetly scented with honeysuckle and the mild fragrance of daisies.

It helped a little.

Taking one hand off the reins, he leaned down and picked up the paper lying at their feet. "Here… I got today's copy of the *Herald*. Why don'tcha read it to me?"

She couldn't refuse. Perusing the paper on their way home had become a weekly custom, and she couldn't bring herself to disappoint him.

Dinah opened to the first page and started reading. Salina's residents celebrated the advent of May and the abating of the plague that had recently afflicted Saline County. The grass grew green and tall, and the corn flourished, watered by frequent rains. Too frequent for Dinah's liking.

A concert company would perform at the opera house next Wednesday. Her heart leaped with excitement, but her eager suggestion that they attend died on her lips. They couldn't afford to go. Not anymore.

Her mood turned even fouler as she read of new expansions and construction and a fast-approaching railroad. "We already have a depot. We don't need another one."

"Ain't about need," her father grumbled. "It's about greed."

"'Enemies to civilization,' they call those who disapprove," she scoffed. "'We should *rejoice* at the puff of the engine, the clank of the shaft, and the hum of the machine, proclaiming that industry reigns within our border.'"

"I'll rejoice when those Eastern bigwigs make themselves scarce 'round here."

Dinah grunted in agreement and skimmed until a certain section caught her attention. "'There is nothing half so sweet in life, half so beautiful, or so loveable as a nice girl—not necessarily a pretty or a dashing or an elegant girl—but a nice girl. One of those lovely, lively, good-tempered, goodhearted, sweet-faced, amiable, happy, domestic creatures, met within the sphere of home, diffusing around the domestic hearth the influence of her goodness, like the essence of beautiful flowers.'"

She snorted. "What *nonsense!* Should we be loved only when we're cheerful and patient and *oozing* goodness wherever we go?"

Her father chuckled. "I don't think the man meant any offense, Dinah. Sounds like he was tryin' to pay a compliment."

"Well, he did an awful job of it. Look at all those adjectives. They're nauseating." She laid the paper in her lap with a huff. "I've had enough of 'civilized society' for today."

"You didn't even go into town," he remarked with amusement.

"Exactly."

———————•————————

The eight-mile journey home took well over an hour at Dusty's plodding pace, and Dinah spent every minute dreading the inevitable lecture she'd endure when her mother read Daniel's letter.

She'll try to talk Dad into sellin'.

Wouldn't be the first time, and it wouldn't be the last.

He'll never give up on this place. Not after sixteen years of fightin' for it.

Grackles and thrashers chirped and trilled as Dusty hauled the wagon over the hill. The land bowed before them, a lush cradle with cottonwoods and hackberries and white poplars blossoming along the river to the north. An old bur oak shielded their house from view as they approached from the west. On their left, the cattle heralded their arrival with a chorus of moos, and on their right, a sorrel quarter horse galloped across the pasture to greet them.

Dinah grinned.

"Hey, Cardinal!" she called as he trotted along the fence. "I'll see you soon, okay?"

They followed the muddy path around the oak, white fluff from the cottonwoods swirling around their heads like falling snow.

Her smile faded as they neared the house. Her father brought Dusty to a halt, and Dinah drew a breath of preparation.

"Go on," he encouraged. "I'll be in soon."

Reluctantly, she jumped down from the wagon. The windmill whined as she headed for the porch.

"Dinah."

She stopped and looked back at her father.

"I'm glad you're here," he said.

Heart squeezing, she smiled and then climbed the stairs. She paused at the door, pulled the envelope from her jacket, and frowned at Daniel's perfect penmanship.

Dad should do this, not me.

Dinah turned the knob and stepped inside, squinting as her eyes adjusted to the dimmer light. Vigorously, her mother swept the floor, her movements brisk and controlled.

Dinah closed the door. The swishing broom stilled, and her mother turned around. Strands of strawberry-blond hair framed her flushed cheeks, the rest of her long tresses pinned up and away from her sweat-glistened neck.

"Dinah," she breathed. Her blue-green eyes widened as they darted to the envelope. "Is that—?"

"From Daniel," she muttered with none of the enthusiasm that had brightened her mother's features.

Her mother leaned the broom against the back of the couch and crossed the room with swift strides. She snatched the envelope from Dinah's extended hand and took out the letter, practically burying her nose in it as she went to the couch and sat, perched on the edge with anticipation.

Dinah unbuttoned her jacket and hung it on a hook. Tugging off her gloves, she looked through the doorway to the left. Sunlight beamed through the window in the dining room, spilling onto the table and revealing swirling particles in the air. Her gaze wandered back to her mother's bowed head, then to the bookshelf in the corner, to the stone hearth and their framed pictures—lingering on the photograph of the four of them together.

Oh, how she hated waiting, especially when she knew *exactly* what came next.

Her mother looked over her shoulder. "You already read this, didn't you?"

Meeting her gaze, Dinah raised her chin in defiance.

Her mother sighed and laid the letter aside. "Dinah, change is never easy, but you shouldn't resent your brother for wanting more out of life than... *this*," she said, gesturing around them.

"He *abandoned* us."

Her mother stood and faced her. "You had your chance to get out of Kansas. If you'd married August—"

"I didn't want to," Dinah cried.

"You were *scared*." Her mother huffed and put her hands on her hips. "We all should've gone back east a long time ago, but you and your father won't let this place go."

Dinah's fury burst from its fragile cage. "You're the one tryin' to run away."

"Who wouldn't?" she snapped, the vein between her brows bulging. "Our life here has been one disaster after another. Fires, blizzards, locusts. Outlaws robbing us of everything we had."

"You can't escape what's happened here," Dinah spat. "Lydia's gone, just like Ophelia. Livin' somewhere else won't change that."

Her mother flinched and paled. Instantly, Dinah regretted her venomous words. Her sharp tongue had reared its ugly head once again. Guilt demolished the iron wall of her anger and pierced her heart, killing the last of her willingness to argue.

She'd seen that look before—blank and glazed over. Unreachable as the depths of a dark and endless pool. Dinah didn't know what to say. Her pride wouldn't allow her to apologize, so she just stood there, eyes pinned to the floor as pressure built inside her.

She had to get away.

Dinah threw her gloves on the floor and strode to the door. As she reached for the handle, it swung inward. She stepped back to avoid colliding with her father, whose blue eyes clouded when they met hers. Dinah ducked past him.

The sun's welcoming warmth invigorated her as she stormed across the yard. Tears welled in her eyes. She pulled the pins from her hair and tucked them into the waistband of her split skirt. Thick waves tumbled down her back, blood pumping through her veins.

Dinah threw open the barn doors, went inside, and grabbed her bridle from the hook.

She set off again, toward the horses' pasture. She gave a shrill whistle, and a neigh answered. Cardinal galloped toward her. As she unlatched the gate, he stopped and tossed his white-starred head.

"Hey, boy," she said, giving him an affectionate pat before slipping the bit into his mouth and the leather over his ears. "Wanna get outta here for a while?"

Dinah led him from the field, closed the gate behind them, and looped the reins around his neck. Grasping a handful of fiery mane, she sprang onto his bare back. The slightest nudge of her heels against his sides made him trot with quick and eager steps.

They turned south at the corner and loped along the fence. The other horses raised their heads from grazing and watched them go—Dusty, Sarge, and Belle—her brother's black mare.

He'd left her behind too.

When they ran out of fence, Dinah let the reins glide through her fingers. Cardinal's neck extended, and he bounded up a grassy slope.

Arriving at its crown, she sat back and said, "Whoa."

The gelding obeyed, but he tugged on the bit as she looked over at a small grave in the shade of a redbud tree.

Lydia Hance
March 25, 1869
Before thou camest forth out
of the womb I sanctified thee.

They'd lost her fourteen years ago. The little sister she'd never gotten to know. To grow up with.

Tears forged burning trails down Dinah's cheeks as she urged Cardinal into a gallop, the wind rushing against her face and brushing them away.

She still remembered the day she'd stepped off the train and seen Salina for the first time. Everything had felt so magical, like something out of a dream. She'd been thrilled to go on an adventure, to go out west. She'd heard all kinds of ridiculous stories—that it flowed with rivers of gold, that the trees grew as tall as mountains.

But the prairie's deceptive beauty hid legions of horrors beneath. Bones upon bones. She realized now how naive she'd been to believe that her family would live happily ever after in this land of endless toil and brutality that tried even the hardiest of souls.

Still, she wouldn't trade it for a gilded cage. She'd seen what "progress" looked like, had watched it rot Salina from within.

Dinah leaned forward and gripped tighter with her legs as they reached a flat stretch of open prairie. Cardinal lengthened his strides, his hooves hardly touching the ground. They eased into a perfect rhythm. Their hearts beat as one, their sights set on an infinite horizon.

This is freedom. This is living.

At the crest of the next hill, Dinah reined in Cardinal and frowned. A wall of ominous clouds lined the western sky. The black shroud hung low, moving fast and casting a sinister shadow over the land.

Time to head back, she decided. *That storm's gonna be a nasty one.*

CHAPTER TWO

"I told you there was rain on the wind."

"More'n that," Joseph grunted. It was a downpour. "Might get a chance to see one of them twisters I've heard so much about. You ever seen a cow fly, Enyeto?"

"No," he answered. Always so serious.

"Me neither."

Joseph clapped his free hand over his hat as a sudden gust tried to steal it. With the other, he kept a tight grip on Steel's slick reins. The mustang arched his neck and plowed on through the darkness.

Lightning flashed on the horizon, brief and blinding. Joseph spied the outlines of buildings ahead before they disappeared. "There—that'll be Salina."

A crash of thunder made Steel spring sideways.

"Easy," Joseph muttered, talking to himself as much as the horse. He pulled his dripping hat lower over his brow. "We robbed the bank here ten years back. It got real ugly, real fast."

"Why come back?" Enyeto asked. The rain had flattened his long black hair against the grizzly pelt he wore over his shirt.

"Somethin' about a moneylender wantin' muscle. If a fella needs roughin' up, Sal always sends me or Marcus. We're good at scarin' folks."

And not much else, Joseph thought gloomily.

"You think you're going to need another pair of fists?"

"You ain't here to fight. You're here to drink."

"Oh," Enyeto said, sounding puzzled. "Why me?"

"You've been doin' your part for the gang, pullin' your weight. More'n some of the fellas who've been runnin' with us a lot longer," Joseph explained, meeting the Indian's gaze. "We ain't talked much, you and me, but I wanted ya to know the work you been puttin' in ain't gone unnoticed."

Still, he seemed unsure. "I appreciate that, Joseph, but I don't know if this is a good idea."

"Nobody saw my face. Gettin' recognized shouldn't be a problem."

"I don't mean that. I mean *me*."

Realizing that he was talking about being an Indian, Joseph waved away Enyeto's worry. "They ain't gonna give us no trouble. Salina has its share of misfits and lawbreakers."

"That was ten years ago," Enyeto reminded him. "Things might have changed."

"Guess we'll find out."

In the three months since he'd joined the gang, Enyeto had gone to great lengths to prove himself useful. He didn't talk much, kept mostly to himself. But he did chores around camp the others thought themselves too good for.

That ain't why ya brought him along.

Joseph stared into the blackness ahead, each step bringing him closer to the last place he wanted to be. He'd tried to get out of it. Marcus had volunteered to go instead, but Sal had insisted.

Is that why he sent me? Because I didn't want to?

The wind howled, the rain blowing sideways across the prairie. Without the moon, Joseph couldn't see more than a few steps in front of him.

When they crossed the bridge into town, he heard the river rushing beneath him. His muscles tensed. Soaked to the bone and chilled with dread, he peered up at the lamps burning in the windows. The bad weather had driven everyone indoors, a stroke of good luck that made the misery worth it.

Joseph read the sign as he rounded the corner.

SANTA FE AVE.

His stomach turned, his heart racing out of control. Rain stung his eyes. Rain or sweat?

Gunshots pop on the sidewalks. In the street. Women scream as they run for their lives. Windows shatter. Bodies fall in clouds of dust and smoke.

A dead girl lies in a bloodstained dress...

Joseph stopped Steel in front of the bank, trying to catch his breath. To shut out the noise. But closing his eyes made it worse.

"What is it?" Enyeto asked.

"Nothin'," Joseph mumbled. He tapped the stallion's sides with his spurs and walked on.

After stabling their horses at the nearest livery, they trudged to the saloon across from the bank and stepped onto the covered sidewalk.

"We must be a sorry sight," Enyeto muttered, adjusting the soggy pelt on his shoulders.

Joseph shrugged. "No worse than the rest of 'em."

His coat whipped around his legs as he pushed through the batwing doors. The lively melody of a piano met his ears, the air thick with the smell of burning tobacco. A big chandelier hung over gamblers hunched behind cards and stacked chips. Another group of men played billiards in a back room.

Several curious stares tightened the knot in Joseph's gut. He strode toward the bar, where a portly man with a gray mustache wiped a glass with a rag. The man glanced up at him, then down at his work. His hand paused, and he glanced up again.

Joseph pulled his pair of Schofield revolvers from the holsters on his hips and put them on the counter. "Two whiskeys."

The man cleared his throat and set down the glass. "I'm sorry, sir. We don't serve spirits. It's the law here in Kansas, and this is a law-abidin' establishment."

Joseph blinked and looked at Enyeto, who shrugged. The bartender's earnest face didn't show even the slightest hint of cracking a smile. "You're serious, ain'tcha?"

"Yessir. Been the law here two years now. The law also says his kind ain't allowed in here," he added with a nod at Enyeto.

Joseph's eyes narrowed, a fuse lighting inside him. He flattened his palms against the bar and cocked his head. "What kind is that?"

The man swallowed. "I'd be more'n happy to fix ya our famous prairie chicken or some stew, sir, but your friend'll have to wait outside."

Joseph glared at him. If he weren't in a room full of witnesses...

"In and out," Sal had said. *"Quick and quiet."*

Sweat beaded on the bartender's brow.

Enyeto put a firm hand on his arm. "Let's go, Joseph. We don't want to start any trouble."

"Hey!" someone barked behind them. "Who let that redskin off the reservation?"

Joseph picked up his revolvers and turned around as a burly man rose from his chair at one of the poker tables. He had a balding head, a bushy beard, and a mean look in eyes, his belly spilling over his waistband.

"That's mighty impolite of you, mister. Why don'tcha apologize to my friend here before I lose my temper," Joseph warned.

"What did you say?" the stranger exclaimed.

"Deaf *and* ugly. Your mama must be real proud of you."

"Take it outside, Frank," the bartender interrupted. "I'll have no fightin' in here tonight."

Frank marched toward Joseph with clenched fists. "You askin' for a whippin', boy?"

Enyeto stepped between them.

Frank stopped and frowned down his crooked nose. "Get outta my way, Red."

He was the biggest man in the room, and he seemed to think that made him invincible.

Bet he ain't ever lost a fight, Joseph thought. He shoved his guns back into his holsters. *'Bout time he did.*

Enyeto didn't budge, and Frank's face turned red with rage.

He took a swing at him, but Enyeto was too quick. He ducked and thrust his fist into Frank's stomach. Frank grunted but didn't go down. He punched Enyeto and sent him reeling.

The piano stopped.

Joseph's burning fuse reached its end, and he exploded into action. As Frank lunged at Enyeto, Joseph caught him and shoved him back.

Joseph's teeth clacked together as Frank retaliated. He staggered, his hand flying to his jaw. Frank grabbed him by his coat and flung him onto the floor.

Pain jarred Joseph's ribs. He scrambled to his feet and spun around. As Enyeto charged at Frank, two men jumped up from Frank's table and rushed to stop him.

"Take it out*side!*" the bartender hollered.

Joseph dodged a clumsy punch from Frank and drove his knuckles into Frank's cheekbone. The impact rippled up his arm. Growling, Frank grappled with him again. As they struggled, Joseph saw Enyeto slam a man face-first into a bowl of stew.

Joseph rammed his knee into Frank's gut. A downward swing knocked one hand loose and—

Frank's skull smacked against his. White light burst before Joseph's eyes. His arms went limp, and Frank threw him backward through the saloon doors. He hit the sidewalk and rolled off, splashing into something wet and sticky.

Mud.

Fingers curling into the cool earth, Joseph pushed himself onto his hands and knees. A deep breath of stormy air revived him. Pain stabbed his sides as he stood. Rain pattered on his shoulders and flattened his hair against his forehead. His hat lay in a nearby puddle.

Tasting a coppery tang on his tongue, Joseph ran the back of his hand under his throbbing nose and found it smeared with blood. *Not again,* he thought with a sigh.

"You had enough, boy?" Frank taunted from the sidewalk.

Joseph didn't fight much anymore—not with his fists—but when he did, he *always* won. He glared up at Frank and squared his shoulders. "I'm just gettin' started."

Lightning flashed as Frank jumped down from the sidewalk. Joseph sidestepped the first reckless swing that came his way, the fire in his blood clearing his head. He landed a pair of quick strikes, but Frank blocked the third and knocked him to the ground.

The small crowd that had gathered on the sidewalk cheered. Sprawled on his stomach, Joseph spat blood from his mouth and pushed himself up again.

A knee dug into his back as a hand shoved his face into the mud. He couldn't breathe. Arms thrashing, he reached for something—*anything.*

His thumb found an eyeball and gouged. Frank howled.

Gasping for air, Joseph threw him off, got up on his knees, and hit him again. Frank fell backward with a splash. Joseph crawled on top of him, ready to finish the fight. Blood pounded in his ears as he pulled back his right fist. He grit his teeth and let it fly.

Crack!

Broke the man's nose.

Again. Make him hurt. Make him pay.

And he did. Again and again and *again,* bloodying his knuckles and making a mess of Frank's face.

"I said, *enough!*"

Someone yanked Joseph's arm, trying to drag him off. Thunder boomed as he rounded on whoever had the *nerve* to interfere.

He found himself glaring into Enyeto's dark eyes. Joseph's chest heaved, blood and rain running down his face.

"Enough," Enyeto repeated.

Joseph shrugged him off and trudged past him, snatching his hat from the puddle as he went. A wave of exhaustion rolled over him as he stumbled to the water trough in front of the saloon. He set his hat on the hitching rail, bent over, and splashed cold water onto his face, washing away the mud and blood.

He shouldn't've drawn attention to himself. Sal would be furious if he found out.

Joseph swore under his breath and looked up at the men on the sidewalk.

"You best ride on to the next town," one of them said. "Cowboys like you aren't welcome here no more."

Joseph scowled. "I ain't no cowboy."

He shoved his hat onto his head and walked away.

"That didn't go as planned," Enyeto muttered as they returned to the livery.

Joseph pinched the bridge of his nose and winced. He didn't think it was broken, but he couldn't be sure. "He got what was comin' to him."

"So did his friends." Enyeto rubbed his knuckles and sighed. "Sal won't be happy when he hears about this."

"I won't tell him if you don't."

Enyeto glanced at him in surprise. "You think that's a good idea?"

No. But facing Sal's wrath would be worse.

"Sal's got enough on his mind. He don't need to be bothered with this."

Even as he said it, Joseph dreaded the inevitable. He'd never been able to hide anything from Sal—not for long. None of them could.

"We goin' back to camp?" Enyeto asked as they led their horses out of the stable.

"You are, if ya want. But I've got a meetin' to keep."

Enyeto stopped and shook his head. "Sorry. With all that happened, I forgot."

He mounted his pinto mare.

Joseph moved to Steel's side, grasped the saddle horn, and hesitated. Guilt weighed on him, battling with his iron-clad pride. He let go of the horn and turned to look up at Enyeto.

"I'm sorry," he blurted, "about what happened back there."

Enyeto shrugged, his solemn expression shifting into a wry smile. "It was more fun than drinking."

Relieved, Joseph smiled back. His jaw twinged, and he grimaced, reaching up to massage it.

Enyeto trotted away, and Joseph hauled himself into the saddle. As he rode farther north down Santa Fe Avenue, he cringed with every step the stallion took. The pain doubled him over, and he cursed that raving fool Frank, the bartender—everyone in that blasted saloon.

The directions Sal had given him brought Joseph to a small office tucked between a shoemaker and a harness seller. Painted above the office door in big black letters was a single word: *LOANS*.

He hitched Steel out front and, seeing a *CLOSED* sign on the door, ventured a knock.

"Come in," a thin voice called.

The door creaked as Joseph stepped into the lamplit room, and he shut it behind him. An older man wearing a black vest and a clean white shirt sat at a desk neatly stacked with papers, holding a pencil in his bony hand.

"Good evening. How may I help you, sir?" he asked with an expectant gleam in his sunken eyes.

"Actually, I'm here to help you," Joseph answered. "You Howard Roach?"

"I am. Please, come closer, though I must ask that you remain standing given your current... condition."

Joseph eyed him warily as he approached the desk, spurs clinking and boots muddying an expensive-looking rug. Maybe he'd care if it were someone else's rug. Someone who didn't latch onto struggling people like a leech and bleed them dry.

He hated these jobs. Hated kicking folks already down on their luck.

"You were sent by Mr. Valentin, yes?"

Joseph nodded and rested his hands on his gun belt. "That's right."

Adjusting the glasses perched on his beaklike nose, Roach put down the pencil. "There's a fellow who lives on a homestead ten miles east of Salina. He borrowed a substantial sum many years ago after an unexpected misfortune and has paid back bits of it here and there. But life on the prairie is... difficult. Setbacks have occurred, and he's missed payments. As a result, the interest has increased exponentially—"

"What do you want me to do?" Joseph said, wishing he'd get to the point already.

Roach leaned forward and steepled his fingers. "Threaten him. Beat him if you have to. I've been far more patient with him than he deserves."

"What's his name?" Joseph asked.

"Jesse Hance."

CHAPTER THREE

Dinah couldn't sleep. The walls creaked and groaned under the strain of a ferocious wind. Thunder rattled her bedroom window, rain pelting the glass as she lay staring up at the ceiling, thinking of August.

Being with him had always been easy. Comfortable. They'd grown up together. Played every day after school. She'd spent many an afternoon with him and Ophelia, making mud pies and baking them in the sun. Chasing lightning bugs on hot summer nights.

She hadn't tired of his company, and she'd cherished his friendship. After she lost Ophelia, he'd been her only friend. But she never loved him. Not the way a woman should love a man who might become her husband.

August had succumbed to the same sickness as her brother—disdain for all things "uncivilized" and reverence for the iron horse, for the industrial machine steaming westward and ravaging everything in its path. Everything she held dear.

What would her life be like now if she'd married him? If she'd gone with him to New York? Would she spend her days alone, trapped in a parlor and staring at the clock? Waste her evenings at fancy parties making shallow conversation with pretenders who'd speak ill of her the moment she turned her back?

How dull. How miserable.

Good riddance, Dinah thought. *I'm better off without him. Maybe I'll never get married. Save myself the trouble.*

A tremendous crash brought the train of her thoughts to a screeching halt.

She bolted upright. Throwing back the covers, she swung her legs over the side of the bed and went to the window. A hackberry tree had fallen on the fence, and their sixty head of cattle stampeded through the gap.

Dinah ran to her dresser and yanked it open. She grabbed the first split skirt she laid eyes on, pulled it up over her drawers, and tugged on her boots. She didn't bother to put on a proper shirt over her white camisole before flinging open her bedroom door.

Her father barreled down the narrow hallway half-dressed, wearing only his pants and boots and red union suit.

"Come on, we gotta head 'em off before they get too far," he said, already wide awake.

Dinah followed him into the hall, down the stairs, and raced past the dining table. She turned the corner as he threw open the front door. He charged out into the storm, and she hurried after him, her breaths coming hard and fast.

The rain drenched her in an instant, weighing down the wide legs of her skirt and plastering her camisole to her skin.

"Dinah!" her mother cried from the porch as she tore across the yard. "You be careful!"

Her father had stabled the horses to keep them out of the bad weather, so they grabbed their bridles and fetched Cardinal and Sarge from their stalls. There was no time to saddle them. They sprang onto the geldings' bare backs and galloped after the cattle.

"They're splittin' up. I'll get this bunch," her father shouted over the howling wind. He jabbed a finger at the cows veering south—almost half of them. "You get those!"

Dinah took off in pursuit. She'd chased down cows over the years, but never so many at once. And never in the dark.

She held on for dear life, clinging to Cardinal's slick back. Rain blew into her eyes, the wind rushing in her ears, and all she could do was pray. That Cardinal wouldn't step in a hole. That she wouldn't slide off. That the cows would stop.

A calf strayed from the herd, and Cardinal lunged to cut it off. Dinah grabbed another handful of mane to keep her balance. The calf darted left and right. But Cardinal was too quick, wheeling on his haunches to block its path of escape. The calf returned to the herd, and the chase resumed.

Must be near the dogwood tree, Dinah thought as the hills flattened, and that meant they were running out of Hance land. She needed to turn them around, and she had to do it quick.

"Yah!" she cried, giving Cardinal a firm kick.

He lengthened his strides, galloping left of the herd. When he drew even with the lead cattle, she nudged him closer, trying to steer them to the right. She whooped and hollered and waved her arm. Their course shifted slightly, but they didn't turn for home.

Dinah's heart pounded as hard and fast as their thundering hooves. The cows scattered, completely out of control. She didn't know what to do. She couldn't round them up alone.

A fork of lightning ignited the horizon, outlining a man sitting astride a horse some hundred yards ahead. No sooner had he appeared than he vanished with a clap of thunder. Dinah swiped at her eyes with the back of her hand.

Had she imagined him?

A muzzle flashed in the darkness, firing two shots into the sky. The herd turned tail and fled toward the homestead, bawling and bellowing as they went, and Dinah moved with them. Relief flooded through her, and she glanced over her shoulder.

"Go on, get!" growled a disembodied voice.

Another streak of lightning revealed him galloping at the back of the herd, on the right side to balance out her position on the left. She caught a fleeting glimpse of a black hat and flapping coattails before he disappeared again.

He barked orders at the cattle, but Dinah didn't risk anymore backward glances. She didn't have a clue who he was or why he'd decided to help her, but she wasn't one to look a gift horse in the mouth.

The cows' heads hung low, their hooves dragging as they approached the gate. The rain had gotten lighter, and the wind had calmed. Her father had already herded the rest of the cattle into the pasture, her mother standing beside him as he mended the broken fence. She held up a lantern for him to see by, her knee-length coat buttoned over her nightgown and her braided hair hanging over her shoulder.

"There you are!" she exclaimed, hurrying to open the gate. "I was about to send your father after you."

"I woulda needed him if this Good Samaritan hadn't lent a hand," Dinah replied, sneaking a peek at the mysterious stranger.

Little more than a shadow, he walked his horse closer to them as the exhausted cattle sauntered into the pasture.

"Does this Good Samaritan have a name?" her mother inquired.

Dinah looked at him again, wondering why he didn't answer.

"Joseph," he said.

"Pleased to meet you, Joseph. I'm Sarah."

Dinah swung her leg over Cardinal's back and slid to the ground. Her boots splashed in the mud, and her knees nearly buckled. She'd exerted herself more than she realized.

"Your daughter's quite the rider," Joseph remarked.

Dinah's heart swelled with pride, and she couldn't help but smile as she patted Cardinal's neck.

"That she is," her mother admitted. "Thank you for helping her."

"Weren't no problem, ma'am."

Holding the gate with one hand and the lantern in the other, her mother gave a pointed glance at her clothes. Suddenly, Dinah remembered that she hadn't put on a shirt over her camisole. Cheeks burning, she shrank behind Cardinal, feeling as if she'd slipped into one of those mortifying dreams where one looks down and discovers they're naked.

"Evenin', sir," said her father in his gravelly voice as he joined them. "Did I hear that you helped Dinah bring back our cattle?"

"He did," her mother replied.

The last of the herd went through the gate, and she pushed it closed. With the cows out of the way, Joseph dismounted and led his horse over to them.

Dinah peeked around Cardinal, admiring the beautiful animal as he stepped into the lantern light. His towering size made Cardinal look like a pony by comparison, his noble head held high and his big black eyes watching them with suspicion. *A mustang?*

Her father's brow furrowed. "Bad night to be out ridin'. You lose your way?"

The lantern's red glow shone upon rugged, handsome features. Dark stubble framed Joseph's slanted lips and the shape of his jaw. Few men stood as tall as her father, but he did, broad-shouldered and well over six feet.

"I didn't mean to trespass, sir. I ain't from around here, just passin' through."

He talked out of the right side of his mouth, the left side stiff and limited in movement.

"Well, I'm much obliged to ya. You've done me and my family a kindness I won't forget," her father said. He stepped forward and extended his hand. "Jesse Hance."

Joseph swallowed as if something had stuck inside his throat. He reached out a black-gloved hand to shake her father's. "Joseph."

Dinah squinted, inspecting him more closely. An angry bruise swelled on the bridge of his nose.

"You must have a ways to go yet," her father mused. "If ya need a place to spend the night, you're more'n welcome to use the hayloft."

"That's mighty kind of ya, but I can't stay."

Dinah's heart sank as Joseph tipped his hat to her mother with a polite, "Ma'am."

Then he turned to Dinah. Half-hidden behind Cardinal's lowered head, half-dressed and soaking wet, she felt completely and utterly ridiculous. Not an ideal first meeting, but she supposed it didn't matter, as it would also be their last.

Joseph's gaze lingered on hers, an unspoken word on his parted lips.

He tipped his hat and mounted his horse. Dinah watched him gallop away until he passed out of sight and hearing, as if he'd never been at all.

There and gone like a bolt of lightning.

CHAPTER FOUR

C *lick.*

Joseph's eyes flew open. He grabbed his Schofield and aimed it at the forehead of the man standing over his bedroll. Slicked-back hair, brown face, black mustache—*Tony*, he realized with a flash of anger.

Tony snickered and holstered his Colt. "Woulda hadja, Joseph."

"Walkin' into a wanted man's tent, pointin' a gun at him—" Joseph sat up with a grimace. "That's a surefire way to get shot in the face."

"C'mon," he scoffed, spreading his hands wide with his usual sense of self-importance. "I'm Tony Vega. Fastest gun in the West."

Joseph squinted up at him, sunlight spilling into the darkness of the tent. Tony had left it open when he came in. "You told Sal that?"

Tony looked at his boots.

That wiped the smirk off his face.

"Speakin' of Sal, he sent me for ya. He wants to talk to you."

"'Bout what?" Joseph asked.

Tony shrugged. "He didn't say."

The canvas flapped in an icy breeze, and a shiver ran down Joseph's spine. "Tell him I'm on my way."

Tony's brow furrowed. He bent over, hands on his knees as his dark eyes studied him. "Hey... You don't look so good. You got in a fight, didn'tcha?"

Joseph's pulse quickened. He'd hoped the hits he'd taken wouldn't leave much of a mark. *Must be bad.*

One look at him, and Sal would know.

Tony straightened and sighed. "Sal's been plannin' this job for months."

"I know," Joseph muttered, tossing the blanket off his legs and pulling on his black boots—caked with dried mud from the night before. He'd been too tired to clean them when he got back to camp.

"He's gonna be mad."

"I *know*," Joseph growled.

Tony shook his head and ducked out of the tent.

Joseph raked his fingers through his hair. Every inch of him ached, his head throbbing like he'd gotten roostered. Except he'd gone without a single drop of whiskey.

He'd messed up—let his temper get the better of him—and he couldn't take it back.

Joseph shoved his hat onto his head. Got up and slung his gun belt around his hips. Filled the holsters with his pair of Schofields and pulled on his coat over his dark blue shirt.

He took a deep breath and stepped out of his tent. The light stung his eyes, and he held up a hand to shield them.

All around him, he saw only grass and sky. Nowhere for hostiles to hide. No signs of civilization but their mist-shrouded campsite.

Just the way he liked it.

Elliott already had a fire going, the glow glinting off his glasses as he stirred the steaming pot hanging over it. The smell of beans wafted along the breeze, and Joseph's stomach growled. Rick sat by a pot packed with fresh biscuits, crumbs stuck in his dark beard as he stared into the crackling flames.

Ponderin' some mystery or another, Joseph supposed.

Gus still sprawled on his bedroll, snoring away.

Scowling and droopy-eyed, Collin went over and kicked him with the toe of his boot. "Hey. Quit your snorin'."

Startled awake, Gus rolled over and squinted up at him. "Huh?"

"I *said,* quit your snorin'," Collin repeated, louder this time. "How am I supposed to sleep with you over here sawin' logs?"

Gus sat up, his shaggy blond hair sticking in all directions and his round face turning red. "I ask myself the same thing *every night.*"

"I don't snore."

"You're the loudest," Tony chimed in, scooping some beans onto his plate. "Must be that big nose of yours."

Elliott chuckled as Collin glared at Tony.

Joseph smiled and shook his head.

Gus, Tony, Elliott, Rick, and Collin—the five of them had grown up together in Ohio. They'd been their own gang before they joined Sal's. Inseparable since they were kids. They bickered like brothers, always teasing and poking fun at one another, just like he and Marcus did.

Enyeto stood across from Rick, his plate in one hand and a biscuit in the other. As Joseph approached the fire, the Indian met his gaze, his left cheek bruised and swollen.

Charlie's jaw dropped at the sight of him, and he nudged Elliott with his elbow. He'd just turned eighteen, but he remained a boy in Joseph's eyes. Sometimes, he still couldn't believe that Charlie was Remy and Donny Guidry's kid brother. He had none of Remy's bloodlust or Donny's violent temper, being instead of a mild and amiable nature.

Elliott looked up and whistled in amazement. "What happened to you? I ain't seen ya so beat up since we got into that scrape with the Norman boys."

"Made the mistake of goin' for a drink," Joseph said as he held his hands over the fire.

"And?" Elliott prompted. "Didja take a fella's girl? Was she a redhead?"

Rick gave a long-suffering sigh. Elliott's preference for redheads was no secret to any of them.

Joseph remembered the girl he'd met at the homestead, Jesse Hance's daughter. Her pretty face glowing in lantern light, half-hidden in shadow.

"A fella and his friends didn't take kindly to Enyeto settin' foot in their saloon, so we taught 'em a lesson."

"Did the law get involved?" Collin asked around a mouthful of biscuit.

"No. We got outta there fast."

Elliott dipped the ladle into the pot of beans and scooped some onto a plate for himself. "Didja get the drink first?"

Joseph shook his head. He pulled his hands back from the fire and rested them on his gun belt. "Barkeep said they don't serve liquor."

Their expressions turned incredulous.

"What?" Gus exclaimed as he joined them. "No whiskey?"

"Dry as a bone. Whole state is, accordin' to him."

"C'mon, we all know that ain't true," Rick said. "People like to drink, and they'll go on doin' it. Nothin' Uncle Sam does is gonna change that."

Joseph was inclined to agree.

"What're they gonna say next?" Tony lowered his spoon and gestured around them. "We can't breathe the fresh air?"

"Better start a swearin' jar," Elliott quipped. "They'll be finin' us for that soon."

Joseph smirked. "Tony'd fill it in a day."

"An hour," Collin added as Charlie and Elliott laughed.

Tony cracked a smile. "Y'know, my dad used to beat me for cussin'."

29

Here he goes, Joseph thought. Tony never missed a chance to tell a story—he had a knack for it. But Joseph often wondered how many of them were true.

"One mornin' when I was gettin' ready for school, I got real mad at my mama. I cussed at her, and my dad stood up faster than Gus scarfs down a sausage. 'I'm gonna tan your hide, boy,' he said. He pinned me against the wall with one hand. Reached for the switch with the other. Tore my shirt clean off my back tryin' to hold onto me.

"I made a run for it and jumped out the window. He was shakin' his fist and screamin', 'Get back here, Antonio!' I said, 'Come and get me, old man!'" Tony grinned at the memory, his dark eyes twinkling. "I didn't come home for a week."

"Wha' happened when ya did?" Charlie asked in his thick Acadian accent.

"He was sittin' right there in his rocker waitin' on me. He whooped me so good, I walked crooked for another week after."

Elliott wheezed, and Rick joined in with his jolly giggling. Their laughter was contagious, and Joseph smiled as he turned to leave.

"Hey, Joseph," Elliott called, "don'tcha want some grub?"

Joseph stopped and cast a reluctant glance over his shoulder. "I've gotta talk to Sal, tell him what happened."

The laughter around the fire died. They'd all been in his position at one time or another.

"Good luck," Rick said with a knowing look.

Enyeto put down his plate and came over to him. "I'm going with you."

Joseph shook his head. "You don't have to do that."

"You aren't the only one who threw a punch," Enyeto reminded him.

But I started the fight. If I'd walked away when I should've, it never woulda happened.

Enyeto didn't deserve the blame, but he seemed to have made up his mind. Joseph sighed and motioned for Enyeto to follow him.

They strode past the bedrolls spread in the grass, past the grazing horses. The air chilled away from the fire, the waking world washed in soft blues, pinks, and purples. Four figures stood against the rising sun, one of them so still he could be made of stone. Sal's rust-colored coat stirred in the wind, his hands clasped behind his back as he contemplated the horizon. The others stood apart from him, Marcus and Donny listening as Remy went on and on about something.

Always yappin', Joseph thought, irritated at the mere sight of his stooped shoulders and crooked hat. He would've sent him packing months ago if

Sal didn't insist on keeping him around. Remy was a decent shot, and he got things done. *But I could throw a rock and hit fifty fellas more agreeable.*

Marcus took his cigarette from his mouth and blew a trail of smoke into the air, his boredom obvious to Joseph. As he approached them, Marcus looked his way, squinting up at him from under his faded brown brim.

"You look like hell."

"I feel like hell," Joseph grumbled.

"Look atcha," Remy chided with mock concern, "all black-and-blue."

"Him too," Donny added with a nod at Enyeto. He clucked his tongue and shook his head. "You can take da savage off da reservation, but he's still a savage."

Joseph shot him a warning glare. Enyeto's hands balled into fists, Donny's hooded green eyes daring him to try something.

Spurs clinked toward them, slow steps crunching through the grass. Sal stopped between Marcus and Donny, regarding the latter with cold disapproval. He was no Indian, but he was half Mexican, and he didn't tolerate such behavior from any member of his gang. Appearances didn't matter to him—only actions—and Joseph admired him for it.

"Enyeto is one of us," Sal declared. "One of *mine*. Treat him with respect. If you don't, I will not punish him for whatever he might do to you."

Donny's eyes flashed, his narrow chin jutting.

Finally, Joseph thought. He'd caught Remy and Donny giving Enyeto a hard time once before, and he suspected they'd been doing it more often than any of them knew.

Sal turned his penetrating gaze on him, his eyes burning like coals.

Joseph's satisfaction evaporated. He was a full-grown man of twenty-eight, but that one withering look shrank him to a boy again, desperate not to disappoint. To prove himself a worthy son. Sal wasn't his father, but he was the closest thing he had.

"I told you not to draw attention to yourself," rumbled Sal, low and foreboding like approaching thunder.

Joseph swallowed. He'd lain awake coming up with a hundred ways to explain what had happened. None of them sounded good.

"We went for a drink. That's all. I didn't think any harm would come of it."

"You didn't think," Sal echoed grimly. "That much is clear."

His words stung like the smoke from Marcus' neglected cigarette. Joseph clenched his aching jaw and hung his head, avoiding the brothers' smirking faces.

"The fault is mine," Enyeto said, and Joseph glanced up in surprise. "I knew my presence might cause trouble, but I went anyway. A man attacked me in the saloon, and Joseph came to my defense."

Sal considered him a moment. His gaze met Joseph's again, and he sighed. "Your loyalty is commendable, Joseph, but your actions wouldn't have been necessary if you hadn't gone there in the first place. If you hadn't taken Enyeto with you. Your recklessness could've brought the law down on us."

Guilt weighed on Joseph's chest, dragging his heart down to his toes. "I'm sorry, Sal. It won't happen again."

"See that it doesn't," he warned. "You know better. I raised you to be better."

The group gathered around the fire had gone silent, their stares boring into Joseph's back. His face burned.

"Did you talk to Howard Roach?" Sal asked.

"Yeah. Homesteader hasn't been makin' his payments. Roach wants me to motivate him."

Sal nodded. "Roach has proven useful in the past. I want his request taken care of."

Joseph shifted uneasily. He was in no position to ask for a day off, but he had to try. "I took a hell of a beatin', Sal. I don't think I'll be very intimidatin' lookin' like—"

"I'm not asking, Joseph."

His excuse died on his lips. Sal's stern gaze left no room for debate. No way out. Much as Joseph hated what he had to do, he couldn't refuse a direct order. Couldn't fail him again.

———————•———————

His ride to the Hances' homestead should've taken an hour, but Joseph walked his horse when he could've galloped, dragging out every minute. Drowning in self-loathing. Dreading the way the girl would look at him when she learned that he was no Good Samaritan.

He liked her. He liked her family. They seemed like decent, hardworking people. How could he beat a man whose beeves he'd saved the night before?

He could say he'd done it. Say he'd threatened him when he didn't.

Joseph shook his head, dismissing the idea the second it crossed his mind. Despite their dishonest way of life, he never lied to his friends, and he never lied to Sal. Partly because he didn't want to. Partly because there was no point in trying to trick him.

He'd tried once, a long time ago, and it had made him so miserable, so racked with guilt, that he couldn't look Sal in the eye. He'd confessed a day later, only for Sal to tell him he already knew the truth.

A pheasant launched out of the grass some fifty yards ahead. Steel stopped in his tracks. A rifle cracked, and the bird dropped.

"Easy, boy," Joseph said as the stallion danced and tossed his head.

A lithe figure strode through the waist-high grass with a rifle slung over her shoulder. Her fiery curls whipped across her face like flickering flames. She walked with purpose, carried herself with dignity and pride.

His chest clenched. *Dinah.*

She picked up the bird by its neck and examined it.

Curiosity sparked in him. *A rancher and a hunter.*

No—he couldn't let her spot him. He had to see this through.

Joseph nudged Steel's sides with his spurs and trotted down the slope, giving Dinah a wide berth as he rode north toward the homestead. Now that her back was toward him, he hoped to slip by unnoticed.

A shrill whistle split the chilly air as he started up the next hill. Joseph swore and reined in the mustang. Dinah's red horse appeared over the rise, loping toward her.

Until he saw Steel.

"Cardinal!" she cried as he changed course.

Approaching Steel without fear, Cardinal walked right up to him, and they bumped noses. Joseph huffed in frustration. He should slap that horse on his hindquarters and strand her out here while he dealt with her father.

"Go on." He waved a gloved hand at Cardinal's head, and he shied away.

Joseph's insides twisted in knots as Dinah came toward them. *I can't do it. Not now.*

He wheeled the stallion east and spurred him into a gallop.

"Hey!" she called after him.

He ignored her, cursing his conscience and urging Steel on. The rushing wind muffled her voice and caught the tails of his coat. The sun glared in his eyes as it rose above billowing clouds. Before him lay a stretch of open land dotted with shrubs and the occasional tree.

"Hey! Stop!"

Joseph glanced over his shoulder, and surprise jolted through him. Dinah had jumped onto Cardinal's back and was gaining fast. He clenched his jaw and smacked the mustang's silver hide with the reins. Steel sprang forward with a burst of speed. He pinned his ears flat against his head, his neck stretching and long legs reaching.

Cardinal's hooves thundered louder.

Joseph looked back, and his temper flared. In the eight years that he'd had him, there'd never been a horse that could outrun Steel. No lawman's mount. Not even Tony's fancy thoroughbred.

"Go home!" he shouted at Dinah as Cardinal's nose drew even with Steel's flank.

"Stop runnin'!" she hollered back.

Her eyes blazed in silent challenge, and he realized that somewhere along the way this little chase of hers had become a race.

The *nerve* of this girl. Didn't she know when to give up?

A big dogwood tree bloomed at the top of a hill a couple hundred yards ahead, its dark branches and white flowers standing against the deep blue sky.

That'll be the finish line, Joseph decided.

Cardinal's nose moved to Steel's shoulder, and before he knew it, they were matching each other stride for stride. Sweat darkened the horses' necks, stems snapping as they trampled the grass. Dinah gripped the reins with both hands, her face screwed up in determination.

"C'mon, boy," Joseph urged with another tap of his spurs, and Steel surged into the lead.

Despite Dinah's cries of encouragement, Cardinal kept falling behind. *Wore himself out catchin' up.*

Steel charged to the top of the hill, and triumph swelled in Joseph as he galloped under the dogwood's drooping lower limbs.

"Thatta boy."

He reined in the mustang and circled back to Dinah. She'd stopped Cardinal in the shade of the tree, his nostrils flaring as she leaned down and patted his lathered neck. She spoke kindly to him, but the disappointment on her face was plain as day.

She glared at Joseph as he approached her. "Don't look so smug. You had a head start."

"You're the one who wanted to race," he said as she slid down from her saddle. Its faded brown leather was stained and frayed, coming apart at the seams.

"I *wanted* to talk to you," she corrected, "but you ran away."

That stung. He sat up straighter. "I wasn't runnin'."

"Oh *please,*" Dinah scoffed, rolling her eyes and putting a hand on her hip. "You turned tail faster than this poor fella."

She gestured at the dead bird stuffed in a sack on her back.

The blow to his pride riled him. *She's got no idea who she's talkin' to.*

Joseph dismounted, his spurs jingling when his boots hit the ground. "I've got some business to take care of."

"What kind of business?"

"The important kind."

She arched a thin brow and pointed her thumb over her shoulder. "Salina's that way."

"I wasn't goin' to Salina."

Dinah cocked her head as she studied him. "What happened to your face?"

"Y'know, it ain't polite to pry," Joseph warned, sauntering toward her. "Your daddy never teach ya no manners?"

She raised her chin and drew herself up to her full height, standing a good bit taller than most women he'd met. "Your mama never tell ya not to lie to a lady?"

"My mama was the biggest liar of 'em all." The admission slipped out before he could stop it.

Dinah blinked, the stern line of her mouth curving into a frown. She looked young, maybe twenty, but a wisdom beyond her years sharpened her gaze.

What does she see?

Dinah sighed and put her hands on her hips. "I guess your trouble ain't my business, so long as you haven't brought any with you."

Joseph recognized the weariness in her voice. She'd seen enough trouble in her life. Here she was, hunting alone out in the cold so she could put food on the table for her family.

He couldn't beat her father in front of her. She didn't deserve that.

"I don't tell tales, 'specially not to a lady," Joseph said, "but some things ain't for sharin' with strangers."

He didn't want her to think badly of him, to suspect what he really was. He liked being the good guy for a change.

"We don't have to be strangers," Dinah ventured. "Your horse could use a rest. Why don't you come and sit a minute before you get back to… whatever it is you were doin'?"

Joseph glanced at the hills to the north. "You ain't worried about someone seein' us?"

She shook her head. "No one's gonna see us. No one comes out here but me and my father."

She went to the tree, lifted the strap over her head, and set the sack in the grass.

He didn't know what to make of her. She didn't dress or act like the "proper" women he sometimes saw from a distance, but neither did she strike him as the promiscuous kind common in his world. Whatever she was, she intrigued him.

Don't, the rational part of him warned. He had a job to do, a responsibility to Sal. Never had he shirked that responsibility.

But as Dinah took a seat under the tree, Joseph found himself letting go of Steel's reins and leaving him to graze. He walked over to her and hesitated.

She gazed out at the boundless prairie, legs crossed and hands clasped in her lap. Pink lips and long lashes softened the sharp angles of her face. Auburn waves tumbled down the back of her dark blue jacket, a floral-patterned shirt buttoned up to her neck.

Dinah peeked up at him, and he looked away.

Stop gawkin' and say somethin', you moron.

"Looks like a nice catch ya got there."

"Should make a fine meal," she agreed.

Joseph sat beside her, leaving some space between them. "You like huntin'?"

Her eyes brightened, and she nodded. "My father taught me. My brother and I used to take Ginger with us and spend hours out here. Sometimes we'd catch four or five roosters in one trip."

"Ginger?"

Dinah's smile faded. "Our dog. She died a few years back. Bird huntin's a lot harder without her—and my brother."

"Somethin' happen to him?" he asked.

She frowned and looked down. Her chin jutted as she picked at the grass. "He left. Decided he was too high and mighty for Kansas and moved to New York. It's just the three of us now."

Joseph grimaced. He'd run across some fellas from the big cities back east, all of them sapheads and tenderfoots.

"No husband?"

Realizing how that sounded, he cringed, feeling as if he'd shoved one of his boots into his mouth. Dinah raised her head, and he stared at the horizon, avoiding her gaze.

"No," she answered with an edge in her voice.

He'd touched a nerve. Better change the subject.

"And you?" she prompted. "Do you have a family?"

"Yeah. I mean, not a wife and kids, but I've got folks I care about. That I'd die for."

He shouldn't be doing this. Pretending to be normal. Pretending he wasn't an outlaw with a five-thousand-dollar price on his head.

Joseph stood with an anxious knot in his chest. "I should get goin'."

Her face fell. "I didn't mean to—"

"You didn't do nothin' wrong," he assured her. "It's just—like I said, I've got somethin' to take care of."

He went to Steel and bent to pick up the reins, his heart pounding at the thought of facing Sal. *I'll tell him everything. Explain what happened with the cows and the storm. Maybe he'll understand.*

He doubted it, but whatever the consequences were, he'd deal with them.

Joseph glanced over his shoulder. Dinah had gotten to her feet and followed him a few steps. He turned to her, wishing he could stay awhile longer. That he could get to know her.

"This was... real nice."

She smiled faintly, and he climbed into the saddle.

"Don't be a stranger," she said, sounding like she never expected to see him again.

Joseph made no empty promises, gave her no false hope. Strangers was all they would ever be. This spirited young woman had her whole life ahead of her. And he?

He was a dead man walking.

Long shadows moved across the plains, the minutes dragging by. Steel pawed the ground, and Joseph shifted in the saddle, waiting with Marcus, Sal, and Remy.

Rick and Collin had stayed behind to guard the camp while the rest of the gang made the sixteen-mile journey east to Abilene. They'd split up into four groups when they arrived, each riding into town half an hour after the last. Gus and Tony had gone first to "get drinks" at a saloon on Cedar Street. Elliott and Donny went to a restaurant on Spruce Street. Then Charlie and Enyeto had set out to spark the diversion that would clear Sal's path to the bank.

Joseph leaned forward to look past Marcus. Sal sat silent on his albino stallion, studying his map of Abilene. He always got quiet before a robbery, especially the big ones, but it was more than that. Sal hadn't said much to him since yesterday. Since he'd returned without confronting Jesse Hance and confessed why he couldn't.

Sal's plan occupied him for now, but Joseph knew he wouldn't forget. He didn't let things go so easily.

Half a mile distant, the rising sun hung low over Abilene's hazy shadow. Joseph hadn't seen the once infamous cow town since they'd passed through on their way to Salina in 1873—ten years ago. He hadn't been much more than a kid then, eighteen and still so naïve.

He tried to take a deep breath, but the weight pressing on his chest made it difficult.

"Joseph."

He met Marcus' dark eyes.

"You got your head on straight?"

Insulted by the question, Joseph leaned over and spat on the ground between their horses. Marcus' brow furrowed with lingering doubt, but he nodded and turned his gaze back to Abilene.

"Dey 'ave no idea wha' dey in for taday," Remy said with a yellow-toothed grin.

"We ain't here to kill folk," Joseph growled. "We get the money and get out."

Remy bent over his Palouse's white-spotted neck to meet his glaring gaze. "Where's da fun in dat, Gray?"

Joseph's grip on the reins tightened, his glove scraping his sore knuckles.

Sal tucked his map inside his coat and pulled out his gold pocket watch. "It's time."

They thundered toward Abilene with Sal leading the way, galloping alongside the railroad tracks. Joseph's heart hammered as brick and frame buildings rushed toward him, blurring into shapeless streaks of color. The bridge, the water flowing beneath—they reminded him of Salina.

Riding in from the west, they slowed their horses to a trot to attract less attention, their coats buttoned to hide the guns on their hips. A blond woman sat in a rocking chair on her front porch, humming as she sewed. When she heard them coming, she glanced up and froze.

"Mornin', ma'am," Marcus called.

"Good morning," she answered with a cautious smile as they passed by.

Workers sawed and stacked planks in the lumber yard on their right. On their left, some boys played a game of baseball.

Suddenly, one of them dropped his bat and pointed at the sky. "Fire! There's a fire!"

Joseph looked up and saw smoke on the other side of the tracks. *That's the signal.*

"Steady," Sal muttered.

Joseph barely heard him over the thumping in his ears and the clamor of voices ahead.

At the next corner, people gathered on the sidewalks and crowded the muddy road, gaping at the gray cloud rising into the sky. Sal nodded, and Joseph followed his gaze. Standing outside the saloon, Gus and Tony nodded back.

As they rode on to Broadway Avenue, Joseph's face got clammy, his nerves making him sick to his stomach. It didn't matter how many times he'd done it—how many fights they'd survived or how much Sal had prepared.

Every job could go wrong.

They stopped their horses in front of the grocery store across from the bank. Joseph dismounted and looped Steel's reins over the rail. Unbuttoned his coat and rotated his shoulders. Flexed his fingers.

"Bandanas on, boys," said Sal.

Joseph covered his face and looked up at the bank as they squelched through the half-dried mud. Inside, a vault full of money waited to be emptied. A good take could set them up for months—maybe longer.

Maybe this one could be the last.

Marcus tossed him a pair of empty saddlebags, and Joseph slung them over his shoulder as he climbed the steps. They gathered around the door. Sal drew his ivory-handled Colt, raised a gloved finger, and began a silent count.

One. Two. *Three!*

Marcus barged into the bank, and Joseph charged in behind him.

"Put your hands where I can see 'em and get on your knees!" Marcus barked. "This is a robbery!"

Joseph counted five men—four workers and a customer. The customer fell to his knees in front of him and raised his hands in surrender. Sal walked in with Remy close on his heels. Remy shut the door, and Marcus whipped a bookkeeper upside the head with the butt of his gun. While the man was down and stunned, Marcus snatched a key from his belt.

"Here," he grunted, tossing it to Sal.

The other bookkeeper scrambled backward and tripped over his desk in his efforts to escape from Remy. He slumped against the yellow wall, scattered papers fluttering around his head.

As Sal went to the teller's door, Joseph shoved his revolver in the cowering customer's face. His eyes widened behind round glasses, his lip quivering under a brown mustache.

"Gimme everything ya got," Joseph growled. "Money. Valuables."

The man frantically fumbled in his pockets.

"*Now!*"

"Okay! Okay! H-here," he stammered, throwing a few bills and his watch onto the floor.

Joseph holstered his weapon just long enough to scoop them into a saddlebag.

Sal pushed open the teller's door. It clanged against the wall as he strode toward the two men hiding behind the barred windows.

"Which one of you is the teller?" he asked, calm and collected.

"I am," answered the man in a light blue suit.

"Open the vault," Sal ordered.

"I'm sorry, sir. I—I can't do that."

Sal aimed his Colt at the cashier's head and pulled the trigger. Joseph flinched, ears ringing as the acrid stench of gun smoke filled the room. The cashier staggered back and hit the glass, smearing a trail of blood and brains as he slid to the floor. Joseph's stomach churned.

"Someone's gonna hear that!" Marcus exclaimed.

"Don't matta." Remy pointed at the window. "Law's already on da way."

Joseph turned and looked out the window. Three lawmen spurred their galloping horses toward the bank. Getting out would be messy.

Just like Salina.

"Next time, it's you," Sal warned the teller.

The customer blubbered, and the man kneeling in front of Marcus murmured a desperate prayer.

"Open it, for heaven's sake!" begged the other bookkeeper.

Gunfire erupted outside, men shouting and hooves thundering.

Glass shattered, and Joseph swore. Dragging his hostage with him, he threw him into the corner and took up position next to the broken window. He pressed his back to the wall, heart slamming against his ribs. Joseph glanced at the man huddled in the corner, hair disheveled and glasses askew. Scared out of his wits and probably wondering if he'd make it home to his family.

We weren't supposed to kill nobody.

Sweat glistened on the teller's blood-speckled face. His mouth opened and closed, mustache twitching as he swallowed. Sal leveled the Colt at his head. Joseph stared, holding his breath.

"All right," the teller said. "I'll do it."

The door burst open and banged against the patterned wallpaper as Elliott ran into the bank.

"We gotta go," he panted. "The whole town's shootin' at us!"

Bullets ripped into his back. He fell facedown in the doorway, his brown vest filled with holes. Marcus cursed, and Joseph holstered his Schofield. He hurried to his friend, grabbed his arms, and hauled him out of the line of fire.

"Hang on, partner. I gotcha."

He rolled Elliott over, pulled down his bandana, and discovered a wide grin on his face. They'd always thought it strange how the worse he got hurt, the harder he laughed. But this time, the tears welling behind his broken glasses betrayed him.

"I been shot, ain't I?"

Joseph didn't know what to say. He couldn't even think.

Gunshots popped outside. The vault stood open, Marcus and Remy rushing in to get the money.

"It don't look good," Joseph admitted.

Tears slid down Elliott's paling cheeks. He clutched Joseph's sleeve with one hand and his bloodstained glove with the other. "I can't go yet. I ain't done right by my wife. My kids."

He coughed, blood dripping from the corner of his mouth.

A lump stuck in Joseph's throat as he gripped Elliott's hand. "You been a good friend to me. To all of us."

Elliott's eyes met his, glazing over as he croaked, "Don't wait, Joseph. Don't wait."

His hand went limp. Joseph breathed a shuddering sigh and closed Elliott's eyes. Remy ran past him with stuffed saddlebags and didn't give Elliott a backward glance.

"We gotta leave him, Joseph," Marcus said.

Joseph looked up at him, then back down at Elliott. Gathering his wits about him, he let go of his hand and got to his feet.

As they headed for the door, Marcus called over his shoulder, "C'mon, Mr. V!"

Joseph drew his right revolver and followed him out into the smoky haze. Shouts and screams bombarded him from every direction. Off to his left, from the back of his liver chestnut, Donny shot at anything that moved.

As Remy raced toward his horse, a local stepped out of the barbershop next to the grocery store with a shotgun raised to his shoulder. Remy stopped and blasted a hole in his chest. The stranger staggered forward and tumbled down the stairs, dead before he hit the ground.

Another dead man lay in the middle of the street. Were there others? Had anyone died in the fire?

Don't think about it. Just keep movin'.

Joseph ran to Steel and slung the saddlebags over his back. He unwrapped the reins from the hitching rail, shoved his foot into the stirrup, and sprang into the saddle. Steel tossed his head and snorted, his gray neck already dark with sweat.

"Easy, boy," Joseph said, gripping the reins in his left hand and his Schofield in the other.

"Where's Sal?" Marcus yelled.

A shot went off inside the bank, and they exchanged an anxious glance. Marcus spurred his black Morgan forward, bringing along Sal's white stallion. Joseph galloped after him, and they skidded to a halt in front of the bank. Sal strode through the open door, his face and coat spattered with blood.

Joseph's stomach turned. He didn't have to ask what he'd done. He knew Sal had killed the teller for slowing them down.

Sal came over and swung onto Hado's back with graceful ease. How could he shoot two unarmed men and look so aloof? So guiltless?

Donny reined in his horse nearby, wild-eyed and breathing hard. "Anyone seen Charlie?"

No sooner had he said it than the kid sped toward them with a lawman hot on his heels. Behind the lawman were Tony on his brown thoroughbred and Gus on his Belgian Draft. Joseph lined up a shot, but Tony fired first. He put a bullet in the lawman's back, and he fell face-first into the mud.

"Whew!" Charlie exclaimed as his horse skidded to a halt. "Dat was a close one."

"You're bleedin', Charlie," Donny told him, and Joseph's eyes darted to Charlie's right shoulder.

His blue shirt was soaked through.

"Make sure he stays on his horse," Sal instructed. "We'll tend to him when Abilene is behind us."

Following his lead, they turned onto North Second Street and galloped alongside the railroad tracks. As the flames roared higher on the south side of town, riderless horses stampeded through the streets.

"Ya got the money?" Gus called from the back of the group.

"Lots of it!" Marcus yelled over his shoulder.

Joseph glanced back, and his heart pumped faster. "We're bein' followed!"

Remy twisted around in his saddle and fired at the two lawmen on their tail.

"Watch it!" Gus hollered. "Ya almost shot off my good ear!"

Anger coiled in Joseph's gut. *They're not takin' nobody else.*

When they reached the next junction, he steered his horse into the alleyway behind the opera house. Bricks and windows flew past on his left, and for several seconds, he couldn't see his friends or the lawmen as gunshots popped on the other side. Every breath he breathed, every thud of Steel's hooves seemed louder. Slower.

Finally, Joseph found an opening. He turned Steel on his haunches, slipped between a livery and another frame building, and came out in a perfect position to ambush the lawmen.

Joseph took the reins in his teeth and drew his other six-shooter. He closed his right eye and squinted down the sights. He couldn't miss. If he did, he risked hitting a friend instead.

He breathed in, then out. On the exhale, he pulled the trigger.

Bang!

The lawman slumped over and tumbled from the saddle. Joseph shut his left eye and aimed his right revolver. Fired again. The other lawman slid off, and his spooked horse dragged him away with his boot stuck in the stirrup.

They'd never seen it coming, both taking a bullet between their shoulder blades.

The gang whooped and hollered.

Did I kill 'em? Joseph wondered as clouds of remorse gathered.

Guilt's shadow loomed on the horizon as he left the burning town behind, his rage scorching like lightning.

Elliott's gone...

He rejoined the rest of the gang, and they kept up a blistering pace for another mile before giving their mounts a brief rest.

As he sat catching his breath, Joseph's gaze swept over the group. When his count stopped at seven, his heart dropped like a hanged man.

"Where's Enyeto?"

"I—I don' know," Charlie stammered, his hand pressed to his bleeding shoulder. "Afta we started da fire, we got split up."

Joseph turned Steel toward Abilene and squinted at the smoke in the sky. "We've gotta go back for him."

"You crazy?" Remy exclaimed. "Dey'd lynch us all."

"Wait—where's Elliott?" Gus asked.

Joseph swallowed. He couldn't bring himself to tell him. Marcus' jaw clenched, his face taut and stoic, but Joseph knew he shared his grief.

"He didn't make it," Sal answered gravely.

"What? What do you mean 'he didn't make it?'" Tony demanded.

"He got shot," Marcus said, his somber gaze fixed on the ground. "Weren't nothin' we could do."

Tony's dark eyes widened, and Gus' mouth hung open, both looking as if something had broken inside them.

"We have to keep moving," Sal reminded them. "We need a place to lay low. Somewhere close. Somewhere the law won't think to look."

No one offered any suggestions. As Joseph racked his brain for ideas, only one came to mind.

"Joseph, what about the homestead you visited?" Sal asked him.

No—not there. He couldn't bring Dinah the trouble she'd suspected him of.

"It's outta the way," he admitted, "but I don't think—"

"Take us there."

CHAPTER FIVE

Strawberries glistened in the sunlight, red and ripe for the picking. Dinah crouched beside a leafy cluster, pulled one free, and placed it in her basket. Then she plucked another. She'd just had dinner, but she couldn't resist taking a bite. Closing her eyes, she savored the juicy burst of sweetness.

Dinah stole a glance over her shoulder before wiping her mouth on the back of her primrose-covered sleeve. Her mother picked peas nearby. They'd barely spoken to each other at dinner. Or breakfast. Or the whole day prior.

The longer the silence lasted, the harder it got to break it. Several times, she'd almost apologized. She knew she'd gone too far, but why couldn't her mother admit her part of the blame?

Dinah huffed and put more berries in her basket. She hadn't told her parents that she'd seen Joseph again yesterday. Neither of them would approve of her spending time alone with a man without their consent, especially one they weren't well acquainted with.

Doesn't matter. He won't be comin' back.

How long had they talked? A few minutes? Was she really so insufferable?

He'd seemed interested. Asked if she had a husband. But she'd learned nothing about him.

Where'd he come from? And why's he so secretive?

Someone had beaten his face black-and-blue. Over what, she couldn't begin to guess.

Joseph seemed a decent man. He'd gone out of his way to save their cattle. But there was something about him… Something wild. Something dark.

Dinah moved to the next cluster of berries. Reaching out to pick one, she hesitated, her hand hovering as the wind whispered through the grass.

The birds weren't chirping. She looked east, a stray curl tickling her cheek. A fly buzzed by her ear.

Leaving her basket on the ground, Dinah stood and shielded her eyes with her hand.

A rider appeared atop the hill—a man on a pale horse.

Her throat tightened like a noose. *It can't be.*

She blinked to banish him, but there he stayed.

A second rider came over the rise. Then another. Soon, eight shadows sat shoulder to shoulder.

"Mama," she croaked.

But her mother had already spotted them.

"Dinah, *run.*"

She couldn't breathe, her feet frozen in place as she stood staring.

"Dinah!"

Her mother dashed to her and grabbed her arm, dragging her toward the barn as the riders charged down the hill. Her father threw open the barn doors and rushed out into the yard. When he saw them coming, he went back inside and emerged with Cardinal's bridle in hand. Hooves thundered behind them, Dinah's pumping legs feeling like lead as her father ran to meet them.

He shoved the bridle into her shaking hands. "Go. Ride to Mr. Miller's place. He'll know what to do."

"Jesse!" her mother exclaimed as he sprinted toward the house.

He's goin' for his gun, Dinah realized.

They had to move, and they had to move fast.

"Come on," she urged, pulling her mother toward the horses' pasture.

Arms swinging and feet flying, Dinah raced across the yard, hearing nothing but her rapid breathing and the violent beating of her heart.

Until her mother screamed.

She stopped and wheeled around. Her mother had fallen on her hands and knees, two riders penning her in like cornered prey.

"Leave her alone!" Dinah cried, a primal instinct driving her toward them.

A speckled mass impeded her. Her boots skidded out from under her, and she landed hard on her backside, arms splayed and chest heaving.

"Well, now," said the man on the spotted horse, "wha' we got here?"

His black hat sat crooked on his mop of shaggy brown hair, its leather crown creased and caving in. His narrow mouth twisted into a smirk, and Dinah scrambled to her feet. She tried to get past him, but he spun his horse on its haunches.

"Where ya goin'?" he taunted.

A second rider circled behind her, his shaven face and hooded eyes strikingly similar to the man on the spotted horse. They had to be brothers.

Dinah cast a desperate glance toward the house.

Her father hadn't made it. Sal Valentin and three other riders had blocked his path to the porch—one of them on a big blue roan.

Joseph.

The sight of him hit her like a slap in the face. Every silly little dream shattered in an instant.

The man on the Palouse dismounted and swaggered toward her, shoulders stooped and brown coat swaying around his knees. He was shorter than her, hollow-cheeked and beady-eyed.

"What do you want with us?" Dinah demanded with as much bravado as she could muster.

His lecherous gaze flitted over her figure. "I got a few ideas."

She backed away in disgust. "Don't you come one step closer."

"Skittish one, ain' she?" he said, grinning up at the rider behind her. "Don' be shy. I don' bite. Less ya wan' me ta."

"You stay away from her!" her mother cried, fighting to free herself from the burly blond man holding her back.

Dinah's nails dug into the bridle's tough leather, the headstall in her left hand and the reins in her right. He kept advancing, and she gritted her teeth, resisting the urge to run. There was nowhere to go. Nowhere to hide.

Legs trembling and pulse pounding, she waited till he came within reach. Then she lashed out with the reins, wielding them like a whip. One slapped his shoulder. The other struck his cheek.

The blow stopped him cold. His hand flew to his face. The second rider let loose a slew of French-sounding words, but Dinah dared not turn her back on the man in front of her, blood pumping wildly through her veins. He lowered his hand and glared at her, a red welt already forming on his left cheek.

She swallowed.

"You little slut," he spat.

He lunged at her. One hand clamped around her wrist, the other trying to wrench the bridle from her white-knuckled grasp. Dinah clung to it with all her strength, holding on even as he shook her like a rag doll.

"Give it ta me."

"No!"

He threw her to the ground. The impact jolted her back and jarred her ribs. "Get—off of me!" she growled as he straddled her.

Smack!

The back of his hand struck her cheek. Dinah gasped. In her shock, she let go of the bridle.

He sneered, greasy hair hanging over his eyes as she pressed her fingers to her burning skin. "Don' feel sa good, huh?"

Dinah rolled onto her stomach and crawled out from under him, elbows digging into the dirt.

"I'm not done witcha yet."

His spurs clinked behind her. The bridle jingled, and she went rigid.

Leather smote the small of her back. Her whole body lurched as she yelped. He hit her again, the sharp sting of the reins stealing the breath from her lungs.

As a child, she'd been switched on more than one occasion, but the pain it had inflicted paled in comparison.

Her mother begged him to stop, but he didn't. Blinded by tears, Dinah covered her head with her arms. She turned onto her side and curled into a ball as he thrashed her, each stroke tearing a cry from her throat.

"Remy! That's enough," Joseph barked, his voice piercing a haze of misery.

Suddenly, the whipping ceased. She peeked up in surprise as a broad-shouldered man in a gray-brown hat and coat lifted her attacker off his feet and flung him face-first into the grass.

"Ya like beatin' women? It make ya feel big and tough?" he snarled. Bending over, he yanked Remy up by the front of his coat and shook him. "*Huh?*"

Remy squirmed in his grip. "Let go a' me, Crane. She 'it me! She 'ad ta be taught a lesson."

"Y'know what kinda man hits a woman? A spineless one. If I ever catch ya doin' it again, I'll rip yours outta your back."

Crane shoved him into the grass and straightened. He turned and looked at her, his eyes dark and his features stern. Dinah stared at him, too terrified to move. Tears scalded her cheek, stripes blazing on her back.

"It's all right, miss. He ain't gonna touch ya again."

Remy shot him a nasty glare as he shoved his hat onto his head. He got to his feet and glanced past him. "Whatchu lookin' at, Gray?"

A few yards from her, Joseph sat silent on his stallion, his brow furrowed and his eyes narrowed. Remy straightened his coat with an indignant huff and stomped back to his horse.

Joseph Gray.

She'd seen that name in the papers beside Marcus Crane's—beside Sal's. Banks, trains, coaches—he'd robbed them all. He was a notorious outlaw and a known member of the Valentin Gang.

The gang whose leader had killed Ophelia in cold blood.

How ridiculous she felt. How *disgusted.* A "Good Samaritan," she'd called him.

"Get her up and take her inside," Marcus told Joseph. "We don't need her causin' no more trouble."

Leading his black horse behind him, he returned to Sal. A mustached man in a striped vest pointed his gun to her father's head, forcing him up the porch steps.

"Let go of me," her mother demanded as the big blond man dragged her toward the house. "That's my daughter, you animals!"

Dinah scrambled to her feet and launched toward them in a fury. A gloved hand seized her arm and reeled her back in. Finding herself face-to-face with Joseph, she raised her free hand to slap him. He caught her wrist, and she fought to escape his grip.

"How dare you?" she snarled. "How dare you bring them here?"

"No harm'll befall you or your family," he said as she struggled. "We ain't here to rob ya."

"You expect me to believe that? I know who you are, Joseph Gray. Ten years ago, you shot up my town and left my family with nothing. You *ruined* us."

He grimaced and glanced down before meeting her gaze again. "Then you know we ain't to be trifled with, so no trouble from you, ya got that?"

"I don't care wh—"

Joseph tightened his hold and pulled her so close that Dinah saw brown rings at the center of his hazel eyes. "If you care about *them,* you'll do what you're told."

She glared up at him, bitterly marveling at how suddenly the daring hero who'd saved their cattle had been unmasked as a villain.

"I thought you were a good man," she said. A lump burned in her throat as she shook her head. "I've never been more wrong."

His eyes dimmed, and his lips pressed together.

"Everything under control, Joseph?" asked a gravelly voice with a Mexican accent.

Joseph blinked and looked to his left. Following his gaze, Dinah felt the blood drain from her face.

Sal Valentin was ten years older now, but his deep-set eyes were unmistakable. His bronze skin and shoulder-length hair. His rust-colored coat and the gold-studded band of his black hat.

For months after the robbery, his name and his bandana-covered face had been plastered all over Salina. Everywhere she went, she'd seen him, heard whispers of him, never escaping those desolate eyes.

Dinah didn't hear Joseph's reply, only the frantic thumping in her ears. She shook uncontrollably, her teeth chattering. She jerked against Joseph with such sudden force that she managed to slip out of his grasp.

She stumbled away from them. Crippled by the excruciating squeezing in her chest, she stopped and bent over, one hand braced on her knee and the other on her stomach as she gasped for breath.

He isn't real. It's just a dream. Just a dream.

"Miss?"

"Don't touch me," she snapped, shrinking from Joseph as he reached for her.

He dropped his hand to his side and turned to his boss. "She's scared outta her wits, Sal."

Dinah's mouth went dry, her insides twisting in knots as she slowly raised her eyes. Sal looked right at her—*through* her—his cold stare turning her to stone. Something flickered in the Stygian depths of his eyes. Curiosity? Recognition?

Does he remember me? Remember her?

He propped his wrists on the saddle horn and asked, "Do you know who I am?"

Dinah gulped, and Sal leaned toward her.

"Do you know who I am?" he asked again, his voice dropping an octave.

Should she lie? Would it matter if she did?

"Yes," she croaked, hoping she hadn't just made a fatal mistake.

Satisfied, Sal straightened and shifted his gaze back to Joseph. "Put her to work. Have her feed and water the horses. Then she can join us inside."

———— •———

Once Sal had stalled his horse and gone into the house, Dinah made the short trek to the windmill next to her mother's trampled garden, Joseph's spurs clinking a few paces behind her. Gingerly, she touched a place where the reins had struck her, and pain lanced through her lower back. She flinched and bit her lip.

"You all right?"

Dinah's rage thawed the fear that had frozen her. She rounded on him and jabbed a finger toward the house.

"My parents are in there with that *monster*, who's doing God knows what to them, and you have the *gall* to ask me if I'm all right?"

"He won't hurt 'em without cause."

"May 3rd, 1873," she shot back. "It was her birthday. She'd just turned eleven, and he shot her. My best friend."

Joseph's eyes widened, and Dinah drew a shuddering breath.

"Her crime?" She shrugged, her voice breaking around the lump in her throat. "Wrong place, wrong time."

He bowed his head, and Dinah turned her back to him, wiping away her tears. She picked up a pail and dipped it into the large tub of water by the windmill. Joseph silently trailed her as she carried the pail to the barn. Four mounts had been tied at the hitching rails on either side of the open doors, the four stalls already occupied.

As her eyes adjusted to the dimness inside, Dinah saw Marcus' black horse and Joseph's blue roan in the stalls on the left. On the right stood Remy's Palouse and Sal's cream-colored stallion, glowing like some kind of otherworldly creature in the sunlight shining through the high window at the back of the barn. He had his head over the door, his pale eye watching her.

She swallowed and headed into the first stall on her left. Marcus' horse appeared to be a Morgan, about fifteen hands tall. He looked at her when she entered, ears flicking forward. As Dinah poured the water into his bucket, she scrambled to come up with a plan.

If she could somehow incapacitate Joseph, she could ride to Salina, tell the marshal what had happened, and return with a posse. But what would Sal do to her parents if he was cornered? Would he use them as a bargaining chip? Would he kill them? Was he planning to kill them anyway?

Dinah looked at the house as she went to refill the bucket. *I have to try.*

When she returned to the barn, she discreetly glanced around as she walked down the aisle, searching for something she could use as a weapon. *The pitchfork? No... Wait.*

Her father's hammer lay on a bale of hay.

That'll do, she thought. It wouldn't be pretty. Such a blow could kill Joseph. *He deserves it for bringin' 'em here.*

Dinah slid back the latch and stepped into the stall. The stallion pinned his ears and stamped his hoof.

"He don't care for nobody but me," Joseph said, sauntering over to her and reaching for the pail. "Here."

She handed it to him, and he went to fill the bucket.

This is my chance.

Dinah crept backward out of the stall. Her fingers curled around the hammer, gripping the handle so tight her knuckles turned white. Mustering her courage, she inched toward Joseph with a trembling hand.

She'd never killed a man before. Much as she despised him, she realized she didn't want to do this.

Dad needs me. Mama needs me.

Dinah lowered one foot into the straw, then the other, trying not to think about what would happen if she failed. She raised the hammer above her head and—

Joseph spun around.

Too late to change her mind now. Dinah swung, and he dropped the bucket. Catching her hands with his, he reversed her momentum and shoved her against the side of the stall.

She felt as if boiling water had splashed onto her back. Dinah cried out, her arms going slack. Joseph yanked the hammer from her grasp, snatching away her last hope of escape.

"Are you crazy?" he exclaimed. "That whippin' weren't enough for ya?"

Her chest heaved as she stared up at him. The wild look in his eyes pinned her to the wall, made her wonder if he would use her own weapon against her. Bash her skull in with her father's hammer.

Something doused the flames. Joseph's clenched jaw relaxed, and he stepped back. He picked up the spilled bucket and held it out to her.

"Go on. I ain't dumb enough to turn my back on you twice."

———————◆●————————

Dinah sat on the floor of her room, wrists bound to the bedpost. She'd been there all afternoon, alone and straining to hear the conversation below. She hadn't discerned anything of importance, nor had she heard the voices of her parents.

When Joseph had brought her into the house, she hadn't seen her father. Sal had taken the seat at the head of their table, ordering her mother to serve him a meal like he was some kind of king. His arrogance had pro-voked a violent impulse in Dinah, but Joseph had dragged her up the stairs before she could act on it.

Miserably, she looked over at the well-worn Bible on the corner of her desk.

Why here? Why us? Haven't we suffered enough?

How many nights had she lain awake on her tearstained pillow, praying that justice would find Sal Valentin? Yet, here he was, alive and in her house.

Dinah shifted, her back cramping and her legs aching. She gazed out the window, the sky bathed in the fiery glow of the setting sun. She couldn't be sure of the time, but her stomach had been growling for a while now. Her head throbbed with a dull, persistent pain, and she felt faint.

Dinah jumped as the door opened.

The mustached man who'd aimed his gun at her father's head strode into the room. He drew a knife from his belt, and she lurched sideways with a jolt of panic, her boots scuffing against the floor. The bed budged a couple of inches, and he held up his hands.

"Easy," he said, "I'm not gonna hurtcha."

"Stay away from me," she warned, voice tremoring and wrists twisting inside the rope.

"Hey, between you and me, Remy had it comin'. He's got no idea how to treat a lady."

"And you do?" Dinah growled. "Leavin' me tied up like a prisoner?"

"Well, we can't have ya runnin' off to squeal on us." He canted his head with an infuriating smirk. "You should count yourself lucky. You'll have quite a story to tell. Ain't many farm girls who can say they've met Tony Vega."

I wish I couldn't.

Everything about him repulsed her. His liberal use of pomade. His garish gold tie. He reeked of vanity.

Tony crouched beside her, and she jerked her knees up to her chest, every muscle tensing.

"Sal sent me to getcha," he explained.

Her empty stomach churned at the mention of his name. "What does he want with me?"

Tony shrugged. "Don't know. Didn't ask."

He reached toward her, and Dinah recoiled.

"Look," he huffed, "I've had a real rough day, so hold still, wouldja?"

She sat rigid, watching him out of the corner of her eye as he tugged at the knots. The knife sawed back and forth. The rope loosened, then released.

She exhaled in relief and rubbed her wrists. Her cuffed sleeves had kept them from being scraped raw, but they were sore. She burned at the memory of Joseph shutting her in, ignoring her pleas for him to let her go.

Gripping the bedpost, Dinah hauled herself upright.

Tony rested one hand on his holster and gestured for her to walk in front of him. "All right, come on."

She stepped toward the door and swayed, her legs stiff and unsteady. Dinah hesitated, taking a moment to regain her balance. She ventured into the hallway.

"Don't try nothin'," he told her, following close behind.

She'd given up trying to escape. Both attempts had failed, and Dinah feared that a third would have deadly consequences.

She figured that a robbery must've gone awry, and now the gang was hiding from the law. She could only hope that the gang would soon be on their way—or that a posse might track them here.

How many were caught in the crossfire this time?

The stairs creaked under Dinah's boots, and Sal's voice rumbled up from below. It might as well have risen from the depths of hell. Her face grew hot, breaking out in a sweat.

She stopped and braced herself against the wall. Her heart hurled itself so violently against her ribs that she thought it would burst. That she would collapse right there on the stairs.

"Hey, what're ya doin'?" Tony asked impatiently.

Resuming her descent, Dinah dragged her hand along the wall, and it seemed to push back. To be closing in on her. The normally enticing smell of roasted pheasant turned her stomach as it wafted up the steps, and when she rounded the corner, her hands curled into fists.

Sal sat at the head of their table, where her *father* should be, cutting into the bird she'd killed that morning. The flat profile of his face glowed in candlelight, his hooded eyes fixed on his plate as he forked a bite into his mouth. He'd taken off his hat to dine, and so had the others. Marcus and Remy's backs were turned to her, Joseph and the man she assumed to be Remy's brother sitting across from them.

Joseph glanced up from his plate, a dark lock of hair falling over one eye. Sweeping it back with his fingers, he straightened in his chair. He'd shed his coat and bandana, the sleeves of his dark blue shirt rolled up to his elbows.

Dinah glared daggers at him, but he made no attempt to match her hostility, his expression blank and apathetic.

"I brought her like you asked, Sal," Tony said as he drew alongside her.

Sal lowered his fork and considered her. Dinah suspected that he'd become aware of her the second she walked into the room.

He indicated the empty chair at the opposite end of the table. "Have a seat, Miss Hance. You must be hungry."

Not anymore, she thought, but she doubted she'd be allowed to refuse him.

Inching toward the chair, she peered through the doorway to the right and saw a fire blazing in the hearth. The big blond man leaned against the mantle with a plate of food in his hands, her father's Springfield rifle and her Winchester mounted on the wall above his head. Another man sat on the couch. He seemed about her age, maybe even younger, and he also bore a strong resemblance to Remy.

What looked like part of a bedsheet had been wrapped around his shoulder. Had he been shot?

Seeing no sign of her father, Dinah sank into the chair. Her head swam, shadows dancing behind the outlaws like manifestations of their wicked spirits. She gripped the arms of the chair, anchoring herself to the floor. Tethering herself to reality.

Someone entered from the kitchen, and she glanced up. Relief flooded through her.

"Mama."

Her mother's eyes met hers and welled with tears. Anxiety creased her forehead and knitted her brows, but she appeared to be unharmed. She came over and set a plate of food in front of her, then took Dinah's face in her hands and drew her close, clutching her to her chest.

Dinah shut her eyes tight and asked, "Where's Dad?"

"Upstairs," she whispered back.

"Your mother tells me you've lived here all your life," Sal interrupted with apparent interest.

A chill ran down her spine, chasing away the warmth of her mother's embrace, and Dinah opened her eyes.

Her mother spun to face him and snapped, "Don't talk to her, you snake."

Remy jabbed his knife at her. "Show some respek, or I'll cut ou'ya tongue."

Her mother's bravery amazed her, but Dinah feared for her safety.

"Nearly," she blurted in an effort to quell whatever anger the insult might've kindled in Sal. "We... we came to Kansas when I was five years old."

Chewing, he nodded thoughtfully, his black beard accentuating the angles of his wide jaw. "You like it here?"

A complicated question, but she gave a simple answer. "Yes."

"It would be unfortunate to lose the farm because of your father's foolishness."

Dinah's nails dug into the arms of the chair. "What're you talkin' about?"

"Don't listen to him, Dinah," her mother interjected.

"Joseph told me about the debt," he replied as casually as if he were discussing the weather.

Fury surged in her, and Dinah's eyes darted to Joseph. His gaze stayed on his plate as he poked at some peas with his fork.

Wait—how did *he* know about her family's debt?

"Foolishness had nothing to do with it. Not on Jesse's part," her mother shot back. "You left him no choice when you robbed us."

Sal leaned forward, his dark eyes unblinking. "Time and chance happen to everyone, Mrs. Hance. Our choices are all we have, and your husband made a poor one."

Dinah seethed. How *dare* he.

"You're a thief and a murderer," her mother growled. "Your time is coming, and when it does, you'll beg your maker for mercy."

Remy came out of his seat, but Marcus yanked him back down.

Dinah reached over in alarm and squeezed her mother's wrist, imploring her to be silent. Her mother ignored her, eyes wide and the vein in her forehead bulging.

"So, you're a woman of faith." Unaffected by her threat, Sal sat back and studied her. "Do you wonder why God didn't stop us from robbing you? Why he took Lydia from you before she drew her first breath?"

Her mother gasped as if he'd knocked the wind right out of her. "How do you—?"

"I saw her grave."

Forget control. Forget the consequences. Dinah's simmering rage boiled over, and she grabbed the knife beside her plate. He'd meet his maker *today*.

She flung it at Sal's head. He twisted to his left, and the knife flew past his face. The window behind him shattered, raining down glass with a tremendous crash.

Dinah's chest heaved as she stared at the jagged hole behind him. Wind rushed into the room, tossing his hair and stirring the tablecloth. The candles quivered, and Sal's gaze met hers. She felt as if a pair of icy hands had closed around her throat.

I'm dead.

The black coals of his eyes ignited, an eerie smile flickering across his face. "I like you."

———

Dinah asked to be excused to the privy, and Sal ordered Tony to escort her. By her estimation, six or seven hours had passed since she'd been left in her room, and she couldn't endure the burning pressure a second longer. Nor could she stomach Sal's fascination with her attempt to kill him. Relieved as she was to be alive, she felt like a mouse trapped between his claws.

Does he think it's funny? Treating us like playthings?

The door creaked as Dinah stepped out of the privy and into the crisp evening air. Dark clouds blew like billowing smoke across a blazing sky. Crickets chorused in the grass as she scanned the hills to the east. Her heart sank.

No sign of a posse.

"You got guts, I'll give ya that," Tony said as they walked around to the front of the house. "He's killed folk for less."

Wait till Dad gets him in his sights, she thought, her gaze lingering on her parents' bedroom window. Her father was a soldier, a *hero*. He'd come up with a plan. Find a way to escape. And when he did, Sal wouldn't know what hit him.

"Donny," Tony called to the man pacing in the yard, "how's Charlie doin'?"

So, Donny was his name—the spitting image of Remy who'd watched as he whipped her, who'd sat next to her at the dinner table.

"He's tougha dan he looks," Donny answered, meeting her glare with his own. "He'll pull through."

Dinah hoped he didn't. One brother of Remy was bad enough.

Donny stayed in the yard when she climbed the porch steps, but Tony followed right behind her. She approached the door, hand trembling as she reached for the handle. She drew a deep breath, bracing herself for whatever came next.

Pushing it open, Dinah ventured inside and stopped short.

Their furniture had been turned to face the piano, where her mother perched on the edge of the bench. Sal sat alone on the couch, stiff and straight with his palms on his thighs. Remy slouched in a chair to his left. Charlie shifted beside him with obvious discomfort, the bloodstained fabric still wrapped around his shoulder.

The big blond man in the chair to Sal's right had his elbows on his knees and his face in his hands. Tony shut the door and went over to him.

"It's gonna be okay, Gus," he said, giving his shoulder a firm pat.

Did they lose someone?

Leaning against the end of the hearth with his arms crossed over his chest, Joseph raised his bowed head. His sullen gaze met hers, and she looked away, blinking as smoke stung her eyes. Marcus stood behind Sal, his elbow propped on the mantle and a cigarette between his fingers as he stared into the crackling fire.

Moving the furniture wasn't enough? Now they had to stink up the whole house? Dinah's blood boiled at the way they lounged about, acting as if everything belonged to them.

"Do you sing, Miss Hance?" Sal inquired as though she hadn't thrown a knife at his head five minutes ago. His stone-cold composure unnerved her more than any outburst.

"Sometimes."

He nodded. "Sing for me."

The knot in her chest tightened. She didn't like singing in front of people, despite the compliments she'd received. "I— I don't think I can—"

"I don't ask for anything twice, Miss Hance."

Dinah gulped and winced. Her throat was bone dry. She hadn't eaten a single bite off her plate, and her tongue swelled with thirst.

Her mother gave her a sympathetic look and put her fingers on the keys. As Dinah drifted closer to the piano, Joseph left the room.

Just as well, she thought, fidgeting under Sal's steady gaze. She ducked her head and tucked a curl behind her ear, her hair disheveled and falling from its pins.

Would Sal punish them if she chose a song he didn't like?

Joseph came from the dining room with a glass of water. He offered it to her, and Dinah stared at him, caught off guard. A vengeful impulse tempted her to slap the drink out of his hand, but she couldn't. She needed it.

Dinah's fingers brushed against his glove when she took the glass. She jerked back her hand, and the water sloshed. Her cheeks burned as she raised the drink to her lips, Remy's narrowed eyes following Joseph as he returned to the hearth.

The long sip soothed her throat, and she set the glass on top of the piano. She looked around at the grim faces staring back at her, remembering simpler times. Happier times.

She leaned down and murmured, "The Meeting of the Waters."

Her mother nodded and gave her hand an encouraging squeeze before she started playing. The gentle melody stirred up a yearning in her, a longing for innocence lost.

"There is not in the wide world a valley so sweet as that vale in whose bosom the bright waters meet," Dinah sang. "Oh, the last rays of feeling and life must depart, ere the bloom of that valley shall fade from my heart. Ere the bloom of that valley shall fade from my heart.

"Yet it was not that nature had shed o'er the scene her purest crystal and brightest of green. 'Twas not her soft magic of streamlet or hill. Oh, no—it was something more exquisite still." Her voice wavered on the last word.

She's a young girl again, her arm locked with Ophelia's as they spin round and round, dizzy and laughing. Her father leans on the piano while her mother plays and sings, tapping his foot and attempting to harmonize. Not very well, but he never seems to care. Daniel grins and claps and joins in as Ophelia's parents belt "Nelly Bly" in their thick Swedish accents.

The vision faded, leaving her surrounded by silent strangers. *Intruders.*

Dinah swallowed and soldiered on. "Oh, no—it was something more exquisite still."

She met Sal's black unblinking eyes, defiance sparking in her heart. Resentment strengthened her voice. Emboldened her.

"'Twas that friends, the beloved of my bosom, were near. Who made every dear scene of enchantment more dear, and who felt how the best charms of nature improve when we see them reflected from looks that we love. When we see them reflected from looks that we love."

Tony sniffed and cleared his throat. Gus wiped his eyes. A draft sighed into the room from the east, red shafts filtering through the western window. The flames shivered behind Sal, his fixed features void of emotion.

Dinah clenched her fists, her nails digging into her palms as hot tears spilled down her cheeks. "Sweet vale of Avoca! How calm could I rest in thy bosom of shade with the friends I love best, where the storms that we feel in this cold world should cease, and our hearts, like thy waters, be mingled in peace." She struggled to utter the concluding words, her voice on the verge of breaking. "And our hearts, like thy waters, be mingled in peace."

The last slivers of sunlight faded with the final note of the piano, and Sal became a hellish silhouette. The fire popped and hissed, the walls shifting in the howling wind.

"Help!" someone cried.

Charlie sat up in alarm. "Dat's Donny."

Her mother rose from the bench as Remy ran to the door, and Dinah waited with bated breath.

"It's Hance!" he exclaimed. "He's got Donny."

I knew it. I knew he'd save us.

Heart leaping, she spun and met her mother's anxious gaze as the outlaws drew their six-shooters.

"I want my wife and my daughter!" her father demanded. "Bring 'em out to me, and we'll be on our way. Nobody's gotta die tonight."

"Easy, boys," Sal said, putting on his hat. He stood and strode closer to the door. "I warned you not to do anything foolish, Mr. Hance."

"There's nothin' I won't do for my family," her father shot back. "Can you say the same?"

"I can," Remy answered.

He stormed toward Dinah.

"Don't take her," her mother begged, clinging to Dinah's right arm as he grabbed her left one. "Take me instead!"

Gus wrestled her mother away from them, and Remy forced Dinah out the door and into the dim blue dusk.

"*Please!*" her mother cried.

Cool air hit Dinah's face. He rammed his revolver against the small of her back, angering the welts under her shirt. She yelped at the pain as Remy pushed her down the steps, his fingers digging into her arm as she struggled to keep her balance.

"You wan' ya daughta?" he snarled. Yanking her to a stop at the bottom of the stairs, he shoved the barrel against her temple. "Gimme my brotha."

Her father stood thirty feet in front of them, holding his Colt to Donny's head. Donny was tall, but her father was taller. His stalwart build made the outlaw look like a scared little boy by comparison. He squirmed in her father's grasp, his arm twisted behind his back.

"My daughter first," her father insisted, dark curls whipping across his unflinching features.

"Ya tink I'm playin'?" Remy clicked back the hammer. "Send 'im ova, or I'll blow 'er brains out."

Tears sprang to Dinah's eyes. "Dad, please."

"Shut up!" Remy snapped, making her jump.

"Do it, Jesse!" her mother pleaded.

Her father glanced up, desperation plain on his face, and Dinah followed his gaze.

The whole gang had come out onto the porch. Joseph had his hands on her mother's shoulders, holding her back.

"All right. All right," her father yielded. "Just... don't hurt her."

Lowering the gun, he released his hostage. Donny took a hesitant step forward.

"Go," her father urged with an impatient gesture.

Donny crossed the yard, and Dinah prayed that Remy wouldn't pull the trigger, the cold metal still pressed against her temple.

"My daughter," her father entreated.

"You're in no position to make demands, Mr. Hance," Sal replied, his spurs clinking down the steps. "You've gambled and lost."

Dread chilled Dinah's bones.

Her father's brow furrowed, his mouth twisting with quiet fury. "Haven't you taken enough from us?"

"Not yet," Sal answered as he drew alongside her. "You haven't paid your debts, Mr. Hance. I'm here to collect."

Her father's face went slack as understanding dawned. "Tell Roach I don't have his money. I need more time."

"Time is a luxury you can't afford."

Panic squeezed Dinah's heart, her eyes darting back and forth between them.

Her father waved his gun toward the pastures. "Then take our horses, our cattle."

"You misunderstand," Sal said. "Tonight, you bet your life, and you must pay with it."

Terror gripped her. "You can't do this."

Sal turned to her without a shred of remorse on his callous countenance. "Your father made a choice, and now his debt falls to you."

She couldn't breathe, pressure building in her chest as her mother appealed to Sal's humanity.

"Dinah. Sweetheart, look at me," her father implored.

She met his gaze, tears scalding her eyes.

"I love you," he said, "and I hope you can forgive me."

She choked back a sob, unable to speak. He raised his eyes, gazing past her, and she knew he was looking at her mother. He swallowed, the rusted blades of the windmill grating as they spun like the hands of a clock.

Dinah shut her eyes tight and prayed for a miracle.

Please, God.

The windmill screeched in a sudden gust, and her eyes flew open. Her father stood unshaken, his face set with grim resolve as Sal stared him down.

Sal's right hand reached across his body. Her father raised his revolver. Two barrels flashed in the darkness.

Ears ringing, Dinah watched her father fall. Heard her mother scream. Shock numbed her, every thought obliterated. He lay in the waving grass, and she waited for him to get up.

He can't be. He can't be…

Blood dripped down Sal's cheek as he looked at her. "Now you see, Miss Hance. God doesn't care, and if he does, he's powerless to stop me."

An all-consuming rage erupted inside her. Wrenching herself from Remy's grasp, Dinah lunged at Sal.

Her head snapped back. Remy had a hold of her hair. Twisting in his grip, Dinah hit him everywhere she could reach. His chest. His chin. His nose.

Pain split her skull as Remy whipped her upside the head with the butt of his gun.

She collapsed in the grass, dazed and defeated. Blankly, she stared at her father, her scarred heart tearing apart at the seams as she slipped into oblivion.

CHAPTER SIX

Time passed in a blur, and even after they'd left the homestead miles behind them, Joseph still heard Mrs. Hance's screams. Felt her collapsing in his arms as she watched her husband die. He'd held her back when she tried to run to Jesse. Subdued her when she lashed out at him, wailing that they'd all be damned for what they'd done.

Another nail driven into his coffin. He knew the wages of his sins. It was only a matter of time.

Earlier that afternoon, he'd ridden out on Hance land with Marcus and Sal, who'd decided that half of the fifty thousand they'd taken from the bank should be hidden away till they'd thrown the law off their trail. Joseph had led them to the dogwood tree where he'd sat with Dinah yesterday morning, and they'd buried it there. He wondered if they'd ever get a chance to come back for it.

They'd killed more men today than they had in a month. Posses would scour the prairie for them. Pinkertons would never stop hunting them. They'd spilled too much blood. Stolen too much money.

"Dose gals are gonna run straight ta da town marshal and blab about us," Remy complained as they neared their campsite southeast of the Hances' homestead. "Shoulda shot 'em."

"I shoulda shotcha for whippin' that girl," Marcus growled.

Joseph gripped the reins tighter, his blood boiling at the memory. *And now she's got no daddy.*

"I can't believe I'm sayin' this, but I'm with Remy," Gus said. "We gotta disappear. We can't keep leavin' loose ends."

Joseph cast him a sideways glance, surprised and disappointed. Gus agreeing with Remy?

Losin' Elliott's got him on edge. Tony too.

Sal looked at them over his shoulder. "We'll be long gone before the law tracks us here."

I hope so.

Any posses that might've come from Abilene would've had all day to search. To contact the marshals of surrounding towns.

We've gotta get outta Kansas—fast.

They found the camp quiet and without a fire. Four horses grazed under the stars, tails swishing as the tall grasses thrashed in the breeze. They raised their heads, and Rick's dun horse neighed a greeting.

"There you are," Rick called as he and Collin walked out of the darkness. "We were startin' to think things had gone sideways."

"They did," Gus said, never one to beat around the bush. "We got the money, but..."

"What?" Collin prompted.

Gus swallowed and met his gaze. "We lost Elliott."

Rick flinched as if he'd struck him. Joseph didn't think Collin's bearded face could get any whiter, but it did.

"What happened?" Rick asked.

Joseph dismounted and led Steel toward his tent. He didn't want to hear it. Didn't want to talk about it. Watching the life leave Elliott's eyes would haunt him the rest of his days.

"*Don't wait, Joseph,*" he'd said.

Wait for what? To change? To leave his outlaw ways behind?

This gang was the only family he had to fight for. All he had to live for.

"Joseph."

He turned and saw Marcus striding toward him with his black Morgan in tow.

"Hell of a day, huh?"

Joseph nodded. "One of the worst I can remember."

Marcus stopped and frowned. "What happened to Elliott weren't your fault. You know that, don'tcha?"

Of course he did. That didn't make his death any easier to swallow.

Joseph sighed and stared at his boots. Should he keep his thoughts to himself? If he couldn't tell Marcus, he couldn't tell anyone.

"It ain't just Elliott," he admitted.

He glanced over Marcus' shoulder, took a step closer, and lowered his voice so the others couldn't hear. "Sal didn't have to shoot the teller. He'd already let us into the vault."

"The teller slowed us down," Marcus said. "If he hadn't, we might not've lost Elliott."

"And Jesse Hance?" Joseph challenged.

"He coulda killed Donny."

"But he didn't," Joseph argued with building frustration. "How's his family gonna make ends meet? How're they gonna pay the debt without him workin' the farm?"

Marcus' dark brows furrowed. "What're you sayin', Joseph?"

He hesitated, figuring how to put it. "I'm sayin' it don't sit right with me."

"Pack up, boys," Sal told the others as they swung down from their saddles.

"Where're we goin'?" Tony asked.

"Back to the Strip. To Dead Man's Dune."

Lawless and sparsely settled, the Neutral Strip was just south of Kansas and stretched all the way to the western border of Indian Territory. It didn't belong to any state or any man—not officially, anyhow. Cattlemen, squatters, and Comanche fought tooth and nail for the areas they laid claim to.

Dead Man's Dune was a ghost town the gang had holed up in six years ago when Texas Rangers had chased them out of the state—a perfect place to lay low for a while. At least, it used to be. Joseph hadn't been back there since.

He turned from Marcus, leaving Steel standing by his tent as he ducked inside.

No one had breathed a word about Enyeto since they'd left Abilene. Didn't Sal care what happened to him? Did any of them?

Enyeto had stepped between him and the man in the saloon without hesitation. He'd worked hard to provide them with fresh game to eat. To be accepted. He'd shown the gang complete loyalty, and he deserved the same in return.

Joseph rose with his bedroll tucked under his arm and pushed through the tent flap. Marcus and Sal had gone to break down their tents, Sal's pitched between theirs.

Joseph set the bedroll behind his saddle, and his hands lingered, his fingers curled around the leather straps that bound the wool.

Gears grind as his frantic eyes scan the windows for his mother's face. The train chugs away from the station, belching clouds of smoke into the winter air.

"Come back!" he cries as he runs down the platform, a blaring whistle drowning out his screams.

Joseph dropped his bedroll in the grass. *I can't abandon him.*

He took a deep breath and trudged toward Sal with a heavy heart. The journey to Dead Man's Dune would be a perilous one. Sal would need him, and he wouldn't be there to watch his back. Ever since he'd gotten into that fight in Salina, he'd done nothing but disappoint him.

"Sal," he said before he could change his mind, "I'm goin' back for Enyeto."

Sal had just secured his bedroll behind his saddle, and he turned to him with a frown. "Enyeto's dead, son."

"Maybe not."

"You gotta be kiddin', Joseph," Marcus exclaimed, marching over to them. "Ridin' back into Abilene is suicide."

"It ain't the smart thing to do, but it's the right thing." Joseph looked around, all of them staring at him with shocked expressions. "How many times've we stuck our necks out for each other?"

Collin sighed. "I don't want him to hang any more than you do, but there's nothin' we can do about it."

"We kicked a hornets' nest," Rick said. "Posses'll be swarmin' all over these hills."

"Rick's right," Tony agreed. "Live to fight another day, Joseph. That's what Enyeto would want."

"I can't help noticin' he ain't here to speak for himself," Joseph grumbled.

Gus huffed. "C'mon, Joseph. We needja. Don't throw your life away for a fella ya barely know, 'specially not for an Injun."

"*Enyeto is one of us,*" Sal had said, but the others didn't see him that way. The Ohio boys had joined the gang eight years ago. They'd been around much longer than Enyeto and the Guidry brothers, and because of that, they treated them differently. Kept them at arm's length.

If Elliott were sitting in a cell in Abilene, Joseph knew they'd be singing a different tune.

He looked at Sal, at the bloody mark on his left cheek where Hance's bullet had ripped off his skin. A rare reminder that even he wasn't invincible.

"Joseph, if you get caught, I won't be there to get you out," Sal warned him.

"I know." Joseph swallowed, wondering if he'd ever see him again. They risked death every time they pulled one of these jobs, but this time felt different. "I'll meetcha at Dead Man's Dune."

Sal wasn't one for sappy goodbyes, and neither was Joseph, so he walked away without another word, his heart pounding at the thought of going it alone.

"Joseph."

Marcus grabbed his arm and spun him around.

"Stop and listen for a second, wouldja?" he growled, his voice just above a whisper. "I know what this is about, and this ain't the way to make amends."

A lump stuck in Joseph's throat. He couldn't deny it, so he deflected. "I ain't dead yet, Marcus. If I end up six feet under, you can put 'I toldja so' on my tombstone."

———————————

Once everyone else had packed up and gone, Joseph tried to get some rest before he set out for Abilene. He tossed and turned for hours. No fire kept out the cold. No tent shielded him from the wailing wind. With his gloves on, his coat wrapped around him, and his head on his saddle, he lay staring at two veins of light flowing like a river through a field of twinkling stars.

What would Dinah and her mother do now? They couldn't afford to hire cowhands. Roach would take their ranch, and then what? With her brother gone and her father dead, what lengths would Dinah be driven to? What would poverty reduce her to?

Joseph looked at the saddlebags sitting beside him. Marcus had given him his share of the take before he left—twenty-five hundred dollars. More money than he'd ever had in his pocket. Much more than he needed.

He couldn't right the wrong. He couldn't bring her father back. But if he lived to see another sunrise, he'd do what he could.

A sudden clamor of barks and howls made Joseph sit up so fast his head spun. He grabbed his rifle and put the stock to his shoulder, squinting into the surrounding darkness. Steel raised his head and gazed north, his ears forward and alert. The coyotes cried again.

They were a long ways off.

Joseph set the Winchester aside, reached into his coat, and pulled out his pocket watch.

One thirty.

Time to head out.

Wearily, he rose and picked up his saddle and blanket.

"Y'know, it's a good thing you can't talk," he said as he hoisted them onto Steel's back. "You'd be tellin' me what a crazy fool I am for doin' this, and you'd be right."

The mustang gave him that same sidelong glance, his big black eyes always seeing straight through him. It both unnerved and comforted him— that strange wisdom horses seemed to have.

Joseph rolled up his bed and buckled the leather straps, tucked it under his arm, and slung the saddlebags over his shoulder. He secured them behind his saddle, retrieved his rifle, and pushed it into the scabbard. Once he'd nudged the bit between Steel's stubborn teeth, he stuck his boot in the stirrup and mounted.

He looked back at the ashes of the fire that had burned that morning, half expecting to see Elliott sitting on an overturned box and stirring a pot of beans. Instead, he saw an empty campsite. Smelled no biscuits. Heard no laughter.

He'd never been away from the gang before—not like this. It felt wrong. Lonely.

"Just you and me, boy."

He pointed Steel east and tapped his sides with his spurs. As the stallion's hooves pounded and the wind rushed in his ears, Joseph couldn't stop thinking about the robbery and what happened at the homestead, trapped in a miserable cycle of "what ifs" and "should haves."

Focus, he reminded himself. *What's the plan? How're you gonna get Enyeto outta there?*

He'd shot two lawmen during their escape, and Tony had killed a third. *That'll have dealt 'em a serious blow. They'll be shorthanded, 'specially with more folks out lookin' for us.*

Joseph weighed his options, considered several situations and how they could play out. Some riskier than others. If he managed to find Enyeto without getting caught, could he subdue the guards without firing a shot? Any commotion would bring the wrath of the whole town down on them, and they'd be done for.

With no moon to light his path, navigating the steeper slopes proved difficult. *Won't be goin' nowhere if Steel breaks a leg.*

Joseph slowed his pace. A shiver ran through him, and he sniffed, nose burning and eyes watering as the wind stung them.

Movement drew his gaze. He stopped and peered into the darkness. A hundred yards to his left, floating lights drifted westward.

Lanterns.

Joseph ducked his head and tugged his hat farther over his brow, his heart thumping faster. Posse or not, he had no intention of being spotted. Steering well clear of them, he glanced over his shoulder, waiting for shouts to rise above the wind. For hooves to thunder behind him.

The lights disappeared over the next hill, and Joseph sighed in relief. *Good thing there ain't no moon, after all.*

The hills flattened as he kept riding east, and he guessed that he was less than five miles out from Abilene now.

The knot in his chest pulled tighter, his buried fears bubbling to the surface. *What if Sal's right? What if Enyeto's dead, and I came all this way for nothin'?*

Something moaned in the darkness ahead.

Startled, Joseph brought Steel to an abrupt halt. The stallion stood at attention, the wind ruffling his mane and whispering through the grass.

"You hear that, boy?"

There it was again. A cry for help.

Joseph spurred Steel forward, his hand on his holster as he ventured closer to the road. He shouldn't show himself to anyone. Shouldn't risk getting recognized. But a line had hooked somewhere behind his breastbone, reeling him in.

Was it guilt? Curiosity? A sense of responsibility?

Whatever the reason, Joseph couldn't ignore it.

A big box-like shape appeared out of the blackness. He leaned forward and squinted. He could just make out two wheels turned sideways.

A wagon.

Joseph circled in front of it and found broken crates littering the ground, their contents scattered in the grass. A stranger lay pinned under the wagon, squirming and struggling.

"You're in a pretty bad way there, partner," Joseph called.

The man froze and looked up at him. "Please, help me. I can't move."

Joseph feigned indifference. "Quite a bind."

"Please, sir! My— My leg—"

Joseph rolled his eyes and sighed, his conscience pestering him like a fly. "All right. Quit your naggin'."

He dismounted and approached him, stepping over broken eggs and splintered wood. "What're you doin' out here so late, anyhow? That's just askin' for trouble."

"I might ask you the same, sir."

His eyes darted to the farmer's wizened gaze. *Does he recognize me?*

Joseph turned his face away and braced his gloved hands against the underside of the wagon. "Get ready to crawl, old man."

Teeth clenched and muscles taut, Joseph pushed with all his strength. The wagon shifted, and the stranger wriggled out from underneath. Once his leg had been freed, Joseph let the wagon fall with a heavy thud.

The farmer's bearded face twisted as he got to his feet. Balancing on one leg, he clutched his ribs, his bony shoulders stooped with age. He wore a wool cap on his head, his clothes covered in patches.

"Thank you," he panted. "Them that robbed me—they stole my horse. My goods. I was takin' these supplies to Abilene, to folk who need 'em."

"That's… real unfortunate," Joseph mumbled, looking down and scuffing his boot in the dirt.

"If it ain't too much trouble, mister, my cabin's just a couple miles north of here. Can you take me there?"

He shook his head. "Sorry, partner. I ain't got the time. Someone else'll come—"

"I know I'm askin' a lot, sir, but I'll compensate ya," the stranger pleaded.

Joseph pinched the bridge of his nose, and pain flashed between his closed eyes. It still hadn't healed from the headbutt he'd taken in the saloon a couple of nights ago. He hissed through his teeth and lowered his hand.

"Stand up on that crate over there."

He pointed, and the man's wrinkled brow creased deeper in confusion. Joseph didn't bother explaining himself. He returned to Steel and climbed into the saddle, his limbs stiff with cold and the many miles he'd already ridden that day.

"Mind your manners now," he muttered, the mustang's ears flicking back at the sound of his voice. "If ya buck him off, you'll break him."

Joseph walked the stallion over to the crate, where the stranger stood shivering. Leaning to his left, he stuck out his elbow and said, "Get on."

The farmer's face brightened. "Oh, thank you, sir! Thank you."

He reached up and grasped Joseph's arm with a weathered hand. Joseph braced as the man pulled, and he hauled him up onto Steel's back. The mustang snorted and tossed his head.

"Easy," Joseph warned. He glanced over his shoulder. "You on?"

"Yeah," the stranger grunted, letting go of his arm.

Joseph started off at a slow and steady pace. "Couple miles north, you said?"

"That's right. Ya got a name, mister?"

"Joseph," he answered reluctantly.

"A fine name. A strong name. I'm Obadiah."

Awful cheerful for a fella who just got robbed.

"Long way from home, ain'tcha?" Obadiah remarked.

Joseph's eyes narrowed as he stared at the starry horizon. "How do ya mean?"

"I know a Dixie drawl when I hear one. I was born and raised in Tennessee. Moved out here after the war ended."

"A place ain't home just 'cause you're born there," Joseph grumbled.

"True." Obadiah sighed. "I didn't know what to do with myself when the fightin' stopped. I was angry and restless. Thought I needed a change of scenery, somewhere that weren't so familiar. I traveled eight hundred miles, only to realize that my home had been right beside me all along. It weren't a place. It was my wife."

Is he in the habit of sharin' his life story with strangers?

"We'd lived in the same house almost thirty years. She musta reckoned I'd lost my marbles, but she left her family, her town, everything she'd ever known to follow me to Kansas. I don't deserve 'er, my Martha. Ya got a woman, Joseph?"

His heart sank, and he clenched his jaw. "No."

He never had. Not for longer than a night.

"Why not?"

Obadiah's interest seemed genuine, but Joseph's patience was wearing thin. "I ain't the settlin' type."

"In my experience, a wanderin' man's lookin' for somethin'. Searchin' for a thing he's missin'."

"I ain't missin' nothin' but *silence*," Joseph snapped.

Liar.

"If you're plannin' to pass through Abilene," Obadiah ventured after a pause, "I should tell ya that a bank was robbed, and there was a big fire on the south side of town."

Joseph swallowed.

"A gang of outlaws came through yesterday mornin' and cleaned out the vault. Killed a lotta good men, includin' the sheriff. Terrible business. *Terrible.* They caught one of 'em—locked him up in the calaboose on First Street. The marshal's out lookin' for the rest."

Joseph breathed a quiet exhale. *Enyeto's alive.*

And now he knew right where to find him.

———————— • ————————

Joseph stopped Steel in front of a little log cabin with a garden and a chicken coop. Sheep baaed and bleated in a nearby pen as Obadiah slid down from the stallion's back.

71

"Thank you," he said, eyes crinkling as he smiled up at him.

Joseph nodded. Warmth spread through him, the same warmth he'd felt when he saved the Hances' cattle. It felt… good. To help instead of harm. To be thanked instead of cursed.

"Here." Obadiah reached under the collar of his shirt and pulled out a necklace. A cross dangled from the chain, glimmering in the darkness. "As promised. That there is real silver. My pa wore it many moons ago—and his pa before him."

Bitter claws dug into Joseph's heart.

Joyful singing fills his ears. The voices of the adults around him rise above his own, the piping organ vibrating his chest. The sweet and acrid smell of the marshes and the spice of star jasmine waft through the church's open doors. His mother looks down at him and smiles. She holds his hand when they leave, the briny breeze of the Lowcountry blowing brown curls across her face.

Joseph shook his head. He wanted nothing to do with that cross. "I can't accept somethin' like that."

"Please," Obadiah insisted, holding out the necklace. His black brows drew together. "It would mean a lot to me."

Joseph avoided his gaze. "I ain't no saint."

"Neither am I. We're all sinners. Some of us tryin' our best, others doin' their worst."

Joseph huffed an angry, guilt-ridden cloud into the air and looked at him. He didn't understand why Obadiah wanted him to have it or how he could so easily part with something that had been in his family for generations. But, having no desire to insult or offend the old veteran, he reached down and took the cross from his outstretched hand.

"That's seen me through many a battle," Obadiah told him. "It'll never lead ya astray."

Joseph tucked the necklace in his coat pocket and said, "Take care, Obadiah."

He wheeled the mustang around and galloped southeast toward Abilene.

———————

Stars flickered in a pitch-black sky as Joseph rode into the slumbering town, the stillness a far cry from the havoc they'd wreaked yesterday morning. He checked his watch.

Four o'clock.

That meant two more hours of darkness. More than enough time to get in and out before the sun came up.

When he stuffed the watch back into his pocket, the edges of Obadiah's cross poked his gloved fingers. Joseph withdrew his hand as quickly as if the silver had burned him. He'd done a good deed—so what? It was impossible to balance the scales, to ever outweigh the evil he'd done.

Joseph stopped Steel at the corner of Cedar and First Street. A row of charred skeletons stood across from the jail—wood structures the fire had destroyed. One brick house had survived the blaze.

All that for a bag of money.

This didn't feel like sticking his thumb in Uncle Sam's eye. These were homes. Businesses. Everyday people just trying to get by.

Joseph walked Steel up to the small plank jail, a livery looming on the other side of it. Quietly, he slid to the ground. A chill ran through him—partly from the cold, partly from nerves. Joseph took a deep breath, curling and uncurling his stiff fingers as he looked up and down the street.

Not a soul in sight.

Heart thumping, he crept around front, hoping the wind masked the clink of his spurs. A lantern burned near the door, sitting on the ground at the feet of—

Joseph's stomach dropped, and he stopped in his tracks. Elliott's body lay in a lidless coffin leaning against the jail, a sign hanging from his neck that read *YOU'RE NEXT.*

A direct threat to the gang. To every outlaw who still walked free.

Every misgiving Joseph had went up in flames. He pulled his bandana over his nose and pressed his back against the wall. Drawing his left revolver, he reached out his right hand and rapped on the door.

"Who's there?" a male voice called. He sounded young. Afraid.

Joseph didn't answer.

The door swung open, shielding him from sight.

"Hello?" The lawman stepped into view, his hand on his holster. "Is someone there?"

Joseph lunged. He clamped his glove over the man's mouth and shoved his gun against his temple.

"Scream, and I blow your brains out," he growled. "Nod if you understand me."

Slowly, the man nodded, taking his hand off his holster.

Joseph steered him inside and shut the door behind them. He had no trouble controlling him—his hostage was as short as Tony and as skinny as Collin.

The jail consisted of a single room with a desk pushed against the far wall and a cell in the back left corner. Enyeto stood up from his cot, eyes wide with surprise.

Joseph's relief turned to rage when he saw new bruises on his face, and he holstered his Schofield. He grabbed fistfuls of his captive's green shirt and shoved him against the wall.

"Are you the one that beat him?" he demanded.

"Please, sir, I—"

"*Are ya?*"

"No! No! I had nothin' to do with that, mister. Honest."

"He's telling the truth," Enyeto said.

Joseph grimaced. He wanted to hit something. Needed an excuse to after seeing what the townsfolk had done to Elliott.

But this fella? He's an overgrown kid. Harmless.

Keeping one hand on his shoulder, Joseph relieved him of his weapon. "Quit your snivelin'. Ain'tcha got some pride?"

"I ain't no lawman, sir. There weren't no one else to watch him."

Joseph pushed him away in disgust. "Open that cell before I lose my temper."

The young man's hands shook as he unhooked the keys from his belt.

Joseph went over and laid the Colt on the desk. A framed photograph of Wild Bill Hickock hung next to a picture of a mustached man he didn't recognize. Lamplight reflected in the glassy black eye of a pronghorn mounted on the wall beside them. He turned from it as the cell door creaked open.

Enyeto walked out and gave him a grateful nod. "It's good to see you. I didn't think anyone was coming back for me."

"You're one of us," Joseph said. "I don't leave nobody behind."

Enyeto's eyes brightened.

Joseph marched over to the guard and yanked the keys from his clammy fingers. "I have half a mind to put *you* in one of them pine boxes. Maybe, if you keep real quiet till we're gone, I'll letcha off easy."

He shoved the young man into the cell and locked the door.

The new prisoner rushed forward and gripped the bars. "Please, sir, don't leave me in here."

"Consider yourself lucky," Joseph warned, stooping so that he was face-to-face with him. "If you ever spill a drop of Valentin blood, I'll come for ya, and our next meetin'll end differently."

The young man swallowed, white as a sheet.

Joseph turned to Enyeto, who'd gone to get his belongings from the corner. "You ready?"

"Yeah," Enyeto grunted, putting his bow on his back. "Let's get outta here."

CHAPTER SEVEN

Everything's brilliant and golden. The prairie ripples like polished amber in a brisk October breeze, the bur oak's falling leaves fluttering around them as her father watches her with twinkling eyes.

She's supposed to be picking up acorns, but she wants to prove herself, to show him that she can do anything Daniel does. She's wearing her father's hat, despite it being much too big for her. When she swings the rope above her head, the hat slips over her eyes, and his hearty laughter fills her ears. She wants to give him the meanest look she can muster. Instead, a grin splits her face, and she laughs with him.

Tears streamed down Dinah's cheeks as she sat in the shade of the oak's mighty branches, grinding acorns into powder. She'd gathered them last fall, blissfully unaware that she'd use them to dye all her clothes black. A whimper escaped her as she beat and battered them, pain pounding her skull like tiny fists.

Dinah reached up with searching fingers and traced the throbbing in her head to a scab above her right temple. The mark Remy's revolver had made was a couple of inches long, the area around it bruised and sensitive.

As soon as the gang had left, her mother had gone to fetch Dr. Stone.

"*She'll be all right,*" he'd said after a brief examination. "*She just needs to rest.*"

Dinah didn't remember much else from last night. When she'd woken early that morning, she'd found that her father's body had been taken away, and her mother had shut herself in her bedroom.

She set the mortar and pestle aside and slumped forward, burying her face in her hands. She gasped and shook with strangled sobs, an invisible fist squeezing so relentlessly that she was sure her heart would rupture. Oh, how it *hurt*.

Roach would take their house. Their land. Their cattle. Everything her father had worked so hard for. Had dedicated his *life* to.

She couldn't let it happen.

Dinah collected the mortar and pestle and her bag of acorns. When she rose, dizziness assailed her. She teetered sideways, blinking to clear her blurry vision.

Drifting clouds smothered the warmth of the rising sun, their shadows dimming her path as she returned to the house. Dinah shivered and steeled herself against the biting wind.

Once inside, she tramped through the silent living room and went into the kitchen, where she deposited her supplies onto the counter. She dumped the crushed acorns into a steel pot, poured in water from a bucket, and stirred the contents.

Leaving the pot to simmer on the already heated stove, Dinah crossed into the dining room, an icy gust rushing through the broken window as she climbed the stairs.

Be strong, she told herself, each step harder than the last. *Be strong for her.*

Dreading what she would find, she approached her parents' bedroom and stopped at the door to listen. All was quiet within.

"Mama?"

A muffled sniffle. "Yes?"

Dinah swallowed. "I'm goin' into town."

"Why?" her mother asked with strained suspicion.

"There's… there's somethin' I've gotta do. I'll be back soon."

Expecting her mother to protest, she waited.

"Just go," came her resigned reply. "I know I can't convince you otherwise."

Dinah wished she'd objected. She'd rather be scolded. Would rather bicker and quarrel.

Anything would be better than this cold indifference.

LOANS.

Dinah gazed at the black letters painted above the door, wondering if she looked as anxious as she felt. Roach hid his shady operations in plain sight, in a small office on the busiest street in town. Today, however, Santa Fe Avenue was sparsely populated. Most were attending the Sunday services, and she hoped to be long gone before they ended. She didn't want to see or speak to anyone.

No one except Roach.

She'd never met him before. Her father had always made her wait outside. He'd called Roach a crook. A swindler and a liar. And when it came to matters of finance, Dinah was already at a disadvantage, having a mind not at all inclined toward numbers and equations.

If Daniel were here…

But he wasn't. The men who'd transported her father's body to Salina had sent him a telegram about what happened, but part of her wondered if he would come to the funeral. If anything—even his father's death—could bring him back to Kansas.

Dinah smoothed her wind-tossed curls, straightened her jacket, and took a deep breath. Numbly, her legs carried her up the stairs. Her fingers closed around the handle and pulled.

The door swung open with an ominous creak. Before she could second-guess herself again, Dinah crossed the threshold.

Hazy sunlight spilled into the room, but the other side of the office remained in shadow.

"Welcome," a thin voice called.

Darkness swallowed her when she shut the door. Cautiously, she advanced, and a ghoul in the guise of human flesh appeared behind a large desk stacked with papers. Sunken eyes peered up at her, round glasses perched atop a beak-like nose.

"Are you Mr. Roach?" she asked hoarsely.

"Yes."

Anger coiled in her gut. She fiddled with her glove, fighting to keep her composure. "I'm Dinah Hance. Jesse's daughter."

He frowned. "Ah."

"I've come to request an extension on—"

He held up a bony hand. "That won't be necessary."

Her brow furrowed. "What do you mean?"

"The debt has been paid," he said.

Dinah stared at him, stunned speechless. *Impossible.*

"All of it?" she croaked.

"Every penny."

Baffled, she shook her head. "By who?"

"I'm afraid I cannot divulge that information. He insisted that he remain anonymous."

"He?"

Roach pressed his lips together and refused to elaborate.

"Then... the debt's settled?" Dinah ventured. "Our business is finished?"

"Indeed," he replied, pushing a sheet of paper across his desk. "You are free to leave, Miss Hance."

She picked up the receipt and read the amount that had been paid—*twenty-three hundred dollars.*

Who could've done it? And why? Why now, after all these years?

She walked out of his office in a daze and collapsed against the hitching rail, palm pressed to her mouth as tears blazed burning trails down her cheeks.

Free. Free from the chains of debt.

Was it Reverend Yerkes? No—not by himself. He had to have help.

Did the whole congregation pitch in? Dr. Stone could've told them about her father's death. *If he did, how'd they come up with the money so quickly?*

Why didn't they pay the debt before it was too late? Before she lost her father?

Dinah gazed south down the avenue, toward the bank and the jewelry store. A suffocating weight sat on her chest.

"Should I get that locket?" Ophelia ponders as they leave the store.

"That's what they gave you the money for, isn't it?" Dinah reminds her. "To buy yourself something nice?"

"Yes, but what if I find a pretty dress, or... Dinah? Dinah, are you listening?"

"Mhm," she grunts, admiring the cream-colored horse tied across the street.

"Oh," marvels Ophelia, "how beautiful. I've never seen one like it."

"Me neither."

"There's something royal about him, isn't there? A steed fit for a king! Or a queen." Ophelia grins and lifts her chin, prancing along and dramatically swinging her arms.

Dinah giggles.

A colored man wearing a yellow plaid vest with crimson stripes, a matching puff tie, and a brown coat tips his hat to them as he leans against the wall of the general store. "Good mornin', gals."

Dinah doesn't recognize him, but she smiles and says, "Good morning."

As they turn the next corner, Ophelia stops in her tracks.

"I'm going to get the locket," she declares. "Wait here for me."

Cardinal nudged her shoulder with his nose. Dinah reached up to rub his forehead and breathed a shaky exhale. She would never be free.

Not until Sal Valentin faced justice.

She didn't know if he'd be in on a Sunday morning, but the marshal's reputation as the hardest working man in Saline County made her think there
was a chance. Dinah sniffed and dried the last of her tears as she stepped
onto the boardwalk.

"They had him, sir," someone said on the other side of the door.

"But they don't got him now," a man responded with obvious irritation.

"No, marshal."

"How'd they lose him?"

She leaned in close to listen.

"Witness said one of the gang members came back for him."

"One?" the marshal repeated.

"Yessir. Big guy. Southern soundin'."

Her heart beat faster. Were they talking about the Valentin Gang?

"He walked in, took what he come for, and walked back out?" the marshal said, his voice dripping with skepticism.

"Yessir."

"And this 'lawman' didn't think to put a bullet in him?"

"Well, he... he was locked up," the first man explained with some hesitation, as if he was embarrassed on the witness' behalf.

"Locked in his own cell?"

"Yessir."

"Lord Almighty," the marshal sighed. "Who they got runnin' things in
that town?"

Dinah pushed the door open and poked her head inside. A man of
above average height with short neatly combed brown hair turned around,
a badge pinned on his blue vest. He didn't look much older than herself.

"Oh." He smiled nervously. "Good mornin', miss."

Forcing a tight-lipped smile, she ventured into the sunlit office. "Good
morning. I hope I'm not intruding."

"Not at all, miss," he assured her.

"I wondered if I could speak with Marshal Tupper."

"That's me," said the marshal, leaning sideways in his chair to see past
his deputy. "What can I do for ya?"

The deputy moved aside, allowing her to approach the desk. Middle-
aged with a grizzled beard and dour features, Marshal Tupper was an
intimidating figure.

"Marshal, I'm Dinah Hance. I— I don't know if you've been made aware, but my father—" She stopped and swallowed hard. "My father was murdered last night."

The marshal propped his elbows on the desk and clasped his large hands. His dark, heavy brows drew together over dark eyes. "I was informed, Miss Hance. I'd met your father. He seemed like a good man. I'm real sorry about what happened."

Her heart gave a painful squeeze. "Thank you. I wanted to ask, sir, are you puttin' together a posse to pursue the Valentin Gang?"

"I am," he answered without hesitation. "I'm puttin' notices in the papers, spreadin' word around town. And I've reached out to an old friend of mine. As soon as he arrives, and there's a solid lead, we'll get after 'em."

Relief flooded through her. "I'm glad to hear that, marshal. I only wish somethin' had been done about them sooner."

He glanced at his hands, the furrows in his high forehead deepening. He sat back in his chair and straightened his tie. "Miss Hance, I was a Texas Ranger for ten years. Tracked all kinds of badmen and downright scum of the earth. I'll find 'em."

Two days Dinah waited. Twice, she'd returned to the marshal's office and asked if there'd been any sightings of the gang.

"*Nothin' yet,*" he'd said.

She'd written detailed descriptions of every member—even drew them, unsophisticated as her abilities were—and given them to him on her second visit, just to feel like she was doing something.

Dinah dropped her mother's blouse into the simmering pot and submerged it in the black bath, the kitchen filled with the acorns' earthy aroma, the metallic tang of rust, and vinegar's pungent odor. This was the last of the acorn powder.

She pulled off her work gloves, tossed them onto the counter, and went into the living room. *He's all talk,* she thought as she sank onto the couch. *They'll get away. They'll disappear.*

Raising her tired eyes from the flames flickering in the hearth, Dinah stared at the rifles mounted above it—her Winchester and her father's Springfield. She imagined raising the Winchester to her shoulder and blasting a hole in Sal's chest. Not his head—that would be too quick. She wanted him to suffer. Wanted his cold heart to bleed as hers did.

Vengeance is mine; I will repay, saith the Lord.

Dinah's nails dug into her palms as a violent wind beset her haunted house. *When? How long do I have to wait? How many more have to die?*

The fire cracked and popped, spitting sparks onto a bed of wood and ash.

She'd always worried that the Valentin Gang might return to Salina. Dreaded it so severely that she'd avoided going into town as often as she could. Shadows lurked around every corner, outside every window. People called her crazy—a hermit and a recluse—though never to her face. They were too cowardly for that.

Now, the very thing she'd feared, that had driven her to such isolation, had come to pass.

Hooves pounded up the path.

Dinah's heart lurched. Standing so fast her head spun, she grabbed her Winchester from the hooks and wheeled to face the door. Her hands shook. Sweat beaded on her forehead, the fire burning at her back. Her finger hovered over the trigger.

Three firm raps on the door.

"Who's there?" Dinah called, hating how her voice wavered.

"It's me. Daniel."

Her eyes widened, and she lowered the rifle. She put her Winchester back on the hooks and hurried to open the door.

There he stood, every inch a city-dwelling gentleman in his black three-piece suit.

"You came."

"Of course I did," he replied as the stagecoach rattled away. He looked tired, like he hadn't slept, his brown curls tousled by the wind.

He'd left home only a month ago, but it felt like years. Dinah didn't know what to say, what to do. She'd screamed things at him, things that couldn't be unsaid.

Has he forgiven me?

Her mother flew past her and threw both arms around him, and Daniel bent to embrace her. How small and frail she seemed in his arms, her long hair hanging down her back in a messy braid.

"I'm so glad you're here," her mother wept.

Daniel's big blue eyes met Dinah's, his brows slanting with concern. She realized how jarring it must be for him to see their mother like this, so pale and all in black.

Sniffing, her mother drew back and pulled a handkerchief from the waistband of her wrinkled skirt to dab her eyes. "Come inside. You must be exhausted."

I forgot to make supper.

Embarrassed, Dinah headed for the kitchen. "I'll fix us somethin' to eat."

"Wait," Daniel said.

She turned to face him.

He set his luggage by the couch and straightened with a frown so much like their father's. "How did it happen?"

She swallowed and glanced toward the door. Her mother's red-rimmed eyes were downcast, her pretty features drawn with exhaustion.

"The gang that robbed us ten years ago, the man who killed Ophelia…" Dinah forced a breath into her shrinking lungs. "He came back."

Shock widened Daniel's eyes and parted his lips. "What?"

"They'd just hit the bank in Abilene and were hiding from the law. They held us hostage here in the house. Dad tried to save us, but he—" Her voice broke. "Sal Valentin shot him."

Daniel clenched his shaven jaw and bowed his head. He paced in front of the fire, raking his fingers through his hair.

Finally, he stopped and looked at them both. "Where is he? I want to see him."

"He's in town," her mother murmured.

"With the undertaker," Dinah clarified.

Daniel's broad shoulders slumped as he sighed. "I'll take Belle and ride to Salina."

Her mother wrung her hands.

She doesn't want to go. But someone had to. No matter how furious she was with him, he was her brother, and he shouldn't have to grieve alone.

"I'll go with you," Dinah said.

CHAPTER EIGHT

Clouds fumed over Joseph's head like pillars of smoke, red in the glow of the setting sun as he and Enyeto followed the Arkansas River southwest toward Dodge City. They'd spent three days taking the long way around ranchers' fences and sneaking through freshly planted wheat fields whenever they found gaps in the wire, hoping the farmers wouldn't see them and their dogs wouldn't smell them. Despite the detours and the prairie's rolling hills, they'd managed to put more than a hundred miles between them and Abilene.

The open range ain't so open no more, Joseph thought gloomily.

Pawnee Rock rose out of the grassy flat in front of him, smaller than he remembered. Someone had chiseled the sandstone surface and worn it down.

Still a good place to camp. No one can ambush us. We'll see 'em long before they see us.

He'd been so young when he first passed this way, seven years old and alone in the world, his only companions a runaway slave and a stolen horse. Joseph supposed it was compassion that had moved Jeremiah to take him under his wing. He'd taught him how to survive, raised him like a son. In exchange, Joseph had taught him how to read.

"The names written here—who do they belong to?" Enyeto asked.

Names too numerous to count had been carved into the rock's craggy face. Big and small. Long and short. Weathered by the passage of time.

"Folk of every sort goin' west," Joseph answered, "lookin' for a better life."

"Did you write yours?"

Joseph shook his head. "Weren't no room when I came through."

"Did you make the journey alone?"

"No, I was just a kid. I had a friend who made sure I didn't get shot or eaten. We both had a lotta learnin' to do, a lotta hardships we couldn't've dreamt of. He was younger than I am now, had lived on the same plantation his whole life. We never stayed in one place long."

"Why not?" Enyeto asked.

"Well," Joseph sighed, "we were flat broke, so I learned how to pick pockets, and Jeremiah took up connin' folk. Sooner or later, we'd always wear out our welcome."

The West had felt so boundless to him back then. Every time they'd cut and run, they'd found another town. Somewhere they could start over, where no one knew them.

"*To put down roots is to become bound to something,*" Sal had told him years ago. "*Planting yourself in one place makes you vulnerable. When the axe swings, you can't flee. When lightning strikes, there's nowhere to hide. To linger is to die.*"

Joseph lived by those words. They all did. But the West was getting smaller, cities and fences hemming him in. Tightening like a noose around his neck.

"What made you part ways with him?"

Enyeto's question ripped open a wound that still hadn't healed. Eight years of wrestling and trying to find some measure of acceptance hadn't made it any easier for Joseph to talk about. "Consumption. He rode with us till he couldn't no more."

"I'm sorry," Enyeto said.

Joseph clenched his jaw, avoiding his gaze.

Steel lowered his head as he started up the rocky slope, and Joseph leaned forward, Enyeto's pinto mare close at his heels. They'd found her in the stable yard next to the jail the night he'd rescued Enyeto.

Squinting south, Joseph spotted a small town that had sprung up less than a mile distant. Too close.

We should break camp by sunup.

Earlier that day he'd gone into Great Bend to buy ammunition. A risky move, but if a posse caught up to them, he'd need bullets—lots of them. The gunsmith had looked at him funny, and Joseph had been on edge ever since.

When they reached the top of the rock, he swung down from the saddle and patted Steel's neck. Boots crunching through the grass, Joseph led him over to the western side and gazed out at the plains as dusk fell. A dry wind rustled scattered shrubs and a lonely tree as he pondered.

Those who'd written their names on the rock—how many of them had survived? How many had starved or succumbed to disease? How many had met violent ends?

When they died and their names faded away, what legacy would they leave?

What will I be remembered for? When folk think of Jesse James and Billy the Kid, will they think of me? Is an outlaw all I'll ever be?

He used to look up to them. Had followed their escapades in the papers as often as he could. Both had led the law on a hell of a chase.

And both of 'em ended up the same way.

Joseph reached inside his coat and pulled out the cross Obadiah had given him, its silver surface glinting in the dim light.

"Look up," his mother had told him as she wiped away his tears, *"and always remember, as surely as the sun rises each morning, so do his mercies shine on us anew."*

He grimaced, his hand curling into a fist. *It don't matter what she said. She didn't mean a word of it.*

Resisting a sudden urge to throw the cross over the cliffside, Joseph stuffed the necklace back into his pocket and turned his face from the sun.

———————•———————

After a simple but filling supper of canned beans, Joseph leaned back on his saddle and stretched out his stiff legs, his lantern burning beside him. He hadn't dared to start a fire. The saddle's hard leather aggravated his ribs, and Joseph shifted, trying to find a more comfortable position. They'd pushed themselves and their horses to their limits, and he was in dire need of a decent night's sleep.

Enyeto sat across from him, watching him with furrowed brows. "We set a good pace today," he said, as if sensing his agitation.

"Yeah," Joseph grunted. "But we're still five days' ride from Dead Man's Dune. Six if we slow down a bit. Let the horses rest their legs."

Enyeto bowed his head and resumed cleaning his carbine with an oily rag. "I hope Charlie's doing all right. He seems like a good kid."

The knot in Joseph's chest tightened. He thought about Charlie often, wondered if he was struggling to keep up with the others. The bullet hadn't stayed in his shoulder, but Joseph worried about gangrene.

"Ain't got a mean bone in his body," he said. "I can't help feelin' that he never woulda chosen this life if his brothers hadn't dragged him into it. His parents died when he was real young. Remy and Donny are all he's got."

"I never knew my father," Enyeto reflected. "Coyote claimed him before I was born."

Joseph's heart sank. He barely remembered his own father. He'd lost him when the Yanks attacked.

Enyeto's frown deepened, his pensive features focused on the rifle laid across his legs. "I was born a prisoner. Miners had enslaved my tribe on our own land. They worked our men till they dropped dead. Violated our women. Stole our children. I left to look for those who went missing."

Joseph had never asked him where he came from, why he'd joined them. *Always too busy,* he thought with a twinge of guilt.

Sal had told him Enyeto had a score to settle with Uncle Sam, and that had been good enough for him.

"Did you find 'em?"

Enyeto shook his head and met his gaze. "I searched for six years."

He sighed and set aside his rifle, the wind whipping his hair around his fur-clad shoulders.

"Do you ever regret it?" Joseph asked before he could stop himself. "Leavin' your tribe?"

Enyeto considered a moment, his face grave in the glow of the lantern. "If I hadn't, I'd probably be dead."

Sometimes Joseph wondered where he'd be if his mother hadn't left him that day. If he hadn't gone with Jeremiah. Gotten on that train.

Reaching into his saddlebag, he pulled out a stick of charcoal and his leatherbound journal and opened it to the next blank page.

"Your friend you mentioned before—Jeremiah—did he introduce you to Sal?"

Joseph's hand paused, and he glanced up. Enyeto's curiosity continued to surprise him. All this time, he'd thought him quiet and withdrawn. But ever since they'd left Abilene, he'd been full of questions.

"Marcus has known Sal longer than any of us. He didn't have nobody, and Sal took him under his wing, like Jeremiah did with me." Joseph's hand moved up and down the page, back and forth. Some here, a little there. "We ran into 'em one day, Jeremiah and me. Sal didn't have a gang back then, but he had big ideas. The four of us stuck together, became a family of sorts, and the rest is history."

His charcoal scratched away in the silence, thin lines forming slanted roofs and store corners. Smudged shapes walked a dark street.

"When I met Sal, he said he could help me," Enyeto mused. "He said that every bank, every train I robbed would hurt the invaders who'd enslaved my people. I don't see how killing a man on his own land helps anyone."

It don't. His grip tightened, the charcoal digging into the paper. His strokes were quick and instinctive—angry. *Lighten up, or you'll break it.*

"That was a generous thing you did, paying their debt."

"I robbed her and her mama of somethin' far worse than money," Joseph muttered. "People ain't replaceable. Love 'em or hate 'em, family can't be forgotten."

"You didn't kill her father," Enyeto reminded him. "Sal did."

Joseph started a drawing on the next page, never raising his eyes.

Enyeto took the hint. He lay down on his bedroll, and Joseph drew in silence. His throat closed as he sketched crinkled eyes and oval glasses. A broad grin and a bearded chin.

Joseph sits beside the hospital bed, clutching his hat in his hands. Jeremiah lies under white sheets, coughing and shaking with chills that even the driest climate can't rid him of.

"The path I led you down all those years ago… it weren't right," he rasps. "I'm sorry, Joseph. I truly am. You deserved bettuh than us. It's too late now foah me to atone foah the things I done, and Sal—he ain't evuh gonna leave this life behind."

Jeremiah reaches out and grasps his arm, his brown eyes pleading. "But you still got time. A chance to make a propuh man of yourself."

The charcoal snapped in two. Black specks scattered onto Elliott's portrait. Joseph stared at them, the hole inside him yawning wider. Another friend he'd never see again. Another piece of him gone.

Dust to dust.

CHAPTER NINE

Morning mist curled around her feet as Reverend Yerkes opened his Bible. A bitter wind sighed through the redbud's winding branches, its magenta blooms trembling against a gray sky. Dinah stood at her mother's left side, Daniel on the other side, the three of them gathered around the hole in the ground beside Lydia's grave.

"To every thing there is a season, and a time to every purpose under heaven," the reverend read, steady and fervent.

Dinah clenched her jaw, the high collar of her black dress choking the life out of her. *What purpose? What reason?*

"A time to be born, and a time to die. A time to plant, and a time to pluck up that which is planted."

She fought to keep her quivering lip pressed into a tight, emotionless line, the eyes of the congregation boring into her back. They'd tiptoed around her. Murmured their condolences and treated her like she was made of glass. Like she was balanced on the tip of a knife, and the slightest breeze might push her over the edge.

So what if it was true? She didn't want their pity. Their sympathetic stares or wagging tongues eager to gossip about her latest misfortune. She just wanted to be left alone.

"A time to kill, and a time to heal. A time to break down, and a time to build up. A time to weep, and a time to laugh. A time to mourn, and a time to dance."

A time to kill.

Dinah's gaze darted to the reverend's moving mouth. She clasped her gloved hands so tightly that they hurt, the hollowness inside her bubbling like an empty pot suddenly filled with boiling water.

"A time to rend, and a time to sew. A time to keep silence, and a time to speak. A time to love, and a time to hate. A time of war, and a time of peace."

Rend. Hate. War. Traitorous tears burned in her eyes. *If not now, when?*

Reverend Yerkes closed his Bible and looked at the mourners. Everyone from church had come. People from town. Their neighbors—August's family and Ophelia's parents.

The reverend's white brows drew together. "Jesse Solomon Hance was a brave, kind man. In our nation's time of war, he fought for peace, to pre-serve this Union. He was a man of honor and principle. A faithful provider. A devoted husband and father.

"In the presence of evil, he did not cower. He died as he lived—con-fronting the enemy head-on. Protecting his family. May we all face life's trials with such unshakeable courage."

The charismatic conviction with which he spoke had always inspired and uplifted her, but today his words buried Dinah under a mountain of shame. She didn't feel brave. She felt lost. Torn in two directions.

Daniel had urged her mother to sell the farm and invited them to join him in New York. Dinah had no doubt that her mother would give in, and then what? The last place she wanted to move to was a big city, but the thought of being separated from her family terrified her. Where would she go? What would she do?

"Though we as a church and a community mourn this tragic loss, we can take comfort in the knowledge that today and forevermore, Jesse is with our Lord in paradise," Reverend Yerkes concluded.

Dinah only felt a gut-wrenching ache.

He asked them if they would like to say a few words, and her mother gave no answer, her devastated features shrouded by her rippling veil. Daniel shook his bowed head, his eyes downcast.

Reverend Yerkes thanked those who had attended the service and dis-missed them. As the congregation dispersed, her mother sank to her knees, weeping as two men tossed the first shovels of dirt onto her father's coffin. Daniel knelt beside her and wrapped his arm around her bent shoulders.

Dinah couldn't bear it.

She walked to the edge of the hill and gazed upon the house and the barn her father had built with his own hands. The fences and the chicken coop. Cardinal, Belle, and Dusty grazed in the field below, but Sarge stood like a statue, his head high and his ears pointed toward them. He knew. He'd probably seen it happen.

If she'd done something, *anything* differently—

"Dinah."

She turned and discovered Ophelia's parents standing behind her. A lump stuck in her throat. She hadn't spoken to them in well over a year.

"I'm so sorry for your loss," said Mrs. Larson in her thick Swedish accent. Wringing her hands, she ventured closer, her black skirt billowing in the wind. "Is it true? Sal Valentin did this?"

She whispered his name like a curse. A taboo.

Dinah nodded.

Mrs. Larson gave a quiet gasp of horror, and Mr. Larson ran an anguished hand over his bearded face.

"That monster should have been dealt with ten years ago," she spat. "We waited so long, *pleaded*, but Marshal Garrett never cared to do anything about it."

Dinah remembered him less than fondly, a man of complacence and self-indulgence who'd been replaced by Marshal Tupper five years back.

"The posse from Abilene found nothing but an abandoned campsite," Mr. Larson complained. "Marshal Tupper should step in before it's too late."

"He told me he's puttin' a posse together, but he's waitin' on someone," Dinah said. "An old friend of his."

Mrs. Larson huffed and put her hands on her hips. "Well, he'd better hurry, or there won't be a trail to follow."

Mr. Larson greeted Reverend Yerkes with a nod as he came over to them. "Harold."

"Erik," the reverend replied with a kind smile. "Sofia. May I have a word with Miss Hance?"

"Of course," said Mr. Larson.

He pressed his hand to his wife's back and guided her away.

Reverend Yerkes clasped his hands behind him and heaved a sigh. "Dinah, I know telling you this won't ease the pain of your father's passing, but I want you to know that you and your family aren't alone in this. If there's anything you need, anything at all, please don't hesitate to ask."

Ever since she'd spoken to Roach, she'd wrestled with the question of who'd paid their debt. Though he'd told her the person wanted to remain anonymous, her curiosity had become unbearable.

Dinah took a breath and met his keen blue gaze. "Actually, there's somethin' I've been wantin' to ask you about, Reverend. Three days ago, someone paid the debt we've been strugglin' with. But I don't know who."

His eyes widened, his lips parting in surprise.

"Was it you?" she ventured.

He shook his head. "No, not me. But that's wonderful news, Dinah. Wonderful news."

It wasn't him? She'd been so sure. If not him or the congregation, who? Most people didn't have that much money lying around.

Dinah's heart sank as she looked toward the house again. She supposed it didn't matter. It didn't change the fact that she was about to lose her home.

"Is there something else on your mind?" Reverend Yerkes prompted patiently.

Dinah hesitated. How honest should she be?

"Those verses you read… They spoke of a time to hate. To kill." She swallowed hard. "Sal Valentin took Ophelia from me—now my father. I *hate* him. I want someone to make him pay. I wanna see him *hang*."

Dinah met the reverend's wizened gaze. "Am I wrong for feelin' this way?"

He studied her, considering carefully. "There is such a thing as righteous anger. Seeking justice is good, but hatred poisons the soul. We're called to love our enemies. The wicked are God's to punish."

"But he acts through us. He uses us to accomplish his will."

"Yes," he said, "which is why we have laws and men who enforce them. Trust Marshal Tupper. He knows what he's doing."

She shook her head and turned from him. "The law's been after 'em a long time, Reverend. I've got no reason to believe things'll turn out any different than they have before."

"They might, Dinah. They might. But if they don't, remember this: no man can outrun his sin. Not even Sal Valentin."

———— ● ————

When Dinah arrived at the marshal's office, a Kentucky Saddler was hitched out front. A striking bay with a blaze. As she tied Cardinal at the opposite rail and headed for the steps, the Saddler's curious eyes followed her, one brown and the other blue. She wondered if he belonged to Marshal Tupper.

"I passed through Abilene on my way here," a man said as she pushed open the door. "Town's burned and shot all to pieces. Eight men dead. He's gettin' worse, Lee."

The marshal shook his head and glanced up at her from his chair. "Miss Hance, come on in. There's someone I wantcha to meet."

The stranger standing at his desk turned to face her. Tall and lean, he looked to be her father's age. A gray felt hat sat atop his head, a pair of cat-like eyes glinting under the brim. He wore a matching frock coat over an emerald vest and a black puff tie, his right leg encased up to his thigh in a leather prosthetic.

"This is Jasper Lawrence, the friend I toldja about."

Lawrence tipped his hat, the neatly trimmed edges of a brown mustache rising with the curve of his lips as he smiled at her. "Pleasuh to meetcha, miss," he said with the slow drawl of a Southern gentleman.

"Lawrence, this is Dinah Hance. She's been a big help to me these past two days. Gave me drawin's and descriptions of the gang members who woulda been in Abilene that mornin'."

"Mind if I take look?" Lawrence asked.

Marshal Tupper grabbed a stack of papers from the shelf behind him and slid them across his desk. "Have at 'em."

Dinah's cheeks flushed with embarrassment. "I'm no artist, sir, but I tried my best."

Lawrence picked up her drawings and rifled through them, reading the names she'd written under the portraits. "Marcus Crane, Joseph Gray—where there's one, the othuh's not far behind."

Her brow furrowed. He spoke of them as if he knew them. "You've seen 'em before?"

"Once or twice," he mumbled.

"Are you a lawman?"

"He's a man hunter," the marshal answered. "Been at it a long time. He's one of the best there is."

"You flattuh me, Marshal." Lawrence's smirk faded, his eyes narrowing as he stared at her sketch of Remy. "The Guidry boys've joined up with Valentin?"

Marshal Tupper frowned. "I ain't heard of 'em. What's the story on 'em?"

"Remy Guidry's got three thousand dolluhs on his head down in Louisiana. Started robbin' folk when he was a kid, and I guess he took a likin' to it. So did his two brothuhs. He fled the state aftuh he killed a woman."

The story didn't surprise her, but it frightened her. Dinah pressed her gloved fingers to her spine. The lashes still burned when she touched them.

"Sounds like a nasty piece of work," the marshal remarked.

Lawrence looked up from the drawings and met her gaze. "You saw all these men?"

"They went to her house to hide," Marshal Tupper explained. "Killed her father."

Hearing someone mention it again recalled the crushing reality of it. Dinah felt like she was going to be sick.

Understanding dawned on Lawrence's face. "My condolences. You're fortunate to be alive, Miss Hance."

"I don't feel so lucky," she muttered.

"Well, I do have some good news for ya, Miss Hance," the marshal said. "I got a telegram reportin' a potential sighting of Joseph Gray in Great Bend. Lawrence and I are takin' six men out on the first train tomorrow."

Excitement surged in her, feral and feverish. Dinah dared not voice her desire aloud, but a secret part of her desperately wished she could go with them. That she could stare into Joseph's eyes when he had nowhere left to run. When he got what he deserved.

"Thank you, Marshal. Thank you for doin' this."

"I toldja I'd get 'em, Miss Hance, and I aim to do just that."

———◆·◆———

She unfastened his halter, and Cardinal sauntered out into the pasture. Dinah latched the gate and trudged up the sloping path, past the oak tree and the clucking chickens, the weather as saturnine as her spirit.

She didn't doubt Marshal Tupper's competence. If anyone could track them down, he could.

But finding the gang was only half the job. Sal Valentin had never been caught. Never been arrested. He'd killed every man who tried to put him behind bars, and she couldn't shake the fear that the marshal and his posse would meet the same bloody fate.

"Where have you been?"

Dinah spun to see her mother sitting on the porch steps, still in her funeral dress, her hair in a wind-tousled chignon.

"I went to see the marshal again."

"And?" her mother prompted.

"He's got a lead. He's leavin' with a posse first thing tomorrow."

"Good." Her mother sighed and shifted, her hands gripping her knees. "Dinah, I need to talk to you about something. I know now's a bad time, but there'll never be a good one."

Warily, Dinah approached her.

Her mother drew a deep breath and met her gaze. "I don't know who paid our debt or why, but it feels like a sign. A chance to start over. Oh, don't look at me like that, Dinah."

"He hasn't been in the ground a *day,* and you're ready to throw it all away," she exclaimed with a wave of her arm.

"He gave his life for *us,* not this farm," her mother asserted, pulling herself to her feet. "We can't manage it without him. Even if we could—I don't want that for you, and neither would he. You've been stuck here long enough because of what that gang did to us."

"Don't pretend this is about me," Dinah growled.

Daniel strode out onto the porch, his brow furrowed with concern. "What's going on?"

"You just couldn't stay away, could you?" she fumed, glaring up at him.

"*Dinah,*" her mother scolded with a pained expression.

Undeterred, he came down the stairs and took an imploring step toward her. "I know what this house means to you. This land."

"No you don't," Dinah snapped, straining to speak past the lump in her throat. "You never did."

He sighed in exasperation. "Aren't you tired of this violence? Don't you want to live somewhere safe?"

"I wanna live somewhere free."

Daniel huffed. "How can you hate a place you've never been?"

"I've seen enough of it right here in Salina."

"Don't make this harder than it has to be, Dinah," he persisted. He came closer and added quietly, "Mama's been through enough. Sometimes we have to make sacrifices for the people we love."

"What do you know of sacrifice?" she challenged. Her blistering rage had devoured the fuse of her patience, and all that remained was the dynamite. "I'm the one who stayed. If you hadn't left us, he might still be alive."

Daniel swallowed, her venomous retort effectively silencing him. Blinded by tears, she turned and stormed toward the barn.

"Dinah—" her mother called.

"*Go!*" she cried, wheeling to face her. "Go, if that's what you want! But you're goin' without me."

Tears splashed onto the picture in Dinah's shaking hands, their smiling faces staring back at her. Being the taller one, she was seated in a chair, Ophelia standing behind her with a mischievous grin. Ever since that day, she'd kept the photograph buried at the bottom of a drawer.

Now, Dinah placed it in the saddlebag where she'd stuffed an extra shirt and skirt. The other she'd packed full of canned provisions and ammunition.

She buckled her father's gun belt around her hips, his Colt .45 in the holster. His brown Stetson sat on the patterned quilt at the end of her bed, mocking her. A storm raged inside her as she reached down and gently picked up the hat.

Reverend Yerkes was right. Her father faced his fears head-on. Running into danger when others fled. Putting everyone else ahead of himself, despite the things he'd seen and suffered.

All I do is hide and ignore.

And where had that gotten her? She'd been passive long enough.

The least I can do is go down fightin'. I owe him that much.

Dinah took a deep breath, pushed her father's hat onto her head, and—

It fit.

Fresh tears sprang to her eyes, but she blinked them back. She went over to her desk, opened her inkwell, and dipped her steel-tipped pen.

Revenge ain't very Christian, I know. But my soul can't rest until his is in hell. I'll hunt him till kingdom come if that's what it takes.

Dinah put down her pen and closed the inkwell. She glanced at her Bible. Heart clenching, she straightened and returned to her bed, leaving it on the corner of her desk. She slung her rifle across her back, threw the saddlebags over her shoulder, and went to the window. As quietly as she could, Dinah raised it and climbed out onto the porch roof.

She crept along the shingled surface, careful not to lose her footing. The sun hadn't yet risen, the moon an ivory sliver in the sky. A cold breeze stirred Dinah's neckerchief and tossed her unbound curls as she inched to the roof's edge.

It was a risky plan, but she was convinced that the house's squeaking stairs and creaking doors would've betrayed her.

Balancing on the precarious slant, she slid the saddlebags off her shoulder, held them out over the yard, and let them fall. The cans clanged when they hit the ground, and Dinah winced, hoping the crickets masked the clatter of the impact. Slowly, she turned around and maneuvered herself into position, hanging from the roof by her gloved fingers.

She dropped into the grass. Her knees nearly buckled, but she managed to stay on her feet. Dinah breathed a sigh of relief.

She fetched and saddled Cardinal in the darkness of the barn. He craned his neck to look at her, his soft eyes watching with concern. Somehow he always knew when something was wrong. She let go of the tightened cinch and wrapped her arms around his neck. Shutting her eyes tight, Dinah clung to him, trusting that his steady strength would keep her upright.

He rested his head against her back, and she fell to pieces all over again. She missed her father so much, and she ached for one last chance to tell him how dearly she loved him.

How could she leave her mother? Leave home? Leave everything she'd ever known behind?

If you don't leave her, she'll leave you.

Wiping away her tears, Dinah led Cardinal out of the barn and swung into the saddle. She walked him down the sloping path, gazing up at the oak's towering silhouette and bidding silent goodbyes to the horses and the cattle and the land she loved.

When she reached a safe distance from the house, she urged Cardinal into a gallop, riding west toward Salina.

CHAPTER TEN

The morning dawned cold and breezy, the eastern horizon bathed in an orange glow, streaked with yellow and wisps of gray clouds. A couple of miles to the west, the Santa Fe Railroad ran across the open plains, the Arkansas River winding alongside it. They'd stayed well away from the tracks. Trains meant towns, and Joseph had taken his last chance with those.

Pawnee Rock was a day's ride behind them. By tomorrow evening, they'd be within sight of Dodge City.

"This place we're going to—Dead Man's Dune—you've been there before?" Enyeto asked as their horses tramped through knee-high grass.

"Once," Joseph said. "That was six years ago. We'd stirred up some trouble, gotten the Texas Rangers and a man hunter after us. We needed a place to lay low, somewhere they wouldn't follow.

"I don't remember how it got its name. Somethin' about lost treasure and people goin' missin'. Some folks think the dunes are an old Indian burial ground. They swear they've seen ghosts there."

"Do you believe them?"

Joseph shook his head. "Whatever really happened all those years ago, the memory is what haunts folks, not the dead who've passed on."

"My people believe that when we die, our spirits fly west across the sea, following *hinnan mooka*," Enyeto said. "Only a restless ghost remains here, one who has not yet completed their journey."

Joseph's brow furrowed as he cast Enyeto a sideways glance. "What's hinnan mooka?"

"The path of the wind. It brings us to Coyote's village, where we reunite with those who have gone before us."

Like heaven.

Joseph tried not to think about where he'd go when he died. Many took comfort in the idea that they'd someday find themselves in paradise.

He didn't. If heaven was real, so was hell, and he knew the pearly gates weren't opening for him.

"I always believed that if I was standing still, I was wasting time," Enyeto said, staring into the distance. "If I wasn't fighting, I was a coward. I spent a long night in that cell back in Abilene, thinking about the fire I started, the damage I caused. I thought about Elliott, losing his life for a bag of money. *That* was a waste."

The truth of Enyeto's words struck him like a punch in the gut.

"I begged Coyote not to take me yet. Prayed for a second chance. But now that I have that chance, I don't know what to do with it. I've fought all my life because that's all I know."

His confession hit too close to home. Joseph shifted with discomfort. How could he give answers he didn't have?

Enyeto sighed. "Maybe it's time I try something else. My uncle once told me there are two wolves fighting inside all of us, and we must choose which one we feed. I didn't understand then, but now... I think I do."

Joseph stopped Steel, an old fear gripping his heart. "What're you sayin'? You're leavin'?"

Enyeto turned Taipah toward him and shook his head. "Not yet, but soon."

Joseph's jaw clenched. Try as he might, he couldn't hide his disappointment. He understood Enyeto's decision more than he cared to admit, but a selfish part of him resented him for it.

Enyeto's solemn features softened. "You've been in this life since you were a child. Haven't you considered settling down?"

Joseph grimaced. Of course he had, but those hopes had faded with each year that passed him by. Each crime he committed in the name of survival.

"There's no gettin' out. Not for me."

"You won't know unless you try."

Much as they had in common, Enyeto couldn't understand the burden he carried. No cabin in the woods could quiet Joseph's mind. No boat on a lake could calm the storm inside him. Being alone with himself would be a punishment worse than death.

Joseph swallowed and met his gaze. "I can't leave 'em. They need me."

And he needed them. Needed the chase as much as he hated it.

Enyeto nodded, his keen eyes studying him. "They're family. I admire your loyalty, Joseph. I hope Sal proves worthy of it in the end."

CHAPTER ELEVEN

T he Union Pacific depot was quiet as the sun rose over the Smoky Hill River. Railcars lined the tracks to her right, the river glittering between the gaps. Dinah sat on a bench on the empty platform, tapping her foot as she watched the bridge to the north.

She'd been there for more than an hour. *Must be about seven thirty now.*

Every minute, she feared that Daniel or her mother would discover her missing and come riding across that bridge. She'd asked the clerk if any trains had left the station that morning.

"Not yet," he'd said.

Dinah couldn't see much of Iron Avenue, her view obscured by a mattress factory and a woodworker's shop. She looked west toward Fifth Street.

No sign of the marshal. Just a man on a bay horse and another rattling by in a wagon.

An icy gust sent a shiver through her. Dinah sniffed and squirmed on the uncomfortable bench. She straightened her dark blue jacket—so dark that it was the only article of clothing she hadn't dyed black. Cardinal waited patiently at the hitching rail, and she glanced at the saddlebags on his back.

I should check 'em one more time.

Dinah stood and strode to the edge of the platform. Cardinal raised his head when she hopped down beside him. She unbuckled the left saddlebag and rummaged through her supplies.

She didn't know how long twenty dollars would last her, but it was all she had. Food? Enough for several days if she had nothing else to eat. If Marshal Tupper had a cook fixing every meal, she wouldn't have to dip into her provisions at all.

He wouldn't want her traveling with them. Dinah expected him to try to change her mind, but she couldn't take no for an answer. Somehow, she'd convince him. She'd beg if she had to.

Dinah looked up at the sound of approaching hooves.

Marshal Tupper trotted toward the station on a big buckskin, Lawrence beside him on his Saddler. Six men of varying ages accompanied them, each wearing a star-shaped badge on his chest.

Heart racing, she fastened the saddlebag and went to meet them. The marshal's dark brows rose at the sight of her, and he halted his horse. The others followed suit.

"Miss Hance," he said with a tip of his high-crowned hat.

Dinah's rehearsed speech spilled from her lips in a breathless plea. "Marshal, I know a woman joinin' a group of men on a journey like this isn't considered proper, but I'm askin' you to make an exception. I won't be a burden to you. I've brought my own food and—"

"Miss Hance," he said, holding up a gloved hand, "I understand that you want justice for your father. But trackin' down badmen is an ugly business, violent and dangerous and nothin' a young lady should find herself caught in the middle of."

Exactly the answer she'd anticipated. "Please, sir. I can ride and shoot, and I won't slow you down."

Marshal Tupper sighed and shook his head. "If anything were to happen to you, your mama would never forgive me."

Dinah's heart sank, desperation building inside her. *There's gotta be something.*

"Does she know you're here?" he asked.

Her jaw clenched. She met his gaze, and Marshal Tupper nodded, his suspicions confirmed.

"Go home to her."

"Marshal, *please*—"

"My decision's final, Miss Hance," he responded firmly. "Go home to your family."

Lawrence gave her a sympathetic look as he turned to follow the marshal, and Dinah stared at their retreating backs as they went to load their horses onto the train. The conductor stepped out of the caboose and greeted them. It seemed that he'd already been informed of their impending arrival.

Dinah returned to Cardinal with a heavy heart. She had no home to go back to—not for long. Whether it was next week or next month, her mother would sell their land and move to New York, and she'd be left with nothing but her horse and the clothes on her back.

Dinah watched a few passengers climb aboard, men in their thirties and forties. Two wore derby hats and nice jackets, the other a flat cap and a striped shirt. A blaring whine vibrated her chest—a warning that the train was about to depart.

She could buy a ticket. Get on and ride till she ran out of rail. Put all this behind her and start over someplace far away.

One by one, the marshal and his posse entered the passenger car at the front of the train. Dinah's heart hammered, her feet frozen with indecision.

Would she ever be able to live with herself, knowing that she'd given up? That she'd failed Ophelia? Failed her father?

Droning dismally, the train pulled away from the station and steamed southward. The engine picked up speed, racing the rushing river.

Ten years, she'd stood stagnant. Resisting time's current. Drowning in her efforts to defy it.

No more. I'm done runnin'.

Dinah jumped onto Cardinal's back and snatched up the reins. "Yah!"

He sprang into action, chasing after the chugging machine with reckless abandon. She leaned forward—let the leather slide through her fingers as his neck extended. The rising sun set his red mane ablaze, his strides eating up the ground like a wildfire. They flew past the last scattered dwellings on the outskirts of Salina. Beyond civilization and into the unknown.

The engine loomed larger as she closed the distance, puffing smoke into the air and kicking dust into her face.

"Stop the train!" Dinah cried as she drew alongside a passenger car, the wheels thundering over the tracks like hooves of steel.

The man in the cap gaped at her through the glass, and she waved her arm above her head. "Stop the train!"

He ignored her, and she pushed on to first class. Lawrence's face appeared in one of the windows, his mustache drooping and a furrow forming between his brows.

"Stop the train!" she begged. "Please!"

He vanished from the window, and Dinah dropped her arm in defeat. Cardinal's strides shortened, his neck lathered with sweat.

They aren't gonna stop.

Sparks sprang up from the tracks, gears grinding and screeching. She sat back in the saddle, eyes wide as her heart leaped with renewed hope.

Slowly but surely the train ground to a halt. Dinah stopped Cardinal and stared into the swirling dust, waiting.

Lawrence emerged and squinted up at her. "You're welcome," he said. "Load up your horse and get on."

Relief crashed over her. Tears welled in her eyes, but Dinah blinked them back. She couldn't cry—he might change his mind. She didn't know why he'd decided to stop the train, but she didn't question it. Not aloud.

She hurried to comply, swinging down from the saddle and leading Cardinal toward the stock car. Lawrence accompanied her.

The conductor stepped down from the caboose and frowned as he approached them. "She doesn't have a ticket, sir."

"I'll pay whatever it costs to get to—" Dinah cast a sideways glance at Lawrence. "Where are we goin'?"

"McPherson." He canted his head and added, "Shouldn't be a problem, conductuh. The train ain't exactly full."

"All right," the conductor sighed. "Next time, miss, just buy a ticket."

———————•◂———————

Once she'd paid the conductor and loaded Cardinal into the stock car, Dinah walked with Lawrence to the front of the train. He climbed on and turned, offering her his hand. She hesitated, heart pounding and knees trembling. His angular face softened with a smile. Dinah drew a deep breath and took his hand, hoping she wasn't making the biggest mistake of her life.

She followed him into the passenger car. The marshal's men stared up at her, one of them twisted around in his rear-facing seat. They looked none too pleased with the situation. Dinah swallowed, her cheeks burning.

Marshal Tupper sat at the back of the car, wedged onto a bench with an equally broad-shouldered but much younger man. "If you bring her along, she's in your charge, Lawrence," he warned.

"Unduhstood, Marshal," Lawrence replied. He stepped aside and gestured for her to go on.

She squeezed past him. Heard him shut the door as she approached the empty seat facing Marshal Tupper and his companion.

No goin' back now.

Dinah sank onto the bench and scooted over to the window, clasping her gloved hands in her lap. Lawrence sat beside her, and she stiffened.

"Just so we're clear, Miss Hance, I don't approve," said Marshal Tupper, his dark eyes boring into hers. "I don't like it one bit. But I see there's no dissuadin' you."

"I'm sorry to make a scene, Marshal," Dinah responded with as much dignity as she could muster, "but I have to do this for my father. I won't get in your way, and I'm not expectin' special treatment."

"Your father wouldn't wantcha gettin' yourself killed on his behalf."

Her heart clenched, and she grabbed the windowsill to steady herself as the train lurched into motion.

"No harm'll come to her, Marshal," Lawrence assured him with cool confidence. "I'll see to it."

Tupper's frown deepened. "You can't make that promise."

Lawrence's hand curled against his thigh.

"Best to tell it like it is," Tupper went on, meeting her gaze again. "Ain't no such thing as a sure thing, 'specially in this line of work."

"I'm no stranger to violence, Marshal," she reminded him. "The Reaper's been tailin' me a long time. If he takes me, so be it."

"Hmph," he grunted. "That's easy to say when you ain't gotta explain to your mama why you ain't comin' home."

Dinah stared at her gloves, her palms sweating inside them. Her mother had forced her hand when she decided to move to New York. She would've been parted from her whether she went after the gang or not.

"Won't be the first time I've disappointed her," Dinah muttered.

The man seated across from her cleared his throat, and she glanced up. She'd forgotten he was there. Blond-haired and blue-eyed, he wore a brown vest over a light gray shirt, his hat propped on his knee.

He smiled at her. "Well, seein' as you're here, allow me to be the first to welcome you aboard."

"This is my nephew, James Mercer," Tupper said.

Politely, she inclined her head and forced a smile in return. "Nice to meet you, Mr. Mercer."

"Call me James," he replied, studying her with a fascination that made her squirm with discomfort.

"So, why McPherson?" she asked Lawrence.

"If the man the witness saw in Great Bend was Joseph Gray, that means he's headin' southwest," he explained. "I think he's tryin' to get across the borduh into the Strip."

"Wouldn't be the first time," Tupper remarked.

The tinge of bitterness in his voice didn't escape Dinah's notice. "What's the Strip?"

"A lawless place," Lawrence answered grimly, "right next door to Indian Territory. The only justice to be found there is of the vigilante sort. The rule of the mob."

"Lawrence and my uncle chased the gang outta Texas six years ago," Mercer chimed in with pride. "Uncle wanted to keep after 'em, but he was ordered to El Paso."

Tupper shot his nephew a warning glare, and he fell silent. Clearly, that was a sore subject for him.

That's how Lawrence knows so much about 'em, Dinah realized. *Is that why he came all this way? He's got a score to settle?*

He seemed so certain, but it sounded like a big gamble. "How can you be sure that's where Joseph's goin'?"

"I'm not," Lawrence admitted, "but it's the only lead we've got. And if we find Gray, we find Valentin."

———————————•———————————

When they reached McPherson, they boarded a train on the Santa Fe line and traveled on to Great Bend. Speaking with the gunsmith who'd reported the sighting convinced Lawrence and Marshal Tupper that the man he'd sold ammunition to was indeed Joseph Gray.

"What now?" Dinah asked as they rode past an impressive three-story courthouse that stood at the center of the public square.

"We take the next train to Dodge," Lawrence replied.

The most wicked town in Kansas. A violent place rife with every kind of sin and vice. She shuddered at the thought of going there, but she kept her reservations to herself, refusing to give him even the slightest excuse to send her home.

"We'll stay the night there," he said, "then make the rest of the journey on horseback."

They hitched their mounts outside a two-story white frame building across from the courthouse—a restaurant with a millinery next door. Squinting in the afternoon sun, Dinah turned toward the bustling tree-lined street to her left. Being in a new place felt so strange. Every face an unfamiliar one.

108

It would've been exciting if it weren't for the circumstances that had brought her here.

"Miss Hance," Lawrence called from the sidewalk, "you comin'?"

Startled from her thoughts, she realized that everyone else had already gone inside. "Yeah."

She took some money from her saddlebag and hurried after him.

The restaurant was open and airy, a winding staircase leading to the upper level. Patterned rugs covered plank floors, olive green curtains tied back from sunlit windows. Two high-backed booths flanked the door, and three square tables with white tablecloths were grouped near the stairs. A man in a dark brown hat and a tawny jacket ate alone at the farthest table. Two more sat in the booth to the left of the door.

Marshal Tupper and his men had gathered around the counter at the back of the room to order their food. Lawrence joined them, Dinah trailing behind him. She'd been introduced to everyone, and they seemed decent enough, but they'd offered nothing more than their names. Made no attempts to converse with her. She saw the way they looked at her when they thought she wouldn't notice. The glances they exchanged.

They didn't want her here, Lawrence being the only exception.

And Mercer, she thought, rolling her eyes.

Flint, Brooks, and Donovan took the booth in the corner, and Dinah scooted into the one next to it. Marshal Tupper and his nephew claimed the table closest to them. Lawrence sat across from her, Kenny Badger sliding in beside him.

Lean and wiry, Badger had short brown hair and a close-trimmed beard, his manner and speech distinctly and unapologetically Southern. According to Lawrence, he'd come to Salina from Alabama a few years back. The man who sat to her left couldn't be more his opposite—stout and round-faced and taller than Badger, his dark hair slicked back with pomade. Ralph Morris was his name, and he'd moved his family all the way from Boston.

"That's a fine horse ya got, Miss Hance," Badger said as they waited for their meals to be served. "He a quarter horse?"

On an average day, small talk with strangers was unpleasant but tolerable. Today, it was unbearable.

"Yeah."

"What's his name?" he asked.

"Cardinal."

Her one-word answers failed to deter him. "Because of his color?"

She shifted in her chair. "Well, that's part of it."

He stared at her, expecting an explanation. Dinah's cheeks heated, her gaze dropping to the table as a waiter came over and set a glass of water in front of each of them.

When he'd gone, she took a breath and said, "The first time I rode him, before he was mine, we passed by this tree, and a cardinal landed on a branch. Sounds silly, I know, but somehow, I just… knew it was meant to be. That we were gonna be partners for life."

"That don't sound silly at all," Badger replied. She glanced up in surprise, and he smiled at her. "I call my mare Kicks."

"She got a habit of buckin'?" Lawrence asked as he picked up his drink.

"No. She killed her last owner. Kicked his skull in while he was pickin' her hooves."

Dinah's mouth fell open. Morris snorted and cleared his throat to mask his amusement.

Badger grinned. "I like to find the humor in things, even when I probably shouldn't. Helps me stay sane."

Morris looked at Lawrence. "Yours is a Saddler, right?"

Lawrence nodded and set down his glass. "We've been togethuh a long time, Mister and me. Seen a lot. Suhvived a lot. My wife gave him to me—Lord, that was moah than twenty years ago. He was a much younguh and spriuh fella then, as was I."

Dinah's eyes widened in amazement. A horse more than twenty years old still serving as a man hunter's mount…

"How does your wife feel about you chasin' outlaws around the country?" Morris asked before taking a sip of water.

"Hmph," Lawrence grunted, his gaze drifting to the window. "I s'pose she feels much the same as she did when I went off to war. She didn't like it, but she unduhstood."

"My wife don't like it *or* understand," Badger grumbled. He leaned forward and propped his elbows on the table, his brows furrowing as he glanced back and forth between the two men. "But when the marshal said he was puttin' a posse together, I had to volunteer. This gang ain't gonna stop till somebody does 'em in."

"And if we don't, who will?" Morris added. "How many banks and trains have they gotta rob before the government takes action?"

Dinah's heart swelled. The hunt wasn't personal for them, but they recognized the threat. They *cared.*

"The Pinkertons sent two detectives aftuh 'em a couple months back," Lawrence said. "Both of 'em turned up dead. I doubt the agency took kindly to such an affront."

"Two?" Badger rolled his eyes and shook his head. "That ain't near enough."

"As evidenced by their demise." Lawrence sighed and sat back with a haunted look on his face, a look Dinah knew all too well. "In the war, I killed a lotta God-fearin' men. But now, when I shoot a fella or send him to the noose, I know he's goin' straight to hell. With every devil I kill, I'm makin' amends foah a saint whose days I cut short. This nasty group of devils, these *outlaws*—they've had it comin' a long time."

His eyes burned like blue flames, the weight of his words settling on Dinah's shoulders. They emboldened her. Justified her need for vengeance.

One devil for every saint…

The Valentin Gang owed her two.

———————•———————

The sinking sun glared down the dusty street outside Dinah's window as the train charged into Dodge City. The Santa Fe Railroad ran right through the center of town, dividing the north from the south. A big white building with a slanted roof and an adjoining billiard hall rushed toward her. She peered at the sign on the second-story balcony, but the depot blocked her view before she could read it.

"'Respectable' folk keep north of the tracks," Lawrence explained with obvious skepticism.

Leaning past him, she gazed out the opposite windows as the train slowed to a crawling pace. "The southern side looks the same as the north."

"Wait till the sun goes down."

Dinah swallowed.

Gears hissed and went quiet. White fumes engulfed the railcar, and Lawrence stood up.

Moving into the aisle, he gestured for her to go first and said, "Aftuh you."

She rose on stiff legs and hobbled to the door.

A bone-dry wind buffeted her the moment she disembarked, clouds of steam swirling around her. Dinah's chest tightened. Her hunting trips with her father had never been more than a day's ride from home.

How many more miles to the Strip?

Someone grasped her shoulder, and she spun around with a gasp.

Lawrence stepped back and held up his hands. "Sorry, Miss Hance. I didn't mean to startle ya."

Eyes wide and heart pounding, Dinah realized her hand was on her father's revolver. Embarrassed, she let go of it and reached up to adjust her hat. *His* hat.

"I'm gonna need that gun," Lawrence said.

Her gaze darted to his apologetic features. "What?"

"No guns north of the tracks. That's the law here. If they catch ya wearin' one, they'll throw ya in jail."

"Then I'll stay on the south side."

"You're stayin' at the Dodge House with the rest of us," he responded firmly.

"This is my protection," she persisted. "My father's Colt."

Lawrence sighed. "Look here."

Dinah followed him to the edge of the platform, and he pointed farther down the tracks.

"See that calaboose across the way? Your fathuh's gun'll be safe there with the town marshal."

"What if I need it?" she asked, terrified to be unarmed in a place like this.

He turned to her, as serious as she'd ever seen him. "Stay close to Marshal Tupper, and you won't."

"Where are you gonna be?"

He nodded south. "Twistin' the tiguh's tail. Maybe one of those gamblin' fools'll know somethin' useful."

Dinah drew the revolver and held it in her hands. Cold, heavy—deadly. The Great Equalizer.

"Don't get bit," she muttered, grudgingly handing over the Colt.

<hr />

While Morris, Brooks, Flint, and Donovan went with Lawrence to turn in everyone's guns, Dinah helped Badger, Mercer, and Marshal Tupper lead the horses to a livery behind the white building she'd seen as the train pulled into the station. The Dodge House, it was called, a large hotel where they'd all be staying the night.

The fifty cents she spent to rent a room, in addition to the three train tickets she'd bought, dinner at the restaurant, and boarding Cardinal at the stable, left her with half the money she'd started with. There wouldn't be any more trains to worry about, but there was still the matter of meals and lodging. If this kept up, she'd be flat broke in another day or two.

When the rest of the men decided to go for drinks at a nearby saloon, Mercer and Marshal Tupper stayed at the Dodge House, and so did she. They went to get some supper inside, and Dinah sank into a chair on the front porch with a can of beans she'd taken from her saddlebag.

Finally, she thought, relieved to be alone for the first time since she'd boarded the train in Salina.

Her backside was sore from all the sitting. A walk would do her good, but exhaustion glued her boots to the planks. All day, she'd worn a dispassionate mask. Donned a façade of composure.

Players hollered at the billiard hall next door, already getting rowdy as darkness fell. Dinah hung her hat on the back of her chair, her stomach growling as she spooned a bite of baked beans into her mouth.

She'd seen more towns today than she had since she moved to Kansas. Her whole life she'd longed for the thrill of adventure, the allure of the unknown. But she'd never wanted it like this.

What am I doing here? What was I thinking?

The front door swung open. Dinah cast it a sideways glance as Mercer stepped out onto the porch. She scowled and lowered her spoon.

Was five minutes of peace and quiet too much to ask?

"Hey," he said, strutting over to her, "aren't you gonna eat with us?"

Wasn't plannin' to, she thought crabbily.

He frowned as he noticed the can in her hand. "You can do better than that, Miss Hance. C'mon, I'll take you somewhere nice for supper."

Caught off guard, Dinah scrambled to come up with a polite refusal. "That's kind of you to offer, but I'm fine here."

Mercer arched a blond brow at her. "Really?"

"Really," she replied.

Dinah scooped another bite of beans into her mouth, hoping he'd get the hint and leave her be. Instead, he moved in front of her and leaned against one of the porch columns, blocking her view of the train station. He crossed his arms over his chest, his almost shoulder-length hair blowing in the evening breeze.

He was handsome, with a strong, scruffy jaw and piercing blue eyes, but his insistence was decidedly unappealing. His nose creased, his lip curling in a smug, irritating kind of way. Apparently, he thought himself irresistible.

"Might as well keep you company," he said. "Must be lonely, bein' such a long way from home. No familiar faces."

She averted her gaze, staring into the gathering darkness.

"Y'know, you're somethin' of a local legend in Salina."

Dinah's eyes darted to his, her cheeks flushing and temper flaring. "If this is your idea of a joke—"

"It's true, Miss Hance. I've lived in that town six years and never seen you. Always wanted to. Whispers and rumors—that's one thing. Hearing the story from the girl who was right there in the middle of it all—that's another."

Shaking with fury, she shoved her spoon into the beans and set the can on the chair as she surged to her feet. "My friend died that day, Mr. Mercer."

"I meant no offense, Miss Hance," he said, seeming surprised.

"No offense?" she responded incredulously. "You think I don't know what they say about me? That they think I'm crazy?"

Mercer uncrossed his arms and stepped into the lamplight shining through the window behind her. "You're a mystery to them. They can't understand what they don't know. And you're far too pretty to hide yourself away."

Dinah swallowed as he loomed over her, his unrelenting gaze holding hers captive.

"I wanna know the woman behind the mystery. The real Dinah Hance."

She shrank from him, backing against her chair. "You don't. Trust me."

"What are you so afraid of?" he persisted, advancing with increasing frustration. "You've got plenty to say to Lawrence. Why not me?"

"I've indulged you long enough, Mr. Mercer," she answered curtly. "Now kindly leave me be."

His jaw clenched, his eyes narrowing as he leaned in close. "Y'know, some men aren't so civil, Miss Hance. You might wish you'd kept me around."

He turned and went back inside, leaving Dinah stunned and outraged. When the door closed behind him, she stormed to the front of the porch. Breathing hard, she braced her hand against the white post, heart pounding and temples throbbing.

Did he just threaten me?

She had a good mind to tell Marshal Tupper about his nephew's boorish behavior.

He won't believe you. It's your word against Mercer's.

And he might use her complaint as an excuse to send her packing.

Dinah sank to the floor and let her legs hang over the edge. Leaning her head against the post, she watched a train chug away from the station. Longing for the safety of home.

———————

Dinah slung her saddle over Cardinal's back as he stood at the fence near the livery's open doors. Except for a few nicks, he appeared otherwise unscathed after spending the night in a yard crowded with strange horses. She wondered if he'd slept much. She sure hadn't, tossing and turning in an unfamiliar bed. Wrestling with regret. Nightmares startling her awake every time she managed to drift off.

Lawrence's evening of gambling had yielded no information about the Valentin Gang, and he'd ridden out with Marshal Tupper to search the surrounding area as soon as the sun came up. His mood had improved considerably upon their return. They'd discovered fresh evidence of a camp a couple of miles outside town and a trail heading south. They couldn't be certain that the tracks belonged to the outlaws, but what they'd found convinced them that heading for the Neutral Strip was the right idea.

Flint's gravelly voice filtered through the livery doors as she tightened Cardinal's cinch, and Dinah's hands stilled.

"It's almost a hundred miles from here to the Strip," he said. "That's a lotta ridin', a lotta rough livin'. She ain't gonna make it."

Frowning, she ducked under Cardinal's neck and crept closer.

"I told her to go home," Marshal Tupper replied. "You all heard me. That girl's hard-headed as a mule. Gonna get herself or one of us killed."

Guilt hit her like a gut punch, and she slumped against the exterior wall.

"You can take the matter up with Lawrence, but I already tried," he grumbled. "There ain't no changin' his mind."

"Why's he so set on bringin' her along?" Flint asked.

"We all got ghosts. Things we wanna forget. Things we wanna hold on to."

"Miss Hance?"

Pushing away from the wall, Dinah spun to her right. Brooks waved at her, holding her horse by his rope. Cardinal had taken the opportunity to wander down the fence and visit Brooks' mare, a small sorrel with a flaxen mane and tail.

Dinah strode toward them in a hurry. "I'm sorry, Mr. Brooks."

"Friendly little fella," he said, patting Cardinal's neck.

"He is," she agreed sheepishly. "Thanks for holdin' him for me."

"Sure."

The youngest of the group apart from herself, Brooks wore plain clothes with mismatched patches and a faded black hat over his dirty blond hair. Dinah took Cardinal's rope and turned from him, sighing as she led him away.

Among her peers, she'd always been treated like an outsider. At school. At church. She'd gotten used to it, even come to expect it, but anticipating rejection never softened the blow. Knowing how others felt about her didn't stop their words from hurting.

The last thing she wanted to be was a burden.

Something hardened inside her, and she tightened her grip on the rope. *Prove 'em wrong.*

Dinah dragged her weary body into the saddle as the posse broke camp. Hissing through gritted teeth, she straightened her spine and squared her shoulders. Her backside hurt. Her legs ached, and her arm twinged when she reached for her canteen. She opened it and took a big swig, the crisp, breezy air keeping her water nice and cold.

Lawrence nudged his horse closer to Cardinal. "Everything all right, Miss Hance?"

"Right as rain," she answered tersely, shifting her weight in search of a more comfortable position.

She'd spent the last three days riding from sunrise till sunset, following the Jones and Plummer Trail toward the southern border. Loping across the prairie to the songs of sparrows and meadowlarks during the day and sleeping under the stars at night. She'd never lacked for water with Crooked Creek winding along their path, but the long hours of relentless travel were about to do her in.

A blazing sun rose behind gray and purple clouds slashed through with raging reds and violent yellows, the tall grasses snaking back and forth like shadowy flames. Wildflowers bloomed all around her, but their delicate beauty failed to melt Dinah's frozen heart—frigid and immovable as a bear in winter.

She fell in behind Lawrence as they set out, Mercer in front of him and Marshal Tupper leading the way. She'd steered clear of Mercer ever since he'd cornered her on the porch that night, but that hadn't stopped his eyes from lingering. Yesterday evening, she'd snuck down to the creek to bathe, praying he wouldn't follow her. Much as she wanted to be alone, Dinah had stuck close to Lawrence and the others, hoping they would keep Mercer at bay if the need arose.

Marshal Tupper leaned over to study the hoofprints in the dirt. "These tracks are fresh."

"Less than a day old," Lawrence added.

"Valentin's in for a nasty surprise," Mercer said.

"Don't underestimate him," Lawrence warned. "He ain't like the othuhs I've hunted. Ain't scared of nothin'. He'll letcha get close just so he can savuh the look on your face when he slips away. Or kills ya."

What would they do when they found him? Sal wouldn't come quietly.

Dinah's chest clenched, and she shut her eyes. She'd never been in a gunfight. Never shot at anything that could shoot back.

Breathe, she reminded herself, opening her eyes and forcing air into her lungs.

Soon thereafter, Marshal Tupper stopped his horse on the bank of the Cimarron River. Dinah's jaw dropped. The waters ran as red as the Nile turned to blood, a hundred yards of it standing between them and their destination.

Tupper swore—she hadn't heard him do that before.

She swallowed nervously. "Is it always so wide?"

"No." Lawrence sighed and rested his wrists on the saddle horn. "Rains've flooded it."

"Can we cross?" Morris asked from his bay Morgan on the marshal's right.

"The current ain't nothin' to worry about. The quicksand's whatcha gotta watch out foah," Lawrence replied.

Quicksand? she almost exclaimed aloud.

"Line up behind me, single file," Tupper hollered over his shoulder.

Dinah stared at the rugged land across the water, her heart in her throat. What awaited her beyond the river frightened her far more than its size or the quicksand lurking beneath.

Tupper spurred his buckskin into the river. Mercer followed on his black Saddler, Lawrence right behind him.

"In the presence of evil, he did not cower," Reverend Yerkes had said about her father. *"He died as he lived—confronting the enemy head-on."*

Dinah mustered her courage and squeezed Cardinal's sides. He lurched forward, splashing cold droplets onto her clothes as he trotted into the river.

"Easy, boy," she soothed, his head so high it was almost in her lap. He'd never crossed anything so deep and wide.

Cardinal sank lower and lower until the water stopped just below his shoulders. He slowed to a walk as he caught up with Mister, and Dinah leaned down to give his neck an encouraging pat, her wet skirt clinging to her legs.

"Stay close," Lawrence warned, glancing back at her. "Don't stray to eithuh side."

Badger followed her first, then Morris, Brooks, and Flint, with Donovan bringing up the rear. Sunlight sparkled on the surface of the water, huge clouds billowing across the sky. An icy gust tossed her braid, and Dinah shivered. Heeding Lawrence's advice, she focused all her attention on keeping Cardinal's nose close to Mister's tail. Her inability to see where he'd step next kept her in a state of constant apprehension, her muscles tensed and her stiff fingers clenching the reins.

Every minute felt like an eternity, their progress agonizingly slow.

Halfway there, she thought as the opposite shore loomed larger.

"Whoa!" Badger exclaimed.

Heart jolting, Dinah twisted in the saddle. She didn't know how it happened—maybe Kicks had lost her footing—but she'd slipped five feet off course. Now ten.

The horses panicked, tossing their heads and dancing sideways. Dinah gasped as Brooks' mare charged past her, soaking her clothes and startling Cardinal. He surged forward, and she quickly reined him in before his chest could ram into Mister's hindquarters.

"Get her back on track, Badger!" Marshal Tupper hollered.

Badger turned the mare's dappled neck toward them. Kicked and clucked. Nostrils flaring, she took a step, stumbled, and slid another ten feet downriver. She sank to her shoulders. Then Badger's feet went under the water. Kicks bellowed in distress, fighting to escape.

"She's in the quicksand!" he cried above the commotion of her splashing and struggling.

"I'll get him," Lawrence said.

"Stay where you are," Tupper barked as his buckskin spun toward the southern shore.

Reacting instinctively, Dinah freed her rope and tied one end around the saddle horn with fumbling fingers.

"Ya gotta leave her, Badger!" Tupper yelled as she yanked the knot tight.

Swinging the other end of the rope over her head, Dinah gauged the distance and threw it to Badger, who was now waist-deep in the river. He let go of the reins and grabbed hold of it. Pulling the rope taut, he dragged himself toward her, kicking his legs and straining to hold his chin above the water.

Donovan's horse slammed into Flint's and sent him tumbling into the river. Morris hurried to his aid, reaching down and snagging Flint by the back of his jacket.

Through it all, Cardinal stood like a statue, never budging an inch until Badger reached them. Planting his feet on the treacherous riverbed, Badger stood and returned Dinah's rope. Then he grasped her forearm with a red-stained hand and scrambled up onto Cardinal's back.

"Ya got him?" Tupper shouted over the screaming mare.

Tears scalded her eyes as Kicks' muzzle vanished from view. "Yeah, I got him."

When Cardinal followed Mister up onto the opposite bank, Dinah slumped forward with a sigh of relief. Brooks was already there on his wild-eyed mare, panting and pale-faced as he stared at the river.

"Quick thinkin', Miss Hance," Lawrence remarked.

She couldn't take any pride in it, her heart aching for the horse they'd left behind. As Morris, Flint, and Donovan emerged drenched and shaken, she glanced back at Badger. "I'm sorry."

Avoiding her gaze, he sniffed and said, "Me too."

Silent tears trailed down Dinah's cheeks as she gazed at the place where they'd lost her. Watching the mare drown, hearing her screams—she wished she could forget it, but she knew she never would.

CHAPTER TWELVE

They crossed the Cimarron River without any trouble, hot on the trail of an unknown group of riders. Joseph hoped it was the gang, but his gut told him different. As they splashed up onto the bank, Enyeto slid from Taipah's back, his buckskin boots hitting the damp earth without a sound. Crouching, he plucked something from the clay.

"What is it?"

Enyeto held it up for him to see. "A badge."

Joseph frowned at the rugged slopes to the south. "Sal's got a posse on him."

"A big one," Enyeto said. "They aren't more than a few miles ahead of us. We could ambush them. Thin their numbers before they catch up to the others."

"If they haven't already," Joseph muttered.

Why had the lawman lost his badge? Had he drowned in the river? Gotten shot?

He couldn't be sure, couldn't know what he'd find, and that was the worst part. The distance between him and his friends seemed impossibly vast. He hated how helpless he felt.

But he had to be smart. Had to play his cards right.

"Let's hang back awhile longer," Joseph decided. "Keep our distance. No sense in showin' ourselves till we have to."

Enyeto nodded. He tucked the badge into the pouch on his belt and stood. Grabbing the saddle horn, he sprang onto Taipah's back without using the stirrup.

Joseph spurred Steel into a lope, and Enyeto matched his pace.

Who would follow them all the way to the Strip? Who would be brave enough? Angry enough?

It wasn't a Pinkerton badge Enyeto had pulled from the clay. It was a deputy's. Had the posse come from Abilene? Salina?

More importantly, how had they picked up the trail so quickly? How did they know where to look?

Unless, Joseph thought, *they've followed us here before.*

———————•◦———————

A blustery wind blew from the east, the cool air getting warmer as the sun climbed higher in the cloud-strewn sky. Sand seeped between clumps of sage and spiky yucca as Joseph and Enyeto wound through a maze of buffalo carcasses. The stench of death hung heavy, maggots crawling over their spoiled hides. They'd been shot dead and left to rot.

"Dead Man's Dune," Enyeto muttered darkly. "I only see dead bison."

Joseph had stumbled upon such scenes before, and he doubted this time would be the last. *What a waste.*

He squinted at the vultures cawing and circling overhead. As his gaze wandered to the sand dunes a couple of miles ahead, a cloud of dust went over a rise and then disappeared.

"That's them," Joseph said, his heart beating faster. "Come on. We've gotta stop 'em before they get to Sal."

He made a beeline for the dunes, the wind rushing against his face as his mind raced.

The posse hadn't lost the trail as he'd hoped they would. Soon, they'd be within sight of Dead Man's Dune. All he had to do was slow them down—survive till the gang showed up. They'd be close enough to hear the gunfire, and when they spotted him, they'd come running.

Up and down the dunes he went with Enyeto at his heels, their horses plowing through the deep sand. Steel's black mane waved in the wind, his silver neck glistening. Joseph reined him in at the base of a thirty-foot bank and glanced back at Enyeto.

"Let's get a look at 'em from up there."

They dismounted. Joseph pulled his Winchester from its scabbard and took his binoculars from his saddlebag. Leaving their horses, they trudged up the steep slope, clawing their way to the top. Enyeto lay in the sand with his rifle in his hands, and Joseph got down beside him. Propping on his elbows, he raised his binoculars and peered through them.

Half a mile to the west sat Dead Man's Dune, a haphazard cluster of less than a dozen soddies. Two miles south of it, just beyond a winding river, a small town had sprung up.

Not good.

"I count nine of them," Enyeto said.

Joseph turned his binoculars to the riders in the valley below.

A tall, lean fella in a gray coat and hat sat on a big bay horse that had a white face and stockings. Joseph's jaw clenched. Lawrence—that was his name. The man hunter who'd been a thorn in their side in Texas six years back. So had the bearded man on the buckskin beside him.

But Tupper was a Texas Ranger.

What's he doin' here?

Tupper gestured angrily, arguing with someone on a sorrel horse.

Wait…

Long legs and a trim waist. Braided red hair. A sharp chin and straight nose under the brim of an old brown hat.

Joseph swore under his breath.

"What is it?" Enyeto asked.

He lowered the binoculars, hardly believing his eyes. "Dinah Hance."

"The girl from the homestead? What's she doing here?"

Baffled, Joseph shook his head. Things had just gotten much more complicated.

Tupper wheeled his horse around, leaving Dinah and a man without a mount behind as Lawrence and the other five riders followed him toward Dead Man's Dune.

"Now's our chance." Joseph set aside the binoculars and lifted his rifle from his back. Bracing his left elbow in the sand, he closed one eye and squinted through the scope. "I'll take the fella on the buckskin. You take the man in gray."

He breathed in, his finger hovering over the trigger. It wouldn't be easy. His target was more than a hundred yards away.

"You got a shot?"

"Yeah," Enyeto grunted.

The wind stood still. Joseph exhaled.

Bang!

Tupper lurched in the saddle, his hand flying to his right shoulder. His horse surged forward as Enyeto fired the second shot. The bullet meant for Lawrence hit the buckskin, and Tupper and his mount went down in a cloud of dust.

Lawrence's horse sprang sideways. He pulled his rifle from its scabbard.

Joseph ejected his spent cartridge and fired at Lawrence. Missed.

Spotting them, Lawrence raised his weapon and fired back. Sand sprayed into the air a few feet below him, and Joseph ducked behind the crest of the hill.

"We've gotta go, Joseph."

"I know," he growled, slinging his Winchester across his back and retrieving his binoculars.

"No—" Enyeto grabbed his sleeve and pointed past him. "*Look.*"

Joseph glanced over his shoulder. His eyes widened in alarm.

A brown billowing band stretched across the eastern horizon, rumbling like approaching thunder as it rolled toward them like a monstrous wave.

A sandstorm.

He looked down into the valley. Lawrence and the other riders were galloping toward him. No—not just them.

"Dinah, wait!" Lawrence hollered as she left the rest of them in the dust.

In leaving her behind, the posse had unwittingly given her a head start.

"C'mon," Joseph said, scrambling to his feet, "we're gonna lose 'em in that storm."

"Ghosts dance in whirlwinds," Enyeto protested.

"You got a better idea?"

Without waiting for an answer, Joseph hurtled headlong down the dune, plunging through green thickets and fighting to keep his balance in the shifting sands. The storm roared louder, beating and drumming. Its shadow fell over him as he stumbled to the foot of the slope. He shoved the binoculars into his saddlebag and slapped Steel's silver rump.

"Get outta here."

The mustang bolted, Taipah running with him as they fled the coming storm.

Joseph pulled his bandana over his nose and turned to Enyeto. He'd just caught up to him, panting and wide-eyed. Shooting him a resigned glare, Enyeto yanked his bandana off his head and tied it around his face.

Crack!

Dust sprang up from the ground next to Joseph. Wheeling around, he saw Dinah standing at the top of the hill with a six-shooter pointed right at him. He took off running, whipping out his Schofield and firing a warning shot over his shoulder. He didn't want to hit her—he just needed to make her think twice.

Enyeto drew alongside him, his steps as light and swift as a deer's. Black clouds swallowed the sky and blotted out the sun. Dark dunes rose around them, shielding them from their pursuers. Joseph tore through a tangle of shrubs and raced on, chest heaving and pulse pounding.

The storm rushed forward to devour him. Filled his field of vision and drowned out every other sound. Joseph planted his feet and peered up at the swirling mass, bracing for the impact.

"See you on the other side!" he yelled to Enyeto. Pulling his hat farther over his eyes, he shut them tight and bowed his head.

The gale crashed over him, engulfing him in dust and suffocating sand. It ripped at his clothes and raked the hand he raised in front of his face, his pants and coat beating against his burning legs. Joseph opened his eyes a sliver and found himself standing alone in a dense red haze.

"Enyeto?"

No answer—just the wailing wind.

Holding his bandana tighter against his face, he started walking, every step buffeted by violent gusts. He'd lost all sense of direction, but he had to keep going. Had to put more distance between himself and the posse. At least the storm would force them off their horses and slow them to the same crawling pace.

"Turn around!" demanded a muffled voice.

Joseph stopped in his tracks. *No... Not her.*

"*Now!*"

He swallowed, heart thumping as he faced her.

Dinah's braid had come undone, her hair lashing her shoulders and a black neckerchief covering her face. The wind knocked her a step sideways, and she struggled to keep the six-shooter aimed at his chest.

Joseph reckoned there was less than ten feet between them. Rushing her when she was holding a loaded gun was a gamble, but he liked his odds. It wouldn't fire in a storm like this—he hoped.

Joseph lunged. As he grabbed her wrists, she pulled the trigger. Panic jolted through him, but nothing happened. The gun didn't go off.

Shoving the revolver away from his chest, Joseph tried to wrestle it from her stubborn grasp. His fingers clamped around hers. Dinah yelped, desperately clinging to the six-shooter as brutal winds beat and battered them. He pushed closer. Forced her back.

Dinah dug in her heels, and Joseph clenched his teeth. He surged forward. Her eyes widened as she fell backward, taking him with her. They tumbled down a sharp incline, their bodies a tangle of flailing limbs. Joseph's hat flipped off his head. Sand scraped his hands raw.

They rolled off a ledge, and then there was nothing. No ground. Just air. Dinah cried out as they plunged into darkness.

CHAPTER THIRTEEN

Joseph broke her fall, landing on his back with a grunt. Dinah lost her grip on the Colt as she rolled off him, her momentum carrying her down another mound of sand.

Darkness above her. Darkness below her. Darkness all around.

Dinah sprawled on her stomach, dazed and disoriented. She raised her head and pulled down her neckerchief. Gulped a breath of cool air free of whirling dust.

A cave.

White-hot pain pricked her right calf. Dinah yelped, and something slithered out from under her legs. She moved faster than she could think, flipping over and scrambling backward with a startled whimper. She couldn't see it, but she heard a droning rattle.

"Snake!" Dinah shrieked, jerking her knees up to her chest.

Her heart hammered as she sat there shaking. She didn't dare move. What if there were more of them?

A match hit the ground in front of her and revealed the coiled rattler. Dinah gasped and glanced to her left as Joseph skidded down the hill of sand feet-first. The snake hissed and bared its fangs at him as he stood and pulled his six-shooter in a single motion. The muzzle flashed, and she flinched, the crack of the gunshot ringing in her ears.

Joseph holstered his revolver and ground the rattler's head under his heel for good measure. She stared at him, stunned that he'd leaped to her defense. Sand clung to his clothes, his face smudged with dust and dirt.

Breathing hard, he looked at her. "Did it bitecha?"

Dinah nodded. She reached for the place where the fangs had punctured her skin, dreading what she would find if she peeked under her skirt.

Her fingers grazed the tingling wound through the holes in the fabric, and pain stabbed her leg. She grimaced.

She'd never been bitten before, but she knew people who had. Some had survived. Others weren't so fortunate.

"Looks like you're gonna get the last laugh."

"I can help you," Joseph offered, "but I have to do it fast."

The match went out, and Dinah gaped at his vaguely defined shadow. Her simmering anger exploded like a bundle of dynamite. "*Help me*? You're crazy if you think—"

"Do you wanna live?"

She clenched her jaw. Her leg was on fire. "Just shoot me and get it over with."

"I ain't lettin' you off that easy."

"Why?" she spat as he struck another match. "I haven't suffered enough already?"

Joseph's eyes softened with something like guilt. "No one was supposed to get hurt."

If she didn't know better, she'd think he meant it. "Which time?"

He bowed his head and walked away, holding out the match as he scanned the sand-coated floor of the cave.

"What're you doin'?" Dinah asked.

"Makin' sure there ain't more of 'em."

Sweat beaded on her brow, her head spinning with a sudden onset of dizziness.

Joseph returned with an armful of brush and sticks and set them on the ground. He lit a third match and tossed it onto the pile. The fire chewed at the wood, giving them better light to see by.

He knelt beside her and drew a knife from his belt. Dinah's eyes widened. He reached for her leg, and she recoiled.

Hesitating, Joseph met her hostile gaze. Asking for permission.

Dinah swallowed. Much as she hated it, hated *him*, she needed him.

Wincing, she stretched out her leg again. Joseph grasped the red-stained hem of her skirt, so lightly and carefully that she couldn't believe this was the same man she'd fought tooth and nail with a few minutes ago. Dinah stiffened, resisting the instinct to shrink back as he rolled her skirt up to her knee.

Her lips parted in dismay when she glimpsed two puncture marks on the outer swell of her calf. And *swell* was the only word for it.

Nausea crashed over her.

Dinah averted her gaze, her fingers curling into the sand. She didn't like needles or knives or anything sharp poking at her. *Skinnin' an animal's one thing. This is another.*

Craning her neck, she found the gaping hole they'd fallen through, high above them and impossible to reach even with the sand blowing in and piling on the ground.

Something cold pierced her skin, startling a yelp out of her. Her leg jerked, but Joseph had a firm hold on her ankle. The searing pain of the knife digging into that already tender place made her screw her eyes shut and bite her lip to keep from screaming.

"Sorry," he muttered.

A second later, she heard him sheath the knife. Dinah opened her eyes, heart slamming against her ribs as the storm raged outside the cave.

Joseph had made two small cuts in the shape of an X. His right hand gripped her ankle again, the other slipping under her knee and lifting her leg.

What's he—? Oh no.

His lips latched onto her leg and sucked—*hard.* Cheeks flushing and fists clenching, Dinah fought the urge to punch him. Kick him. *Anything* that would give her the slightest bit of relief. That would spare her this pain and humiliation.

Joseph turned his head and spat.

Why me? Why not him? Dinah glared into the blackness, soaked with sweat and trembling with fever. *Is this your idea of justice?*

Joseph's mouth returned to her wound, and she gritted her teeth. He spat again. The third excruciating pull of his lips made her punch the sand.

Finally, Joseph lowered her leg. "I got some of it."

Dinah met his gaze with heavy-lidded eyes, her strength dwindling faster than the flames. "I... need a doctor."

"I know." His lips were stained with blood—*her* blood. He wiped them with the back of his hand. "I'll look for a way outta here."

He took off his bandana, tied it around the bite, and rolled her skirt back down to her ankle.

"My hat," she croaked as he stood.

"I'll find it. Just stay put."

He left her sitting by the dying fire. Dinah shivered, wanting nothing more than to lie down and sleep.

Focus. Stay awake.

A tiny flame ignited in the darkness. She concentrated all her attention on its yellow glow as Joseph carried it through the shadows, listening to the sound of his spurs and the howling wind.

CHAPTER FOURTEEN

This was a disaster. The cruelest twist of fate.

I'm cursed, Joseph thought. *I've gotta be.*

He'd risked his life going back to Salina to pay off her debt, to make sure she got a fresh start, and now she might die down here in the dark.

Because of me.

He returned to Dinah with her hat in one hand and a burning branch in the other. He'd put his own hat back on and stuck her gun in his belt.

She sat right where he'd left her, eyes closed and head hung low.

"Dinah?"

She flinched awake as he crouched beside her.

"I found a tunnel. Might be a way out."

Joseph held out her hat. She snatched it from him and clutched it to her chest, sweating and shivering. He threw away the branch as the flames neared his hand.

Dinah struggled to her feet, and she swayed. He rose just in time to catch her.

"You're gonna be the death of me," she grumbled, "pushin' me into this cave."

"You ain't dyin'," Joseph growled, trying to convince himself as much as he was her. "Put your arm over my shoulders."

Reluctantly, she did. Her legs were about as steady as a newborn foal's as he guided her forward, his arm wrapped around her waist.

The fire went out, leaving them in total darkness.

"You got another match?" Dinah asked nervously.

"Yeah, but I ain't usin' it yet."

When he found the adjoining passage again, Joseph felt his way along a wall of solid rock with his free hand. His throat was as dry as the dunes, his thighs burning from plowing through the sand.

Dinah huffed and squirmed. "Move your hand."

Suddenly, he became very aware of the curve of her waist. The heat of her body against his. "Where?"

"I don't know," she answered irritably. "Just—not there."

He shifted his hand higher. "Y'know, if you hadn't come after us, this wouldn't've happened. What self-respectin' lawman lets a lady ride with a posse, anyhow?"

"Marshal Tupper's a brave and decent man, and you shot him like a coward," Dinah snapped.

Joseph's blood boiled. "Would you rather I killed him?"

"I'd rather you were dead," she shot back.

Her words stung, and he hated that they did. Hated that he cared. "It ain't too late for me to leave you in this cave."

"Go ahead," she dared, "'cause that's the only way you're gettin' rid of me."

Joseph clenched his jaw, inwardly cursing her stubbornness as he inched through the tunnel. He couldn't get distracted. One wrong step could prove fatal.

Dinah's nails dug into his shoulder. "Sal's gonna get what's comin' to him."

Joseph sighed in frustration. He understood her anger and the grudge she held against them. He'd lost his father a long time ago. But the thought of her throwing away the chance he'd given her, throwing away her *life*—

He almost told her about the debt. The risk he'd taken on her behalf.

"Never seen a girl so downright determined to get herself killed," he muttered.

"As if you care," Dinah scoffed.

"You're the one who tried to shoot me," Joseph reminded her.

"That's what enemies *do*. That's what we are."

Her answer echoed in the silence. The blustering wind had faded away, leaving only their clunking footsteps and her heavy breathing. He suspected that it was all she could do to keep putting one foot in front of the other, and he couldn't help but marvel at the iron will of this grieving young woman who'd endured so much and traveled so far.

No more arguin', he decided.

Sal didn't like loose ends. He'd tell him to shoot her or leave her for dead. That was the smart thing to do. The easier thing.

Joseph pushed the pace, a clock ticking in his head. How long had they been down here? He couldn't be sure, and he had no idea where this winding passage would lead them. To the surface, or deeper underground?

If she dies—

He stopped that thought in its tracks.

"Are you a prayin' woman, Miss Hance?"

"Yes," she answered hoarsely.

"Best get to it then. I doubt he'll listen to me."

Joseph took a deep breath, smooth rock gliding under his sweating palm. He didn't talk to God anymore. Hadn't in years. But he didn't know what else to do.

We ain't on good terms, you and me. I ain't askin' for that to change. What I did is unforgivable. I know that.

It's my fault she got dragged into this mess, so punish me, not her. She believes in you, believes you can save her. Prove her right. Don't desert her like you did me.

As she limped along beside him, her grip on his shoulder slackened. She stumbled, and Joseph clutched her to his side.

"Dinah?"

"Mm?"

"I know it ain't easy, but I needja to keep walkin'," he said, his arm aching from holding her upright.

She struggled on, and with every step they took, he tested the ground with the toe of his boot.

They hadn't gone but another ten feet when its silver tip struck something hard. Joseph stopped, and Dinah sagged against him. He extended his free hand in front of his face, and his palm flattened against cold stone.

No.

He reached to his left and felt another wall. Stretched past her and found another on their right.

A lump stuck in Joseph's throat. He couldn't bring himself to tell her they were trapped.

"Do you feel that?" Dinah asked.

His brow furrowed. "Feel what?"

"Air," she murmured, "comin' through from the other side."

She pulled away from him.

"There's a hole down here," she said, sounding like she'd crouched.

Great. He didn't like small spaces, especially ones he couldn't see the end of.

"Come on."

Dinah grunted as she wriggled into the tunnel.

"Right behind you," Joseph grumbled.

He took a deep breath, got on his hands and knees, and crawled through the opening. It was a tight fit, his shoulders scraping and scuffing against the sides. His head bumped against solid rock, and Joseph cursed. Heart thumping in his ears, he inched forward, complete darkness crushing in on him from every direction.

Don't stop. Just keep goin'.

He couldn't see her, but he heard her ragged breaths. Cool air caressed his face, promising escape. A way out.

Then he saw it—light up ahead. Hope sparked inside him.

Dragging his weary legs out of the tunnel, Joseph got to his feet and dusted himself off. He stood in a cave much like the one they'd left behind, sunlight shining through a nearby opening about ten feet high.

Relief flooded through him. "You were right. This is our way outta here."

She didn't answer.

"Dinah?"

"I don't… I don't think I'm gonna make it," she mumbled.

Realizing that she was sitting on the ground, he crouched beside her. "Yes you are. We're almost there."

Dinah's tearstained cheeks glittered in the gloom. "Just leave me."

He shook his head. "No. You ain't quittin' on me now."

Wrapping his right arm around her shoulders, Joseph wedged his other hand under her knees. She made a weak attempt to free herself as he hoisted her into his arms. She felt so light—so fragile.

"Stop your squirmin'. We're runnin' outta time."

Something cracked under his boot, and he froze.

"What was that?" she asked.

Joseph remembered the legend of the dunes and the Indian burial grounds. Peering into the shadows, he saw hundreds of bones piled all around them. His eyes widened.

It was true. In part, at least.

"Nothin'," he muttered.

Quickly, he carried her past them, heading for the mouth of the cave. With each step, the light grew bigger and brighter until finally, Joseph found himself squinting at a clear blue sky. The storm had passed.

"We made it," he breathed.

Judging by the height of the sun, it wasn't yet noon. A small pond sparkled below, bordered with shrubs and a tree rustling in the breeze. A blue roan stallion stood drinking, and he raised his dripping muzzle.

Joseph couldn't believe his luck.

"Hey, boy," he said as Steel trotted toward him.

Dinah's head rested against his shoulder, eyes closed as she clutched her father's hat in her lap. Fear gripped him.

"Hey. Dinah. Stay awake, okay?"

Her lids fluttered open as Steel stopped in front of them. He snorted and shook sand from his mane.

"Easy," Joseph said, slowly approaching him.

The stallion pinned back his ears, his big black eye watching him with suspicion.

"I've gotta get her to a doctor."

Joseph took another step. Then another. Steel didn't budge.

Carefully, he lifted Dinah into the saddle. She slumped forward but caught herself against the horn. Joseph shoved his foot into the stirrup and mounted behind her. Reaching around her, he took up the reins and spurred the stallion's sides.

Steel galloped around the mouth of the cave and bounded up the dune. Joseph stopped him at its crest and surveyed his surroundings. The tunnel had led them southwest, Dead Man's Dune sitting half a mile to the north. Much closer than he'd expected.

He saw no sign of the posse. Maybe they'd gone to the town across the river. Tupper would need a doctor.

Joseph grimaced. If they were with the doctor, he couldn't take Dinah there. They'd arrest him or shoot him on sight. Much as he wanted to help her, he couldn't risk it.

He had to take her to Dead Man's Dune.

———————•———————

Galloping into the abandoned town, Joseph reined in Steel in front of the old saloon. A buffalo skull hung above the batwing doors, flat-roofed soddies arranged around it in the shape of a horseshoe. He swallowed, bracing himself for the questions—the outrage.

Enyeto pushed through the saloon doors. His face brightened as he stepped out onto the porch. "Joseph! You made it."

Joseph breathed a little easier at the sight of him. "Sal and the others—are they—?"

"Everyone's here."

Joseph sighed in relief. He dismounted and held Steel by the reins as Enyeto came down the stairs.

"What's she doing here?" Enyeto's frown deepened as he got closer. "She doesn't look so good."

Dinah stared at him, pale and feverish.

"Snake bite," Joseph said. "She needs a doctor."

"She's in luck." Enyeto gestured to the nearest soddy. "There's a doctor here. The Guidrys took her from that town across the river. Charlie isn't doing well."

Joseph's heart dropped. *Must be bad for 'em to do somethin' so desperate.*

"One thing after another…"

Enyeto nodded. "Always."

Joseph led Steel across the dusty street and hitched him outside the soddy. Dinah was barely conscious when he carried her to the door. She mumbled something as he gave it two hard taps with his boot.

Moments later, it swung open. A woman stood in the doorway, early thirties, blond-haired and blue-eyed. She wore a gray vest over her white shirt and a navy skirt that matched her neckerchief.

She looked scared.

"You the doctor?" Joseph asked.

"Yes."

"She's been snake bit," he explained, striding past her as she stepped back to make way for him.

He supposed this dim and dusty place had once been someone's home. It had a wooden counter and cabinets, a small table with a couple of chairs, and two beds on the right side of the room. Charlie lay in the farthest one, shaking and shivering. His eyes were closed, his hair flattened against his sweaty forehead.

Joseph's chest clenched with worry.

"I don't believe it," said a familiar voice.

He turned in surprise as Tony stepped away from one of the windows.

"First, Remy and Donny kidnap a woman. Now this?" Tony exclaimed. "What the hell is she doin' here?"

"I ain't got time for this," Joseph grumbled, taking Dinah to the empty bed and lowering her onto the narrow mattress.

She grunted, her face screwing up in pain as his arm brushed against the bite.

"Sorry," he muttered.

"What kind of snake?" the doctor asked.

"A rattler."

"How long ago?"

Joseph turned and shrugged as she took the lid off a barrel and dipped a bucket into it. "Half an hour. Maybe more."

Her lips pressed into a tight line. She hurried to Dinah and set the bucket beside the bed. Dinah was covered in sand from head to toe, her hair wild and windblown. Red strands stuck to her brow and cheeks, her face as white as the bedsheets. She looked like she'd been through hell, and Joseph suspected that if he held up a mirror, he wouldn't look much better.

"Where were you bitten?" the doctor asked her.

Dinah rolled up her skirt and pointed at the right side of her calf.

"Ah, I see you've already received some treatment," the doctor observed, sounding pleasantly surprised.

Dinah looked as embarrassed as he felt. Joseph stared at the floor, avoiding Tony's gaze.

The doctor took off Dinah's boot, her sock, and his bandana. When she put her leg in the water, Dinah yelped, her fingers curling against the sheets.

"Some whiskey, I think," the doctor said.

Dinah grimaced and shook her head. "I don't drink."

"Just enough to ease your pain," she assured her.

"Is she gonna be all right?" Joseph asked.

"Should be, but it's too soon to say for certain. I'll be able to make a more accurate prognosis in twenty-four hours."

A whole day? He might not be here then. The posse could show up any minute.

Would the gang pack up and move on, or would Sal stay and fight? If he chose the latter, Dinah's troubles were just beginning.

"Where are you goin'?" Tony demanded as he headed for the door.

Joseph stopped and looked back at him. "To talk to Sal."

He glanced at Dinah. Her green eyes stared into his, wide and terrified.

Sal would be angry with him. That was a given. But he'd done the right thing.

What he had to do.

Joseph stepped out into the nippy breeze and closed the door behind him. Clouds fanned across the open sky as he stood in the empty street. He sighed and took off his hat, raking his fingers through his hair and shoving it back onto his head.

Something moved at the corner of his vision, and he turned. Marcus leaned against the soddy, arms crossed and a scowl on his face.

"How long've you been standin' there?" Joseph asked irritably.

"Long enough to know you've forgotten what's important."

Joseph huffed and strode toward the saloon. *Here comes the lecture.*

"What the hell were you thinkin', bringin' her here?" Marcus growled as he followed close behind.

Joseph rounded on him. "She don't deserve what we did to her."

"No, she didn't, but what happened at the homestead shoulda been the end of it."

"She lost her father."

"We've all lost folk," Marcus said, unmoved.

Joseph turned from him and put his hands on his hips, wrestling with his guilty conscience. *Ain't just about her father.*

"What's gotten into you?" Marcus demanded. "Ya gettin' soft on me?"

Joseph glared over his shoulder. "I ain't gettin' soft."

"You like her. Is that it?"

"I hardly know her," he muttered, gazing out at the rolling dunes.

"That ain't an answer."

Joseph clenched his jaw, confused and conflicted emotions stirring in him. Dinah wanted him dead, yet he was drawn to her like a moth to a flame. She was fierce and determined and—

Forbidden.

"Men like us... We always want what we can't have," Marcus reflected with regret. "Sometimes I wonder what happened to Mollie Luther. Where she is now. But I'm better off without her—I know that."

Rarely did he mention her. Even after all these years, the pain in his voice was so raw that it tugged at Joseph's heart. He turned to face him. Harsh as Marcus' words had been, Joseph knew he'd said them because, more than anyone, he understood his struggle. Didn't want him to make the same mistakes he had as a young man.

"Did you ever think about runnin' away with her? Startin' over someplace?"

Marcus hesitated, his dark brows drawing together over drooping lids. "Yeah, I did. But a thought's just that, ain't it?"

I s'pose so. Joseph stared at the sand under his feet, a nagging emptiness gnawing at him.

"You thinkin' about leavin', Joseph?"

"Course not," he answered, more defensively than he'd meant to.

Marcus nodded, his rigid posture relaxing. "Good. You and me—we ain't fit for settlin' down. We're drifters. Wanderin's in our blood."

Reality had forced Joseph to accept that he would never again have a home, never have a wife or kids or a plot of land to call his own.

Still, he couldn't help imagining it. Longing for it.

"C'mon," Marcus said, heading for the saloon steps.

———— • ————

Joseph pushed through the batwing doors and followed Marcus inside. Slowly, his eyes adjusted to the dingy darkness, the air stale and stuffy. He hadn't seen this place in six years, but he remembered the cobweb-covered heads mounted on the walls. Rabbits, foxes, coyotes—even a buffalo behind the bar.

"'Bout time, Gray," Remy called, leaning against the wooden pillar at the center of the room. "If ya done tryin' ta crawl inta bed wit da enemy, we got a posse ta deal wit."

How nice it would be to put a bullet between those beady eyes of his.

"Least I ain't kidnappin' doctors and riskin' the wrath of a mob," Joseph growled.

"Charlie's our brotha," Donny snapped, "not a stranga."

Sal turned from a glassless window—one with a clear view of the soddy Joseph had carried her to. "You should've put her out of her misery."

Joseph's fists clenched in frustration. "Why? She ain't no threat to us."

Sal's black eyes flashed, and Joseph's mouth went dry. He hated it sometimes, Sal's uncanny ability to read his thoughts. To see right through him. Nothing was off limits. Nothing was his own.

"Ya wan' me ta deal wit 'er, Sal?"

Joseph's gaze darted to Remy's eager face. His heart slammed against his chest, pounding in his ears as Sal considered in silence.

"No," he decided. "We can use this to our advantage. Remy, Donny, go to the soddy next to Tony and Charlie. Gus, take Rick and Collin to the old store across the street. When the posse rides into town, we'll have them surrounded."

"You think we can take 'em?" Collin asked.

Marcus nodded, always confident. "Enyeto said there were nine of 'em countin' the girl."

"We shot one of 'em," Joseph added. "Killed his horse. It was that Ranger who chased us outta Texas six years back."

Sal's eyes narrowed. "Tupper."

Marcus sighed. "Thought we'd seen the last of him."

"So did I," Joseph said. "He's got that man hunter with him—Lawrence."

To his surprise, Sal cracked a smile. "Lawrence… Still chasing his white whale."

Another reference Joseph didn't understand. He didn't do much reading.

As the others trooped out of the saloon, Marcus stood by the door, watching the dunes to the east. Enyeto sat at a table close by, checking his rifle.

"Can I count on you, Joseph?" Sal asked suddenly, leveling him with his penetrating gaze.

Joseph stared at him, insulted and incredulous. "Always, Sal."

"You sound surprised, Joseph. Do you think I'm blind?"

Joseph sighed, his eyes searching the room's dark corners for the right words. "I couldn't leave her to die. You know how I feel about—"

"How you *feel*," Sal echoed scathingly, "doesn't matter when our survival is at stake. The gang comes first."

Of course it did. But he had rules he couldn't break. Lines he couldn't cross.

Sal's disappointment cut like a knife, pinning Joseph's gaze to the floor. Marcus and Enyeto stayed silent, but he knew they heard every word.

"Joseph."

He swallowed and raised his eyes to Sal's.

"You've been with me from the beginning. I trusted you to do whatever I asked of you, to do the job and do it well. But you've become careless. Distracted."

"I know," he admitted. "I'm sorry."

"Nothing you do will ever be enough for her—for 'civilized' society. You know that, don't you? They don't tolerate men like us. They're weak, narrow-minded slaves of a broken system. A false religion."

A dull ache gripped Joseph's chest as Sal stepped closer. "Your guilt is holding you back. Let it go."

Helplessly, he shook his head. "I don't know how."

"Remember what I told you about the lightning and the tree. Bind yourself to nothing but this gang." Sal put a firm hand on his shoulder. "All we have is each other. I need you focused. Committed."

Joseph nodded, and Sal withdrew his hand. He didn't want to care about Dinah, but he couldn't help feeling a sense of responsibility for her. To make sure she got out of this alive.

"They're here," Marcus announced.

———————•———————

The posse galloped into Dead Man's Dune, kicking up a trail of dust in their wake. Joseph counted four of them and frowned. There should be more. Where were the rest? Had they lost them in the storm?

"Looks like Tupper's sittin' this one out," Marcus said. "You musta got him good."

"Where's Lawrence?" Joseph muttered.

Passing between the soddies where the rest of the gang had hidden themselves, the man in front stopped his black horse near the saloon, and his companions followed suit. Joseph recognized them as the men he'd seen with Lawrence and Tupper out in the dunes.

Marcus pressed his back to the wall by the door, his hand on his revolver. Joseph took up position on the other side and peeked around the corner.

Badges gleamed on the riders' chests, three of them stern-faced and the fourth looking like he'd pissed himself. He was the youngest of the group, maybe Collin's age.

"There's no use hiding," called the man on the black horse. "We know you're here."

He glanced to his left—his right—the wind whipping his blond hair across his scowling face. "My name is James Mercer. I'm acting on behalf of U.S. Marshal Lee Tupper. You've got a lot to answer for, Valentin. To be frank, I'd rather finish this here and now. But in the interest of avoiding further violence, I'm gonna make you a one-time offer—surrender, and we'll bring you in alive."

"Likes hearin' himself talk, don't he?" Marcus grumbled.

"Joseph, cover the back door," Sal instructed.

He smells it too. An ambush.

Joseph headed for the bar and motioned for Enyeto to follow.

"You're in no position to dictate terms, Mr. Mercer," Sal answered with stone-cold confidence. "I hear your marshal needs a doctor. You won't find her in town. She's here, and if you open fire, she dies."

Joseph's heart beat faster, his insides twisting in knots. Sal didn't make empty threats. *Is that what we're doin' now? Killin' women?*

"Prove it," Mercer demanded. "I wanna see her."

As Joseph went behind the bar, he looked out the southern window. In the soddy across the street, Tony shoved the doctor into view, holding his gun to her head as she squirmed and struggled.

Joseph swallowed and turned into a short, dark hall. He passed a small room that must've been the kitchen and strode to the back door. Reaching for the handle, he glanced over his shoulder. Enyeto nodded, his rifle at the ready.

Joseph drew his left revolver and opened the door. He blinked, blinded by the light that flooded through the doorway.

Bang!

He jumped back, throwing the door between him and whoever had just taken a shot at him.

"Move!" he exclaimed, shoving Enyeto into the empty kitchen.

Bullets tore through the door as they ducked around the corner. Pulse pounding, Joseph pressed his back against the wall. Enyeto stood on the other side of the doorway, breathing hard as gunfire erupted outside.

"Did you see them?" Enyeto asked.

Joseph shook his head, his hand still trembling. *That was close. Too close.*

The back door crashed open. Enyeto raised his rifle and fired.

Ears ringing, Joseph poked his head out into the smoky hall. A man lay facedown on the floor.

"Go on! Yah!" someone hollered.

Sal's horse galloped past the saloon. Then Remy's.

Joseph swore. Stepping over the stranger's body, he rushed out onto the back porch. One of the posse members held the paddock gate as all the gang's horses charged through. Lawrence waved them on from the back of his dark bay Saddler.

Joseph's blood boiled. *There he is.*

Enyeto slung his rifle across his back and hurried down the steps. As Taipah ran by, he grabbed her black mane and sprang onto her back.

Joseph fired at Lawrence but missed. Lawrence spun his Saddler around and spurred him into action, galloping alongside the horses as he aimed his revolver.

The wooden post to Joseph's right splintered a foot from his head. Heart thumping, he ducked and sprinted the other way. He vaulted over the railing and landed on his feet, his boots sinking into the white sand below.

The man by the paddock let go of the gate and took a shot at him from across the street. Joseph sent two bullets flying back at him. The man staggered and collapsed against the fence with a bleeding hole in his chest. His gray horse shied away, and Joseph made a mad dash for the soddy where the women were being held—where Steel was still tied outside.

All hell had broken loose. Three riders raced to and fro, Remy and Donny shooting at them through the windows. A dead man and his horse lay in front of the saloon.

Suddenly, Charlie stumbled out of the soddy, his gun swinging at his side.

In his shock, Joseph skidded to a stop. *What's he doin'? He's gonna get himself killed.*

"Charlie!" Tony shouted through the window on the right. He couldn't go after him, not with the doctor still fighting to break free.

Mercer charged around the corner on his big black horse. Standing right in his path, Charlie fired once—twice—and missed. He didn't look like he could see straight, let alone shoot straight.

"Help!" Dinah screamed from the left window. "I'm here!"

Mercer took aim at Charlie. Joseph raised his Schofield, pulled the trigger and—

Nothing. His gun didn't fire.

Mercer's did. The shot launched Charlie backward, and Joseph's heart dropped. Mercer's horse swerved around Charlie in a cloud of dust and flew past Joseph, Tony yelling as he fired round after round.

Joseph stared at his Schofield in disbelief. Why'd it jam? Why now?

Marcus hurtled around the corner. "They're runnin'! Get the—"

He stopped short at the sight of them, breathless and wide-eyed.

Numbly, Joseph went to Charlie and crouched beside him. He was already gone. Joseph bowed his head, pushing his clenched fist into the sand.

Charlie was just a kid. He'd had his whole life ahead of him.

Burning with rage, Joseph stood and stormed toward Steel.

"Hey," Marcus said. "Joseph, wait."

Ignoring him, Joseph unwound the reins from the hitching rail. When he looked up, sad green eyes met his. Dinah stood in the window, pale and crestfallen. Her hopes dashed.

He turned from her and climbed into the saddle.

"Joseph!" Marcus hollered after him as he galloped away.

Tearing east out of Dead Man's Dune, Joseph spurred Steel to the top of the nearest bank and reined him in. Lawrence, Mercer, and their two surviving companions were making a beeline for the town across the river.

He wouldn't be able to catch them before they got there.

Joseph drew his rifle and glared at Mercer through the scope. He fired, and Steel tossed his head. He pumped the lever and fired a second shot. A third.

They were too far out, moving too fast.

Joseph lowered his rifle, shoved it back into the scabbard, and returned to Dead Man's Dune with a heavy heart.

CHAPTER FIFTEEN

Charlie wasn't the only outlaw who'd been killed. Gus had come out of the soddy across the street, red-faced and yelling that the posse had gotten Collin—whoever that was.

Good riddance, Dinah thought. Her nails dug into the sill, tears stinging her eyes as she stood at the window.

Morris lay in the dusty street, his dead horse beside him.

He had a family. Kids he wouldn't go home to.

Dinah's chest squeezed with an awful ache. Who else had been killed? Had Lawrence made it out?

Was he even here?

She hadn't seen him.

Remy sat in the sand, holding Charlie in his arms. Tears ran down his cheeks, his lip quivering and his eyes glaring east. Donny stood at his shoulder with his fists clenched at his sides.

"I'm gonna kill 'im," Donny fumed. "I'll make 'im wish he was neva born."

"Dinah."

She turned from the window. Dr. Hart waved her toward the back door. In his grief, Tony had gone to Collin and left the two of them unguarded.

Dinah took a step, and fiery pain shot up her leg. She bit her lip to keep from crying out.

Dr. Hart hurried to catch her as she swayed. The room spun, her body aching and clammy with fever.

"You go, Dr. Hart," she croaked. "I'll slow you down."

Her brow furrowed. "I'm not leaving you here with these animals. And please, call me Jill."

Too dizzy to argue, Dinah draped her arm over the doctor's shoulders and limped toward the door.

"It's two miles to Beaver—where they took me from," said Jill, her voice just above a whisper. "We can get help there."

Quietly, she turned the handle and pulled open the door. It creaked, and Dinah cringed. She cast an anxious glance over her shoulder as Jill bent to pick up her bag of tools and medicines.

She'd left her father's hat at the end of the bed.

"Wait. I forgot my—"

"There's no time. We have to hurry."

Jill guided her out the door, and Dinah gasped. There stood Remy and Donny. Remy shook with fury, his mouth twisting and nostrils flaring.

"Ya wan' outta here?" he snarled.

Dinah's heart hammered as she stared at him.

He seized her arm and tore her from Jill. Her leg gave with a jolt of pain, and Remy threw her to the ground. Dinah grimaced as her palms scraped against the sand. She flipped over, chest heaving as she scrambled backward. Donny tried to grab Jill, but she swung her bag of supplies and smacked him square in the head.

Remy drew his knife, stalking toward Dinah as she crawled away. "I'll sendja straight ta ya papa."

Her back hit the wall of the soddy. There was nowhere to go.

Jill yelped as Donny ripped the bag from her hands and tossed it out of reach.

Dinah's fingers curled into the sand, her burning leg heavy as lead. Remy stooped over her with bared teeth and a fiendish gleam in his eyes.

She couldn't stop him. Couldn't save Jill. Not without her Colt.

But she wasn't going down without a fight.

Remy reached for her, and Dinah flung a fistful of sand into his face. He sprang back with a cry, his free hand flying to his eyes.

A man in a black coat stormed past her, and she glanced up in surprise. *Joseph.*

He tackled Remy to the ground, and she stared open-mouthed as he started beating the living daylights out of him. Remy squealed like a stuck pig, fighting to reach the knife that had fallen from his hand. But Joseph had him pinned, pounding his face with his fist.

She'd never seen Joseph so savage, so enraged. It would've frightened her if she wasn't so relieved.

Donny stomped toward him, and Jill went for her bag. Joseph had no idea he was coming.

I've gotta do something.

Spotting a shovel propped against the wall beside her, Dinah grabbed the handle and struggled to her feet. She limped up behind Donny, gritted her teeth, and swung as hard as she could. The shovel clanged into his back, and he fell to his knees.

"Enough," rumbled a voice that turned her blood cold.

Joseph's raised fist froze, and he looked over his shoulder. Dinah followed his gaze.

Sal and Marcus stood by the open door.

"The next man who throws a punch doesn't get the rest of his share," Sal threatened.

Slowly, Joseph lowered his fist and got to his feet.

Blood poured from Remy's nose, running into his mouth as he sat up and spluttered, "Gray attacked me!"

"Musta had a reason," Marcus grunted.

Remy scowled and swiped the back of his hand under his nose. "Da women tried ta escape, an' we stopped 'em."

"You had more'n that in mind," Joseph growled.

"*Enough*," Sal said again, less patiently this time. "We have horses to catch."

Groaning, Donny dragged himself upright, his hand pressed to his back.

Sal's black eyes met Dinah's, her shaking hands still gripping the shovel. "Marcus, keep an eye on this one."

Dinah sat at a little round table in the middle of the room, staring into the tin cup Jill had put in front of her. Watching the water's shifting, reflective surface.

What now?

They'd had their chance. She doubted there'd be another. Not with Marcus watching them like a hawk. He paced in front of the soddy, glancing through the windows every time he passed by.

"How's your leg?" asked Jill, sinking into the chair across from her.

"Hurts," Dinah muttered.

"You should get some rest," she suggested. "I'll need to treat your wound again soon."

Dinah gave her an incredulous look. The bite was the least of her worries. Remy would've gutted her if Joseph hadn't shown up when he did.

"*Rest?* Here?"

"You've had quite a day, and it's not even noon."

"So have you," Dinah reminded her. How could she be so calm?

Jill arched a thin brow and raised her cup to her lips. "I didn't get bitten by a rattlesnake."

What happened in the cave felt like a bad dream, some moments still so vivid in Dinah's mind. Others she couldn't even remember.

She picked up her cup and took a long drink. Though lukewarm, the water soothed her parched throat.

"They wanted you to save Charlie?"

Jill nodded gravely. "I tried, but it was too late. Infection had set in. I think he knew."

"Why keep you here?" Dinah mused as she set down her cup. "He's dead now, and the posse attacked anyway, knowing you were a hostage."

Jill frowned, her gaze drifting past Dinah. "Maybe they're planning to…"

Dinah glanced at the beds behind her. Realizing her meaning, she shook her head. "I don't think so. Not with Joseph and Marcus around."

"You say that like you know them."

Dinah took a breath, remembering the fiery stripes Remy had lashed across her back. Her fingers tightened around her cup. "Marcus protected me once before, and you saw what Joseph did to Remy."

Jill's brow furrowed. "Once before?"

A lump lodged in Dinah's throat.

"Eight days ago, the Valentin Gang came to my family's farm. Held us prisoner in our own house. When my father tried to free me and my mother, Sal killed him." She swallowed hard. "That's why I'm here with the posse."

Jill's eyes widened, her lips parting in surprise. "I'm so sorry."

Dinah stared at the table, her vision blurring and a sob clawing its way up her throat.

Jill sat back, and her chair creaked in the silence. "I lost my husband five years ago."

Dinah's heart tugged with sympathy, and she glanced up.

Jill sighed, her gaze wandering to the window. "For a long time, I was a shell of a person. I didn't know how to move on without him. Sometimes I still don't. But my mother once told me: 'From the depths of our deepest sorrow springs our greatest joy.' I hold on to that hope every day."

Tears spilled down Dinah's cheeks, and she bowed her head in shame.

"I was sure I was gonna die in that cave. Part of me wanted to," she confessed. "Why didn't God let me?"

"Because he's not done with you yet," Jill said gently but firmly. "He's brought you this far, and when you can't take another step, he'll carry you. You just have to trust him."

Dinah's heart squeezed, and she drew a shuddering breath. God hadn't sent her into that cave alone. *He had a plan. Gave me a way out.*

She looked out the window at the sound of approaching hooves.

"They're back," Jill whispered.

Joseph, Tony, and the Indian hadn't been gone long. Maybe half an hour.

Joseph trotted past the soddy on his big blue roan, holding the reins of a black horse and a small sorrel.

"Cardinal," Dinah breathed.

She stood so fast her leg buckled and her head spun. She caught herself against the table as Jill jumped up from her chair.

"What's wrong?"

"My horse," Dinah panted. "That's my horse. He can't take him. I won't let him."

"Dinah, wait," Jill implored as she limped toward the front door.

Dinah stopped and huffed. "I need to see him. I have to—"

"You can. Just… hang on."

Jill strode to the back door and picked up the shovel Dinah had left leaning against the wall. She laid it on the table and went to her bag of supplies.

Dinah's brow furrowed. "What're you doing?"

"Your leg can't bear much weight yet. It'll take some time to recover its strength," Jill explained. "Until then, you'll need to use a walking stick."

Dinah hated the idea, but she knew better than to refuse. Carrying a stick would be less humiliating than falling on her face.

Jill pulled a bone saw out of her bag and returned to the table. She nodded at the shovel's long wooden shaft. "Hold this still, will you?"

Dinah did as she asked, keeping a firm grip on the handle as Jill started sawing. "Marcus is gonna hear that."

Jill shrugged. "We have nothing to hide."

The front door burst open—right on cue.

"What's goin' on in here?" Marcus growled as he stormed inside.

Jill paused her sawing and looked up at him. "Dinah's having trouble getting around on her own, so I'm turning this shovel into a walking stick."

He raised a skeptical brow. "That so?"

Dinah gestured to her injured leg. "Do I look like I'm goin' anywhere? I just wanna see my horse."

"That whatcha told Remy?"

She heaved a frustrated sigh. "Watch me. Follow me if you want. I don't care."

Jill resumed sawing, and Marcus crossed his arms. Dinah turned her back to him again, holding the shovel in place as the teeth scraped back and forth. Nervously, she glanced over her shoulder, his dark eyes studying her with suspicion.

She didn't know what to make of him. He seemed so cold, so stern. Had he taken pity on her the day he'd stopped Remy from beating her? Or had he seized an opportunity to lash out at someone he hated?

He sure didn't care that Remy's face had been beaten to a pulp.

The shovel blade clanged onto the floor, and Dinah jumped, startled from her thoughts.

"There," said Jill. "That should do just fine."

Dinah lifted the shaft from the table and put the sawed-off end on the ground. It was nice and sturdy. Not too heavy.

"Thank you."

Jill nodded and put a proud hand on her hip. "I always take care of my patients."

Dinah mustered a smile and limped toward the open door.

"Don't try nothin'," Marcus warned, trailing behind her. "Sal won't be so merciful a second time."

She stopped in the doorway and glared up at him. "Merciful? Is that what you call it?"

Wheels rattled outside, and he pointed toward the street. "You see them?"

Gus was pushing a cart past the soddy—a cart carrying two bodies. *Flint and Donovan.* Dinah gasped, her stomach turning as the cart rolled by.

"That should be you," Marcus said. "Keep runnin' that mouth of yours, and it will be."

She swallowed. Already, the posse had lost three members, and Marshal Tupper had been shot. They couldn't possibly take on the gang now—not without help.

Dinah gazed at the saloon across the way, the empty town still and silent in the aftermath of the gunfight. *Is Sal in there?*

Her heartbeat quickened as she ventured into the street. She turned left and hobbled toward the stable yard, her leg throbbing and her stomach growling.

A glance at the sky told her it was almost noon. She had food in her saddlebags. Maybe she could get a can—one for Jill too.

Dinah looked over her shoulder. Marcus stood outside, watching her every move.

She passed in front of another one-room soddy and approached the stable yard. *Almost there,* she told herself, dragging her boots through the sand. *Almost there.*

Joseph latched the paddock gate behind him. He'd just turned his stallion out with the rest of the horses.

The Indian was with him.

Cardinal whickered a greeting when he spotted her, his reins looped over the fence rail. Low as her spirits were, Dinah couldn't help but smile.

"Hey, boy. It's good to see you too."

"What do you think you're doin'?" Joseph demanded, striding toward her.

She squared her shoulders and raised her chin with as much dignity as she could muster. "Funny. That's what I was gonna ask you."

He stopped and rested his hands on his belt, her father's Colt still tucked next to his left holster. "We're leavin' soon, and you ain't in no shape to walk to Beaver."

Dinah gaped at him. She couldn't believe her ears. "Sal's letting me go?"

He shrugged. "No reason to keep ya."

Her brow furrowed. Marcus had made no mention of that. Something didn't seem right.

"You've talked to him?"

Joseph clenched his jaw, the tails of his black coat stirring in the breeze. "Not yet."

Dinah's eyes widened. *He'd* decided to let her go—not Sal.

Gratitude sparked in her, and she immediately stamped it out, grinding it under the heel of her hatred. "I don't understand. Why are you helpin' me?"

Joseph sighed and looked away. He seemed so miserable. So *tortured.*

Dinah couldn't reconcile the man standing before her—the man who'd saved her life—with the monster who'd shot Marshal Tupper. Who'd robbed her family and caused her father's death.

"Why haven't you left?" she asked. "Why stay with him?"

Joseph glared at the ground. "You wouldn't understand."

"You're right. I don't," Dinah said. "You're not like him. He enjoys killing. Revels in ruinin' people and leavin' 'em with nothing."

She swallowed hard, straining to speak past the lump burning in her throat. "But when I look at you, I see a killer who doesn't wanna be."

His gaze met hers. Searching. Longing.

"Is that all you see?"

She stared at him, caught off guard by the question. Tongue-tied by the look in his eyes. "If it's pardon you want, you're askin' the wrong person."

Joseph frowned, her answer snuffing out the hope she'd glimpsed like a candle in the wind. "There ain't no pardon for me."

His bitter resignation wrenched at her heartstrings, and Dinah scrambled to remedy her mistake. "Salvation's never more than a prayer away."

"You tryin' to save my soul, Miss Hance?" he scoffed. "Don't bother. I've heard it all before."

She bristled at the mockery in his voice. Why *had* she bothered?

"Joseph."

Panic jolted through her as Joseph glanced over her shoulder.

Sal.

Heart pounding, Dinah turned and saw him standing outside the saloon. How long had he been watching them?

"A word," Sal said. He looked displeased.

Dread gripped her as Joseph trudged toward him, her hopes of escape dwindling. Sal wouldn't let her go. He had no compassion in his heart—only cruelty.

Dinah recalled the cart rolling past her. How callously Flint's body had been thrown over Donovan's. Like they were refuse.

Her knuckles turned white as she clung to her walking stick, her body trembling with a sensation she couldn't shake.

It felt like doom.

———————

Dinah sat by the window, watching night fall, the curtains fluttering in a balmy breeze. She and Jill had been left alone all day, Tony standing guard in front of the soddy. He hadn't spoken a word to them, though he'd done plenty of pacing and muttering to himself.

Thunder rumbled in the distance as she tapped her boot on the floor. *Why haven't they left yet? What're they waiting for?*

Should she try to sneak out again? Use the darkness as cover? If she could get to Cardinal, she and Jill could ride to Beaver and find Lawrence. He had to be there. According to Jill, there wasn't another town for miles around.

A shadowy figure strode toward the soddy. Dinah sat up in her chair. *Joseph.*

Heart thumping, she scooted out of sight.

"What is it?" Jill whispered from her seat at the table.

Dinah held a finger to her lips and leaned toward the window to listen.

"It's time," Joseph said. "Sal told us to saddle up."

"What about the women?" Tony asked.

"We're leavin' the doc."

"And the girl?"

A pause. Dinah swallowed.

"Sal wants her gone," Joseph muttered.

"Gone? You mean…?"

"Yeah."

Her chest pulled tight as a knot.

"He told me to take care of it."

"I'll go with ya," Tony offered.

Her wide eyes met Jill's, her heart hammering out of control.

"You don't have to do that," Joseph said.

"No, I mean it," Tony insisted. "C'mon, let's get this over with."

Dinah struggled to her feet, bracing herself against the windowsill as the door swung open. Tony marched inside, Joseph right behind him. Jill rose from her chair.

"It's your lucky day, Doc," Tony said. "Soon as we're gone, you're free to go."

She frowned. "Both of us. Right?"

He shook his head, took off his derby hat, and wiped his brow. "Sal's got other plans for Miss Hance."

"What plans?"

"To kill me," Dinah answered. Despite her best efforts, her voice wavered.

"*What?*" Jill's brow creased in distress. "You can't do that. She's my patient. My responsibility. I won't let you—"

"Let us?" Tony sneered. "Remember who's in charge here, Doc."

"Please, let her go," Jill entreated as he strode toward Dinah. "She's in no condition to fight. She's no danger to you."

Dinah shrank from him, but Tony seized her arm, all out of patience. He yanked her toward the door. She dug in her heels, and her leg buckled.

"Get up and get movin'," he ordered. "We ain't got all night."

"She can't," Jill said. "Not without this."

She grabbed Dinah's walking stick from the table and hurried toward her.

Tony whipped out his revolver and aimed it at her face. "Stop right there," he warned. "Give that to Joseph."

Jill swallowed and grudgingly handed over the stick.

"Don't do this," she whispered to Joseph. "You care for her. I know you do."

"That's enough outta you," Tony threatened. "Let's go, Joseph."

He jerked Dinah to her feet and dragged her out the door. The wide legs of her skirt snapped in the blustery wind, her hair flying across her face.

"Get it over with," she growled. "Why wait?"

His fingers dug into her arm as he pulled her close—too close. "Not in front of the doc. We ain't stupid."

Joseph joined them outside, and as he passed Dinah the walking stick, his eyes met hers. Silently, she pleaded with him. He didn't want this. Sinner that he was, Sal hadn't killed the good in him completely.

Joseph turned away.

"Rick," Tony called to the man who'd just stepped out of the saloon, "watch the doc till we get back."

Jill stood in the open doorway with her hand over her heart.

"Go on," Tony grumbled, pushing Dinah forward.

As she trudged past the saloon, she spied an unmistakable silhouette in the lamplit window. The spark of a cigarette ignited Sal's black eyes and sent a chill down her spine. A raindrop plopped onto the brim of her hat, her pulse pounding.

If only she had her Colt. She'd point it at his smug face and pull the trigger. That would get her shot full of holes, but it'd be a better end than this. Walking to her own slaughter.

A steady drizzle was falling by the time they reached the stable yard. Cardinal and Joseph's blue roan had already been saddled, Remy and Donny cinching up their horses farther down the fence as Gus brought a Belgian Draft out of the paddock.

"Mount up," Tony said.

He shoved her toward Cardinal, and she stumbled. Planting her stick in the sand to keep herself upright, Dinah surveyed her old saddle and the empty scabbard. Someone had taken her rifle.

Of course they had.

Scowling, she stuffed her stick into the scabbard and looked down at the stirrup. As easy as it was for her to mount a horse as small as Cardinal, Dinah didn't know if her injured leg could support her weight.

She limped to the fence, unwrapped the reins, and looped them around Cardinal's rain-slicked neck. Gripping the horn, she drew a deep breath. Lifted her left leg and—

Searing pain stabbed her right calf. Dinah clenched her teeth and lowered her leg with a shaky exhale. She'd walked less than a hundred yards down the street, but the effort had exhausted her.

Spurs clinked behind her. She turned in surprise.

"What're you—?"

Joseph put his gloved hands on her waist, and Dinah yelped as he lifted her into the saddle. Cheeks flushing, she started to scold him, but he left without a word and went to his horse. *The nerve of him.*

Fuming, Dinah raised her right leg. It burned and throbbed, impossibly heavy, but she managed to maneuver it over the horn and wedge her foot into the stirrup. As she sat there catching her breath, Tony slipped his bridle over a thoroughbred's ears and led it toward the gate. She shivered, her wet clothes clinging to her skin.

"Joseph."

Dinah looked to her left and saw the Indian man approaching with a pinto horse in tow.

"I spoke to Sal," he said, "told him I've decided to go my own way."

"You're leavin'?" Joseph's back was turned to her, but he didn't sound happy.

The Indian nodded. "I came to say goodbye. And to thank you. True friends are hard to come by, but you've proven yourself one of them."

"I'm sorry to see ya go," Joseph admitted, "but I understand. Things are goin' downhill fast. Have been since Abilene."

Enyeto stepped closer, rain running down his solemn face and dripping from his chin. "Remember the wolves, Joseph. Don't betray yourself for anyone. Not even Sal."

Dinah's brow furrowed. What wolves? What did he mean?

Enyeto looked up at her, his eyes softening with… compassion?

"Lead the way, Joseph," Tony called, riding toward them on his dark horse.

Joseph turned from Enyeto and climbed into the saddle. He tipped his hat to him in farewell, then pointed his horse east—back the way they'd come.

She nudged Cardinal's sides and followed him, a sickening dread coiling in her gut. Would Joseph listen to Enyeto? Or would he end her life tonight?

Rain pattered on the saloon's slanted roof. A flash of lightning blinded her. Wincing, Dinah cast a sideways glance at the window. A crash of thunder shook her to her core.

Sal had vanished.

———— • ————

Jagged forks jumped from cloud to cloud. Plunged from the sky and struck a black horizon. Dinah pressed a hand to the crown of her hat, the howling wind blowing rain into her eyes and soaking her to the bone. Cardinal danced under her as they rode east across the dunes.

"What about there?" Tony shouted above the downpour. "That's as good a place as any."

She glanced over her shoulder, following his pointed finger north to a lonely tree in the wilderness. Terror seized her. Were they going to hang her?

"No," Joseph yelled back.

"Come on, Joseph. We've wandered long enough," Tony complained.

Joseph turned his horse north and started down the steep slope. Cardinal followed close behind him. Leaning back in the saddle, Dinah braced her legs, and pain knifed through her calf. She bit her lip to keep from crying out.

It came as a great relief when the ground leveled out and she could finally relax her burning muscles. But as they crossed the vast stretch of sand between them and the tree, Dinah's heart hammered. Should she try to make a run for it? She'd have a better chance of slipping away in the dark and the rain.

They're too close. They'll shoot me.

Paralyzed by indecision, she kept riding, praying that Joseph would change his mind. Dinah peered out from under the dripping brim of her hat, watching his swaying back. Since they'd left Dead Man's Dune, not once had he looked at her, let alone spoken to her.

Joseph stopped, and so did she, just short of some shrubs and what appeared to be a hackberry tree. Dinah frowned, reminded of the one that had fallen on the fence the night she'd first met him. The night that changed everything.

Tony drew alongside her and halted his horse. "Go on. Get down."

She hesitated. Some small part of her remained in denial. It couldn't end like this.

Eyes narrowing, he pulled back his coat and put his hand on his six-shooter.

Numbly, Dinah swung her right leg over Cardinal's hindquarters and slid to the ground. Her boots sank into the wet sand, and she clung to the saddle to keep from collapsing.

Glancing over her shoulder, she glimpsed Tony trudging toward her just before he shoved her against Cardinal's side. Cardinal jerked up his head, and Dinah tried to wriggle free as Tony wrenched her arms behind her back and bound her wrists with rope.

"Joseph, look at me," she panted, but he ignored her.

Tears of frustration stung her eyes. Tony gripped her elbow and yanked her away from Cardinal.

"Look at me!" Dinah screamed as Tony dragged her past him.

A violent gust of wind ripped her father's hat from her head. It snagged on a shrub, mocking her as Tony hauled her to the base of the hackberry tree, whose gnarled arms reached toward the roiling heavens. He forced her back against its knobby trunk and wrapped the rest of the rope around it, tying her in place.

"All right, Joseph," he said. "She's all yours."

He stepped away, and Dinah threw herself against the rope, twisting and straining and rubbing her wrists raw. Slowly, Joseph walked toward her. He drew his revolver from his right hip, and her shoulders slumped in defeat.

"Don't do this, Joseph," she pleaded. "Not after everything—"

"Shut up," Tony growled.

Joseph stopped ten feet from her and raised his bowed head, his anguished gaze finally meeting hers.

So, this is Sal's punishment, she thought, *for him and me.*

He clenched his jaw. Aimed the revolver at her heart and pulled back the hammer. Lightning streaked behind him, time slowing to a crawl.

Never had Dinah been so aware of everything. Her nails digging into the bark. The flattened curls clinging to her cheeks. The thumping in her chest. Every breath she breathed.

Joseph's finger moved to the trigger, hand shaking as his face screwed up in determination.

"Compassion," Dinah confessed, too desperate to hold back. "That's what I see."

He blinked. Something shifted in his countenance—as if he'd snapped out of a trance.

"What're you waiting for?" Tony demanded. "Shoot her."

Joseph lowered the revolver and shook his head. "I can't."

Her heart leaped with renewed hope.

Tony swore and drew his six-shooter. "If you won't, I will."

"Tony, no!" Joseph exclaimed.

She froze as she found herself staring down the barrel.

Bang!

Dinah flinched and shut her eyes. Waiting for the pain. For blood to start spilling out of her.

But she didn't feel anything. Just the rain pouring down her face.

She opened her eyes.

Clutching his side under his right arm, Tony staggered. "Son of a…"

His hat tumbled from his head as he collapsed in the sand. Breathing hard, Joseph stared at him, eyes wide and wild as thunder rolled.

Dinah gaped at Tony's sprawled limbs and blank expression. *He killed him.*

Joseph holstered his revolver. Hiding his face behind a gloved hand, he groaned and turned away. "What've I done?"

She didn't know what to say. What to think. "Joseph…"

He looked at her as if surprised, then strode toward her in a hurry. It seemed that, in his distress, he'd forgotten he needed to free her.

Joseph unsheathed his knife, stepped behind her, and cut the rope tied around the tree. The tension stressing her back and shoulders released, and Dinah sighed in relief.

"Hold still," he said, slipping the blade between her skin and the bindings on her wrists.

She didn't move a muscle, trusting his gentle precision. Trusting him more than she'd ever thought possible.

The rope dropped to the ground. Free at last, she massaged her aching wrists.

"You all right?" Joseph asked as he sheathed his knife.

Fine, she almost replied out of habit. But she wasn't fine. She'd nearly died, and he'd saved her life—again. A simple "thank you" didn't suffice.

Dinah raised her eyes to his, her stomach turning somersaults. Would he shrink from her? Push her away?

Before she could change her mind, Dinah stepped forward and threw her arms around him. Joseph stiffened, and she panicked. *I shouldn't have.*

Strong arms embraced her.

Tears sprang to Dinah's eyes as she buried her face in his shoulder, and he drew her closer. It didn't seem at all wrong or strange. It felt… right.

How nice it was to be held. To feel so small and safe.

A strangled sob escaped her, everything she'd bottled up inside bursting forth like a broken dam. His hand moved up from the middle of her back, crushing her against him as he bowed his head.

"I'm sorry," he said, his voice muffled by her hair. "I'm so sorry."

He released a shuddering breath, and Dinah clung to him with every ounce of strength she had left. Maybe, she thought, he needed this as much as she did.

The rain lightened, the wailing wind quieting to a murmur. She didn't want to let go, but she knew they couldn't stay like this forever.

Dinah sniffed and reluctantly withdrew, wiping away the last of her tears. "I'm okay, thanks to you."

"Don't thank me. I'm the one who broughtcha here in the first place."

Joseph sighed and gazed out at the dunes. He looked lost. Afraid.

"I can't go back to 'em now."

"What're you gonna do?" she asked.

He stared into the darkness, his pensive frown deepening.

Dinah's brow furrowed, and she followed his gaze. "What is it?"

"Someone's comin'."

CHAPTER SIXTEEN

A half-moon shone through the parting clouds, revealing four riders galloping toward them. Joseph pulled Dinah's Colt from his belt, his pulse pounding as he turned to her.

"Here."

She snatched it from his outstretched hand, and he drew his Schofield. Striding past Tony's body and the shrubs scattered around them, he positioned himself between Dinah and the approaching riders.

That hat. That horse. The man in front had to be—

"Lawrence!" Dinah cried behind him as the man hunter reined in his mount.

Joseph's finger shifted to the trigger, and Lawrence put his hand on his holster.

"Hand her ovuh, Gray. I won't ask again."

Two riders lined up on Lawrence's left, Mercer on his right. Joseph glared at Mercer's sneering face, fighting the temptation to blast a hole in it.

"Wait," Dinah panted, limping forward to stand at Joseph's side. "Don't shoot. Joseph saved my life."

Lawrence's hostile expression softened. "It shoah is good to see you alive, Miss Hance."

"How'd you find me?" she asked.

"Your doctuh friend came to us in Beaver. Said the gang had taken you out into the dunes to kill ya."

"Dr. Hart?" she exclaimed. "How'd she get away?"

He shook his head. "Somethin' about chloroform."

The knot in Joseph's chest clenched tighter. It wouldn't be long before Sal found out Dr. Hart had escaped—if he hadn't already—and that meant the gang would be out looking for her. Looking for *him.* They'd want to warn him in case the posse showed up.

Lawrence cocked his head, studying him. "I nevuh thought you'd turn on 'em."

"I know you've got no reason to trust him, but he killed one of Sal's men to protect me, and there's a body to prove it," Dinah told him, pointing behind her.

"So what?" Mercer said. "He's a thief and a killer, and I say we give him the death he deserves."

Joseph glanced down in surprise as she stepped in front of him—to *defend* him.

"Much as I'd like to," one of the men admitted, "we're the law. If we don't keep it, we're no better than he is."

Lawrence nodded. "Well said, Badger. We'll bring him in alive, as we ought."

"You're outnumbered," Dinah reminded him. "There's still six of 'em left. Joseph can help you."

"I ain't offerin'," Joseph growled, miffed that she'd spoken on his behalf.

She glared at him. "Do you wanna get pardoned or not?"

A war raged inside him. He felt like a leaf being tossed about on the breeze, torn in two directions and falling fast. Of course he wanted a pardon, but he wouldn't turn traitor to get one.

"A man doesn't change ovuhnight, Miss Hance. Don't forget what he is. Why you're here," Lawrence warned.

"Enough talk." Mercer drew his revolver. "Step aside, Miss Hance."

She didn't budge.

"Look!" exclaimed the young man next to Badger.

He pointed behind him, and Lawrence twisted around in his saddle. Joseph stepped to his right to see past the posse.

Some hundred yards south, at the crest of a dune, a man sat on a pale horse.

Joseph's heart jumped into his throat. Sal wasn't alone—five riders were with him.

"It's the gang!" the young man cried.

Lawrence turned to Joseph. "Get her outta here."

Mercer gaped at him. "What?"

"But—"

"*Now,*" Lawrence ordered, silencing Dinah. He wheeled his horse south. "Ride with me," he told his men, and he galloped toward the gang as they charged down the dune.

Joseph sprinted to Steel and Cardinal, snatched Dinah's hat from the shrub it had snagged on, and brought the horses over to her. "C'mon."

She hobbled to Cardinal's side. Joseph pushed her hat onto her head and lifted her into the saddle. As he strode to Steel, he cast a glance south.

Three riders had separated from the rest of the gang and were heading straight for them.

Marcus.

Heart pounding, Joseph sprang onto Steel's back and pointed him north. "Follow me," he said.

And she did, staying close on his heels as they raced across the sand, gunfire ringing out like peals of thunder in the night.

———————

They loped side by side through a moonlit wilderness, ten miles between them and the dunes they'd left behind. Stars glimmered through gaps in silver-lined clouds, a restless wind stirring the grass. Joseph gripped the reins so tight his hand had gotten stiff, clenched his jaw so hard it ached.

He'd done the right thing. Sal had gone too far this time. Making him kill an innocent woman to prove his loyalty?

Somethin's broke inside him.

Still, an accusing voice whispered, *Traitor. Murderer.*

Tony hadn't left him any choice, but they wouldn't understand that. None of them would accept that he'd chosen Dinah over one of their own. Gus and Rick—they'd want him dead for what he'd done.

Joseph looked back, scanning the rugged hills to the south. He couldn't see the riders who'd chased them out of the dunes—hadn't for a while now. He didn't know who was with Marcus. He hadn't let them get close enough to tell.

Dinah held on to the saddle horn with her free hand, shoulders slouching and a grimace on her face. She seemed awful uncomfortable. Exhausted and struggling to keep her balance.

Joseph didn't have to check his pocket watch to know it was nearing midnight, but they couldn't stop yet. Not till they'd crossed the Cimarron River.

For the last hour, he'd been racking his brain for a place they could lay low for a week or two. But every hideout he knew of, Sal had shown it to him.

One option had come to mind. Somewhere Sal had never been. That he wouldn't even know existed.

Returning to Obadiah's was about as risky as riding back into Abilene to rescue Enyeto, but it would bring Dinah close to home.

And I ain't stayin' long.

Suddenly, there came a sound like distant drumbeats, fast and faint, breaking the monotony of Steel's hooves crunching through the grass.

Joseph glanced over his shoulder, his gaze sweeping across the dark horizon. He didn't see anything, but the rhythmic pounding kept getting louder.

There.

Three shadows charged over a rise some two hundred yards behind them.

"Oh no," Dinah breathed.

"C'mon," he said, "let's beat 'em to the river."

He spurred Steel into a gallop, and Cardinal sprang forward to match him. The wind rushed against his face, howling as they ran across the open plain. Joseph leaned low over Steel's stretched neck, the mustang's black mane flying and his ears flattened against his head.

Cardinal splashed through a puddle and stumbled. Joseph's heart skipped a beat, but Dinah didn't lose her seat. Quickly righting herself, she thrust her hands forward and urged him on.

Joseph looked back and muttered a curse. *They ain't givin' up the chase.*

Two miles slipped by in a blur, and as they neared the Cimarron River, Steel slowed, his breaths coming hard and fast.

"C'mon, boy. Gimme a little bit more."

The stallion surged with another burst of speed. Cardinal's eyes were wild, his nostrils flaring as his hooves thundered beside Steel's, trampling the tall grasses in their path.

The eastern current ran strong with fresh rainfall, glittering in the moonlight. Joseph reined in Steel, and Cardinal skidded to a halt on the river's muddy bank.

"You go first," he told her. "I'm gonna watch your back."

Dinah gulped and stared at it. "I— I don't think I can—"

"There's no time to argue. *Go.*"

Her frightened gaze met his, and he added, "If anything happens, I'm right behind you."

Dinah's face steeled with resolve. She took a deep breath and gave the gelding a kick. Cardinal bounded into the river, and the mustang plunged in after him. Wading up to his shoulders, Steel pressed on, sloshing through the water and wetting Joseph's drying clothes all over again.

He couldn't see under the surface. Didn't know if the stallion's next step would carry them forward or drown them in quicksand. So he focused on what was in front of him—Dinah's back and Cardinal's tail. The northern shore drawing closer.

Steel's stride faltered. Joseph fell forward onto his neck, panic jolting through him.

"Joseph!" Dinah screamed as he slipped downstream.

He lost all control, the mustang's legs flailing in a frantic attempt to find his footing.

"Don't stop!" he shouted back at her. "Keep goin'!"

Steel planted his feet, and Joseph's boots went under the water. He looked down in alarm.

"Quit fightin' him, Joseph." Jeremiah's words came to him unbidden as he clung to the stallion's dripping mane. *"It ain't about who's boss. You're partnuhs. Trust the horse, and he'll trust you."*

Steel bellowed in distress, and Joseph patted his neck.

"Easy, big fella. Take it slow."

He nudged the mustang's sides, giving him all the slack he needed. Steel snorted and took one step forward. Then another.

"Thatta boy."

Pushing against the current, Steel fought his way back to Cardinal and Dinah, who waited right where she'd been when they got swept off track. She took her hand off the rope attached to her saddle and blew a big breath.

A warm feeling thawed fear's grip on Joseph's heart. "I toldja to keep goin'."

"I didn't listen," she answered with a backward glance.

Following her gaze, he spotted the three riders galloping toward the river.

"Yah!" Dinah cried.

Cardinal leaped into action, and Steel charged after him. As they made a mad dash for the water's edge, Joseph expected bullets to whiz past his head.

But they didn't.

"Joseph!" Marcus called as Steel climbed up onto the bank.

Joseph spun the mustang to face him.

"Stop runnin'!" he shouted from the opposite shore, Gus and Remy on either side of him. "I just wanna talk."

"Talk?" Gus exclaimed. "After what he's done?"

"I didn't wanna do it, Gus," Joseph told him, knowing he wouldn't care. "Tony was my friend."

Gus raised his rifle, but Marcus shoved it down.

"All them years, Joseph. All we've been through," Marcus fumed. "Sal raised us as *sons!*"

Joseph grimaced. Marcus' words clawed at him, ripping him apart. "He's lost his way."

"No, you ain't seein' clear no more. She's usin' you. You don't mean nothin' to her!"

"He's stallin'," Remy said, spurring his horse toward the water. "Let's get 'em."

"No!" Marcus barked. "We ain't chasin' 'em no farther. We gotta get back to Sal."

Joseph's shoulders relaxed, relief flooding through him. *He's lettin' us go.*

He gave Marcus a grateful nod, but the man he called brother made no gesture in return. Frowning, Joseph turned Steel around and headed north. Dinah fell in beside him.

"I'm gonna kill you, Gray!" Gus erupted. "You hear me? *I'm gonna kill you!*"

Joseph pulled his saddle and blanket from Steel's sweaty back and carried them over to his bedroll. He dropped the blanket in the grass and set the saddle at the head of his bedroll, as was his custom. Crouching, he opened his saddlebag, took out his brush, and trudged toward Steel with a sigh.

He'd already unsaddled Cardinal for Dinah, despite her insisting she do it herself. She stood brushing him as Joseph approached Steel. How she was still on her feet after all she'd been through, he didn't know.

Running the stiff bristles over Steel's silver coat, he swept away the dirty clumps clinging to his back, his strokes brisk and instinctive. It gave him something to do, something to focus on. But it failed to distract him from the crippling awareness that he was once again alone in the world. That he'd left the gang for good. His only friends—his family.

Joseph brushed harder.

"That can't've been easy for you," Dinah said.

His hand paused. "No."

Grass swished against his boots as he resumed his task, the air thick and damp in the aftermath of the storm.

"What're we gonna do now?" she asked.

"There's a cabin on the plains, a few miles from Abilene." Joseph bent to brush Steel's belly. "You should be safe there."

"You think the gang'll come after us?"

He straightened and moved to the stallion's hindquarters. "Not you—me. You heard Gus. The sooner you're away from me, the better."

She frowned at him over Cardinal's back. "That's your plan? You're just gonna keep runnin'? From the gang, the law—everyone."

"I've been runnin' all my life, Miss Hance. You get used to it after a while."

"All your life," Dinah echoed doubtfully. "You weren't born an outlaw. You had to come from somewhere. What about your parents? Brothers or sisters? Don't you ever wanna see them again?"

Joseph huffed. His past was the last thing he wanted to talk about right now. But how else could he make her understand?

"I left home when I was a boy."

Her brow furrowed. "Why?"

Joseph walked around to Steel's right side and turned his back to Dinah as he started brushing again. "My daddy was stationed at Fort Walker when the Yanks showed up. They killed him."

It felt strange to talk about him. About the war. The early years of his childhood seemed like a dream. A life someone else had lived.

"They took Beaufort, and then they took our house. My mama moved us to Charleston to stay with my uncle. But she…" He drew a deep breath—the knot in his chest made it hurt. "She was in a bad way. One mornin', she got on a train. Didn't even leave a letter to say where she'd gone."

"How old were you?" Dinah asked.

Joseph gazed up at the stars. He remembered lying under them on muggy summer nights, his mother telling him that God had made each and every one. That he called them all by name.

"Seven."

"What happened then?" she prompted quietly.

"I met a man named Jeremiah. He'd just escaped from a plantation. Said he was goin' as far west as the rail would take him. That sounded swell to me, so I went with him and never looked back. It was just the two of us for a while, till we ran into Sal and Marcus."

He lowered the brush and sighed. "So y'see, Miss Hance, I ain't got no one waitin' for me."

Soft steps approached him, and he turned.

Dinah was right in front of him, the two of them standing in the narrow space between their horses. Joseph's mouth went dry.

"Life hasn't been kind to either of us," she said, "but I have to believe that I've suffered for a reason. That we met for a greater purpose than destroyin' each other."

How could she say that? How could she see anything good in him? Feel anything but hatred?

She wouldn't if she knew. If I told her everything.

Joseph reached inside his coat and pulled the necklace from his pocket, the silver cross glinting in the moonlight. "The mornin' after we robbed the bank in Abilene, I met a stranger on the road. He mistook me for a decent man, insisted on givin' me this. But it don't belong with me."

Dinah's lips parted as she met his gaze, her eyes like mirrors. Reflecting his pain. His shame.

"I'm no more deserving than you are." She reached out and gently closed his gloved fingers over the cross. "He meant it for you. You don't have to prove yourself worthy of it."

She withdrew her hand. Joseph stared after her as she limped toward her bedroll, still feeling the tender pressure of her fingers. Wrestling with the notion of accepting something he hadn't earned, something he wasn't worthy of.

"There's no such thing as selfless," Sal once told him. *"Nothing is given freely. There's always a cost. Conditions that must be met. Only a fool gives without expecting something in return."*

Early the next morning, they saddled up and continued their journey north, veering east to avoid the soddies scattered along the Jones and Plummer Trail. After what happened with the gunsmith in Great Bend, Joseph wasn't taking any chances.

Rolling hills became rugged slopes with red flat-topped rocks rising all around them. Shrubs and sagebrush and cedar trees gathered near clear-running streams.

When they paused to fill their canteens and let their horses drink, he noticed Dinah gazing up in wonder.

They hit the trail again, winding through a narrow canyon with a jagged strip of blue sky overhead. He drew a deep breath of crisp air and settled into the routine rhythm of travel, listening to the crunch of Steel's unshod hooves on the gritty path. The wind whistling between the canyon walls. Out here, so far away from everything and everyone, he could pretend that his life hadn't been turned upside down.

That he hadn't killed one of his friends.

As they rode out of the canyon's shadow, Joseph squinted up at the noon sun. It was time to break for their midday meal. He picked a spot on a high treeless hill, reckoning that Dinah would appreciate its wide view of the surrounding landscape.

He brought Steel to a halt and dismounted, giving his speckled neck a pat as she slid from Cardinal's back. They'd been in the saddle since sunup, their only rest a brief one.

And she ain't complained once.

Joseph rummaged in his saddlebag till he found a can of baked beans and his can opener. He sawed off the lid, took out his spoon, and joined her on the grassy hillside. Dinah sat staring at lush green plateaus and their rusty edges, her knees bent and arms braced behind her. Her clothes splattered with the same reddish stains his were.

Joseph scooped some beans from the can and studied the western horizon as he chewed.

Wait. He glanced down at her again. *Where's hers?*

His brow furrowed. "You ain't hungry?"

"I am. It's just..." Dinah leaned forward and hugged her knees to her chest. "That can of peas I had this morning was my last one."

"Why didn'tcha say so?"

She shrugged, and Joseph sat beside her.

"Here," he said, offering her the can and spoon.

She looked at him in surprise, then shook her head. "No. I can't take yours."

"C'mon," he insisted, "I ain't givin' ya all of it. We're sharin'."

Dinah's cheeks turned pink. "All right, fine."

She accepted the can and spoon and took a bite, her shy eyes avoiding his. Joseph shifted his gaze back to the horizon and stretched out one leg, propping his arm on the other. He didn't want her to feel uncomfortable with him. To think she couldn't ask for things.

"Can't have ya slowin' me down," he teased with a sideways glance.

Dinah lowered the spoon and arched a brow at him. He smirked, and her razor-sharp eyes twinkled, a smile tugging at the corner of her lips. Her *eyes*—green as a summer meadow with russet flowers blooming at their center.

Joseph caught himself staring after she'd looked away. As she dipped the spoon into the can again, he said, "You're tough as nails, you know that?"

A shadow passed over Dinah's features, her smile vanishing like the sun behind a cloud. "I don't feel so tough."

He swallowed, struggling to put it into words. To tell her how brave, how *special* she was. "All I'm good at is gettin' even. Breakin' faces and shootin' folks. It ain't easy to show kindness to a fella who's done ya wrong. You've got a strength in you I don't rightly understand."

"I pulled the trigger, Joseph," she reminded him. "I coulda killed you."

"You were defendin' yourself."

Dinah drew a shaky breath and met his gaze.

He smiled at her, wanting nothing more than to glimpse the sun again. "Enemies, right?"

Her eyes brightened, a sheepish smile peeking through as she passed him the beans.

———————◆———————

Joseph awoke to the sound of distant thunder, a pale sky and gray clouds overhead. Wincing, he sat up, stretched his stiff neck, and glanced around the campsite. The fire had died. Dinah lay on the other side of it, her back turned to him. Her blanket rising and falling with each deep breath.

The horses stood nearby, heads raised and alert.

Joseph frowned. There was no break in the thunder. No pause in the rumbling that drummed louder and louder.

He grabbed his rifle and got to his feet, not bothering to put on his hat. He ran to the edge of the hill and peered into the basin below. A dark mass stampeded through the valley, heading north as gold rays split the clouds in the east.

Buffalo.

The herd wasn't half as large as the ones he'd seen roaming the open range in years past, but he was glad to see them again. He'd started to wonder if they'd all disappeared.

Dinah limped to his side, winded and wide-eyed.

"Oh," she breathed in awe. "I haven't seen 'em in so long."

She grinned from ear to ear as she watched them, the rising sun casting an orange glow over her face and setting her hair ablaze. Joseph didn't dare move or breathe. There was something sacred about this moment. Sharing this with her.

He realized that he didn't mind it being just the two of them. That he'd rather spend his days with her than wander alone. He didn't want to leave her—or her to leave him.

And it terrified him.

CHAPTER SEVENTEEN

A s dusk fell, they approached a winding miles-long band of trees growing beside a creek or a river Dinah couldn't yet see. They'd left the undulating hills of the buffalo valley far behind, the land leveling out again into smaller, gentler slopes. She hadn't spotted anything familiar since yesterday morning. Joseph had taken an easterly course, completely abandoning the trail she'd followed with the posse. She had no idea where they were now.

She hoped he did.

A commotion of shouting voices and striking hammers made Dinah peer deeper into the darkness ahead. She discerned the faint outline of a house and a bigger unfinished structure beside it.

Joseph shifted in his saddle. "What's goin' on up there?"

Men crouched on the slanted roof and carried planks on the ground while women chatted, laughing children racing between them.

The familiar sight tugged on Dinah's heartstrings. "They're havin' a barn raisin'."

"What's that?" he asked.

"We had 'em back home. Whenever a neighbor was puttin' up his barn, the whole community would come together and build it in a day. There was food and dancin'…"

She sighed.

"Sounds like good memories," Joseph replied.

He steered well clear of them, and she followed him. But she couldn't help staring as she passed by.

A tall, dark-haired man lifted a little girl in his arms and spun her around as she squealed with delight. A smiling woman stood watching them.

Dinah's throat burned, tears stinging her eyes. She blinked them back and looked away.

Riding northwest alongside towering elms and leaning walnut trees, they walked their horses another half mile before Joseph stopped and said, "Let's camp here."

He turned Steel into a row of cottonwoods, fluff-covered seeds floating along the breeze. One tickled her cheek, and she glanced at the strong branches sprawling overhead, their heart-shaped leaves whispering of home. A wistful ache filled the hollow of her chest as she ventured into the shadowy grove.

Willows wept over the burbling creek, their drooping boughs sighing as Dinah sat cross-legged on her bedroll. Her fingers worked to unbraid her hair, frogs croaking and crickets chirping all around her.

Flames sprang up from the pile of broken sticks Joseph had gathered. He gave them an encouraging blow before scooting back against a cottonwood's stalwart trunk. His coat and gloves lay in the grass, his rolled-up sleeves exposing his sinewy forearms. He set aside his hat and wiped his brow, a lock of dark hair falling over his forehead.

As Joseph reached for his saddlebags and dragged them closer, her gaze lingered on his flexed muscles, his broad chest and strong shoulders. How easily those arms had carried her. How tightly they'd held her...

His eyes met hers, and Dinah's fingers fumbled.

"How much food've you got left?" she asked, her cheeks flushing with embarrassment.

"Couple days' rations," he replied as he opened a leatherbound book in his lap. "We'll have to get more."

"We're goin' huntin'?"

He shook his head, his charcoal-wielding hand hovering over the page. "No. I mean goin' into town."

She frowned. "You aren't worried about gettin' caught?"

"I ain't goin'. You are."

Dinah's eyes widened. "By myself?"

"Mhm," Joseph grunted, his charcoal scratching on the paper.

Stunned, she stared at him. He trusted her not to run off and leave him?

"What town?" she asked.

"The next decent-lookin' place I see."

Dinah's eyes narrowed with suspicion. Her fingers fell from her unbraided hair. "Do you know where you're goin'?"

Joseph's hand paused. "Well enough."

"You don't sound like you do."

His eyes flashed to hers. "If we keep headin' east, we'll hit Wichita, and I'll know the way from there."

Wichita. She'd never been there, but she'd heard of it. Seen the name on a sign when she got off the train in McPherson.

Wichita was on the line that ran north to Salina.

"Are we takin' a train?"

"Not if I can help it," he muttered.

Dinah's heart sank.

He didn't want to get recognized. She understood that. But she didn't know how many more days she could spend in the saddle, achy and weary as she was. Her fever had broken last night—that was an improvement. But she had a ways to go yet.

Firelight flickered on Joseph's concentrated features, and Dinah's curiosity got the better of her. "You draw?"

"Sometimes," he mumbled.

"I can't draw to save my life," she said with a wry smile.

"Mine ain't no good either."

"Can I see 'em?" she ventured.

His hand froze, his eyes darting to hers. "No."

Dinah flinched at the gruffness of his answer and lowered her gaze to the crackling flames. *Shouldn't've asked.*

"Trust me, they ain't worth seein'," Joseph added, softer this time.

The charcoal resumed its quiet scratching, and she picked up a twig, turning it over and over in her fingers. She could try to sleep, but she doubted she'd be able to. She couldn't stop thinking about that family and their blissful happiness. Their peace and contentment. Their wholeness.

Will I ever have that?

The twig snapped, and Dinah threw it into the fire. The flames sparked and spat as she looked over at her hat, at the rifle Joseph had returned and her walking stick.

Not this time, she decided. Maybe her leg would recover faster if she didn't rely on the stick so much.

Grimacing, Dinah got to her feet, and he frowned at her.

"Where ya goin'?"

"For a walk," she said.

———————•▪———————

The rustling of the cottonwoods was like gently falling rain, soothing her restless spirit as she followed the creek southeast. Dinah glimpsed its flowing waters through gaps in the trees on her left, the silvery light of the waxing moon drifting through their leaves.

Against all odds, she'd survived. Escaped Sal's clutches when he'd tried to snuff her out.

But what about Lawrence? Brooks and Badger? Jill and Marshal Tupper?

Jill had risked her life going to Beaver to warn the posse, and Lawrence had risked his riding out into the dunes to find her.

A crushing weight drove an anguished sigh from Dinah's lungs. She couldn't bear the thought of losing another friend—losing them because of her own failure. Her reckless, *foolish* mistake. Lawrence had yelled at her to wait, but she'd ignored him. Chased after Joseph and Enyeto anyway.

The lively plucking of a banjo and the strumming of a guitar stalled her spiraling thoughts. Dinah paused and listened. The brisk bowing of a fiddle and the hum of a harmonica drifted along the breeze.

I'm gettin' close.

The cheerful melody reeled her in, drawing her to the edge of the woods. The single-story house sat just beyond the shade of the trees, warm light spilling through a window's half-opened shutters. Her heart squeezed as she glimpsed whirling skirts and grinning faces. Heard stamping boots and merry laughter.

That used to be me.

She thought she'd be married by now. Living on a homestead somewhere or roaming the western frontier. But after she'd refused August's proposal, no other suitor had ever come along.

Of course not. How could she expect to meet anyone when she avoided dances and parties like the plague?

Some silly part of her had believed the right man would magically appear. That he'd find her somehow, no matter how desperately she hid herself away. That she'd *know* the moment she laid eyes on him.

As the song ended, Dinah's nails dug into the trunk of the mulberry she hid behind. A prickling sensation made the hairs on the back of her neck stand up.

I'm not alone.

She spun around and gasped, her hand flying to her chest. She had a good mind to let him have it for startling her, but as she opened her mouth to do just that, Joseph offered her his hand.

Dinah's tongue turned to lead.

Is he mockin' me? Blood boiling, she glared at him, but she didn't detect a trace of humor on his face. He'd taken off his gun belt and his spurs. *He's serious,* she realized.

Dinah swallowed and took a hesitant step toward him. She hadn't danced in years. Would she remember how?

What would her mother think? Her father?

"Don't forget what he is," Lawrence had warned her.

Heart pounding, she placed her hand in Joseph's. Hers seemed so small in comparison.

I haven't washed it, she remembered, panicking as he drew her to him. That mortifying thought—and every other thought—was obliterated when he put his left hand on the small of her back. Dinah averted her gaze as she rested her right hand on his shoulder.

"Why'd you follow me?"

"I was worried aboutcha," he said.

The players took up a slower, more tender tune that she instantly recognized as "Rose of Killarney." A ballad. A *love song.*

Her cheeks flushed, and Joseph stepped to the side, leading with confidence. Easing into a leisurely rhythm at odds with the violent beating of her heart.

He's no stranger to dancin'. She'd always been decent enough at it, but she had a tendency to step on her partner's feet. Dinah glanced down as they swayed with the lilting melody.

How many women had he danced with? How many of them better than her?

Joseph squeezed her hand, and she looked up at him. His mouth slanted in a crooked smile, and Dinah felt as if a cage of butterflies had been freed in her stomach. He raised her arm above her head, and she gave him her best twirl, ignoring the twinge in her leg. A grin split her face, the warmth of his fingers and the light in his eyes melting the icy walls guarding her heart.

The spring snow of the cottonwoods fluttered around them as they pulled apart, hands grasped and arms stretched to their limits. Dinah giggled when they came together again, and Joseph laughed. Actually *laughed*. A soft, throaty sound that was music to her ears.

Round and round they went, and each time she spun back into his arms, they came a little closer. The fiddle crooned through the window, moonlight dappling the leaf-scattered ground. He dipped her backward, and Dinah glimpsed the stars, gripping his hand as she kicked up her heel.

Her heart soared as he raised her, her spirit singing as the final notes faded into silence. Their feet had stilled, but the world kept spinning. Breathless and captivated, she stared up at him, their faces inches apart.

Joseph laced his fingers through hers, pressing their palms together, and a shiver ran through her. The fire blazing in his eyes both terrified and excited her.

I shouldn't. But, oh, how she wanted to.

He stooped farther, drifted even closer. Dinah didn't retreat. Something had taken hold of her, something she could no longer deny or resist.

Joseph leaned in, and she closed her eyes, frozen and trembling. She felt the warmth of his breath, and then—

He kissed her.

Nothing could've prepared her for it, gentle but mind-numbing in its power. Strange and new but not at all unpleasant.

Dinah's eyes fluttered open. *Why'd he stop?*

Joseph stayed close, his burning gaze searching hers. Waiting. Asking.

She untwined her fingers from his and reached up. Reverently, she touched his face, her thumb brushing his cheekbone and her hand coming to rest against his stubbled jaw. Dinah glanced at his mouth, an overwhelming impulse banishing every fear and doubt.

She stretched up and pressed her lips to his, her heart thumping so wildly she felt as if it would burst from her chest. She didn't have a clue what she was doing, but she had no intention of disappointing.

Dinah kissed him harder, wrapping her other arm around his neck and threading her fingers through his soft hair. She'd been wanting to do that for a while now.

If the sigh he breathed was anything to go by, maybe she was doing something right.

Joseph pushed forward, his hands on her waist. She clung to him for balance, almost tripping over her own feet. Her back hit the nearest tree, and he pinned her there, his kisses deepening.

It took her by surprise when his tongue skimmed across her lips. Dinah hated herself even as she parted them. He delved into her mouth, and a moan escaped her.

She savored each thrilling sensation, the taste of him and the way their tongues tangled. Losing herself in the blinding heat of it.

A chorus of voices spilled out into the night, and Joseph broke the kiss.

Dinah's eyes flew open. Dazed and disoriented, she glanced over at the stream of people issuing through the door of the house and saying their goodbyes.

Suddenly, she remembered where she was. That they weren't far from a crowd of strangers who'd consider them trespassers. Shielded only by darkness and clustered cottonwoods.

Joseph didn't seem to care. He turned to her, his breaths hot and heavy. The intensity of his gaze made her weak in the knees. He leaned in to claim her lips again, and she almost let him.

"Wait," she managed, and Joseph drew back.

He looked so young in that moment, his brow furrowed with concern and his eyes softer than she'd ever seen them.

"We—" Dinah stopped and swallowed, the gravity of what had just happened sinking in. "We should get outta here. Before someone sees us."

He blinked as if waking up from a dream.

"Yeah." He straightened and raked a hand through his tousled hair. "You're right."

What've I done? she thought as Joseph went to pick up his gun belt. *What've I done?*

CHAPTER EIGHTEEN

Joseph didn't sleep a wink that night. He tossed and turned for hours, forcing himself to by every means he knew how—even counting blasted sheep. Nothing worked. He stared into the dying flames, wondering if Dinah lay awake too.

I went too far. Scared her off.

Joseph sighed and shifted onto his back, watching smoke rise into a star-strewn sky.

Maybe she came to her senses.

Women had always puzzled him, their ways a mystery he couldn't begin to solve.

Dinah was no exception. The same lips that had wished him dead had turned sweeter and more intoxicating than any spirits he'd ever tasted. Her touch sparked a fire in him that burned so hot, roared so loud, that he'd disregarded everything. All the reasons it couldn't and shouldn't happen.

And he couldn't take it back. Couldn't forget it.

For her sake, I've got to.

———————◆———————

The day's ride was a quiet one, tense and downright uncomfortable. Dinah hadn't spoken a word since they'd packed up and left, and neither had he. Joseph cast her a sideways glance as they climbed a grassy slope scattered with cedar trees. She'd washed in the creek before they broke camp, her coppery waves damp and glistening in the sunshine.

What am I supposed to say? That I made a mistake?

He pinched the bridge of his nose, his thoughts foggy with exhaustion. He didn't want Dinah to think he'd changed his mind because of some flaw or shortcoming on her part.

"So," she said suddenly, "how long are we gonna pretend nothin' happened last night?"

Caught off guard, Joseph cleared his throat and adjusted his hat. "I didn't think ya wanted to talk about that."

"I didn't," she admitted, "but… I'm ready now."

He took a deep breath and braced himself. "I'm listenin'."

"Well," Dinah began hesitantly, "where I'm from, there's an order to things. Traditions. With courtin' comes intention."

He stared at her. He couldn't believe his ears. She didn't want out—she wanted commitment.

Joseph's heart swelled even as it shattered. He brought Steel to a halt, and she stopped Cardinal. "We can't, Dinah."

Her face fell. "Why not?"

Joseph swallowed. He hated to disappoint her. Hated hurting her.

"You know why. I'm an outlaw. There's five thousand dollars on my head. That ain't ever gonna change."

"You haven't tried," Dinah persisted.

Not this again.

"I toldja already—I ain't makin' a deal with the law."

"Why?" she challenged. "Because of your pride?"

"It ain't about pride," he growled. "It's about loyalty."

"To the man who ordered you to kill me."

Joseph grimaced and looked away. "It ain't that simple."

He had Marcus to think about.

"Look," she insisted, "I don't know if Lawrence got him out there in those dunes or not, but if he didn't, you can help me catch Sal. He's the one they want most. If you bring him in, they might pardon you."

That's what she's really after. The realization stung, and Joseph shook his head. "I shoulda known. You're just usin' me to get to him."

Her hopeful expression crumbled. "That's what you think of me? Is it so impossible for you to believe someone could care for you?"

A pang of guilt made him clench his jaw and drop his gaze.

"Well, I do," she declared.

All it'd take is a month. A year. She'd tire of me.

"You ain't thinkin' straight," Joseph told her. "Don'tcha understand that bein' with me means livin' on the run? Lookin' over your shoulder? Pardon or not, there's always gonna be folk that want me dead. I can't give ya the kinda life you deserve."

Dinah's eyes blazed with defiance. "I decide what I deserve."

"Listen to me," he urged, nudging Steel closer to her. "A wolf without a pack don't last long, and I ain't got one no more. You're young. You got a bright future ahead of ya. There's no sense in you wastin'—"

"What future?" she choked as tears gathered on her lashes. "My father's dead. My mama's sellin' our farm and movin' across the country."

His heart ached for her.

She sniffed and shrugged. "What've I got to lose?"

"Your life," he scolded, "and that's worth a hell of a lot to me."

"Then take me with you."

A lump lodged in his throat, his resolve on the verge of breaking. He'd never wanted anything more desperately. Never felt more undeserving.

Joseph sighed and ran a hand over his face. He couldn't look her in the eye as he said, "You should go with your mama. Leave all this behind and forget about me."

Pointing Steel east again, he spurred him on, and Dinah followed him in silence.

———————— • ————————

The next evening, they came upon a small town in a river valley, a green oasis nestled amid rough red rocks. Joseph stopped about a mile out and surveyed it from atop a hill covered with wildflowers, the setting sun burning at his back. The town looked big enough to have a general store or two.

He counted out fifty dollars and offered the bills to Dinah. "Here. I think we're still a good ways from Wichita, so we'll need a few days' rations."

She arched a brow at him. "What am I buyin', five-course meals?"

"No, I—" Joseph sighed and glanced at her red-stained skirt. "I thought ya might wanna get yourself some new clothes after crossin' that river."

Her cheeks flushed. "Oh. Thanks."

She took the bills from his hand and put them in the pouch on her belt.

"Don't go wavin' that around," he warned. "And watch out for pickpockets. I don't know this town or what kinda folk live in it."

"Don't worry." Dinah patted the gun on her hip. "I've got this, remember?"

"Don't go wavin' that around neither."

"Says the outlaw," she quipped, and with that, she sent Cardinal loping off down the hill.

———————

Joseph checked his pocket watch for the tenth time since Dinah left. She'd been gone almost an hour. He stuffed it back into his coat and resumed pacing, traipsing through daisies and yellow primroses as the wind howled through the valley below. Steel stood munching a mouthful of grass, his ears forward and his big black eyes following him.

Surely Dinah wouldn't run off and leave him. Not without a railroad to make a quick escape.

Probably wishes she could.

Joseph wouldn't blame her if she did. He'd given her false hope. Fueled a fantasy that couldn't last. Keeping company with him would destroy her reputation. Her family would cut ties with her. Choosing him would mean sacrificing everything else. Everything normal.

Sooner or later, she'd regret that decision.

Cursing the lapse in control that had gotten him into this mess, Joseph stopped and looked out at the western horizon, the sky tinged a vivid pink as the sun sank behind the hills.

If the gang killed the posse or gave them the slip, the law would be the least of his worries. Sal didn't forget, never forgave.

He hadn't forbidden them from leaving the gang, but he didn't tolerate betrayal. Only one had tried in the past, ratting them out to earn himself a pardon, and the other—

The other made him sick to think about. Poor Riley had been their newest and youngest member at the time, and he'd led the law back to camp one day. After they'd gotten rid of the posse, he'd insisted it was an accident, but Sal had declared him a liar and a traitor and shot him in the gut. Joseph had watched the boy bleed out, still begging them to believe him, and he had. He still did.

Would Sal's rage be aimed only at him? Would he want to punish Dinah for the part she'd played?

If he's huntin' both of us, she'll be safer with me than on her own. Maybe leavin' her at Obadiah's ain't the best idea after all.

Joseph turned at the sound of thundering hooves, the weight lifting from his chest as Dinah galloped toward him. He sighed in relief, his clenched fists uncurling. *She came back.*

Cardinal charged to the top of the hill, and she reined him in. He snorted and tossed his head, pulling on the bit as he pranced toward Joseph.

"I got the food," she panted. "Saddlebags are stuffed full."

She dismounted, wincing when her boots hit the ground. She'd traded her shirt for another black one, but instead of a high collar, the blouse had a low neckline trimmed with white lace. Its fitted fabric complemented her slim figure, the hem tucked into the waistband of a new skirt.

Joseph swallowed as she approached him, and she held out two ten-dollar bills.

"I had some left over."

"Keep it," he told her.

"No," she refused, glaring up at him. "I don't want your charity."

He sighed and stuffed the bills back into his pouch.

"I had some money of my own," Dinah said. She pulled a black bandana from her belt. "Figured this was the least I could do after I ruined yours."

Joseph blinked in surprise, a warm fondness kindling in his heart.

She blushed and glanced down. "If you don't like it—"

"No, that's... just what I needed." Moved by the gesture, he took the bandana and nodded. "Thanks."

A smile tugged at the corners of her mouth, and Joseph couldn't help himself.

"You, uh... You look good."

Dinah pursed her lips and put a hand on her hip. "You shouldn't say that to me."

His brow furrowed. "I shouldn't?"

"Not unless you're plannin' to stick around."

He sighed and stared at the bandana. "You make it real hard to say no, Miss Hance."

"I've had enough people in my life come and go, Joseph. I'm lookin' for someone who's gonna stay."

———————•✦•———————

As they got closer to Wichita, fences became a common obstacle, often forcing them to take the long way around. Each encounter with barbed wire wore Joseph's patience thinner, frayed his nerves a little bit more. There were cattle ranches everywhere. At this pace, it'd be another week or two before they reached Obadiah's.

Too long. Dinah had pushed hard enough. She needed a bed and a roof over her head. Time to rest and recover.

"When we get to Wichita," Joseph told her, "we're gettin' on a train."

Her eyes widened. "What if someone recognizes you?"

"I'd rather take one risk than fifty." He glanced at the cows grazing on the other side of the fence. "This ain't free land no more. If a cattleman catches us anywhere near his herd, he's liable to shoot us."

"You aren't thinkin' of goin' to Salina?"

He shook his head. "No. We'll get off at the stop before and take our horses the rest of the way."

"Fine by me," she said. "I could use a break from ridin'."

Joseph drew a deep breath and brought Steel to a halt. Something had been nagging at him ever since they'd left Dead Man's Dune. He'd kept it from her all this time, telling himself it was for her own good, that he shouldn't worry her sooner than he had to.

Now that he couldn't put it off any longer, Joseph realized his real reason for waiting was a selfish one.

"Dinah, there's somethin' I need to tell ya."

She stopped Cardinal and faced him with a frown. Joseph hesitated, dread holding him hostage.

"The money we took from the bank in Abilene—we buried half of it at your farm."

"*What?*" Dinah burst, her concern erupting into outrage. "Where?"

"Under the dogwood tree."

Her face twisted with disgust, and she glared at the plains to the east. As if she couldn't stand to look at him anymore. "Just when I start to trust you..."

Joseph hung his head.

"Why didn't you tell me?" she demanded, and he met her frantic gaze. "If Sal goes back for the money, if my mother's still—"

Her voice broke, her skin paling. "I have to make sure she's all right."

"You can," he assured her. "Sal won't risk goin' back there—not any-time soon."

Dinah's eyes narrowed with suspicion. "And what happens to the money?"

"I'm givin' it back to the folks I stole it from."

CHAPTER NINETEEN

A full moon rose behind the dogwood tree, bold and yellow in the indigo sky. Breathtaking in size and majesty. Dinah hadn't thought she'd be back home so soon. Hadn't known if she'd come back at all.

Her heart squeezed at the sight of her old friend. She'd often climbed the dogwood as a little girl. Read and slept in its shade. Wept and fussed as it listened without judgment, its leaves whispering gentle comforts. She told the tree the things she would've told Ophelia. Big things and small things and everything in between.

As they loped toward the dogwood's sprawling silhouette, Dinah recalled racing Joseph through this very field. Everything had changed since then—not just for her and her family—but between the two of them.

He'd hardly spoken a word to her on the train, and she'd spent most of the trip staring out the window. What was there to say?

She should've known better.

What else is he hidin'? Was he telling the truth about returning what he'd stolen, or was he planning to keep the twenty-five thousand all to himself?

They reined in their horses at the crest of the hill and dismounted. Joseph walked around to the eastern side of the trunk, and Dinah followed him, anxious to see if someone had already dug up the money.

"Should be right… here." He crouched in front of a dirt mound half hidden by waving grass. "Don't look like nobody's been diggin'."

She blew a breath of relief. "Good. I'll get a shovel from the barn."

"Be careful," he warned. "Might be someone else livin' in that house now."

Eleven days ago, she'd snuck out and run off to join the posse. Would Daniel and her mother really pack up and leave so quickly? Wouldn't they worry? Wouldn't they want her found?

Dinah grabbed the horn, stuck her foot in the stirrup, and dragged herself into the saddle. Pointing Cardinal north, she nudged his sides, and he trotted down the hill.

As the ground leveled out, she let the reins slide through her fingers, and the gelding sprang forward. He tossed his head as he galloped across the moonlit prairie, happy to be home.

She wished she could say the same.

Which would be worse—facing her mother's wrath and her brother's disappointment? Or discovering that they'd moved on without her? That they didn't care?

If they haven't already disowned me, they will when they find out about Joseph.

She couldn't tell them. Why bother? She'd confessed how she felt, let him know she was serious, and he'd pushed her away. Kept secrets from her.

Secrets that endangered her mother's life.

Cardinal charged over the last hill, and Dinah sat back in the saddle. He shook his head in protest, but she finally succeeded in bringing him to a halt.

The sight of the two gravestones in the shade of the rosebud tree wrenched her heart and blinded her with tears. Reminded her why she'd left.

Dinah looked away and continued on, wiping her cheeks as she went. Dusty and Sarge whickered at her approach, and she gave a quiet gasp. *They're still here.*

She didn't see Belle.

Did Daniel sell her? she wondered as Cardinal trotted along the edge of the pasture.

When they came to the gate, Dinah stopped and swung down from the saddle. She looped the reins over a fence rail, her insides twisting in knots. Sweat beaded under the brim of her hat, the evening breezy but warm. And uncommonly quiet.

She turned to look at the field across from the horses, and her heart sank. The cows were gone.

Her disappointment gave way to resignation, a bitter taste in her mouth as she trudged up the path. As she passed under the imposing oak, a voice drifted along the wind. A male voice. Angry and shouting.

Dinah went rigid. *That's not Daniel.*

She sprinted toward the house, blood pumping and feet flying. Lamplight shone through the living room windows.

Nothing else mattered now. Not her fear. Not the pain stabbing her leg.

A spotted horse stood at the hitching rail—Remy's horse. Dinah stopped in her tracks, chest heaving as she gasped for breath.

"Where is it?" Remy demanded, his voice filtering through the open door. "Wha' didja do wit it?"

"I told you, I don't know what you're talking about!"

Mama.

Panic jolted her into action. Remy went on yelling as she ran to the porch. Dinah gripped the railing with her right hand and drew her gun with her left, forcing herself to go slow as she crept up the stairs.

"Maybe dis'll loosen ya tongue."

"Please!" her mother cried. "I'm telling you the truth!"

Dinah pulled back the hammer and stepped through the open door. She found her mother sitting in a chair in front of the windows. Remy stooped over her, pinching her face between his fingers and holding his knife inches from her cheek.

A primal instinct surged in Dinah, and she aimed the Colt at his head. "Remy!"

He wheeled around.

"Dinah?" her mother exclaimed, sounding both horrified and relieved.

"Well," he said with a wicked gleam in his eyes, "look who it is."

"Let her go," Dinah growled.

His lip curled. "Nah, I don' tink I will."

He slipped behind the chair and grabbed her mother's hair. Dinah sucked in a breath as he yanked back her head and pressed the knife to her throat.

Remy's bruised face twisted with loathing, his pale eyes flickering dangerously. "Eye for an eye," he spat. "I lost my brotha. You lose ya mama."

"Let her go. She's done nothin' to you," Dinah pleaded.

"Dinah," her mother choked, tears glistening on her cheeks. "Dinah, I don't want you to see this."

He jerked her hair, and she gave a strangled sob. "Shuddup!"

Rage exploded in Dinah's belly. Her finger moved to the trigger. "I'm not gonna ask again. Let her go, or—"

"Or wha'?" Remy challenged. "Ya got no badge. Ya gone outlaw, Miss—?"

Bang!

The gun lurched in her hand, the muzzle flashing in front of her face. Her mother screamed as he dropped the knife and staggered back against the glass. She'd hit him dead center, right between his bewildered eyes. He slid to the floor, Dinah's ears ringing as her arm fell to her side.

I killed him.

It didn't seem real. She felt like an outside observer, a stranger in her own body.

Her mother sat hunched over in the chair with her chin to her chest, hands covering her ears as she wept. Dinah holstered the Colt and went to her on trembling legs.

"Mama." Her own voice sounded distant and muffled as she bent and grasped her mother's shaking shoulders. "Mama, it's okay. He's gone."

Her mother's watery gaze met hers. Grief had transformed her, framing her bloodshot eyes with dark circles and hollowing her tearstained cheeks.

A pang of guilt pierced Dinah's heart. *I shouldn't've left her. Not like that.*

As her mother's weary eyes searched hers, she feared that she'd push her away. That she'd never forgive her.

Instead, her mother reached up and threw her arms around her.

Tears sprang to Dinah's eyes, and she hugged her tight. How she'd missed that familiar warmth, the comfort and safety of her mother's embrace. There was so much she wanted to say, so much she wished she could tell her.

But all she could manage was, "I'm sorry."

Her mother just held her, stroking her hair as Dinah's tears soaked the shoulder of her black dress. Dinah opened her eyes, staring at the brain-spattered windowpanes. At the blood smeared down the glass. Remy's hand gripped his revolver, unable to draw, his gaze glaring and vengeful even in death.

Dinah's stomach turned. She pulled back to look at her mother. "Where's Daniel?"

Her mother sniffed and blinked, troubled and distracted. "Salina. He went to meet with some men in town. Marshal Tupper and that man hunter, Lawrence."

Dinah's heart skipped a beat. *They're alive.*

"Sal Valentin—did they…?"

Her mother's jaw clenched at the mention of his name. "They captured him. He's in the marshal's custody."

Stunned, Dinah stepped back and braced herself against the couch. Would he finally face justice after all these years?

Her mother rose from the chair. Ill at ease, she turned and considered Remy.

"He said they buried money on our land, and he'd come to claim it." She sighed and swept her hair out of her eyes. "I thought it was over. I thought they'd leave us be. How many of them are still out there?"

Dinah shook her head. She needed to talk to Lawrence, find out what had happened. Who'd been arrested or killed and who'd gotten away.

One thing she knew for certain—Daniel and her mother needed to pack the wagon and go to Salina first thing in the morning.

"It isn't safe here, Mama. Not till they're all dead."

Spurs jingled as footsteps pounded up the porch stairs. She reached for her Colt, heart slamming against her ribs.

Joseph charged into the house with his gun drawn. He stopped short at the sight of her, breathing hard. Dinah's shoulders slumped in relief, and she took her hand off her Colt.

"I heard a shot," he panted. "What happened?"

She cast a sideways glance at the body half hidden behind the chair. "Remy came lookin' for the money. I told him to let her go, but he wouldn't. He was gonna kill her."

Her mother stepped away, staring up at him as he approached the blood-stained windows. Joseph holstered his revolver, pushed aside the chair with his boot, and looked down at Remy.

He rubbed his bearded chin and sighed. "You did whatcha had to do."

Hearing a grunt and a scraping sound behind her, Dinah turned toward the hearth. Her mother had taken down her father's rifle, and now she trained her scorching gaze on Joseph.

"Mama, no!" she cried in dismay.

"You aren't welcome here," her mother growled at him.

He held up his hands. "I ain't here to cause ya no more trouble, ma'am."

"You expect me to believe that?" she fumed. "After what you did to us?"

"I'm… I'm real sorry, ma'am. For all of it," Joseph said, his eyes racked with guilt.

"Get out of my house."

Dinah stepped between them. "He isn't with the gang anymore. He saved my life."

"I don't care what he did," her mother snapped.

Dinah knew her anger better than anyone. Her pain. If only she could make her understand.

"Get out!" her mother shouted past her. "Get out now!"

"Mama, *please*—"

"It's all right, Dinah," he said. "I'm goin'."

Her mother's chest heaved, the vein in her forehead bulging as she clutched the gun with white-knuckled hands. Tears welled in Dinah's eyes as he headed for the door. Her mother stared at her aghast. As if she didn't know her anymore.

"Have you lost every bit of sense you ever had?"

Dinah didn't answer. She hurried to the door and followed Joseph out into the darkness.

"Dinah!" her mother yelled, but she ignored her.

———◆———

He'd left Steel out in the yard, and he was almost to him when she caught up.

"Joseph, wait! There's somethin' I need to tell you."

He stopped and faced her.

She drew a deep breath, bracing for his reaction. "Lawrence and Marshal Tupper made it back to Salina, and they've got Sal."

Joseph's eyes widened. "What about Marcus?"

"I don't know."

He huffed and ran a hand over his face. "They'll hang 'em all."

He sounded so upset, so devastated.

"That's what they deserve," she reminded him.

"Marcus ain't Sal," he growled.

Dinah stared at him in disbelief. "You'd break 'em out if you could, wouldn't you?"

Joseph turned from her, hands on his hips as he gazed west toward Salina.

Her heart sank. What a fool she'd been to think he'd changed. That they could find a way to be together.

"Whose side are you on?" she demanded. "You can't live two lives, Joseph."

He rounded on her. "I gave up my life. I gave up *everything* for you."

Tears pricked Dinah's eyes. "All that you said about livin' on the run, that I deserved better—you were tryin' to get rid of me."

"I was tryin' to protect you."

"Protect me?" She jabbed a finger toward the house. "Mama almost died tonight because of you."

Dinah regretted the venomous retort the moment it left her lips, but the damage had been done. She saw it in the blink of his eyes, the twitch of his mouth.

"One more thing you'll never forgive me for," Joseph said bitterly.

He strode to Steel, and her lip gave a traitorous quiver.

"Where're you going?" she asked, marching after him. "What about the money?"

Joseph climbed into the saddle and glanced toward the porch. She knew her mother must be watching them, but she didn't care.

"Give it to the marshal. He'll take care of the rest."

"Where are you going?" Dinah repeated, more insistently this time.

He shifted in the saddle, avoiding her gaze.

Terror gripped her. Furious as she was with him, she didn't want him to leave—not without her.

"Go to Salina and stay there," he said. "Lawrence and Tupper'll look after ya."

"When will I see you again?" Dinah pressed, hating the tremor that stole into her voice.

Finally, Joseph looked down at her with an anguished expression. "I don't know."

Fresh tears stung her eyes as she stared up at him.

He turned Steel away and spurred his sides. Dinah raced after him, heart bleeding and vision blurring.

"*Joseph!*" she screamed above the rushing wind and the stallion's thundering hooves.

But he didn't stop.

Her leg gave, and she collapsed in the grass. Grimacing, Dinah pushed herself onto her hands and knees and snatched up a rock. She scrambled to her feet as he galloped down the path. Breathing hard, she flung the rock as far as she could with a feral cry.

For the first time in her life, she knew what she wanted. *Who* she wanted. And it had all slipped right through her fingers.

───────●───────

Early the next morning, Dinah set out for Salina with Daniel and her mother, Remy's bundled body slung over Cardinal's hindquarters and twenty-five thousand dollars stuffed in her saddlebags—plus the couple thousand she'd found stowed on Remy's horse. Never had she lain eyes on so much money, and being in possession of such a massive sum had her wound so tight that she couldn't seem to catch her breath. Couldn't focus.

It wasn't just the money. She couldn't stop thinking about Joseph. Couldn't stop wondering if she should've gone after him. Did he miss her? Or was he glad to be rid of her?

He didn't say he was leavin' for good.

Was it possible that he'd gone to Obadiah's cabin like they'd planned? Was he waiting to see if she'd show up?

Probably not. Maybe he needs time, like I did.

She glanced at Daniel as he drew alongside her, Belle's black head held high and her steps brisk and eager to please. The mare held no grudge against him for his neglect, but Dinah wasn't so forgiving. In his absence, she'd fed her, brushed her—taken her for rides so she wouldn't feel unwanted.

Daniel peeked over his shoulder, and she followed his gaze. Some distance behind them, Dusty plodded along as her mother held the reins, Sarge walking behind the jostling wagon.

"You almost killed her," he said, "running away like that after what happened to Dad."

Dinah's chest panged, and she clenched her jaw.

"Wanting justice I can understand, but riding with an *outlaw,* a member of the Valentin Gang..." Baffled, he shook his head. "What were you thinking?"

"I got separated from the posse," she answered sternly. "I was Sal's prisoner, and he was gonna have me killed. Joseph saved my life. He turned on 'em, and when the gang came after us, he protected me. Made sure I got home safe."

Daniel's eyes widened, and she realized how outlandish it must sound.

"That's quite a thing to do for a stranger," he remarked with obvious suspicion.

She averted her gaze, her heart beating faster.

"Makes me think... the two of you were more than that."

He said it with such dread, such unease. As if the mere idea repulsed him.

Dinah's cheeks heated as she stared at the blue horizon. She'd never had a good poker face, never been good at hiding anything, especially not from family.

"Tell me I'm wrong, Dinah."

She couldn't. Not without lying to his face.

"Tell me you aren't going to see him ever a—"

"I can't, and I won't!" she burst, chest heaving as she shook with fury. "You've got no right to lecture me. You lost that the day you left us."

"What's going on up there?" her mother called anxiously.

Daniel glanced over his shoulder before meeting her livid gaze. "It wasn't just about getting out of Kansas, Dinah."

"What then?" she demanded. "Gettin' away from me?"

194

"No, I—" He sighed and looked out at the green hills rippling in the sunlight. "I was saving money so I could help Dad pay off the debt. Not just for him and Mama, but for *you*."

She'd heard wrong. She must have.

"Me?"

Daniel met her astonished gaze and nodded. "I didn't want you to be stuck working that farm for the next ten years, and I knew you didn't either."

Dinah's heart softened, her anger waning. "I… had no idea."

"Yeah, well, it doesn't matter now."

"It matters to me. All this time, I thought you just… didn't care."

"I didn't tell anyone," he admitted. "You know how Dad was. He never asked for help, never wanted to burden anyone. If I'd told him my plan, he would've refused. He was stubborn like that."

She smiled sadly. "Yeah, he was."

He cast her a sideways glance. "Like someone else I know."

Dinah swallowed, throat burning as she stared at the path ahead.

"When I found your note, I was terrified."

Guiltily, she met his gaze.

"I know things've been difficult for you since Ophelia passed, and now Dad. But you aren't the only one grieving," Daniel reminded her. "You don't have to bear that burden alone. Next time, Dinah, *talk* to me."

Tears spilled down her cheeks, and she hastened to wipe them away.

"Promise?" he said.

Dinah sniffed and nodded. It was good to have him back, to know what he'd tried to do for her. But he wouldn't be around much longer. With the cows already gone, all her mother had to do was sell the homestead, and today, she was going to meet with a man in town who was interested in buying.

"Are you sure you wanna face Valentin alone?" Daniel asked after a pause.

She didn't *want* to face him—she *had* to. "I'm sure."

He took a deep breath and nodded. "Seeing him behind bars, knowing he can't hurt anyone else—I hope it gives you the peace you've been searching for."

⸻

When they crossed the bridge into Salina, Daniel and her mother headed for Cornelia Bailey's house on Fourth Street, and Dinah rode on toward the marshal's office. Cornelia was a longtime friend of the family, and her mother hoped she'd be willing to take them in until the gang had been dealt with. Lawrence had told Daniel the posse hadn't gotten them all, but he hadn't said who still roamed free or how many.

With Enyeto gone and four of them now dead, that left Sal, Marcus, Donny, Rick, and Gus still alive.

Dinah got more than a few strange looks as she walked Cardinal down Iron Avenue. People whispered to one another and pointed at the man-shaped bundle stowed behind her, and she tried to ignore them. She didn't have the desire or the patience to indulge their curiosity.

A chill ran down her spine, each step bringing her closer to Sal.

Dinah turned south onto Seventh Street, passing by the Opera House, the Metropolitan Hotel, and frame dwellings. As she neared the marshal's office on the next corner, she noticed a group of men gathered out front—Marshal Tupper, whose right arm was in a sling—Lawrence, Mercer, Deputy Thomas, and five finely dressed strangers. They appeared to be deep in conversation.

Or an argument, she thought as Mercer jabbed his finger at one of them, a much shorter man wearing a black coat and derby hat.

Lawrence spotted her first, and he turned in surprise. "Dinah. You shoah are a sight for sore eyes."

He limped toward her with a smile, and she smiled back, relieved to see him alive.

"What've ya got there, Miss Hance?" Tupper called.

Dinah's smile faded. She dismounted and led Cardinal closer. "I brought you something, Marshal."

His thick brows furrowed as his gaze shifted from her to the bundled body. "That looks like a some*one.*"

Dinah stopped and glanced at the five strangers. At the badges gleaming on their chests.

Pinkertons.

Her heart beat faster. She hadn't planned to make her confession in the company of national detectives.

"What happened, Dinah?" Lawrence questioned with quiet concern.

She swallowed hard and met his gaze. "Last night, Remy Guidry rode to our house and took my mother captive. He wanted to avenge his brother, and he was gonna kill her to hurt me. He wouldn't let her go. I had to—"

The gun kicks in her hand. The muzzle flashes. An ear-splitting crack plunges her world into silence. Remy's accusing eyes glare up at her as blood runs down his face.

Dinah's chest clenched, her insides twisting in knots. She blew a shuddering breath. "I killed him."

The men looked at each other in astonishment.

Tupper put his left hand on his hip and nodded at the body. "You tellin' me that's Remy Guidry?"

"Yes, sir."

His dark eyes studied her, his stern countenance softening. "I underestimated you, Miss Hance."

She'd underestimated herself. What she was capable of when backed into a corner.

Lawrence stepped forward and pulled back the sheet covering Remy's face.

"Is it him?" Tupper asked.

"It's him all right. Heck of a shot too. Right between the eyes."

Tupper turned to his deputy. "Thomas, get him down from there and toss him in the cart out back. Have the undertaker come by."

"Yessir."

"There's a thirty-five-hundred-dollar reward for bringin' in Guidry," Tupper told her. "I'll have it ready for ya in the next couple days."

Dinah's mouth dropped open. *Thirty-five hundred?*

Thomas slung Remy's body over his shoulder and carried him away.

The money, she remembered suddenly. She hurried to grab her saddlebags.

"That reminds me," she said, hoisting them from Cardinal's back. "I brought this—half the money the gang stole from the bank in Abilene."

They stared at her, eyes wide and mouths agape.

"Where did you get that?" one of the agents demanded.

Lawrence shot him a glare out of the corner of his eye. "Miss Hance, this is Agent Cutler of the Pinkerton Detective Agency. You'll forgive his lack of mannuhs. He's a Yankee."

Dinah met Cutler's frigid gaze, his shaven face pale and serpentlike. "The gang buried it on our land. I didn't know till Joseph told me. He showed me where the money was."

Mercer scoffed at that.

Lawrence arched a brow at him. "You got somethin' to say, Mercer?"

"Yeah. She couldn't make a shot like that. I think Gray killed Guidry and took off with the other half of the money."

Dinah's temper flared.

"Gray?" Cutler questioned before she could retort.

Mercer strutted toward her with insufferable arrogance. "Joseph Gray, notorious outlaw and member of the Valentin Gang. Last time I saw Miss Hance, she was runnin' off with him and leavin' the rest of us to fight the gang ourselves."

"You saw me in Dead Man's Dune," she shot back. "You heard me scream, and you didn't even *think* about stoppin'. All you cared about was savin' your own skin."

Lawrence rounded on Mercer. "You knew she was there?"

"There was nothin' I could do," he argued, his voice rising in agitation. "We were getting shot to pieces."

Tupper shook his head in disappointment.

Cutler's eyes narrowed as he turned to Dinah. "Why were you with Joseph Gray?"

Lawrence moved to stand at her side, and she looked up at him in surprise. "She was captuhed by the gang, and Gray turned on 'em. Saved her life. She was gravely injuhed, so when Valentin showed up, I told Gray to get her to safety."

"Where is he now?" Cutler asked her.

Dinah swallowed, the saddlebags getting heavier every second. "I don't know. He left. He didn't say where he was goin'."

"And the other twenty-five thousand?" he prompted.

"The gang has it. My understandin's that they divided it among themselves."

"That's enough, Agent Cutler," Lawrence said when he opened his mouth to question her again. "This isn't the time foah an interrogation."

"That may be, but she's the only lead we've got on Gray."

"Truth be told, Agent," Marshal Tupper interjected, "I've had about all I can stand of ya for one mornin'. If you want Rick Wallace and Donny Guidry, you can have 'em, but Valentin stays with me. He's gonna stand trial right here in Salina."

Cutler's icy eyes flickered with indignation. "We'll see what the governor has to say about this."

"We sure will," Tupper replied, unbothered by his threat.

With a final glare at Lawrence, Cutler turned and walked away, the other four agents following him.

"He's tryin' to take custody of Sal?" Dinah whispered.

Lawrence nodded. "He wants to take him out of state to be tried elsewhere."

Her eyes widened in alarm. "Out of state?"

"Tupper won't let him."

She tried to take some comfort in his confidence.

Marshal Tupper strode over to her with a rare smile on his face. "You've done Salina proud today, Miss Hance."

Dinah's heart swelled. "Thank you, sir."

She handed him the saddlebags, and he turned to his nephew.

"James, go to the telegraph office. Let the folks in Abilene know we've got half of their stolen fifty."

Mercer trudged to his horse, looking very put out.

"I'll take this to the bank for safe keepin' till somebody from Abilene comes for it," Tupper told her. "You rest up now, Miss Hance—take it easy. You've earned it."

Resting was the last thing on Dinah's mind.

Mercer trotted away on his black Saddler, and Tupper wasn't far behind him, sitting astride a big bay roan. His new horse, she supposed.

"Lawrence, Marshal Tupper mentioned Rick and Donny," she ventured. "What about Gus and Marcus?"

"Still at large," Lawrence muttered.

The knot in her chest clenched tighter. So, two of them were still out there, one of whom had vowed to kill Joseph.

"Don't worry, Miss Hance," he assured her. "They'll turn up, and when they do, we'll be ready foah 'em."

"Brooks and Badger—did they make it?" Dinah asked, dreading his answer.

"They did, but Brooks took the deaths of the othuhs hard. I haven't seen him since we got back, and that was three days ago."

"What about Dr. Hart?"

"Safe and unharmed," he replied. "She's quite a woman. Rallied the men in Beaver and got 'em to join the fight against Valentin. Without their help, I probably wouldn't be standin' here."

He turned to her and added, "She came with us, y'know. Back to Salina."

Dinah blinked in surprise. "She's here?"

"Foah the time bein'. She's stayin' at the Metropolitan."

"I'll have to pay her a visit," she said. But first, there was the matter of Sal. "Before I go, Lawrence, there's… one more thing I wanted to ask you."

"Anything, Miss Hance."

She took a deep breath and met his gaze. "I didn't just come here about Remy and the money."

"You wanna see Valentin, don'tcha?" Lawrence frowned and stroked his mustache. "I don't know if—"

"*Please*," she implored with quiet desperation.

He sighed, his shoulders slumping in defeat. "All right."

———————————•———•———————————

Lawrence held open the door, and she stepped inside Tupper's office. Sunlight spilled in behind her, dust floating in the air as she approached his desk. Her tired eyes drifted to the board on the wall, where he'd pinned her drawings of the outlaws. Sal, Marcus…

Joseph.

She swallowed, heart aching as she frowned at her feeble attempt to capture his piercing gaze. He'd kept his word. Left her every penny they'd buried under the dogwood tree.

He wanted to make things right.

Lawrence closed the door, shutting out the cool morning breeze. "You ready?"

Mustering her courage, Dinah faced him and nodded.

"Come on then."

He limped toward the stairs in the far right corner, and she followed him. Her heart pounded, her legs trembling as she climbed the creaking steps.

"Has he said anything?" she asked quietly.

"Silent as the grave," Lawrence muttered.

He opened the door at the top of the stairs and motioned for her to enter first. There were no windows in the long, narrow space—just a couple of lamps on the wall.

Venturing across the threshold, Dinah peeked to her right. In the first cell, a man with dark shoulder-length curls and a bushy beard sat on a cot with his head hung low.

Rick glanced up when her boots thudded on the planks. His thick brows drew together, nose creasing as he glowered at her.

Dinah squared her shoulders and continued on to the next cell.

Donny Guidry paced in the shadows, raking his fingers through his greasy brown hair. He stopped and stared at her, and she stared back. He looked so like Remy, his eyes so empty—so unhinged.

"You…" he murmured.

He lunged at the bars. She gasped and flinched back as he shook them with white-knuckled hands.

"You should be dead!" Donny raged. "You an' all da rest of 'em! You'll wish ya were when I get outta here. Ya little witch! I'll gut ya like a fish!"

He spat through the bars, and it spattered onto Dinah's face. She recoiled in disgust, wiping away the saliva.

Lawrence surged between them with his hand on his holster. "You do that again, Guidry, and I'll putcha down like the rabid dog you are."

"I'd like ta see ya try, ol' man."

She couldn't imagine how Donny would've reacted to her if he'd been told about Remy.

Lawrence frowned at her. "You all right, Dinah?"

"I'm fine," she muttered, sweeping her fingers across her cheek.

Slow, reluctant steps carried her toward the last cell. The air was warm—stifling. The flickering walls seemed to close in on her, the ceiling sinking toward her head. Steeling herself, Dinah drew a strangled breath and peered through the bars.

Black eyes met hers, glinting in the lamplight. Sal stood like a statue, a gargoyle made of flesh and blood. Calm and expectant. His hands hanging at his sides. He'd taken off his hat and coat and laid them on the cot in the corner.

She'd hoped to find him on his knees, miserable and defeated.

Her jaw clenched, and Sal canted his head. Dinah glared up at him, resisting the urge to squirm under his scrutinizing gaze.

"I want to speak to Miss Hance alone."

"Forget it," Lawrence said.

Sal clasped his hands behind his back with an infuriating air of superiority, never taking his eyes off hers.

Why's he so smug? What's he got up his sleeve?

She couldn't leave this room till she knew. "I'll talk to him."

"Dinah, he's got nothin' to say to ya that's worth listenin' to."

"Maybe not," she conceded, but she didn't budge.

Lawrence heaved a frustrated sigh. "Fine, but I've gotta ask ya to give me that gun, Miss Hance."

She hesitated, loathe to hand it over. But she had no choice.

Dinah yanked the Colt from her holster and put it in his outstretched palm.

"I'll wait foah ya right outside that door," he told her. "Don't be long."

As he walked away, the frantic thumping of her heart muffled the scuff of his boot and the clunk of his false leg. Blood pulsed behind her eyes, the lights blinking in and out.

Lawrence pulled the door closed, and Dinah swallowed.

"How did it feel?" Sal questioned with quiet curiosity. "Taking a life."

The blood drained from her face. *How does he know?*

Sal's eyes gleamed with delight. "You enjoyed it, didn't you?"

"No."

He grinned, and Dinah's hands balled into fists.

"I had no other choice."

"You looked at your situation, weighed your options, and did what was necessary. We aren't as different as you think."

"I'm *nothing* like you," she growled.

"Where would you be without me?" he replied, cool and composed in the face of her simmering rage. "Still stuck on that run-down farm, too scared to leave. Those boots don't fit anymore, but you keep wearing them. You can't stop clinging to the girl you were, to the innocence you lost that day."

Dinah's mouth went dry. Nausea crashed over her, her insides churning.

"Yes," Sal purred, stepping closer to the bars, "I remember her. That's where your obsession began, didn't it? If you could get rid of me, the nightmares would end. The wound would heal. But, now, you realize your pain won't die with me."

A lump lodged in her throat as she stared up at him.

His eyes glittered with twisted triumph. "What will you do when you have no enemy to fight? Nothing to distract you? Nothing to hate but yourself?"

Desperately, Dinah blinked back the tears blurring her vision. She'd buried that fear so deep. Ignored and denied and focused every waking thought on tracking him down. Always hunting. Never resting.

If she didn't stop to think, she didn't have to ponder life after him.

Dinah looked up, meeting Sal's imperious gaze with bitter defiance. "You can't stand it, can you? You thought you had Joseph in the palm of your hand, that you could make him dance like a puppet on a string. And he defied you. He chose me over you."

"Is that all it took to blind you to the truth?"

Her brow furrowed. "What truth?"

"All these years, you've blamed me for that girl's death."

"Her name is Ophelia," she snarled. "And you shot her. I saw—"

"You saw what you wanted to see."

Dinah blinked, a strange sense of dread tying a noose around her neck.

Sal turns around, a revolver in his black-gloved hand. He walks away without a word, leaving Ophelia lying in the dust-clouded street.

She didn't see him pull the trigger. Didn't see Ophelia fall.

"I didn't kill her," Sal said. "Joseph did."

She gaped at him in horror. He'd pulled the lever. Dropped the floor out from under her.

Bills lay scattered in the dirt, more fluttering around her head. There's so many. Where did they come from? Who dropped the money?

"You're lying!" Dinah spat.

A wicked grin split Sal's face. He leaned in close, reveling in her distress. "Am I? Why don't you ask him?"

He might as well have plunged a knife into her chest.

Dinah flew at him with a savage cry, but Sal retreated beyond her reach, leaving her clawing at empty air. She grabbed the iron bars and threw herself against them.

"*Liar!*" she shrieked. "You're a liar!"

The door burst open.

"What's goin' on in here?" Lawrence exclaimed.

Fresh tears stung her eyes as she sagged against the bars.

"Dinah, come with me. Come on."

A strong arm wrapped around her waist, and she caught a final glimpse of Sal's devilish grin as Lawrence dragged her away from his cell. She didn't care to resist, shaking so terribly that she could barely stand.

"I knew this was a mistake," Lawrence grumbled, half carrying her toward the door.

"Where ya goin', little fish?" Donny jeered.

He killed her, Dinah thought, too distraught to pay him any mind. *He killed Ophelia.*

"Easy," Lawrence warned as he helped her down the stairs. "One at a time."

She choked back a sob, clinging to him for support as her legs threatened to buckle. When they reached the room below, Dinah tore from his grasp, yanked off her hat, and threw it onto Tupper's desk.

"Heaven's sake, Miss Hance, what'd he say to ya?" Lawrence asked as she paced.

"He knew," Dinah muttered miserably. "He *knew,* and he didn't tell me."

"Who?"

She buried her face in her hands and let out an anguished groan. *Fool. What a fool I am!*

Back and forth she went, weeping and smacking her palms against the sides of her head.

"Dinah, stop it," Lawrence admonished, striding toward her. "*Stop.*"

He grabbed her elbow. She took a blind swing at him, and he caught her wrist.

"Get off me!" she cried, lashing out in a grief-addled frenzy. "Get off!"

Lawrence pulled her to him. She beat her fists against his chest, but that only made him hold her tighter. Dinah collapsed in his arms, sobbing so violently that she couldn't catch her breath. Convinced that her heart would rip in two.

"It's all right," Lawrence said. "It's gonna be all right."

But it wasn't. And it never would be.

CHAPTER TWENTY

The air got warmer as the sun peaked in a cloudless sky, a constant breeze sweeping across the plains as Joseph approached Obadiah's cabin. He hadn't thought he'd ever come back here, and he didn't know what kind of welcome he'd get. But he didn't have anywhere else to go.

Obadiah held a big sheep between his knees as he sheared its wool in the noisy pen next to the cabin. Concentrated on his work, he didn't see Joseph coming.

Joseph walked Steel up to the fence and brought him to a halt. He hesitated, fearing that the old farmer would turn him away.

"Obadiah."

He looked up in surprise, eyes crinkling as he grinned. "Well, I'll be! Look who it is."

"You got a minute to talk?" Joseph asked.

"Sure. Let me finish up this bad boy real quick."

Joseph dismounted and looped Steel's reins over the rail. Leaning forward, he propped his arms on the fence and watched the ram squirm. He wondered if shearing hurt.

Finally, Obadiah stood, and so did the sheep, white and clean as he bolted off. Obadiah gathered the wool in his arms and came to the fence.

"Been shearin' all day'," he panted, hanging the wool over the top rail. "Ain't never a pleasant experience, but that fella right there—he makes it downright miserable."

Leaving the pen, Obadiah closed the gate behind him and dusted off his palms on his blue jeans.

Joseph turned toward him, leaving his right hand resting on the fence. "Does it hurt 'em?"

"Not a bit." Obadiah adjusted his cap, his bald head glistening with sweat. "It'd go a lot faster if they didn't make such a fuss. Frustratin' little critters. Ya try to help 'em, and they fight ya every step of the way."

He scratched his beard and sighed. "But you didn't come here to listen to an old man gripe about his sheep. It's good to see ya again, Joseph. What can I do for ya?"

Joseph shifted, gripping the fence tighter. "Well, I ain't one to ask for favors, but—"

"Don't apologize, Joseph. I owe ya more than one for savin' me that night."

Forcing himself to swallow his pride, Joseph looked him in the eye. "I need a place to stay a couple days before I move on again, and I was hopin' you might have some room to spare."

"We ain't got an extra bed, but there's a couch by the fire if that'll do ya. Though I s'pose I should ask Martha first."

"Obadiah!" a woman called.

Joseph glanced up and saw her leaning out the front door, her dark gray hair tied back from her stern, suntanned face.

"There she is now." Obadiah faced her and motioned her toward them. "Martha, come over here. There's someone I wantcha to meet."

Brow furrowing, she left the cabin and lifted the hem of her plaid skirt as she came down the steps. Small but wiry, she walked with brisk confidence, and Joseph suspected that she was a force to be reckoned with.

"Martha, this is Joseph, the fella I toldja about a couple weeks back."

Squinting up at him in the sunlight, she smiled. "I'm glad to finally have the chance to thank you, Joseph. I'm mighty grateful there was a Good Samaritan on the road that mornin'."

Shame bowed Joseph's head. Dinah had called him that when he'd helped with their cattle, having no idea who he was or what he'd done to her family. "It was nothin', ma'am."

"Humble too," Martha quipped with a glance at her husband. "I like him."

"He's lookin' for a place to stay a couple days," Obadiah explained.

"Well, he's more'n welcome here. I just got the stew ready. It's nice and hot. Come on in, Joseph, and I'll dip out a bowl for ya."

Strange bein' invited into a place. But a welcome change.

"I'm much obliged, ma'am."

———————•————————

The smell of cooked meat and vegetables filled their home, and Joseph's stomach rumbled. The cabin was one room, the kitchen on the right side and a couch and chairs arranged around the fireplace on the left. A narrow staircase in the far corner led to an upper level—their bedroom, he assumed. He noted the window beside the mantle, another next to the dining table, and a second door at the back of the cabin.

An old habit. He did it every time he walked into a room, always looking for a way out—or the ways a bullet might get in.

"You can hang your coat by the door there," Martha told him as she went to the stove.

Joseph shed his coat, took off his hat, and hung them on a hook on the wall. He turned to consider the four chairs at the table, two on each side. All of them would put his back to something.

Better to keep an eye on the doors, he decided.

Martha glanced over her shoulder as she stirred the pot on the stove. "No guns at the table."

He froze mid-step. Grudgingly, he unbuckled his gun belt and draped it over the hook beside his hat.

"Smells delicious, Martha," Obadiah said, hanging his cap on another.

Joseph walked around the table, pulled out a chair, and sat in front of the window.

Obadiah wiped his wrinkled brow with his forearm and came over to join him. "She makes a mean rabbit stew."

"And you ain't gettin' none till you wash the sheep off your hands," she warned.

"All right. All right," he grumbled.

Joseph looked at his own dirty hands and stood from his chair. Obadiah went to a porcelain basin on the counter to wash up, and when he'd finished, Joseph did the same. Martha gave him a nod of approval, and he sat across from Obadiah.

He laid his bandana in his lap, his fingers lingering on the black cotton. *I shouldn't've run off like that.*

It had happened so fast. Finding out about Sal, realizing it was all coming to an end. If Marcus had gotten caught, he couldn't leave him to die.

But what could he do? Abilene was one thing. Salina was another.

"You heard the news, Joseph?" Obadiah asked. "A posse captured the leader of the gang that tore up Abilene—Sal Valentin. The same fella that robbed Salina ten years back."

"He shoulda been dealt with a long time ago," Martha chimed in, setting a spoon and a bowl of steaming stew in front of Joseph.

Stay calm, he reminded himself. *They don't know who you are.*

"Did they get the rest of 'em?" he responded with casual curiosity.

"Two others." Obadiah's blue eyes squinted as he stroked his beard. "I think it was, uh… Oh, I don't remember their names now."

As far as Joseph knew, Marcus, Gus, Rick, and Donny were the only ones left. Rick and Gus would stop at nothing to avenge Tony, and if Donny ever found out what Dinah had done to Remy, killing her would become his top priority.

Which two had been captured with Sal, and who still walked free?

If any of 'em. Whoever hadn't been taken alive might've been shot dead by the posse.

Joseph picked up the spoon and took a bite of stew as Martha gave a bowl to Obadiah. He got a big mouthful of tender rabbit meat, carrot, and potato, and he almost sighed in relief. For the past week, everything he'd eaten had come straight out of a can. He'd missed Elliott's cooking. Having an actual meal to look forward to.

As Joseph scooped another bite, Martha sank into the chair next to her husband.

"Folk in town ain't too happy about Valentin bein' kept in Salina," she said. "They want him tried in Abilene. I can't blame 'em. We lost a lotta good people that day. Not to mention the damage that was done. Some families lost everything."

Joseph stared at his stew, guilt dulling his appetite.

"I know, but the folks in Salina want justice," Obadiah reminded her. "It's personal for 'em, same as us. He killed that little girl, remember?"

Joseph's hand shook. He broke out in a cold sweat.

"Robbery! Robbery at the bank!" a man cries.

Sal points his Colt and pulls the trigger. The man falls off the boardwalk and hits the dirt.

Sal strides toward his horse, unbothered by the chaos. Joseph stays close on his heels, his revolver in one hand and a bag of money in the other. People are running. Screaming.

Someone shoots at them from across the street, and Marcus fires back. Gunpowder clouds the air.

"Come on!" Jeremiah calls, waving them toward him. He's already unhitched the horses.

Joseph's eyes dart back and forth, blood pumping through his veins.

Who's got a gun? Who doesn't? It's all a blur.

Hooves thunder to his left. He spins and sees a horse charging toward them. The rider raises a rifle.

"Look out!" Joseph exclaims.

He aims his gun at the rider.

Bang!

The man tumbles from the saddle. Joseph hadn't shot him—Marcus had gotten him first.

The riderless horse gallops straight toward Joseph.

He springs back so fast he loses his balance. The panicked animal streaks past him as he falls. He drops the bag to catch himself, and pain jolts up his left arm.

Dust and money swirl around his head. Breathing hard, Joseph sweeps scattered dollars and coins back into the sack. He scrambles to his feet and slings it over his shoulder.

A rifle cracks behind him.

Joseph ducks. Movement flashes at the corner of his vision. He wheels around and pulls the trigger.

The impact knocks her off her feet—a young girl. She lies there gasping and bleeding, and all he can do is stare.

She's gonna die, *he thinks.* She's gonna die 'cause of me.

"Joseph." Sal grabs him by the shoulders and shoves him toward the horses. "Go. There's nothing to be done."

"But—"

"Go," he repeats sternly.

Joseph glances down at the girl. He swallows.

Numb and sick to his stomach, he runs and doesn't look back.

"You all right, Joseph?" Obadiah asked.

Joseph blinked and looked up from his bowl. Martha frowned at him, Obadiah's black brows furrowed with concern.

"Yeah," Joseph stammered. "It's just… awful what happened."

Obadiah nodded in agreement. "Tragic."

Neither of them seemed convinced by his response.

"This is real good, ma'am," Joseph said, hoping he hadn't offended Martha.

"Thank you," she answered with quiet pride.

Obadiah grinned. "I toldja."

Joseph returned to his stew and tried to put the girl out of his mind. Would he ever get through *one day* without reliving it? Would he ever stop hating himself for what he'd done?

Obadiah glanced over his shoulder as he headed outside. "I heard that."

After dinner, Obadiah had more work to do. All the sheep had been sheared, but now he had to "skirt the fleece." Whatever that meant.

"Why don'tcha give me a hand, Joseph?" he suggested as he put on his cap.

Joseph shifted in his chair, his face heating with embarrassment. "I would, but… I ain't ever done that before."

Obadiah waved him toward the door. "Come on. I'll show ya how."

"Don't worry," Martha told him, her brown eyes twinkling. "He's gotten soft in his old age."

Obadiah glanced over his shoulder as he headed outside. "I heard that."

Joseph couldn't help but smile. He got up and followed him, leaving his bandana on the hook with his hat and coat. Instinctively, he reached for his gun belt, then caught himself. He felt naked without his Schofields. He carried them everywhere, rarely taking them off.

But I don't want 'em gettin' suspicious.

Joseph turned away and sighed as he stepped out onto the porch. The sticky heat made him roll up his sleeves, the air thick and suffocating. Almost as bad as the marshes back in Carolina.

As he gazed west across the windy plains, something snagged inside his chest. Pulling him. Calling him.

He wanted to see her. To tell her he was sorry. And if she'd talked to Lawrence, she'd know what had happened to Marcus.

"Ya comin'?" Obadiah asked.

"Yeah."

Joseph tore his eyes from the horizon and tramped down the steps. Obadiah led him around to the back of the cabin, where he had a long table lined with huge clumps of wool—creams and grays and even a black one.

"Ain't much to it, really," Obadiah said, "just patience."

He picked up a fleece and pointed. "This section here is chock-full of chaff, so we'll throw that away. Usually happens up around their neck."

He separated that part from the rest of the wool and tossed it on the ground. "At the tail end, there's other bits that get stuck in their coats. Ya might wanna wear gloves to pull those out."

Joseph grimaced.

"We don't let nothin' go to waste. We save as much of the fleece as we can. Get rid of the hair that's matted or black at the tips," Obadiah instructed, holding up a piece for him to see. "Keep the good parts."

He set down the wool, took a deep breath, and hooked his thumbs under his suspenders. "Any questions?"

Joseph shook his head.

"All right. Let's get to work."

———————•———————

Though not intense, the labor was painstaking. Hours passed, and the afternoon got hotter as it wore on. Joseph's shirt clung to his back, hair sticking to his forehead as he picked one fleece after another. When they finished, he'd skirted fifteen of them. Obadiah had done a whole lot more.

Joseph grunted as he stretched his aching back. "You're too fast for me, old man."

"Comes with experience," Obadiah said. "The more ya practice, the faster ya get."

Just like shootin'.

"Thanks for your help, Joseph."

He nodded and rubbed his sore neck. Tired as he was, it felt good to do an honest day's work. Something he could be proud of.

"Was the least I could do to earn my keep."

"Ya got the hang of it pretty quick," Obadiah remarked as they walked past the pen.

Steel seemed to be getting along all right with the sheep, grazing peacefully but staying well away from them. Joseph had never kept him with smaller animals before, and he was relieved that the hot-tempered stallion hadn't decided to trample them yet.

"Y'know, you remind me of my son," Obadiah mused. "I had two. Both killed in the war. My eldest, William—he was a tireless worker. Tall and strong like you. He wanted to learn how to do everything. Martha was so proud of 'im, but she'd always tell me not to let 'im grow up too fast. 'There's time enough for that,' she'd say.

"But there weren't no time," he sighed. "Not nearly enough."

His words weighed heavy on Joseph. Seldom did he find a fella who hadn't lost someone in that godforsaken war.

They climbed the porch steps, and Obadiah sank into one of the old rockers. Wearily, Joseph lowered himself into the other. He looked out at the rustling grass, gold in the evening light. Thinking of the friends he'd lost far too soon.

"I was so hard on 'im." Obadiah shook his head, his grizzled mustache drooping and his eyes glistening. He ran a weathered hand over his face and met Joseph's gaze. "That cross I gave ya—I always meant to pass it on to 'im. But I waited too long."

His pained admission gripped Joseph's heart. All this time, he'd wondered why. Why him?

"I ain't lived a good life," Joseph confessed. "Done a lotta things I ain't proud of. But I'm tryin' to be better."

He forced a deep breath into his lungs, his gaze fixed on the blue horizon. "There's this girl. We didn't meet under the best of circumstances. She hated me—and rightly so. I didn't think I had a chance with her."

"But now ya do?"

Joseph sighed. "She wanted to give it a shot, but I ain't a proper match for her. I couldn't let her give everything up for me. So I left."

"Didja leave to protect 'er, or didja leave to protect yourself?"

Caught off guard, Joseph looked at him. Obadiah's wizened eyes seemed to see right through him, dragging his hidden fears out into the open. But they didn't condemn him. They were sympathetic—understanding.

"Do ya love 'er?"

A lump lodged in Joseph's throat. He hadn't allowed himself to even *think* that word.

He knew the answer, but admitting the truth meant confronting it. Risking rejection. Asking Dinah to make the biggest gamble of her life.

Joseph nodded.

"Have ya told 'er?"

"No," he mumbled.

"Don't wait, Joseph," Obadiah cautioned. "Tell 'er before it's too late. If ya don't, you'll spend the rest of your life wonderin' what coulda been."

Joseph huffed and stood. He strode past Obadiah and gazed west toward Salina. The wind rushed against his face, tossing his hair and whipping through his shirt. He closed his eyes and listened.

"Joseph!" she screams as he gallops away.

He imagined a future without her. Never seeing her again. Never hearing her voice. Never holding her. Her smile living only in his memory. Her touch a sensation that would fade with the passage of time.

The thought broke him.

Joseph opened his eyes, his mind made up.

"Here comes Martha," Obadiah announced.

Joseph turned as he rose from his rocker. The wagon rattled toward them, and she stopped the trotting horse in front of the cabin.

"Obadiah!" she called anxiously.

Obadiah went out to meet her. "What's wrong, Martha?"

She got down from the wagon and hurried toward him. "A group of ranchers and townsfolk just left Abilene."

"What?" he exclaimed.

"They're headin' for Salina," she panted. "Said they don't care who stands in their way. They're gonna bust the outlaws outta that jail and lynch 'em."

Joseph strode to the top of the steps, heart pounding and thoughts racing. He'd told Dinah to go into town and stay there. If she was in Salina, if a gunfight broke out in the streets…

"I gotta warn 'em."

Obadiah turned to him with furrowed brows. "Who?"

"The folk in Salina. They gotta be told."

Martha and Obadiah exchanged a worried glance.

"They all brought guns," she warned. "They ain't thinkin' straight. With tensions runnin' high, things could turn ugly."

"That's why I gotta go," Joseph answered, leaving the porch and joining them in the yard.

Martha's frown deepened, and Obadiah put a comforting arm around her shoulders.

"I understand," he said. "Do whatcha gotta do, Joseph."

He hated to leave like this, but he had no choice.

"Thank you both." Joseph met Obadiah's gaze and swallowed. "For everything."

Obadiah nodded. "Be careful, son."

CHAPTER TWENTY-ONE

Dinah stood before Ophelia's grave, hands hugging her sides as she bowed under the weight of her shame. She sank to her knees in swaying grass, tired and defeated. Feeling like a traitor. She'd been so blind.

Pathetic, chided an inner voice. *So desperate for a man to love you that you fell for a killer.*

Dinah raised her weary eyes to the sky. The sun hung low over Gypsum Hill, its pale yellow light bleeding through blue clouds.

Was this your plan? she demanded of God. *To make a fool of me? To give me what I've longed for just so you could take it away?*

She couldn't face Joseph. Couldn't bear the thought of hearing it from his lips.

But she'd made Ophelia a promise. Sworn that she would bring her killer to justice. She had to finish what she'd started.

Didn't she?

"Your mothuh said I might findja here."

Dinah jumped up and wheeled around. Lawrence stood some twenty feet behind her, holding Mister's reins.

"What're you doing here?" she responded tersely, cheeks hot and fists clenched.

"Sorry to disturb ya, Miss Hance. You were rathuh upset when I took ya to the Baileys' place, and when I came back to check on ya, your mothuh said you'd been gone quite a while. I wanted to make shoah nothin' had happened to ya."

"Well, now you've seen me, and now you can go."

Dinah turned her back on him, guilt nagging at her conscience. She didn't mean to be so harsh. Pushing people away had become second nature.

"Your mothuh told me about Ophelia."

How *dare* she? Fury surged in Dinah as she rounded on him.

Lawrence let go of the reins and slowly approached her. "What Sal said to ya—did it have somethin' to do with what happened to her?"

"I don't wanna talk about it," she warned.

He stopped just short of her, his brow furrowed under the brim of his hat. "If there's anything I can do—"

"There isn't," Dinah snapped. "She's gone, and it's my fault. If I'd—"

"The blame is on Valentin. Not you."

How many times? she fumed. How many times had she heard those very words? Over and over till she was sick of them.

"You weren't there," she shot back, straining to speak past the lump in her throat. "You don't understand."

Lawrence's features darkened. "I've lost many friends, Miss Hance. Men unduh my command. Ain't easy bearin' that responsibility."

Dinah massaged her throbbing forehead, hiding her face behind her hand. The wound had been ripped open all over again, raw and smeared with salt. But her well of tears had run dry. She couldn't cry anymore.

"You were just a kid," he said. "You've gotta stop punishin' yourself."

"You haven't," she countered, glaring up at him. "The war ended eighteen years ago, and you're still measuring your life by the men that you kill. You have a wife you should go home to. Don't you miss her?"

He stared at her, lips parting as his stalwart exterior crumbled.

"Every day," he answered grimly.

Dinah's heart twisted with instant remorse.

Lawrence walked a few paces away and faced the fire-streaked horizon. He stood in brooding silence, the wailing wind flinging the tails of his gray coat.

Dinah's gaze dropped to her boots. She'd gone too far. She knew what the war had done to her father. How it had haunted him.

"She died," Lawrence said.

Dinah went cold. Her wide eyes darted to his as he turned. He looked so broken. So bereft.

"My daughtuh too," he added bitterly. "Instead of bein' there to protect 'em, I was five hundred miles from home, fightin' a war we'd already lost."

But… he'd spoken of them as if they were alive.

Dinah gaped at him, appalled. How cruel she'd been. How thoughtless.

"I'm— I'm sorry, Lawrence. I had no idea."

"I don't go around tellin' it. Easiuh to pretend that way."

He took a step toward her, ducking his head and cupping his hand over his mouth. He stopped and closed his eyes. Lowered his hand and drew a deep breath as he met her gaze.

"I'm tellin' ya because, well, I've been runnin' a long time. Chasin' ghosts. It's a lonesome life, Miss Hance. I don't want that foah ya."

Dinah swallowed, moved by his quiet persistence. His patience and compassion in the face of her outbursts. "You're a good man, Lawrence. I haven't been half as kind to you as you've been to me."

"Nonsense," he replied with a dismissive wave of his hand.

"I mean that," she insisted. "It's... been a long time since I've had a friend."

His eyes shone, the corners of his mustache curving. "We should head on back, Miss Hance. Ain't safe foah ya to be alone up here in the dark."

Dinah cast a final glance at the gravestone before following him to the horses. Lawrence mounted Mister, and she climbed into Cardinal's saddle.

Shadows lengthened as they walked down the path in the dying light. She wrestled in silence, torn between her vow to Ophelia and her attachment to Joseph.

He had so much time. So many chances to tell me the truth.

Instead, he'd let her go on believing the lie.

She couldn't imagine him doing such a thing. He couldn't even kill her—how could he kill a child?

It had to have been an accident. Had to.

Dinah drew a shaky breath and looked at Lawrence. She couldn't keep it bottled up inside a second longer.

"Joseph killed Ophelia. That's what Sal said to me."

His eyes widened. "You think he's tellin' the truth?"

"I didn't wanna believe him, but he told me to ask Joseph, like he didn't think he'd deny it." She sighed. The thought made her sick. "Has Joseph ever...? Have you ever heard of him...?"

"He's killed folk, shoah, but women... children." Lawrence shook his head. "I've nevuh heard of him doin' a thing like that."

Neither had she, but hearing it from him helped.

"You're askin' because you've come to care foah him," he guessed with a knowing glance. "Haven'tcha?"

Dinah's cheeks burned as they reached the bottom of the hill and turned west onto the road. First Daniel, now him. Was she really so obvious?

"You know what that would mean foah ya," Lawrence ventured. "The trouble it'd bring. Have ya considuhed that?"

"I have. But what coulda been doesn't matter now. I don't know if I'll ever see him again."

If she did, what would she say? How would she feel? Even if what he'd done was an accident, could she ever bring herself to forgive him?

"Probably foah the best," Lawrence said.

Hooves thundered behind them, fast approaching from the east.

"What in tarnation?" he exclaimed.

She spun Cardinal around, and her heart jumped into her throat.

A blue roan raced toward them in the gathering dusk.

"Joseph," she breathed.

Lawrence's hand went to his gun. "Get behind me, Dinah."

She stayed by his side, eyes wide as Joseph reined in the lathered mustang.

"What do ya think you're doin, showin' your face around here?" Lawrence hollered at him. "You want me to arrest ya?"

"There's a mob comin' from Abilene," Joseph panted. "I came to tell ya. They'll be here any minute. You gotta get the prisoners outta Salina."

A mob? To lynch the outlaws?

Lawrence frowned. "How do I know this ain't a trick to spring your pals outta jail?"

"Because Sal wants me dead more than anyone," Joseph answered, looking heartbroken as he said it. "I guarantee ya that."

His eyes met hers, and Dinah swallowed.

"How many men?" Lawrence asked.

"Fifteen."

Lawrence sighed and ran a hand over his face. "Don't make me regret this, Gray."

She was inclined to believe Joseph, though a doubting voice whispered in the back of her mind.

"Marcus—is he with them?" he asked her.

She shook her head.

Joseph's jaw clenched, and he nodded.

"C'mon, Miss Hance. We gotta hurry," Lawrence said. He glared at Joseph as he pointed Mister toward Salina. "And you—stay outta the way."

Dinah hesitated, Joseph's longing gaze holding her back. There was something he wanted to say, but she couldn't stay. Didn't want to hear it right now.

It would have to wait.

She wheeled Cardinal west and galloped after Lawrence.

———————•———————

Dinah turned as the Pinkertons brought the handcuffed outlaws outside, Lawrence, Mercer, and Badger waiting with her. Rick's dark hair hung like curtains around his bowed head, Donny shrugging an agent's hand off his shoulder as he marched through the door.

Sal walked out last. Immediately his black eyes found hers, gleaming in the darkness. Fearless and… eager.

Marshal Tupper rode up to the jail and reined in his horse. "A train's waitin' at the station, Lawrence. Got it all arranged for ya."

"Thanks, Lee," Lawrence replied as Tupper dismounted.

Dinah stepped forward. "I'm goin' too."

"Miss Hance, you've done more'n enough already. Lawrence can—"

"I'm not lettin' him outta my sight, Marshal," she vowed with a sidelong glare at Sal. "Not till I know this is done with."

Tupper sighed and adjusted his hat. "Come inside a second."

He turned away, her brow furrowing as he strode past the equally confused Pinkertons. She looked up at Lawrence, who shrugged and shook his head.

Hesitantly, Dinah followed Marshal Tupper into his office and shut the door behind her.

"I know better than to try to talk you out of somethin' you've set your mind to," he grumbled, going to his desk and pulling open a drawer. "Brooks turned this in when we got back from the Strip. Said he weren't cut out for this kinda work. Can't blame him after what happened out in those dunes. Gettin' shot at, seein' friends die—it changes ya."

He closed the drawer and approached her with a star-shaped badge in his upturned palm. Dinah's breath caught as he offered it to her, the star's bronze surface glinting in the lamplight.

"If you're gettin' on that train, you should wear one of these. I daresay you deserve it more than my nephew."

Reverently, she took the badge from his hand, two words engraved on its smooth face.

Deputy Sheriff.

As her thumb traced the star's rough edge, her heart swelled with gratitude. Dinah swallowed and met the marshal's gaze. "Thank you, sir."

His stern eyes softened, and he nodded. "Now get goin'. You got a train to catch."

———————◆———————

Dinah took the window seat, and Lawrence slid in beside her. Agent Cutler sat facing them. Across the aisle, Agents Jennings and Davis supervised Sal, who'd been suspiciously cooperative thus far. At the back of the car, Agents Fletcher and Hughes guarded Donny, and Badger and Mercer kept an eye on Rick.

Per Marshal Tupper's orders, no other passengers had been permitted to board the train.

The Pinkertons were all too happy to help them transport the prisoners, and she suspected their enthusiasm had something to do with their plans to claim custody. Lawrence was less than pleased to have them along, but he knew they needed every man they could get. Even with the aid of the detectives, the mob Joseph had warned them about still outnumbered them.

Much as the Pinkertons' pompous behavior grated on her nerves, she took some comfort in having them aboard. They had a reputation for catching criminals no one else could. Though Dinah disagreed with some of their methods, she hoped they lived up to the stories she'd read in the papers.

"Where're we takin' 'em?" she whispered to Lawrence as the train started moving.

"Wichita," he muttered.

Haven't been there since yesterday.

Peaceful dwellings slipped past the windows across the aisle, clouded by billowing steam. One of them was Cornelia's.

She tore her gaze from the house with a pang of guilt. There'd been no time to tell Daniel or her mother what was happening or where she was going.

With any luck, this would go smoothly, and she'd be home soon.

Home? What home?

Their land would be sold. Her family would go to New York. And Joseph…

Dinah's chest clenched. She looked out her window and clasped her hands tighter. What did he want to say to her? He'd come from the east—been close to Abilene.

He went to Obadiah's. He must have.

Would he still be here when she came back? Had he come to tell her he was moving on? Going west without her?

Where would that leave her?

The Smoky Hill River glimmered in the light of a full moon, racing beside the train. Its waters always flowing. Never resting. Never letting up.

Is this all my life will be? she wondered bleakly. *Ridin' the current and tryin' not to drown? Keepin' my head above water till I reach the sea?*

"Looks like we're in the clear," Jennings said as they left Salina behind.

Silver hills rolled outside her window. A couple of miles flew by.

Dinah sighed and shifted on the hard bench. She couldn't get comfortable. Couldn't put her mind at ease.

Something didn't feel right.

Her eyes dropped from the twinkling sky to the prairie below. Shadowy forms emerged from the darkness, running along the river.

Dinah's heart skipped a beat. She blinked and scooted closer, her nose an inch from the glass. Manes and tails waved like black banners, four riders driving their horses toward the front of the train.

It was the mob Joseph had warned them about. Had to be.

"Lawrence, look."

He leaned past her to peer out the window. "Aw, hell."

"There's more over here!" Davis exclaimed.

The riders shouted and brandished rifles, but the chugging engine smothered their demands.

"What do we do?" she asked Lawrence, hoping he'd have a plan.

The riders fired into the air, then at the train. The window by Badger shattered, and he ducked, shielding his head with his arms as glass rained down.

"They've lost their minds!" he cried in outrage.

The railcar jolted as the train braked.

Dinah's back slammed into the bench as Cutler launched forward, grabbing the edge of his seat to keep from tumbling out of it. Her fingers splayed against the glass, and Lawrence flung a protective arm in front of her. She braced herself, muscles straining and heels digging into the floor.

Finally, the screeching gears fell silent. The train jerked to a stop, throwing her against his outstretched arm. Dinah sat back in her seat, breathless and shaken.

Lawrence lowered his arm. "You all right?"

"Yeah," she panted as riders surrounded the passenger car.

Lawrence rose and drew his revolver. "I don't know if these folks can be reasoned with. Be ready to defend the prisonuhs."

She glanced at Sal, who kept still and composed as the Pinkertons jumped up from their seats. The last thing she wanted to do was protect him.

"Not so fast," Cutler objected as Lawrence stepped into the aisle. "I'm in charge of these prisoners, and I will negotiate—"

The front door of the railcar burst open. A mustached man wearing a short brown coat and a wide-brimmed hat barged inside with a rifle. Dinah's hand flew to her holster as she got to her feet, Lawrence bravely blocking the aisle.

"My name's Reuben Maddox," the stranger said. "I and these other fine folks have come from Abilene. We're here for the scum that robbed our town and killed our people."

"I unduhstand your anguh, Mr. Maddox, and they will answer foah what they've done," Lawrence assured him. "But their punishment will be decided in a court of law, not by a mob."

Maddox frowned and tightened his grip on his rifle. "We ain't leavin' without 'em."

"Unless you and your friends intend to join Valentin in handcuffs, I suggest you return promptly to Abilene," Cutler threatened.

"Ain't too smart of ya to twist my arm, tenderfoot. We've gotcha surrounded."

He wasn't bluffing. Dinah counted fourteen men outside the passenger car, ready to open fire at a moment's notice.

"Don't be rash, Mr. Maddox," Lawrence cautioned. "Think of your family. If you go through us to get to Valentin, you're no bettuh than he is. You and everyone you've brought with ya will be arrested for murduh. Is that how you wanna be remembuhed?"

Maddox swallowed. His gaze shifted toward Sal, then back to Lawrence.

Dinah's heart pounded, her limbs tensed and trembling. Maybe he'd change his mind. Maybe they'd all just walk away.

Pop!

She yanked her Colt from her holster and spun to look outside. One of the riders slumped over and slid from his saddle as a bearded man galloped by on a black horse.

Marcus.

A second shot smashed a window at the back of the railcar. Fletcher cried out and stumbled into Hughes.

A rifle cracked across the aisle. Dinah gasped as Maddox staggered and fell backward through the doorway. An acrid stench stung her nose, smoke curling from the barrel of Jennings' gun. His chest heaved, his eyes wide and wild.

Bang!

She wheeled around. Saw Hughes fall.

Donny had gotten control of Fletcher's gun, and he wrenched it from his hand. Shot him as Badger and Mercer rushed to help.

As Donny turned the revolver on them, Dinah pointed her Colt and pulled the trigger. Her bullet found its mark, and he cursed, clutching his bleeding shoulder.

Rick stood up with Hughes' gun in hand.

Dinah cocked the hammer again, but Cutler fired first. Rick's revolver went off as he collapsed onto the bench. A lamp dropped from the ceiling and busted on the floor.

It burst into flames.

Jennings swore, and a stringy-haired stranger charged inside. He took aim at Lawrence, and Lawrence dropped him with a shot to the heart.

"Get Valentin outta here!" he hollered at Jennings over the gunfire outside.

The Pinkerton pushed Sal into the aisle, and Lawrence stepped aside to let them pass. Davis followed on Jennings' heels, and Cutler went behind him.

The flames crawled toward her, climbing over the seats and filling the car with smoke.

"Dinah, c'mon," Lawrence urged, waving her toward the doorway.

Coughing, she hurried to him. He put a firm hand on her shoulder, firelight flickering on his perspiring face.

"Stay close," he told her, "and stay behind me."

He ventured out into the darkness with his revolver at the ready. Grimacing, Dinah stepped over the man he'd killed. As she emerged from the burning train, she found Maddox. His limbs were sprawled, his body hanging in the gap between the passenger car and the baggage car. His eyes wide open and his shirt soaked with blood.

Her stomach turned.

It all happened so fast. What was Marcus thinking—that the mob would be the distraction he needed to help Sal escape?

She hopped down into the grass, Badger and Mercer dragging a thrashing Donny from the back of the car. Out on the prairie, four riders encircled a large man on a draft horse.

Gus.

Several shots rang out, and he tumbled from the saddle.

"Get back on the train," Lawrence said.

She gaped at him. "What?"

"*Run,*" he implored, pushing her ahead of him. "Get on the next pas-senguh car and get to the horses."

Dinah glanced at the riders, who wheeled their horses around and galloped toward them. Heart lurching, she raced to catch up with Badger and Mercer.

"Go!" she yelled at them. "Get back inside!"

Donny gave them no trouble. He'd probably seen what the mob had just done to Gus.

Dinah sprang onto the train and looked over her shoulder. Lawrence followed as fast as he could but struggled to run. He took two shots at the charging riders.

A rifle cracked, and Lawrence fell onto his hands and knees.

Her breath caught in her chest. *No!*

Dinah jumped off the train and sprinted toward him, heart thumping and blood pumping. She fired at the man who'd shot him, but her aim was sloppy. Hasty.

She missed.

"Damn it, Dinah," Lawrence grunted as she crouched beside him. "I ain't worth dyin' foah."

She wrapped her right arm around him, and he put his left over her shoulders. A bullet struck the railcar with a clang. She ducked and gritted her teeth as she hauled him upright.

Hooves thundered louder. The mob was almost on them.

Dinah struggled forward, back straining under Lawrence's weight as he limped beside her. Blood stained the left leg of his pants. He'd been hit in the thigh.

"One at a time," she panted.

Suddenly, Badger stepped between them and the riders, and he glanced over his shoulder. "Go on. I gotcha covered."

He flashed her a reassuring smile, and Dinah pressed on.

Shots rang out as Lawrence crawled onto the train. She climbed up behind him, and he stumbled through the doorway. Breathing hard, she followed him into the passenger car and rushed to a window.

Three riders remained.

Badger staggered, his free hand flying to his left side. Dinah gasped as panic jolted through her.

But he stayed on his feet. Hobbling toward the riders, he fired again. A horse flipped, flinging one of them through the air.

The second hit sent Badger reeling, and he collapsed in the grass.

She slammed her hands against the glass. "*No!*"

Lawrence dragged her away from the window, reminding her that they had to keep going.

I didn't even thank him.

A muffled shout came from her left, and Dinah looked out the other side of the car. A silver stallion skidded to a halt, and she stopped in her tracks, forcing Lawrence to do the same.

Frozen with shock, she stared as Joseph dropped Steel's reins and drew his left revolver. The rider charging him raised a rifle to his shoulder, and Joseph blasted him off his horse.

"What's he doin' here?" Lawrence growled. "I told him to stay outta this."

She burned with rage as Joseph holstered his Schofield and galloped toward the back of the train. He'd come for Sal. He must have.

And he's not gonna take him.

CHAPTER TWENTY-TWO

Two of the four remaining riders from Abilene raced toward Sal and the three guards escorting him to the back of the train. As Marcus galloped after them, the other two riders moved to cut him off.

Joseph wasn't here for any rescue. He just wanted to make sure Dinah got out of this alive. But that didn't mean he was going to sit back and let Marcus get himself killed on Sal's behalf.

Heart pounding, Joseph spurred Steel faster. He caught up to Marcus as the riders took aim, one pointing a revolver and the other raising a rifle.

Marcus roared and started shooting. They all fired a couple rounds before a bullet made contact. Joseph's third shot blew a hole in his target's chest, and he fell face-first into the dirt.

Marcus pushed a new cartridge into his revolver and fired across his body as he and the second rider flew past each other.

Joseph glanced over his shoulder. The man slid off his horse, and he sighed in relief.

Marcus didn't slow to reload. He holstered his Colt and yanked his Winchester from its scabbard.

"Marcus, wait!" Joseph shouted above the howling wind.

If he could just get him to stop and listen. To *think*.

A rifle cracked somewhere in front of them. One of the charging horses flipped and landed on its rider.

Marcus aimed his Winchester and fired. The last rider slumped over and dropped from the saddle.

Steel swerved around the fallen horse, and Joseph turned his gaze to Sal and the guards. One of them lay on the ground, gunned down by the riders from Abilene. That left only two protecting Sal.

Even in handcuffs, he carried himself with pride. Never in a hurry. Never bothered by the violence he was always at the center of—that he *caused*.

Joseph pulled back on the reins, and Morgan surged ahead of Steel. "Marcus!"

Still, Marcus ignored him.

The bigger of the two guards raised a rifle to his shoulder. The shorter man wearing a black derby hat turned and pointed his revolver at Sal's head.

"Stop right where you are, or Valentin dies!"

Marcus brought his horse to an abrupt halt.

Joseph drew alongside him, his lip curling as he noticed the badges on their coats. "Pinkertons," he muttered.

The railcar to the detectives' left grated open. Inside, Mercer held a gun to Donny's head. Lawrence panted as he leaned against the door he'd just pushed aside, his shoulders stooped with exhaustion.

Dinah stepped out of the darkness and stood between them.

Joseph's heart skipped a beat, but she didn't look happy to see him. Her long hair whipped across her glaring eyes. Smoke curled at her feet, her Colt in one hand and the other balled into a fist.

"Identify yourselves," the agent in the derby hat demanded.

"No need foah that," Lawrence told him with a grimace. "That's Marcus Crane and Joseph Gray."

Firelight flickered over the agent's hollow cheeks and sunken eyes, flames roaring and black fumes pouring from the nearby passenger car. "Mr. Crane, Mr. Gray, I'm Agent Cutler of the Pinkerton Detective Agency, and I have a warrant for your arrest. Get off your horses and lay down your weapons, or we will open fire."

"I got a better idea," Marcus scoffed. "You let Sal and Donny go, and we let you live."

We? Joseph shifted in his saddle. Donny could rot for all he cared, and when it came to choosing between Sal and Dinah, he'd pick her every time.

Cutler scowled and raised his shaven chin. "Look around. You're outnumbered."

"By who?" Marcus countered. "A girl and a crippled old man? I'll take those odds."

Joseph glanced at Dinah. *If everyone starts shootin', nobody wins.*

He couldn't lose her.

"Keep the prisoners," he suggested, "and we all walk away."

Marcus' head snapped toward him. "What?"

"Do you know our maxim, Mr. Gray?" Cutler responded with nauseating superiority. "'We never sleep.' Nor will we turn a blind eye."

"I advise ya to considuh his offuh, Agent Cutler," Lawrence warned. "There's been enough bloodshed."

Cutler pursed his lips, his gun still leveled at Sal's head. "My men are dead because of these degenerates. There's nothing to consider."

Marcus looked at Joseph and muttered, "Follow my lead."

He dismounted, put his rifle on the ground, and stepped forward.

"Your revolver," Cutler prompted.

Marcus drew his Colt and tossed it behind him.

Joseph wasn't sure what Marcus planned to do, but he knew he'd never let them take him alive. He sighed and swung down from the saddle. Dropped his Schofields in the grass and went to stand beside Marcus.

His heart pounded, his shirt clinging to his skin. Every sense heightened. Every inch of him tensed. His finger twitched, but he had no trigger to pull.

Marcus gave him a grateful glance, his dark brows drawing together and his chin jutting as if to say, "We got this, brother."

Joseph drew a deep breath and nodded.

They'd always stuck together no matter what. Still, every man's loyalty had its limits, and Joseph had certainly tested his. He'd expected coldness, maybe even hatred. But Marcus was willing to stand with him—trusted him to have his back. It meant everything to him.

"Jennings, Mercer, cuff them," Cutler ordered.

Jennings lowered his rifle and strode toward them. Joseph didn't like the tight-lipped smile that creased Donny's round cheeks as Mercer jumped down from the railcar. Jennings slung his rifle across his back, took two pairs of handcuffs from his belt, and tossed one to Mercer.

Marcus kept still, holding out his hands in a gesture of surrender. Joseph did the same as Mercer marched toward him. His gaze drifted to Donny and Dinah, his chest clenching tighter.

He's too close to her.

Jennings went to clamp the irons on Marcus, the open cuffs coming up under his wrists. Marcus' fingers curled.

Here we go.

Marcus swung his arms down and knocked the cuffs out of Jennings' hands. Mercer dropped his and drew his revolver. As Mercer spun toward Marcus, Joseph lunged and tackled him to the ground. He didn't give him a chance to fight back, raining blows on Mercer's face till he knocked him out cold.

"That's for Charlie," Joseph growled.

Jennings fell beside him, gurgling as blood spurted from his neck. Marcus stood over him with a dripping knife.

Breathing hard, Joseph rose with bleeding knuckles and saw Sal strangling Cutler with his own chains. His wildly searching gaze found Dinah pinned in the grass, Donny fighting to pry her gun from her two-handed grip.

Joseph charged in a blind rage. Seeing nothing else. Hearing nothing but his hammering heart.

Lawrence got to them first. Joseph skidded to a stop as the man hunter came up behind Donny and grabbed a fistful of his hair. Without a moment's hesitation, Lawrence yanked back his head and slit his throat. Blood sprayed onto Dinah's face, and she cried out as she shielded it with her arms. Lawrence threw Donny aside, sheathed his knife, and reached down to help her up.

"Joseph!" Marcus warned.

He wheeled around. Stared down the barrel of the gun Sal aimed at him. *Bang!*

Marcus slammed into him. Joseph hit the ground hard, pain jolting through his ribs and shoulder. Dazed, he pushed himself upright as shots rang out behind him.

Sal ducked and ran. He grabbed Morgan's reins, sprang into the saddle, and whipped his hide.

As he galloped away, Marcus sat up and yelled, "Get back here you piece of—*agh.*"

He growled and gripped his right arm. Joseph scrambled to his feet and hurried over to him.

"Did he hit ya?" he asked, crouching in front of him.

"Yeah." Marcus lifted his hand from his bicep and looked down. Blood seeped from a hole in his coat sleeve. "Think it went clean through."

"Get that wrapped up," Joseph told him. "Don't wantcha bleedin' out on me."

He stood and straightened his hat, and Marcus' brow furrowed.

"Where do ya think you're goin'?"

"To finish this."

"Not without me you ain't," Marcus argued.

Joseph raised his eyes to Dinah's. Her chest heaved as she stared at him, her face smeared with blood. She'd never be safe, never know peace—not till Sal was dealt with.

His beating heart felt like it would burst, desperate to confess the secret he'd buried so deep. The truth he'd finally accepted. But there was a chance he wouldn't survive. He couldn't do that to her.

I'll tell her when I get back.

Joseph turned from her and went to retrieve his revolvers.

Marcus got to his feet and stormed after him. "Joseph, don't go and do somethin' stupid."

"This has gone on long enough, Marcus." Joseph shoved both Schofields into his holsters. "It ends tonight."

Steel danced sideways as he climbed into the saddle.

"Joseph—" Marcus said again.

But Joseph spurred the stallion's sides and galloped off into the night.

He rode hard and fast with a full moon lighting his path, racing south along the river as he chased after a distant shadow. Morgan's hooves thundered up ahead, just loud enough to rise above the howling in Joseph's ears. The wind drove tears from his eyes, his coat whipping behind him and railroad tracks flying by on his right.

Fire raged in his heart.

Son, Sal had called him. *Family.*

And then he'd pointed a gun at him. Had almost killed Marcus in his attempt to get rid of him.

It was all a lie.

"You can't run forever!" Joseph yelled.

He didn't know if Sal heard him, but he showed no signs of slowing.

On and on they went, charging up high hills and plunging down their steep sides. Joseph never even tried taking a shot at him. He wasn't letting him off that easy.

Sal veered west, and Joseph did the same. Steel breathed hard, his silver neck lathering and hooves pounding.

He can't keep this up much longer. Joseph gritted his teeth and willed the stallion to push on a little farther. *Morgan'll hit his limit. Probably already has.*

Sal headed for a small soddy on a stretch of moonlit plain.

231

Joseph's brow furrowed. *What's he doin'?*

When he reached the house, Sal swung down from the saddle as Morgan skidded to a halt.

Joseph hoped it was abandoned. Sure looked to be. Half the roof had either blown off or caved in, and the front door had fallen off its hinges.

He reined in Steel not far from Sal, who stood still and silent. Waiting.

His chest tightened. Steel tossed his head and restlessly shifted.

Mustering his courage, Joseph dismounted. His boots thudded on the hard ground. He drew a deep breath, his heart slamming against his ribs as he patted the stallion's sweaty neck. Steel's big black eye looked at him, and a lump stuck in Joseph's throat.

"It's been a hell of a ride, partner. Thank you."

He turned away and walked toward Sal. Thunder rolled in the distance, strange shadows crawling over the ground as clouds passed in front of the moon. Sal's coat stirred in the wind, his dark hair blowing across his sober face.

Did he fear death? Did he feel anything at all?

Joseph clenched his jaw, spurs clinking and boots crunching through the grass. He'd spent his whole life running from the law. Dodging the noose. Never realizing that his greatest enemy had been right beside him all along. Had raised him. Had taught him everything he knew and shaped his view of the world. Of himself.

When Joseph stopped, he'd cut the distance between them in half.

Sal never moved. Never even blinked.

"I didn't want it to come to this," Joseph said.

"Yes, you did," Sal responded with a slow nod. "You chose this the moment you betrayed me."

Joseph's blood boiled. "You could've sent anyone to kill Dinah. It wasn't about gettin' rid of her. It was about keepin' me in line."

Sal shook his head in disappointment. "You had so much potential, and one bad day ruined you. One silly little girl."

Joseph's mouth went dry. He swallowed and squared his shoulders. "That's the difference between you and me. I've got a conscience."

Sal's thick brows furrowed, a dangerous flicker in his heavy-lidded eyes. "I told Dinah what you did. That you're the one who killed her friend."

Joseph's heart plummeted.

Sal tilted back his head and grinned. "You should've seen the look on her face."

Joseph's hopes shattered. Every future he'd imagined with her went up in flames.

That explained how she'd acted back at the train—when he'd found her and Lawrence on the road outside Salina. The hatred in her eyes. The heartbreak.

"She will never forgive you," Sal gloated. "And you gave up everything for her."

Fury crashed over him, sweeping aside his fear. Joseph grasped his revolver. "Then I guess I've got nothin' left to lose."

Sal sneered. "You can't beat me."

His hand moved, and Joseph drew. His finger froze over the trigger as Sal threw away Cutler's gun.

"Now it's fair."

Joseph gritted his teeth. He couldn't kill him like this, no matter how badly he wanted to.

"Pick it up," he demanded.

Sal tossed his coat onto the ground.

"Pick it up!"

Sal rolled up his sleeves, and Joseph huffed. He shoved his Schofield back into his holster, shrugged off his coat, and unbuckled his gun belt.

"You ain't so invincible as you think. Jesse Hance proved that."

Sal scowled and stalked toward him. "Jesse Hance is dead, and when we're finished here, his daughter will join him."

A savage instinct overcame him. Unhinged him.

Joseph roared and charged.

Sal planted his feet and crouched like a cougar. Joseph lunged to take him to the ground, but his arms closed around empty air as Sal ducked low. His shoulder rammed into Joseph's gut. Knocked the breath from his lungs and drove him backward. His ribs jarred as he hit the ground, his hat flipping off his head.

Sal raised his fist.

Thunk!

The impact of his punch rippled through Joseph's face. But he felt no pain. Not until Sal's bare knuckles bashed the bridge of his nose.

Joseph's eyes watered, blurring his vision as he reached up and grabbed Sal's vest with both hands. Sal landed another blow as they struggled. Then another.

Finally, Joseph wrestled him onto his back. He tasted blood, and a vengeful impulse surged in him. All those times he'd wished he could fight back, biting his tongue as Sal lectured and belittled him. Suffering his humiliations in silence.

My turn.

The anger he'd muzzled, the back talk he'd swallowed, the guilt he carried—Joseph unleashed it all. He pounded Sal's face with bleeding knuckles, reveling in every sting. Every shock that jolted up his arm.

Sal batted his arm aside. Yanked him down and banged their foreheads together.

When Joseph came to, he was lying on his stomach. A flash of lightning blinded him. Thunder rattled his throbbing head as he pushed himself up onto his hands and knees.

Sal had already gotten to his feet, and he drove the toe of his boot into Joseph's ribs. He landed on his side, groaning as his aching fingers dug into the dirt.

Get up.

He dragged his knees under him, and Sal kicked him again—this time in the jaw. Joseph bit his tongue and grimaced. He spat blood as Sal circled him.

There was a black stain under Sal's broken nose. His upper lip had been cut open, blood dripping into his mouth and trickling into his beard.

Joseph rose on trembling legs. *I've gotta finish him.*

Sal marched toward him, and Joseph rushed to meet him. As they grappled, he grabbed a handful of Sal's shirt and clawed at his vest, battling for control. Sal gave him a violent push, catching him off guard.

He stumbled backward, and Sal swung at him. Joseph stopped his punch with his hand. Countered with a right hook that knocked Sal's head sideways with a fresh spatter of blood.

Joseph's teeth smacked together as Sal brought his fist up under his jaw. He staggered. Sal snatched a fistful of his hair and thrust his fist into his gut. Two—three—four times. Each strike forcing Joseph another step back.

His heel hit something hard, and it didn't give way. Panic jolted through him as he lost his balance. Sal shoved both palms against his chest, and Joseph toppled over an unseen edge.

He reached out for the only thing that could stop his fall, but Sal just watched. His black eyes wild and triumphant.

Too late. The words echoed in Joseph's mind, in those last terrifying moments before darkness swallowed him. *Too late.*

CHAPTER TWENTY-THREE

"**W**here are you?" Dinah murmured, peering into the darkness with watering eyes.

After riding back to Salina and bringing help for Lawrence, she'd set out in immediate pursuit of Joseph and Sal, despite Marshal Tupper's insistence that she wait. There was no time for that. She'd already lost precious minutes.

Thunder boomed behind her, a storm coming from the north as Cardinal flew down the dusty road.

"That's all I need," Dinah muttered.

Sal had headed southwest when he fled, but she couldn't know if he'd changed direction. How far he'd gone. She had no trail to follow, nothing to go on, but she did possess a certain intuition. A strange ability to anticipate, to predict, and that instinct screamed that something awful had happened in her absence. Something she could've prevented.

Even as she hated Joseph for what he'd done to Ophelia, Dinah's worry for him ate her alive. The thought of losing him made her lungs seize up. Tied her insides in knots and crushed her heart in an unrelenting fist.

Please, Lord, don't take him from me. I know he ain't good, but he's all I've got.

Dinah pressed on without rest or pause, desperate to find them. Her hope dwindling with every agonizing minute. Each second an eternity.

She spotted a soddy up ahead, not far off the road. It looked abandoned, but…

A horse stood outside.

Dinah slowed Cardinal to a walk and squinted, her heart beating faster. Was that Marcus' horse?

A shadow rose and strode toward the horse.

She stopped Cardinal and stared. She'd know that walk anywhere. That coat.

Sal mounted and wheeled the horse toward the road.

Frantic fury surged in her. She couldn't let him out of her sight.

"Yah!" Dinah cried.

Cardinal sprang forward, racing past the soddy and chasing after Sal as he galloped south into the gathering fog.

⸻

She didn't have a clue where she was. Sal had left the road some time ago, and she'd had no choice but to follow. With the darkness and a dense gray shroud covering the hills, it was difficult to see much of anything.

Every time he slowed, she'd close in on him, and he'd speed up again. Staying just beyond her reach but never getting too far ahead. His torturous game of cat and mouse had turned her crippling fear into reckless rage.

How long had she been after him? Hours? Why run from her? Why wouldn't he *stop?*

"Face me, you coward!" Dinah screamed.

She dropped the reins, yanked her rifle from its scabbard, and raised it to her shoulder. She didn't care if she hit the horse—not anymore.

Three times she fired. Three times she missed.

Dinah growled in frustration. He was almost a hundred yards off. She couldn't get a good shot.

A massive bluff emerged from the curtain of fog, towering above the river valley.

Sal headed straight for it. Had he finally tired of running? Or was Marcus' horse on the verge of collapse?

Cardinal's labored breathing worried her. She'd never pushed him this hard. But she couldn't stop. Couldn't let Sal get away. Not this time.

Sal charged up the northern slope, and Dinah followed, winding around the bluff's steep sides. Trees bowed over her, bending and groaning like mourners on the hill, their forked branches waving like flailing arms. The wind howled louder as she climbed, fierce and unabating.

When the ground leveled out at the crown of the heights, Cardinal came to an abrupt stop, his head hung low and nostrils flaring. Dinah dismounted and patted his lathered neck with a pang of guilt. Sal had vanished, and she found herself engulfed in a gray haze.

Where'd he go?

Dinah drew her Colt with a shaking hand, brutal gusts buffeting her as she ventured forward. Everything looked the same. Everywhere she turned, nothing. Oblivion so thick the moon couldn't pierce it. Sweat beaded on her temples.

He's here. I know he is. Waiting to pounce.

"Show yourself!" Dinah cried, her frenzied gaze searching the labyrinth swirling around her.

A lone tree loomed ahead, tall and sprawling with limbs spread wide like welcoming arms. She made her way toward it, her skirt beating her legs and her sleeves slapping her chilled arms.

A sudden rush stole her hat from her head. Dinah snatched at it, but it flew beyond her reach. Helpless tears sprang to her eyes as it disappeared. Her empty fist fell to her side, and she bent over with a stifled sob.

Why'd she gone after him alone? Why didn't she wait?

She'd thought Joseph would be here. Why wasn't he? Had Sal thrown him off his trail? Or had something worse happened?

"To the last I grapple with thee," rumbled a voice like death.

Dinah gasped and wheeled around. Her wide eyes darted to and fro, but she couldn't find him.

"From hell's heart I stab at thee. For hate's sake I spit my last breath at thee."

"Where is he?" she demanded, even as she dreaded his answer. "Where's Joseph?"

Silence.

"*Where is he?*"

Thunder crashed as a hand clamped down on her shoulder. Before she could turn, a second hand seized a fistful of her hair and slammed her head against the tree.

Pain split her skull. Dinah staggered, seeing two of everything.

Sal pushed her back against the trunk, driving the breath from her lungs. Despite her best efforts, he wrestled the revolver from her weakened grasp and threw it away.

Dinah's bare knuckles collided with his bloody cheek. The shock rippled up her arm.

Sal grabbed her jaw and forced her pounding head against the bark. Dinah whimpered and squirmed, her neck twisted at an agonizing angle. But he gave her no reprieve.

Wildly, she swung at his face and shoved at his shoulders. Sal caught her wrist, crushing it in his ruthless grip as he leaned in close.

My knife. Maybe she could reach it.

"Joseph betrayed me because of your lies—your interference," he growled.

Dinah's blood ran cold as she stared at his bruised and swollen face. His crooked nose and blackened eyes.

Sal dug his fingers into her skin. "I don't suffer traitors."

Dinah was overcome by a sudden childlike urge to hide herself away and cover her ears. But there was nowhere to run. No escape from his accusing gaze.

"I killed him," he revealed with diabolic relish. "He's dead because of you."

Tears leaked from her eyes, her cheeks pinched between his fingers. She realized now that it was possible to die and still draw breath. For her body to walk the earth as her soul lay in the grave.

"Your God has forsaken you," Sal said, his vampiric eyes drinking in her grief. "Taken everything from you."

"Not yet."

Dinah drew her knife and thrust the blade into his side. He sprang back with a hiss and looked down at the gushing wound. Vengeful satisfaction surged in her as she stepped away from the tree.

Pain stabbed her temples, and she swayed.

"I should've killed you that night," Sal snarled. "I should've killed you every night since."

Dinah burned with a feeling beyond rage, beyond hatred. "If I go, I'm takin' you with me."

She raised the dripping blade in her white-knuckled hand as they began to circle each other. Sal wasn't as tall as Joseph, but to her he was Goliath. Broad-shouldered and strong and an experienced fighter. She didn't stand a chance, not without a weapon that could even the odds.

Risking a glance at her revolver, she inched toward it.

Sal followed her gaze. Eyes narrowing, he charged like an angry bull.

Dinah dropped the knife and dove for the Colt. Hit the ground and grimaced as she stretched her arm to its limit. Her fingers grazed the grip and—

Sal grabbed her leg.

Dinah cried out, clawing at the dirt as she slid backward through the grass. She kicked up her other leg and heard his teeth clack. She flipped onto her back, and Sal pounced.

His hands closed around her throat.

Pinned under him, Dinah gasped for air that wouldn't come. She pried at his fingers, but that made them squeeze even tighter as he bared his teeth, his savage eyes boring into hers. His emotionless mask fractured, exposing his true face. Manic and deranged and the most terrifying sight she'd ever beheld.

Dinah thrashed and struggled, her vision dimming and her lungs on the verge of bursting. She raked her nails down his cheeks, but Sal didn't let go.

All fell silent save the frantic beating of her heart.

She fumbled for the badge on her belt and pulled it free. In a last, desperate effort, she plunged one of the star's five points into Sal's neck and gouged.

Blood spurted when she ripped out the badge, his eyes bulging as his hand flew to the wound.

Dinah rolled onto her stomach and started crawling. She gulped air into her burning lungs, coughing and wheezing as her elbows dug into the dirt. Her trembling fingers found her Colt again, and she scrambled to her feet. Heart pounding, she gripped it with both hands and spun to face him.

Sal was on his knees, his blood-soaked hand still pressed to the side of his neck. His eyes wandered, dull and unfocused.

Then they met hers. Something mad and monstrous kindled in their black depths, and he planted one foot in front of him.

Dinah pulled the trigger. When the flash of the muzzle faded, there was a bleeding hole in his gut.

That's for Ophelia.

Sal swayed, and his raised leg buckled. She cocked the hammer and fired into his chest.

That's for my father.

Fresh tears spilled down her cheeks as he drew a rattling breath.

And this is for Joseph.

She blasted a third hole straight through his heart.

Blood trickled from Sal's mouth as he sat on his knees. He stared at her with a strange look—a flicker of remembrance, of longing. It unnerved her.

What if I can't kill him?

Outrageous as the thought was, that didn't stop it from crossing her mind.

Sal let out a long exhale, his eyes glazing over as his head bowed. His hand dropped to his side, and he fell facedown in the grass.

He's gone.

Dinah blew a shuddering breath. She couldn't believe it.

Slowly, she sank to the ground. Slipped her fingers under her neckerchief and touched her aching throat. She could still feel his fingers digging into her flesh, crushing the life out of her.

A raindrop splashed onto the tip of her nose. More tapped on her shoulders and pattered on the rocks. The storm had finally caught up with her.

Ten years she'd waited for this moment. Always, he'd haunted her thoughts, driving every action and rotting her from the inside out like some incurable disease.

As the fire in her blood dwindled, Dinah found herself empty. Numb. Whatever she'd expected, it wasn't this. She looked down at the Colt in her hand, feeling everything and nothing all at once.

"I did it, Dad."

***

A bitter wind blasted through the valley, buffeting her steps as she led Cardinal through the tall grass. Her unpinned hair hung heavy, her clothes stuck to her skin and rain blowing against her face.

Dinah paused and looked back. A flash of lightning outlined the bluff's towering silhouette against a purple sky.

She turned away and trudged on. Tears stung her eyes as they searched the suffocating darkness. *Joseph's body—he's out here somewhere. In the wet and the cold.*

She couldn't bear the thought. *I should've gone with him.*

An anguished sob escaped her burning throat. She'd been so furious with him. She still was, but that didn't change the fact that she'd give anything to get him back. To have him here with her.

"Dinah."

She stopped dead in her tracks. Had she imagined it?

Again, his voice came to her on the wind. *"Dinah."*

She dropped the reins and spun to her left. "Joseph?"

His call struck a match in her. Conjured her memory of a fleeting but unforgettable meeting. Of a near-fatal reunion amid swirling sand.

I always find you in the storm.

Heart racing, Dinah trekked west across rough, uneven terrain, tripping over rocks and tearing her skirt from thorny clutches.

"Joseph!" she cried hoarsely, arms swinging as she stumbled along.

She shivered, drenched from head to toe and stiff with cold.

"Joseph!" she wailed, her strangled voice drowning in the downpour.

She called for him again and again, aimlessly wandering as the storm raged on. But he didn't answer.

"Where are you?" she croaked.

The aching of her heart became so excruciating that it crippled her.

Dinah fell to her knees. A mournful wind howled, pain drumming against her skull as her nails dug into the mud. He wasn't there. Just a figment of her desperate imagination.

How could a righteous God be so cruel? Was it her lot in life to suffer? To be alone?

Lightning forked across a hopeless horizon, and Dinah screamed at the sky, hating everyone and everything. Herself, most of all.

CHAPTER TWENTY-FOUR

Joseph's eyes opened, and pain knifed through his head. He groaned and blinked, his blurred vision slowly coming into focus. Dark clouds drifted across a black circle. An icy rain was falling, splashing onto his face and sliding down his cheeks.

Where am I?

He sat up, and a wave of nausea rolled over him. Grimacing, Joseph massaged his throbbing forehead, fighting back the bile that rose in his throat.

Thunder rumbled, and he craned his neck to squint at stones laid upon stones, arranged in curving rows that reached thirty feet high.

A well.

It all came back to him in a dizzying rush. The gunfight at the train. Chasing Sal. Falling into darkness.

"Dinah," he breathed.

He had to get to her before Sal did.

Joseph shifted onto his hands and knees, racked with too many aches and pains to count. Gritting his teeth, he stood and caught himself against the rocks.

Had he broken any bones? He wasn't sure, but it didn't matter. Didn't change what he had to do.

Joseph took a breath of damp air and doubled over. He clutched his ribs, stones poking into his back.

Shoulda shot him.

His pride had stopped him from pulling the trigger—not honor or decency. It was about proving himself a man.

Wincing, Joseph stepped forward and reached up, sliding his fingers along the rocks' wet edges. Would they be too slick? He wouldn't know till he tried.

When he found a good grip, he pushed off the ground and started climbing.

Progress was difficult, his muscles tensed and straining. His hands blindly searching in the blackness. A fierce wind howled overhead as he fought his way up, inching toward the opening.

He'd gotten halfway when his foot slipped.

Panic jolted through him. Time slowed to a crawl as he clawed at empty air.

Thunder clapped when he hit the ground.

Joseph stared at the sky in silent terror. He couldn't breathe. His heart pounded, his fingers digging into the mud.

Finally, he sucked a gulp of air into his lungs. Anger burned in him as he coughed, each one stabbing his sides. Joseph was sure that somewhere up there God was laughing at him.

He sat up and hissed a bitter curse through his teeth.

I can do this. I have to do this.

Bracing himself against the rocks, he got to his feet, swaying as he considered the wall a second time. It loomed over him, daring him to try. Mocking him.

Joseph clenched his stiff jaw and limped forward to scale the wall again.

He couldn't ignore the pain, so he used it to fuel him, refusing to rest. Focusing only on the next step. The next rugged edge.

Till he reached the spot where he'd fallen.

Joseph froze. He looked down. His heart beat faster, his legs shaking as he clung to the slippery rocks.

What if I fall again? What if it kills me this time?

A stone came loose.

Suddenly, he was holding onto nothing. He cried out, arms flailing as he plunged to another hard landing.

Crack!

Searing pain pierced his ribs, hot as a brand straight out of the fire.

This is it. I'm done for.

He wouldn't get out of this well. He wouldn't save Dinah. He was going to die down here, alone in the dark, his only legacy the bounty on his head.

Part of him wished the fall had killed him. It would've been quicker. Easier.

He didn't want time to think, to dwell on his many mistakes. He'd wasted his life. Rejected every offer of help. Every chance to get out.

He'd always assumed he'd kick the bucket with his boots on. Go out in a blaze of glory.

Not like this.

Joseph lay there a long while, fearing that his broken rib would puncture a lung. Or worse—that he wouldn't be able to move if he tried. He flinched at each inhale, cringed with every exhale.

Lightning flashed behind his shut lids, rain pelting his beaten face and soaking his clothes. The cold numbed his bruised hands, the walls closing in.

"*Salvation's never more than a prayer away,*" Dinah had said.

Joseph's heart hardened. His mother, his father—they'd both told him that God would never leave him or forsake him. But when the North invaded, forced him from his home and tore his family apart, where was God?

Silent. Absent.

He always had been, and he always would be.

———— • ————

Joseph opens his eyes and finds himself gazing at a drooping, shadowy canopy.

When had he fallen asleep?

A smell like a burnt match makes him wrinkle his nose and sit up. He's in the Lowcountry, but he can't remember how he got here.

Doesn't matter. He hasn't seen it since he was a kid, and he's missed it.

A thick layer of fog hangs over still black waters, and Joseph realizes that he's the only passenger in a small boat. A dark-skinned man in colorful clothes stands at the front and rows, the paddle dipping in and out with scarcely a sound, scarcely a ripple. A lantern burns between them with a sickly yellow glow, doing little to fend off the encroaching gloom. Its warmth smothered by the chill in the air.

Joseph shivers and rubs his arms. "Hey, I think we should head back to shore. I can't see a thing in this fog."

The stranger keeps rowing.

"Hey, didja hear me?" he calls again. "Turn this boat around."

"There's no goin' back once you've made the crossin'."

Joseph's mouth drops open. He knows that voice.

"Jeremiah?"

Thoughtfully, he tilts his head. "Jeremiah... Yes, that was my name, a long time ago. I'd almost forgotten."

"But—" Joseph stops and shakes his head. "You can't be here. You're dead."

"So are you."

His blood goes cold.

"So are they," Jeremiah adds, gesturing at their surroundings.

Boats float beside them. Ahead of them. Behind them. All carrying lanterns and grieving passengers.

Many sit silent, their stares blank and hopeless. Others moan and wail.

Joseph panics and grabs the sides of the boat. "Wait. I'm not ready."

"We don't get to choose our time. Those young-uns—they didn't know they would catch the fevuh. That man ovuh there—he nevuh saw that wagon comin'."

"Where're you takin' me?" Joseph demands. "Where're we goin'?"

"The place of separation," Jeremiah answers. He stops rowing and frowns at him. "Hellfire and torment."

Joseph scrambles to his feet. "I don't wanna go there. I can't go there. Jeremiah, please!"

"I'm sorry, son," he says with grim resignation.

"What can I do? How do I stop this from happening?"

"You can't, Joseph. It's too late."

Desperate, he turns to jump overboard but stops short.

Water lilies float on the surface, their closed flowers dirty and shriveled. Red droplets plop onto their petals and drip onto their heart-shaped pads.

His brow furrows, and he looks up, watching the drops fall from overhanging trees like tears of blood. One by one, the stained flowers sink into murky depths.

Where'd they go?

Joseph crouches and peers over the side of the boat. His eyes search in vain as Jeremiah rows between towering cypress trees. They jut out of the river like the bones of an ancient creature. The ones he'd heard rumors about. What were they called again?

Finally, he sees something. A glow far below. Faint at first but getting brighter.

A lily breaks the surface of the water with unfurling petals white as snow.

Joseph stares, admiring the flower's flickering light—pulsing like a heartbeat. He tries to touch the petals but can't quite reach. He leans farther out of the boat. Stretches his arm and feels a gentle warmth.

Joseph can't bring himself to look away. The lily calls to him, singing softly.

Splash!

A huge set of jaws bursts from the water and clamps down on his arm. Yanks him out of the boat and pulls him under.

The light goes out.

He glimpses a reptilian eye and a flash of teeth. Blood gushes from his arm. The monster has him in a death roll, and no matter how hard he pries at its scaly mouth, he can't force it open.

He can't even scream, holding his breath as his lungs burn and his arm's ripped to shreds. The gator's pale and scarred, but he can't fight it. He's not strong enough.

The beast drags him deeper and deeper till all he can see is a sea of red. A world on fire.

Terror seizes him. He's nearing hell.

In his desperation, Joseph lets go of his pride and reaches skyward.

Save me.

A pierced hand parts the veil of shadows and grasps his. The beast releases him, and he rises toward the light.

———•◆———

Joseph sat up with a gasp. Drenched and trembling, he looked down at his right hand, expecting to see another holding it.

It was a dream, he realized, his left arm intact and free of toothmarks.

A glance at his surroundings reminded him where he was. The storm had passed, and the rain had stopped, leaving him sitting in several inches of water.

I'm not dead.

Relief flooded through him. He never would've imagined that he'd be so glad to find himself trapped at the bottom of a well.

Joseph got on his knees, on his face, thanking God for another chance he didn't deserve. Begging for forgiveness.

Don't leave me. Don't ever leave.

A peace that defied description settled on him. Joseph raised his eyes to the brightening sky, his cheeks wet with tears. A still, small voice murmured words he'd learned long ago:

Fear not, for I am with you. Be not dismayed, for I am your God. I will strengthen you. I will help you. I will uphold you with my righteous right hand.

Dragging his legs through the water and the mud, Joseph crawled to the wall. Pain shot through his ribs as he reached up to grab hold of the rocks, and he grimaced. It seemed impossible.

Fear not. I will help you.

Joseph drew a ragged breath. Mustered his courage and struggled to his feet.

His clothes weighed him down as he started climbing, his dripping hair hanging over his eyes. He fought his way upward, shutting out every doubting thought.

It hurt to breathe, to move. His muscles screamed in protest. But he kept going. Kept trusting.

Almost there. Just a little bit more.

His boot slipped, and his heart skipped a beat.

Joseph caught himself, teeth clenching as his aching fingers clung to the rocks. He held on with everything he had, resisting the temptation to look down.

"*Look up,*" urged his mother's gentle voice.

And he did.

Once he'd found his footing again, Joseph pressed on, keeping his eyes fixed on his destination. Finally, he reached up and over the edge, first with one hand, then with the other.

This is it.

He pushed off with both feet, using his last ounce of strength to haul himself out of the well. Joseph swung one leg over the wall. The rest of him followed, and he collapsed in the grass.

As he sat there leaning on the rocks, a cool breeze blew against his face. He closed his eyes, breathing in the fresh air. Hardly believing that he'd made it.

A bright light burned behind his lids, and when he opened them, Joseph saw the sun peeking over the hills. Blazing against a heavenly canvas painted in vivid strokes of pink, purple, and blue. Bathing billowing clouds in a golden glow.

He'd come very close to never seeing another sunrise, and its splendor gripped his heart. Moved him more than any had before.

A soft whicker greeted him, and Joseph glanced over his shoulder in surprise. Steel stood watching him, his ears flicked forward and his tail swishing.

He shook his head in amazement. "You're some horse, y'know that?"

Steel snorted and came over to him. Bracing his elbows on top of the well, Joseph pushed himself upright, his weary legs barely holding his weight. His face hurt when he smiled, and he winced as he scrubbed the stallion's forehead.

He didn't think he could get in the saddle, let alone ride.

I've gotta find Dinah. But how?

Steel twisted his neck around and neighed. Another horse answered.

Peering around him, Joseph spotted a lone rider galloping toward him—a man on a black horse.

His heart raced. Had Sal come back to finish him off?

Joseph stumbled toward his gun belt, weaving like a drunkard. His ribs twinged with every step, his vision blinking in and out.

By the time he reached his revolvers, the rider was there in front of him.

Joseph's eyes widened, his throat so dry it was difficult to speak. "Marcus?"

"Joseph," he panted, sounding both worried and relieved. "What happened?"

———•—————

Joseph gritted his teeth, fighting to stay upright as Marcus helped him into the abandoned soddy. The one-room house had been emptied of furniture and belongings.

"Where'd you find Morgan?"

"Couple miles north of ya," Marcus said. "Almost ran himself to death. Had to ditch the nag I took from the train."

Joseph withdrew his arm from Marcus' shoulders and grimaced as he sank to the dirt floor. Slumping against the wall, he set aside his hat and gun belt, and Marcus dropped his coat and canteen onto his lap. Joseph pulled out the cork and took a long drink, his weary gaze following Marcus to the eastern window.

"Sal wouldn't've gone on foot," Marcus muttered, "not by choice. Somethin' musta happened."

Joseph lowered the canteen and wiped his mouth with the back of his hand. "He can't've got far. We've gotta find him before—"

"We?" Marcus cut in, turning from the sunlit window. "You ain't in no shape to face him."

"I can still pull a trigger," Joseph growled.

Marcus sighed and shook his head. "Let him go, Joseph."

"Let him go?" Pain stabbed his ribs, and he winced. "This ain't over. Not till he's dead."

"There'll be another time. This ain't it."

"He's gonna kill Dinah if—"

"I don't wanna hear that name again," Marcus snapped, pointing a threatening finger. "None of this woulda happened if it weren't for her."

Joseph's eyes narrowed. "If it weren't for *Sal.*"

"You had no problem with Sal till she came along and gotcha wrapped around her finger."

"No," Joseph said. "For the first time, I'm thinkin' for myself. And he tried to kill me for it."

"You betrayed us," Marcus shot back. "You blew Tony's brains out. What'dja expect him to do?"

Guilt stung him, but Joseph wasn't giving up. There had to be some way to get through to him. "Sal left you for dead, Marcus. He never cared about us. He was usin' us."

Marcus paced with restless anger. "Nobody uses me."

"What about Cimarron?" Joseph challenged.

Marcus rounded on him. "Mollie thought she could control me. I showed her, didn't I?"

"Who put that in your head? Huh?" Joseph prompted. "Sal didn't want you leavin'."

Marcus stormed back and forth, his hands balled into fists and a blood-stained strip of fabric tied around his coat sleeve. He stopped and stared out the window, his dark eyes miles away.

"Ain't nothin' left to leave now," he grumbled. "The gang's finished."

Joseph laid his coat and canteen on the floor and shifted, but he couldn't get comfortable. Couldn't think of a single thing to say. If he'd realized sooner, seen Sal for what he really was—if he'd talked to the others, maybe he could've convinced some of them to leave with him. Maybe they'd still be alive.

"I better get goin', 'fore the law shows up." Marcus took a breath and turned to him. "Are you comin' or are you stayin'?"

Joseph's heart sank. "I can't leave, Marcus. Not till I know Dinah's safe."

Marcus frowned. "Then… I guess we're goin' our separate ways. How many years has it been? Twenty?"

"Twenty-one," Joseph answered glumly.

They'd grown up together. Done everything together. Marcus was more his brother than the ones he'd left behind in Carolina. He couldn't imagine never seeing him. Not knowing where he was or how he was doing.

"Where're you gonna go?" he asked.

Marcus shrugged and met his gaze. "A long ways from here. It's time I disappear for a while."

Marcus strode past him, and Joseph struggled to his feet. Bracing his hand against the wall, he inched forward till he reached the door. A cool gust caught Marcus' coattails as he walked to his horse, boots crunching and spurs clinking.

I should say somethin'. But what?

He couldn't say goodbye.

Marcus' steps slowed. He stopped and faced him. "There's somethin' different about ya. Somethin' I can't quite figure."

Joseph sighed and leaned against the doorframe. "Let's just say I had the fear of God put into me."

"Huh," Marcus grunted. "Who woulda thought?"

He climbed into the saddle and took up the reins. "Till next time, Joseph."

Joseph nodded, his heart heavy as Marcus wheeled Morgan around and galloped toward the western horizon.

⸻

The ride back to Salina was the worst Joseph had ever endured. Never had five miles seemed such an impossible journey. He couldn't go faster than a walk. Holding himself upright in the saddle was enough of a chore.

He checked his pocket watch for the hundredth time. Seven thirty.

It'd only been an hour since he left the soddy. His insides twisted in knots, his chest clenching so tight it ached. He had a plan, but he feared what he'd find out. That he was already too late.

If Sal had failed or if he hadn't yet reached her, what would he say? *Sorry I've lied to you since the day we met?*

Would Dinah believe that he hadn't meant to kill her friend? Would she care?

All these years, she'd blamed Sal. Hated him. Wanted him dead.

Whatever she thinks of me, whatever she decides—I can't change that. All I can do is tell her the truth, and I will. Not just about her friend.

All of it.

CHAPTER TWENTY-FIVE

Something tickled her arm.

Flinching, Dinah opened her eyes and blinked at the offending blade of grass. Squinted at sunlight peeking through rustling leaves.

The night had passed in feverish misery. She remembered collapsing in the rain. Being lifted out of the mud. But everything after was a blur.

Her throat hurt when she swallowed.

Black eyes and bared teeth flashed in her mind's eye. Her lungs burning as Sal's hands crushed the life out of her.

Dinah sucked in a breath, her fingers flying to her neck.

"Welcome back," said a familiar voice.

She sat up so fast her head spun. The colorful blanket covering her fell to her waist, pangs of panic jolting through her chest as she stared at the Indian sitting in the shade of the trees.

He held up his hands. "Don't worry, I'm not gonna hurt you. My name is Enyeto. I'm a friend of Joseph's."

"I remember you," Dinah growled as she trembled, her temples throbbing with a dull pain. "What're you doing here?"

"Joseph once risked his life for mine. To give me a second chance. I could do no less for him," Enyeto answered with solemn conviction.

Her heart shattered all over again. A lump lodged in her throat, tears welling in her eyes. "There's something you should know."

He frowned, his black brows furrowing under his bandana.

Elms creaked as their branches swayed in the breeze. Dinah's blurring gaze drifted beyond the glittering pond behind him and up to the bluff that dominated the landscape.

"Joseph—" Her voice broke, and she hung her head. "Joseph is dead."

Birds chirped in the silence—so *cheerful.* Her nails dug into the blanket as her bitter tears spilled over.

"What happened?" Enyeto asked.

"It was Sal," she choked out, meeting his devastated gaze. "We had him. We had him, but he got away. Joseph went after him, and I— I wasn't fast enough."

His lips parted, and he looked past her, as if searching the shadows for answers. His cleft chin jutted, his dark eyes narrowing as they dropped to the ground. "Do you know where Sal might've gone?"

Dinah nodded toward the bluff. "He's up there, where I left him."

Enyeto glanced over his shoulder, then stared at her in astonishment. "You killed him?"

"Go see for yourself if you don't believe me." Grimacing, she massaged her aching throat.

"And Joseph?" he ventured.

Dinah's eyes stung as she shook her head. "I couldn't find him."

His nostrils flared. He uncrossed his legs and got to his feet.

Her hand flew to the gun on her hip as she shrank from him.

Enyeto's stern features softened. "You have nothing to fear from me. Wherever you need to go, I'll take you there."

She didn't want to go anywhere. Do anything. All she wanted was to lie back down and pretend this was a bad dream. A world without Joseph wasn't one she cared to live in.

"I can't go home."

"Why not?" he asked.

"Because—" Dinah's voice cracked, and she bit her quivering lip.

He sat again, ready to listen. Resting his hands on his knees as he studied her.

Her cheeks heated with embarrassment—with shame. But somehow, telling a stranger seemed easier. She didn't fear what he'd think of her or worry that she'd disappoint him.

"Because Sal was right," Dinah confessed. "I don't know who I am without him. Without what he did to me. Ten years, I've been trapped in this cage. Never getting close to anyone. Livin' like a ghost."

She struggled to continue, tears dripping onto her muddy sleeves. "I finally let someone in, and now he's gone."

"My family was taken from me," Enyeto said gravely. "Some by sickness, others by war. I know what it's like to be lied to. To have a heart filled with pain and hate."

He sighed, his downcast eyes contemplating the whispering grass. "Revenge is a cycle that's difficult to break. But I have to believe it can be. That a wounded spirit can heal."

"What if it can't?" she asked hopelessly.

He met her defeated gaze with quiet determination. "Believing is half the battle."

They'd lived such different lives, but his struggle was surprisingly akin to her own. He'd lost everything, just like her. Just like Joseph.

She saw so clearly now how Sal had exploited and manipulated them. He wanted them to view the world as he did. To be as cruel and miserable as he was.

"Joseph wouldn't want me to tell you this," Enyeto said with hesitation, "but you deserve to know."

Dinah's heart slammed against her ribs. What else had Joseph hidden from her?

"Your father's death, the robbery all those years ago—it weighed on him. He thought you wouldn't accept his help if he offered, so he paid your family's debt in secret."

She gasped. Fresh tears blazed burning trails down her cheeks, and Dinah pressed a hand to her mouth to stifle a sob.

All this time, she'd wondered…

"Dinah!"

Startled, she looked toward the calling voice. So did Enyeto.

I'm not imagining it.

She scrambled to her feet and hurried to the edge of the pond. Gazing across the water, she spotted six riders coming over a hill to the north.

"Mama," she breathed.

Daniel rode beside her—Cornelia, her husband Henry, and Ophelia's parents behind them.

Dinah's heart squeezed. They'd come all this way looking for her.

"You should go to them," Enyeto encouraged.

She turned toward Cardinal, who grazed beside the Indian's pinto mare. Her jaw clenched with newfound resolve.

"I will," she said, meeting Enyeto's gaze. "Thank you. Joseph was fortunate to have a friend like you."

Humbly, he inclined his head. "He gave me a great gift, a chance to begin again. I do not know where I belong or where my path will take me, but I will not live as I did before. I will find my spirit's calling."

The redbud's pink flowers had faded, lush leaves growing in their place. Stooping beneath a violet sky, its drooping boughs whispered in the breeze, shielding the graves in its shade.

As the sun set at Dinah's back, her shadow stretched out from her feet, falling inches short of her father's headstone. The journey home had so exhausted her that she could hardly stand, but she had to see him.

Two weeks ago, they'd laid him to rest on this blustery hillside. She remembered that cold gray morning like it was yesterday. And yet, a lifetime seemed to have passed.

The hollow ache, the burning rage that had driven her—they still lingered. But the time for killing had ended.

Dinah blinked back the tears welling in her eyes, her hands clasped so tight that they hurt. *Is he proud? Or disappointed?*

She'd succeeded, but at what cost? Her quest for revenge had tainted and corrupted her. Turned her into someone else.

Maybe this is who I've always been.

Someone who'd rather pull a trigger than wrestle her demons. Blaming her misery on her circumstances. Blaming her family. Blaming God.

Blaming everyone but herself.

Soft steps rustled behind her. Dinah glanced over her shoulder.

Her mother waded through the knee-high grass, her black skirt gathered up and a few loose curls blowing across her sober face.

"Mind if I join you?"

Dinah shook her head. Her gaze returned to her father's grave as her mother drew alongside her. Guilt gnawed at her insides, a sob clawing up her throat.

"I lost his hat," she confessed, "up on that bluff. Silly to cry over, I know. But… it was a piece of him I could still hold on to."

"That isn't silly at all," her mother said.

"I just—" Dinah swallowed hard, struggling to speak. "I miss him so much."

"Me too."

As they stood in dismal silence, Dinah clenched her jaw, fighting the pressure building inside her. Refusing to break down in front of her mother.

"Every day, I ask God why he took him from us," her mother admitted. "My only comfort is that we'll see him again someday."

Tears rolled down Dinah's cheeks as she met her gaze. Her mother reached over and grasped her hand.

"Until then, let's make the most of the time we've been given. God has a plan for you, Dinah. Never doubt that. Listen, and he will speak to you."

Her mother smiled and gave her hand an encouraging squeeze, her words striking Dinah like a bolt of lightning. Nothing she'd chased had filled the void inside her.

It's temporary, she thought as her mother walked away. All of it could be taken from her in the blink of an eye. What her heart longed for wasn't of this world.

She should've sought him first. Instead, she turned to him last, when all else had failed her.

Her mother stopped and looked back. "It's getting dark."

"Coming," Dinah answered, hurrying to catch up.

Alone in the blackness of her bedroom, Dinah sank to the floor, the solid weight of her Bible familiar and comforting in her hand. Set beside her on the patterned rug, her lamp's warm light flickered over the book's leather-bound cover.

She crossed her legs and laid the Bible in front of her. The walls creaked as she opened it, a strong wind gusting outside her window. She didn't know where to turn, so she let the pages fall where they may.

"For we are saved by hope," read the first words her desperate eyes found, *"but hope that is seen is not hope: for what a man seeth, why doth he yet hope for? But if we hope for that we see not, then do we with patience wait for it."*

Dinah's heart squeezed with a pang of conviction. God hadn't brought her this far for nothing.

She kept reading, meditating on every verse. Words that had been written almost two thousand years ago and traveled through the ages, by land and sea and pen and tongue until they reached her right here, right now. Cutting to the core of her being.

"In all these things we are more than conquerors through him that loved us," she murmured, her tears dripping onto the page.

"For I am persuaded, that neither death, nor life, nor angels, nor principalities, nor powers, nor things present, nor things to come, Nor height, nor depth,

nor any other creature, shall be able to separate us from the love of God, which is in Christ Jesus our Lord."

I'm not alone, she thought, hopeless no longer. *I never was, and I never will be.*

CHAPTER TWENTY-SIX

Joseph snuck into Salina under cover of darkness, keeping his head bowed and his hat pulled low as he made his way to Roach's office. He walked Steel up to the hitching rail, took his foot out of the stirrup, and carefully swung his leg over his back. Grimacing, he slid to the ground. As he looped the reins over the rail, Joseph looked south down the quiet street, where he'd beaten a man within an inch of his life.

Sure, the fella had said something he didn't like. That made him angry. *But that ain't why I hit him.* Joseph sighed as his gaze drifted across to the bank, where he'd shot the girl. *Always fightin' to keep from thinkin'.*

His ribs twinged as he climbed the stairs and stepped onto the boardwalk. Ignoring the *CLOSED* sign on Roach's door, he walked inside without knocking.

Roach spun with a gasp, scattering papers everywhere. Several sheets skimmed across the floor and came to rest at Joseph's feet. As he shut the door behind him, he noticed a case lying open on the desk.

"Goin' somewhere?"

"I— I didn't expect to see you again," Roach stammered with wide eyes. "Not after—well—"

"After what?"

Roach blinked and adjusted his glasses. "You mean, you don't know?"

"Know what?" Joseph prompted, heart thumping as he advanced.

Roach cleared his throat and wrung his wrinkled hands. "Mr. Valentin is dead. Killed by a local girl. It's all the town's talking about."

Joseph stopped in his tracks, numb with shock. "Was it Dinah Hance?"

"Ah, yes," Roach nodded, "that's her name."

Joseph felt as if a bucket of freezing water had been dumped over his head.

She killed him. *She* killed *him*? How had she managed it?

Part of him mourned. A bigger part was relieved. He was free.

"Where is she now?"

"Not in Salina, I suspect," Roach answered, crouching to gather his papers. "She seemed put off by all the attention. The crowds."

Where would she go? Joseph ran a hand over his face, racking his brain as he paced the floor. *Where would she go to get away?*

"This is my last night here," Roach said, stacking the papers in the case on his desk. "I'm leaving Salina."

Good, Joseph thought. Roach's name was a fitting one. He wasn't sorry to see him go.

Roach peered at him over his glasses and added, "I'd advise you to do the same if you don't want to end up like our friend."

CHAPTER TWENTY-SEVEN

Cardinal galloped over rolling hills of green, tossing his fiery mane as the wind rushed against Dinah's face. A shiver ran through her. It was a bracing spring morning, her buttoned jacket warding off the chill. She breathed in the fresh air and looked up at the blue sky.

She had to get out of the house for a while. Daniel and her mother had carried on constant conversation at breakfast, and they'd seemed concerned by her silence. Much as they cared, they couldn't understand.

She hadn't spoken Joseph's name since she'd told them of his death. She couldn't believe that was only yesterday.

Last night, she'd tossed and turned for hours. Drifted off on a tearstained pillow and woken with red, stinging eyes.

She never stopped thinking of him.

Bright rays broke through the clouds behind the dogwood tree, shining on the field where they'd run side by side under sun and moon. Dinah raced toward that distant hill, chasing a vision. A dream.

Joseph's coat billows in the breeze, Steel's black tail flying behind his silver hide. She can catch him. She's so close.

Dinah shut her eyes, listening to the wind and Cardinal's thundering hooves. Losing herself in the not-so-distant memory.

When Cardinal charged up the slope, she half expected to find Joseph waiting for her in the shade with that lopsided grin of his. So smug and puffed up with pride.

We were strangers then, Dinah reflected as she dismounted. *Or so I thought.*

She approached the tree with a heavy heart, its thick leaves rippling in the shifting light. Its white blossoms had long since fallen and blown away. She placed her hand on the trunk, wishing her fingers were entwined with his.

"Rose, Rose, Rose of Killarney, sure I love you," she sang softly.

She walked around the dogwood, trailing her fingers along the scaly gray bark as she gazed east. "Sometimes I see, dear, a devil in your eye. Don't ever leave me. Mavourneen, I would die."

She drew a shuddering breath and circled to the west. "My Rose, Rose, Rose of Killarney, sure I… love…"

Dinah stopped cold. Her eyes widened.

A rider crossed the field below, coming slowly toward her. A man in black sitting on a big blue roan.

Dinah gasped. Her right hand flew to her heart as it gave a great leap, the other braced against the tree. In her mind, she ran to him. Wept and threw her arms around him.

In reality, she stood transfixed. Fearing that if she blinked, if she moved, he'd vanish.

Joseph dismounted at the base of the hill. He left Steel there and started up the slope, wincing as he trudged through the tall grass, his bearing stiff and his strides unusually careful.

He's hurt, Dinah realized with a pang of concern. Her trembling hands fell to her sides as she stepped toward him.

Joseph joined her atop the hill, and she stared, searching his bruised face and blackened eye. He stood a few feet from her, almost close enough to touch. Would her hand pass through him if she tried?

"I hoped I'd find you here," Joseph said.

A lump burned in her throat, her vision blurring. "I thought— Sal told me you were dead."

His brow furrowed as he frowned. "Almost was. I came as fast as I could. He said he was gonna kill ya. I was afraid…"

He shook his head. "That don't matter now. I heard ya gave him his comeuppance."

She found herself at a loss for words, still struggling to believe he was really here.

Joseph reached up and took off his hat. Holding it against his chest, he sank to his knees. "I ain't been honest with you, and I'm sorry. I shoulda been the one to tell you, not Sal. What happened to your friend was an accident. I didn't mean to shoot her."

Tears pooled in his pleading eyes, and Dinah choked back a sob. She hugged her sides, desperately holding herself together.

"I ain't gone a day without wishin' I could undo it. I kept it from ya because—" Joseph bowed his head in shame. "I didn't wanna lose you."

She raised her anguished gaze to the horizon, sniffing and wiping her eyes. Her cheeks. The tremor in his voice tearing her apart.

"I ain't askin' ya to forgive me," he said. "I got no right to. I just needed ya to know. And I wanted to thank you for helpin' me. For seein' somethin' in me."

Dinah's heart squeezed as she looked down at him. There was a softness in his eyes, in the way he spoke, something she couldn't explain but innately understood. He'd changed.

"Say somethin', won'tcha?" Joseph implored. "Yell at me. Tell me you hate me. Ya never wanna see me again. *Somethin'.*"

Fresh tears spilled down her cheeks. "I can't."

"Why can'tcha?"

"Because I—" Dinah swallowed hard. "Because I love you."

How freeing to finally say it aloud!

Joseph stared at her with parted lips. Frozen and speechless. Like he couldn't believe his ears.

Dinah closed the distance between them and got down on her knees. She couldn't contain herself a second longer. She needed to touch him. To somehow convince herself that this was happening.

Her heart pounded as she raised a shaking hand. Lightly, she caressed his cheek, trailing her fingers down his face. As her thumb traced the scar at the corner of his mouth, Joseph leaned into her touch, his ardent eyes gazing into hers. How striking they were in the morning light—olive green with inner rings of chestnut brown.

"And I forgive you," she murmured.

His eyes shone with tears. One escaped and ran down his cheek.

Dinah brushed it away and scooted closer. Moved her hand to the nape of his neck and stroked his hair. Gently, she drew him down to her, and he rested his forehead against hers.

Dinah's heart swelled with joy as she closed her eyes. *You're alive.*

His strong arms wrapped around her, and she melted into the warmth of his embrace, content to remain there forever.

Tears welled behind her lids. "I thought I'd lost you."

Joseph held her tighter, burying his face in her neck. *I'm here,* he seemed to say, *and I'm not goin' anywhere.*

Dinah clung to him with all her strength, delighting in the steady rhythm of his heart beating in tandem with hers. Against all odds, God had brought him back to her. And if she had her way, they would never be parted again.

EPILOGUE

One week later, Dinah accompanied Daniel and her mother to the train station, the morning air crisp and cool. Her mother had put off leaving as long as she could, but Daniel had his job to return to in New York.

Dinah hadn't given their departure much thought. It was easier to pretend it wasn't going to happen.

But she couldn't pretend anymore.

As they approached the platform, Daniel led Belle and Sarge away to load them into the stock car. She looped Cardinal's reins over the hitching rail and carried his luggage toward the stairs.

"Dinah."

She turned, realizing her mother had stopped and set down her bags.

"It isn't too late to change your mind."

Dinah sighed and stared at the dirt path under her feet. She'd expected her mother to make a final attempt to sway her. Part of her was glad. Relieved that her mother still cared enough to try.

Dinah met her gaze with unwavering certainty. "Nothin' in this whole world could get me on that train. I made him a promise."

"A promise?" her mother scoffed. She gestured at the strip of leather wrapped around Dinah's finger. "He didn't even have the decency to give you a ring."

Dinah's grip on the luggage tightened. "You know why he couldn't."

Her mother huffed and cast a sideways glance at the family passing by. "You never have listened to me."

"And it's gotten me into trouble. I know." Dinah took a breath to stifle her rising anger. "I'm not askin' for your blessing. I just— I want you to be happy for me."

Her mother's stern brow softened. She sighed and massaged her forehead. "I always blamed your father for how you turned out. Letting you do men's work when I was teaching you to be a lady. But it's my fault as much as his. I brought you here because I wanted you to have a better life."

Her blue-green eyes grew distant, as if she were thinking back to a time she wished she could forget. "You saw so much. Grew up too fast. Just like I did."

Dinah didn't know what her mother had seen before they came to Kansas. What she'd survived. She never spoke of her past. But Dinah realized now that they had much more in common than she'd ever imagined.

For so long, she'd felt like a bad daughter. A black sheep. Her mother fearing all the while that she'd failed her too.

Dinah approached her and put down the luggage. "If I'm anything like you, then you did something right."

Tears glistened in her mother's eyes. She stepped forward and hugged Dinah tight.

What if I never see her again?

Terror gripped her at the thought. The longest they'd ever been apart was when she'd run off to join the marshal's posse. Would months pass with no news of her and Daniel?

"Promise you won't forget me," Dinah choked.

Her mother drew back and frowned up at her. "Forget you? You're my daughter. I'll wake up thinking of you. Fall asleep praying God's protection over you."

Tears spilled down Dinah's cheeks. Her mother brushed them away and cradled her face between her hands.

"You know what kind of man your father was. Don't settle for anything less."

"I won't," Dinah assured her.

"You want me to take your bags, Mama?" Daniel asked as he returned with their tickets.

"I've got them," her mother replied. "You should say goodbye to your sister."

She picked up her luggage and headed for the platform, leaving the two of them alone.

Dinah sniffed and handed Daniel his bag. "Well, I guess this is it."

"I guess so." He shifted from one foot to the other and adjusted his coat. "You sure this is what you want?"

"I am." His face fell, and she added, "You must think I've gone crazy."

He sighed and shrugged. "We haven't seen eye to eye for a while."

"Maybe that's okay," Dinah ventured. "I've done a lotta thinkin', and… I'm sorry for all those things I said to you. It wasn't my place. We have different dreams. That doesn't make yours or mine any less important."

His eyes brightened.

"All aboard!" came the call.

"No matter what happens," Daniel said, "you'll always be my little sister."

He bent to embrace her, and she smiled through her tears, taking comfort in his promise.

Together, they climbed the steps and crossed the platform. She stopped at the edge, the whistle blaring as he got on the train. Her chest tightened, panic seizing her as the separation became real.

"Write to me?"

Daniel looked back at her and smiled. "I will."

He entered the passenger car and joined her mother, who sat at the window a couple of rows from the front. The wheels started rolling, smoke puffing into a cloudless sky. They waved at her through the glass, and Dinah waved back.

As the train chugged east, her hand fell to her side. She drew a deep breath, watching it go with a sinking heart.

She wished they understood. That they could've set aside their feelings about Joseph for her sake. It hurt that they wouldn't be with her on the happiest day of her life. That her mother wouldn't help her find the right dress or do her hair. That her father wouldn't be there to give her away.

Maybe, she thought with a flicker of hope, *there's someone who can.*

"Dinah, it's been a pleasure," Lawrence said when the time came for her and Joseph to depart. "We didn't meet unduh the best of circumstances, but I'm shoah glad we did."

She'd married Joseph under the dogwood tree that sunny July morning, six weeks after they'd reunited there. At long last, nothing stood between them. No quest for revenge. No secrets. No lingering doubts.

Not only had Lawrence agreed to give her away—he'd also found a reverend to perform the ceremony. They'd sent no invitations. The wedding had been held in secret with Lawrence and Jill as their only witnesses.

Jill had helped her choose the perfect dress—emerald green with a delicate pattern of yellow flowers scattered across its fabric meadow.

After the ceremony, Dinah had packed the dress away with the rest of her belongings and changed into a split skirt suitable for riding. Then she'd joined Lawrence and Jill in the yard, and Joseph had gone into the barn to get the horses.

She looked at the house one last time. Her mother had sold it for a pretty penny. Finally, both of them were free to make a fresh start. To live without debt.

Lawrence extended his hand, and Dinah frowned.

A handshake? After all they'd been through?

She stepped forward and hugged him. Lawrence made a quiet exclamation of surprise, but then his hands came to rest on her back.

"Thank you for being here," Dinah said. She couldn't manage anything more without breaking down completely.

"The honor is all mine, Miss Hance." He grasped her shoulders and drew back to look at her. "Or should I say, Mrs. Gray."

Dinah smiled, wiping her cheeks as his eyes twinkled.

Jill took her hands and gave them a squeeze. "Be well, Dinah. If you ever need me, you know where to find me."

She nodded, noting the way Lawrence gazed at Jill. His discreet glances and Jill's shy smiles over the past few weeks hadn't gone unnoticed by her.

They'd make a good match.

Dinah didn't like goodbyes. They left a bitter taste in her mouth. Left her feeling hollow. But as she turned and went to Joseph, who'd brought their horses out of the barn and stood waiting for her, she found the parting sweeter than any before it. And she lacked nothing.

"You ready?" he asked.

Dinah grinned up at him, brimming with anticipation. "Let's get outta here."

And they did, galloping west across the open prairie. Hooves thundering and hearts soaring under the noon sun as it shone on a new day—a new beginning. This was all she wanted, all she would ever need.

Him and her and the wind.

ABOUT THE AUTHOR

A lifelong artist and writer, **MADISON K. THAMES** grew up riding horses, participated in rodeos, and remains proud that she won her first calf scramble. After graduating from Auburn University in 2018 with a BFA degree, she launched her career as a professional artist, creating a wide variety of commissions for clients and selling her work at comic book conventions. Meanwhile, her love of the American West continued to grow, and an idea sparked in her mind—the story of a woman's revenge and an outlaw's redemption. This idea inspired Madison to make her dream of becoming a published author a reality.

madisonthames.com
@madisonkthames
@goneoutlaw

Made in the USA
Columbia, SC
30 July 2023

20976214R00167